Also by Jackie Notter

Pop Secrets

THE MIRROR'S TOUCH

Jackie Notter

Climate Publishing
Seattle

A Climate Publishing Book

First Edition for North America published by Climate Publishing, LLC

All inquiries should be emailed to info@climatepublishing.com

Written by Markus Taylor under the pseudonym Jackie Notter.
Sr. Editor and Writing Partner: Camille English
Editor: J. Lopez, the mistress with the red pen
Italian Translation: Sofia Cappelloni

Cover: Trif Book Design
Back photograph: Pushis Images
Blurb: Jake Carney

ISBN: 978-0-578-97966-3

Music mentioned or sung:

"Puccini: La Bohème"
Performed by Mirella Freni, Luciano Pavarotti, Elizabeth Harwood,
Nicolai Ghiaurov, Berliner Philharmoniker & Herbert von Karajan
Decca Music Group Limited

"Time to Say Goodbye"
Performed by Sarah Brightman and Andrea Bocelli
Lyrics by Lucio Quarantotto, Music by Francesco Sartori
East West Records

"Imagine"
Performed by John Lennon
Lyrics and music by John Lennon and Yoko Ono
Apple Records

"Balls to the Wall"
Performed by Accept
Lyrics and music by Udo Dirkschneider, Wolf Hoffmann,
Herman Frank, Peter Baltes, Stefan Kaufmann, and Deaffy
RCA (Germany) | Portrait

"St. Louise Blues"
Performed by Bessie Smith and Louis Armstrong
Lyrics and music by W. C. Handy
Columbia

"Remember Me - Sure is Pure (radio edit)"
Performed by Blue Boy
Lyrics and music by Lex Blackmore, Robert Miller,
Richard Evans & Marlena Shaw
Pharm | Jive | Om | Altra Moda Music

Movies mentioned:

Rosemary's Baby
Screenplay and Directed by Roman Polanski
Based on the book Rosemary's Baby by Ira Levin
William Castle Enterprises | Paramount Pictures

Carrie
Directed by Brian De Palma
Screenplay by Lawrence D. Cohen
Based on the book Carrie by Stephen King
Red Bank Films | United Artists | Metro Goldwyn Mayer

The Shining
Directed by Stanley Kubrick
Screenplay by Stanley Kubrick and Diane Johnson
Based on the book The Shining by Stephen King
The Producer Circle Company | Peregrine Productions |
Hawk Films | Warner Bros.

For Bruce

Prologue

Dear Diary,

It would be this one if I could live one day for all eternity.
Tonight Stefano and I made love.

     Our evening was the most amazing and confusing time
of my life. Amazing, because Stefano was my first. Confusing,
because I could feel what he was feeling. Like, seriously feel every
touch Stefano was experiencing. The stinging pain of being
entered was soothed by the mind-numbing pleasure he felt as he
slipped inside me. Each sensation I experienced was amplified by
his own, our passion surging and weaving so intensely I thought
a fuse in my brain would surely blow. I have no idea how our
physical senses were synced or why. Does this happen to
everyone? Is this love?

Janis

Chapter 1

I woke up in a brilliant mood, with thoughts of Stefano resonating through my mind. How shocking that none of the scare tactics about a girl's first time came to fruition. The connection we experienced was nothing short of life-changing. Stefano's tireless sexual creativity would have been astounding on its own, even if I hadn't been able to tap into his physical touch. I understand now what people mean when they say the sex was so remarkable our bodies became one.

Withholding my virginity until I was sixteen proved wise. The longing allowed for a trace of confidence in my naked body. Although, the wait may not have been my own doing. My lumbering frame made me a class freak. A barrage of ridicule kept me there. I'm five-eleven and still growing. My health teacher said girls should stop at fifteen. If it didn't end soon, I'd break the six-foot barrier. My saving grace is I have my mom's soft, subtle doll-like face, so at least I'm not mistaken for a man.

I stretched my arms wide, drawing in the morning, and fell lazily upon my pillow. My hand struck my diary. Something felt amiss as I traced a finger across the spine. My journal was leather-bound. This imposter had the slick sheen of a hardcover. It was an old Nancy Drew mystery that I hadn't read in years. I tossed the book onto my nightstand and searched desperately for my diary. Where the hell had it gone?

My bedroom is at the far end of the house. I headed to the kitchen for a drink of water when Dad's stern voice resonated down the hall. My heart sank as I recognized the words he was spouting. The bastard was reading last night's diary entry.

I leaned against the wall with my hand pressed over my mouth to avoid crying out in anger. The betrayal was soul-crushing. I wasn't sure how I was going to catch my next breath.

"Janis is in grave danger," Grandpa said in his firm yet raspy tone. "I can't believe I'm about to say this. We have to eliminate her boyfriend."

"Fuck," Dad responded.

What the shit? Why would Grandpa need to kill my boyfriend? Stefano is not a threat. He lacks empathy, but we've been working on that. I was hyperventilating and barely made it to the toilet to vomit.

My nausea lingered in the bathroom as if I was out at sea. I rested my head on the cold stone countertop until the world settled.

When I returned to my room, my diary was on the nightstand where I threw the book. Had I dreamt the whole thing? I checked my shelf. The Nancy Drew story was there but in the wrong location in the series. I would never have arranged them like that.

Were Dad and Grandpa really going to kill Stefano? There was no way to warn him. The last fight with Dad ended with him taking away my laptop and cell phone. Calling on a landline was no good; the secrecy of the family business kept one from the house. I had to find Stefano and fast.

I cleaned myself up, dressed simply, and tightened the laces on my track shoes. My anger was a challenge to restrain. I breathed deeply and entered the kitchen.

"Hey, Peaches," my father said, averting his eyes.

Dad is intimidatingly large; this made his avoidance all the more noticeable. He was clenching his jaw, which wrinkled his crooked nose, bringing his unruly Scottish eyebrows to life. Dad squinted in anguish—broadcasting the reality of my grandfather's horrific declaration. I looked over at Bepa, hoping for a change of heart. Grandpa is the toughest man I know, and he couldn't muster so much as a glance.

"Would you mind if I go to the library?" I asked Dad. "I finished all my books."

"Honey, you promised to watch the Fletcher children."

"Oh, shit!" I said.

"Janis," Dad scolded. Grandpa just chuckled.

The time on the microwave was ten to noon. There were minutes left to get to my babysitting gig. Dad really let me sleep in late.

"Sorry, I forgot," I mumbled. "I'll borrow a book from Mrs. Fletcher."

"That a girl," Dad said, putting on his phony 'I'm so encouraging' look.

I found my windbreaker and stared my dad and grandfather down, trying to will them into reconsidering. Bepa just grunted to himself, his face stone. I've seen that expression before when he and Dad were heading out on a case. He slipped his driving cap on and walked from the room.

"I love you, Grandpa," I pleaded.

"I love you too," he said, not looking back.

I was on Mrs. Fletcher's porch trying to stop my tears. She was in too much of a hurry to notice as she raced by.

The three hours of babysitting were the longest in my life. Stefano wasn't answering his phone or emails.

While the kids were snacking, I looked into the weirdness I experienced with Stefano. There were cases of people watching someone get touched, feeling the same sensation, but nothing close to the connection I had with him. It was like his body was mine, every movement and sensation I felt. The search left me more confused.

Mrs. Fletcher arrived late from her book club. The ten extra minutes was an eternity.

"I have to get home," I said, rushing past her car. She would have talked my ear off if I stayed. "I'll pick up the money later."

"All right, Janis," she said, watching me go. "Thank you."

"You're welcome," I yelled and ran to catch a train to the Bronx.

Walking toward Stefano's block, I told myself the black plume of smoke had to be coming from the adjacent neighborhood. The row of fire engines on his street destroyed that hope. I snaked my way through the bystanders and descended into hell. Stefano's rental house was engulfed in flames.

An explosion inside the home shattered the front windows. A blast of heat slammed against me, and I fell protectively to the ground. Stefano's gorgeous face filled my mind, his aqua-green eyes drilling into my soul.

I flowed from person to person in a daze, frantically searching for Stefano or his family. None of the neighbors had seen the Rosotti's. I found a T-shirt of his scorched on the ground. The fabric was still warm to the touch but smelled only of smoke; there was no trace of his scent. Any second I would wake up.

Entering his backyard from the alley, I raced to his treehouse, hoping to find my boyfriend. Inside the doorway was a note pinned to the corkboard with my mother's diamond earring.

Janis,

My family's in danger. We have to leave town. Dad's yelling from the house. Be right back.

I stared at the unfinished note in horror. Stefano was dead. I slipped mom's earring into my pocket and backed down the ladder, away from reality. My foot slipped on the last rung, shocking me awake. I broke into a

6

crying stumble of a run. Blocks away, I crumbled on the sidewalk, bawling uncontrollably.

I needed to get home to confront my traitorous family. An older man walking a dog pointed the way to the metro station.

In our driveway was an unfamiliar Suburban towing a U-Haul trailer. Dad burst through the front door.

"There you are, Janis. We need to leave town. Now."

"What have you done?" I screamed.

He reached out and held my face. "There's no time, Peaches. We're at zero hour. We have to go."

"I fucking hate you!" I yelled and fled to my room. My pulse was racing, waiting for Dad to barge in angrily, but he didn't. The adrenalin receded, and with it, my will.

This wasn't my first move. My family runs a private investigation business that, I was beginning to realize, isn't on the up and up. Either I packed now, or I lost everything. I filled three bags, the first with essentials, the second with items I wanted, and the third with things I could give up so Dad would make room for the second one.

"Time to go," my father said, stepping into my room. He grabbed all three bags, shocking me into silence. "We'll be in the car. Do a quick check to see if you forgot anything."

I left the house in such a daze I ran into the door jamb. Oh my God, Stefano's dance mixes. How could I have forgotten those? I grabbed the USB drive from its hiding place and climbed into the back of the Suburban with my brother.

"This is why we don't have a dog," Dad said. "We'd have to leave it."

"It's more about the danger a walking routine brings," Grandpa said.

It all sounded selfish to me. I sobbed as we drove out of town. My younger brother, David, grinned as if it

7

was fun. Another day. Another run. I knew better. Once again, my life as I knew it was over, but this time was different. My life really was over. Stefano was my everything. School hadn't been easy for me since moving to Connecticut. The girls in my class were ruthless, making it impossible to have real friends. Stefano was the one person who made me like *me*.

Trees lining the freeway raced by endlessly. The stream of motion was hypnotizing. My only option was to jump from the car. If I died, I would be back in Stefano's arms. I grabbed the handle and pushed my weight against the door to freedom.

The child locks were on. I pounded my fists on the back of Grandpa's seat and let out a piercing cry of frustration. It startled Dad, and he wrestled to get us back in our lane. The trailer behind us was fishtailing.

"What the fuck?" he yelled.

My tears were stifling, to the point of constricting my breath.

"It's going to be OK," David said to me. He was having a difficult time concealing the tears pooling in his eyes. I felt guilty for causing him drama.

Chapter 2

The drive from Connecticut to Seattle took five miserable days. I hated every minute of it. Dad and Grandpa acted as if nothing happened, and I was too afraid to talk about it. They stopped trying to make me happy by the second afternoon. Even my brother gave up, and he's a walking fun machine. None of his usual games helped. I was a vapid, empty shell of my former self.

We were holed up at a filthy hotel for a few days while Support worked on our new identities. I had no idea who Support was, but they always came through for us.

David and I had a connecting room to ourselves. He's only two years younger, but his playful nature comes off as more immature than he is. My brother, having eaten half a bag of mini Reese's peanut butter cups, was bouncing tirelessly on his bed.

"Would you stop?" I demanded, harsher than necessary. My misery wasn't his doing.

David jumped once more and landed in a seated position, facing me.

"You know what you are?" he said. "You're a churk burgle."

"What's a churk burgle?" I asked, thirsty to learn something new. I should have known better.

"You, ya stupid churk burgle," he said, bursting into a giggling fit.

"At least I'm not a pest."

David beamed as if that were a compliment. I fell onto my bed with my back to him.

"It doesn't mean anything," he said. "I was just playing."

I put on my headphones and disappeared into the dance mix Stefano made for me. My thoughts drifted to the day I met him.

I was on foot, kitty-corner from the New York Public Library. The beauty of the architecture stopped me in my tracks. It happened every time I laid eyes on the white marble building. At the base of the stairs, two lions guarded the three imposing arched doorways. I chose the middle one and ran gleefully inside. As large as I knew the library to be, a more extensive collection of books was hidden below. The underground bunker held an additional 2.5 million. I was immersed in the written word and couldn't be happier. *Books*, I thought dreamily.

The stairwell on the right led to the Children's Center. Even though I've outgrown it, the room was one of my favorites. I stepped through the entrance and was drawn to the four-foot-long Lego version of the lions out front. Across the room was Winnie the Pooh. Not the books themselves but the stuffed animals that inspired A. A. Milne to write his stories. The characters in the display case were his son Christopher's. It amazed me how five battered toys could be the key to a secret world.

A euphoric feeling washed over me, but it wasn't from the adventures of Christopher Robin. The vibe was coming from the boy standing to my left, staring. He smiled, then placed his hand in mine, sending my heart racing. We walked from the room, our fingers intertwined.

I couldn't believe how handsome this boy was. What drew me in most were his eyes. They were a brilliant aqua-green with a hazel ring near the pupil.

"Do people tell you all day long how stunning your eyes are?" I asked.

"Not *all* day," he said in a funny dismissive tone. "I'm Stefano."

He was Italian. Dad has a habit of leering at Italian men suspiciously, which is hypocritical of his anti-racist stance. It was just my luck.

"Janis," I said, introducing myself.

Stefano repeated my name, letting it flow lyrically. He held my gaze with a warm smile. "I noticed you earlier in Grand Central. You looked like a princess. Not a stupid cartoon one but an actual princess. Pretty blonde hair and all," he said, flipping a piece. "I wanted to be a part of this fairy tale. I hope you don't mind that I followed you."

If he only knew. My life felt more like a nightmare. "I don't mind. I'm just wondering how I could have missed you."

"I'm good at hiding."

"So is my brother."

I was inexplicably drawn to this boy. "Can I hug you?" I asked.

"Of course," Stefano said. I melted into his arms with the scent of his black leather jacket permeating the air. Sunlight radiated upon us as his energy flowed through me. He was my soul mate. I was sure.

I started crying, and my brother placed a reassuring hand on my shoulder.

"What was your favorite part of the day?" he asked.

There wasn't anything positive left in my life. The realization made me bawl. David shuffled onto the bed and spooned up behind me, holding me tight.

He stayed with me until the tears dried, then returned to his bed to find something decent on TV.

I rolled over and looked at him. "What you just did for me was the best part of my day. How about you?"

Without hesitation, he said, "Playing in the park with the giant hat and boots."

"That was fun." I perked up. "I'd like living in that neighborhood. I dug how the planes flew by so close."

"Yeah. That was cool, especially when the Lear Jet passed overhead."

By Monday, Support placed a bid on a house in the Central District, miles from our favorite park. A month later, we moved in. Dad's room was upstairs, David and I had the second-largest space just off the main floor living room, and Grandpa was in the back by the kitchen.

When we arrived in Seattle, I sneaked an email to Stefano hoping to find him alive but have heard nothing back. Each day was a struggle. The worst part is I didn't have a picture of him. Our love was a secret.

Dad gathered us in the living room to dole out our new identity. My family is guarded about what they do for a living. Dad got so mad last time I asked. It wasn't fair. The least they could do is give my brother and me an explanation.

We were now the O'Donnells.

"We're Irish?" I blurted out, my Scottish heritage rearing its ugly head.

"Hey, she talks," Dad said. I was raging inside.

He held up a cocktail. "May our bond be strong and our whiskey stronger." I didn't care for his Irish toast.

Dad's hair was slicked back like a gangster. Earlier in the day, he asked me to trim his unruly eyebrows. He's lucky I didn't shave them off. Dad was adamant about keeping his three-day beard; it went well with his weathered skin and thick sideburns. He always dove headfirst into our new identities. I had to be dragged into them, kicking and screaming.

I unfolded the strip of paper given to me. I was now Bailey Anne O'Donnell. "Great. I'm going to be Big Bailey."

"Honey, no, you won't," Dad said. "You're tall, not big."

"The kids in my class called me Janis the Giant!" I yelled.

"At least you're not Cordy," my brother said. "What am I, a dog?"

12

"Tim isn't much better," Dad said, trying out his new name.

"What the hell is everyone complaining about?" Grandpa said. "I'm not even in the family. I'm Thomas Callister." The tone he used for his name was mocking, like a child.

"Callister is pretty cool," Dad said.

"Yeah, but I'm not a Thomas. How will I strike fear into people with a name like that?"

"Tom Callister scares the hell out of me," Dad said.

"You're just saying that."

"Not at all. You're quite frightening, Pop."

Bepa *was*, especially with his new look. His salt-and-pepper beard was gone, leaving a rough, bushy mustache. Grandpa's balding head was menacing as it encroached on the shortly cropped hair, but not as menacing as his scowl and squinted eyes. He can stare daggers like no other. Bepa, at six-two, was a solid man, all muscle. In another household, he would be tall, but in ours, he was average height. Dad was six-four. My brother, at fourteen, already stood six feet tall.

"Maybe it's not that bad of a name," Grandpa said. He looked over at me. "I like your new hair color. The black works well with your complexion. You'll make a fine Bailey."

"Thanks," I said. I dyed it not to change identities but to match my mood.

"I did a little research on Seattle to help us fit in," Dad said. "To go with our new heritage, and I guess our actual heritage, we should root for the Sounders, the local soccer team. They're surprisingly good. The boys won a couple of nationals." He reached into a tote bag and retrieved a stack of fan paraphernalia.

I hated that Dad found such a cute sweatshirt for me. He wasn't going to win me over that easy. I leaned back in my chair, folding my arms in defiance.

13

"Even though it rains a lot here, the locals apparently don't use umbrellas," he said. "I found this odd because they have a yearly music festival called Bumbershoot, which is literally a British term for an umbrella."

"Wait, what are you talking about? They don't use umbrellas?" I asked. "That's the dumbest thing I've ever heard."

"Maybe they're too cool," my brother said.

"I think it just rains so much they don't care anymore," Grandpa said.

Boy, was he right. It rained endlessly in Seattle, and when it wasn't raining, there sometimes lingers a mist that feels like depression in physical form.

"The best tidbit I learned," Dad said, "is they have something here called the Seattle Freeze, where it's hard to make new friends. That should help keep us to ourselves."

"Speaking of not having friends," Grandpa joked. "Why don't you tell the kids about school?"

"Sure," Dad said, shifting his stance uncomfortably. "You guys never did enjoy public school. If you want, you can learn at home through an online course." The glimmering smile he made to sell his point, I hate to admit, was kind of adorable.

I would have objected out of spite, but I dreaded the idea of finishing my sophomore year at a new high school. Girls can be vicious at my age.

"I'm in," I said. Dad raised his eyebrows in surprise.

"Me too," Cordy responded enthusiastically.

His facial features were beginning to resemble grandfather's. They have the same warm smile that can easily flip to a menacing scowl. The difference between his and Grandpa's face is my brother's had a touch of mother's softness under that towhead. He often used the façade to get out of trouble.

14

"I wasn't prepared for that to go so smoothly," Dad said. "Thank you. I found an online school with teachers and a classroom environment. It'll be like being there physically, except your grandfather and I will teach P.E. We'll use the time to train you how to fight, or as I call it, the art of staying alive. I know we said you couldn't start until sixteen, but you both have to be able to defend yourselves. Training begins tomorrow."

"Yes!" Cordy shouted and performed a poorly executed karate kick.

I gave my father a look of frustration. He treated my brother differently than when I was his age. The double standard upset me to no end.

"This will help," Cordy said. "A couple of black guys gave me the stink eye today."

"Hey, son!" Dad scolded. "That's not how we talk in this family. If you go out of your way to describe someone's race, you're saying they're not white like me. It's bigotry, pure and simple."

Cordy looked at him, dumbfounded. "Sometimes you need to describe a person's skin," he said. "What did my missing child look like, officer? Well, let's see. He has dark hair. A green shirt. Should I tell him about the afro? Oh Lordy, that could be racist."

"Don't get smart with me," Dad said.

Cordy stared him down. "What if I have to describe an Italian man?" he asked.

Dad raised his arm. I grasped his bicep and held firm. "What the hell, Dad?"

"I wasn't going to hit him. Just don't be racist. You can find good in almost anyone. Christ, is it so hard to teach you kids to be decent people?"

I stormed off to my room and threw myself on the bed. I wasn't about to be lectured on morality by the man who killed my boyfriend.

God, I missed Stefano. I closed my eyes and was back in New York City. We had just met that day, yet there was a familiarity like I knew him my whole life.

"You up for coffee?" he asked with a comforting smile.

"How old do you think I am?"

"Eighteen?"

"Not even close. I'm fifteen. How old are you?"

He looked away. "Same, but I'm almost sixteen."

I was surprised by his age. His confidence put him years older.

"You know what? I would like a coffee. I've never had one. And if we're talking in almosts, I'm also almost sixteen."

I sent dad a message that I was grabbing lunch in the park that butts up to the library. Stefano chose the larger outdoor café with stylish modern seating. I'd dreamed of going there but never felt cool enough. He spotted a low table off in a corner. As we walked to it, I noticed how observant he was of his environment. It reminded me of the paranoid way my father acts in public.

Stefano rudely flagged the waitress down as she passed. His behavior was jarring.

"Two mochas and a lunch menu," he said dismissively with a flip of his hand.

"Of course, sir," she said, handing each of us a menu. "Would you like me to bring you water?"

"Whatever," Stefano said, not looking up from his menu.

I forced myself to look at her. "A glass of water for me, please." My voice came out predictably timid.

The woman thanked us and left.

There was a reason for my request. I swallowed my anxiety and spoke. "I read that we consume a credit card worth of microplastic every week. I don't like to use plastic bottles."

16

"A credit card worth? Shouldn't we be maxed out by now?"

His wit made me chuckle. "It's true. A university in Australia did a study." I felt so adult with my conversation. I was glad the article caught my eye last week.

"How's it getting in us?" he said, running a hand through his black hair. It flopped back down in the front, jutting out wildly like a pop star. He was intimidatingly handsome. I couldn't believe I was sitting with him.

"Mostly from bottled water."

"Well, good luck convincing the world. Convenience seems to rule."

I adored this boy. He wasn't immature like the kids in my class.

"Do you have a girlfriend?" I asked, pleased with my boldness.

"Nothing serious. And you?"

"Nope. No girlfriend."

"That's funny," he said instead of laughing. "I'd like to think I have one now." He leaned forward, placing his hand in mine. "No one's ever made me feel like you do. You're what's missing."

I was stunned into silence.

"Are you crying?" he asked.

"I'm just happy. That's stupid, I know."

"No. I'd cry if I could," Stefano said.

"What do you mean, you can't cry? That's ridiculous. You've never cried?"

"Not that I remember."

"What about during the beginning of Up?"

"Nope."

"Bambi, when they shoot his mother?"

"Never saw it. Sounds awful."

"Do you cry if you're hurt?"

"I just deal with it."

"I cry all the time. Probably too much."

17

"You'll just have to cry for both of us. In my family, empathy comes later in life, along with a flood of tears."

What an odd thing to say. I had a feeling my dad would like Stefano. The man doesn't care for tears. He wouldn't let us mourn our mother's death. We left the state so quickly I didn't even get to see her body to say goodbye.

The waitress delivered our coffees. I took a sip, expecting bitterness, but the chocolate made it delicious.

"What did you mean that empathy comes later in life?"

He took my hand and held it tight. "The men in our family aren't born with a lot. It's a fucked up situation." His eyes were focused on mine as if he was looking for a reaction. I shrugged, not knowing how to respond. He smiled and loosened his grip — what a strange boy.

I needed to change the subject. "So, where do you live?" I asked.

"The Bronx."

"And you're telling me you don't cry," I said.

"Yeah, that's no joke. Where's your crib?"

"Greenwich."

"The Village!"

"I wish. Greenwich, Connecticut. It's a train ride northeast. The library is the one place Dad lets me go alone in New York City. I made it super boring when he took me here."

"Where's your mom?"

I lowered my gaze and wrapped my hands around the mug. "She died."

"I am so sorry. Now you're gonna make me cry."

"Really?"

"I wish."

I fidgeted with my silverware.

"What was she like?"

18

I liked the question and looked up at him. "She was the type of mom who would wear the jewelry we made her no matter how stupid it looked."

"That says a lot. How old were you when she died?"

"Ten."

"That's a shitty-ass thing to happen."

"It was a long time ago," I said, pushing the sorrow away before it consumed me. "I'm curious. You're Italian, aren't you?"

"Very."

"Are you not from New York?"

"Nope." He leaned back in his chair. "You were expecting the New York Italian accent, maybe?"

I shrugged and tried to smooth over my rudeness with a smile.

"Dad says it's too dangerous for us to embrace the culture, that we can't stick out. We move around a lot. Maybe we're in a witness protection program," he said with a note of realization.

I wanted to tell him we moved around a lot, too, but Dad was adamant that we never talk about it. Doing so could get us killed. He's so dramatic.

"I'll give you one phrase, fugget about it." He was animated with his hands when he said this.

"That was freaking perfect. You sounded like Tony Soprano."

"I actually have an Uncle Tony."

"You probably shouldn't do that again then."

He laughed. "That phrase was more Hollywood. I'll give you one better. Ti amo."

"What does it mean?"

"I love you," he said, staring into my eyes.

My heart was racing so fast I felt like I was going to puke. Was he saying this to me or just explaining the meaning?

"You respond with anch'io, which is me too."

19

"Anch'io," I said, meaning every word.

Stefano removed a leather bracelet from his wrist—one of many.

"I want you to have this. It's my favorite."

My cheeks heated from the flattery. I don't know why my body reacts that way.

The bracelet was still warm to the touch. "I have something for you," I said and leaned in for my first kiss. Watching his gorgeous face draw to mine was mesmerizing. His lips were sexy, the bottom lush and full, the top extended out as if he were about to say something sultry. I knew I should close my eyes but waited until the last second.

Kissing Stefano was glorious. He barely tried to get his tongue in my mouth. It was nibbles and playfulness. If only our kiss could last forever.

"Do you want to go to Central Park?" he said.

"I can't. Dad checks my phone to see where I've been."

"We can hide it in the library. Come on. I'll rent bikes."

I hesitated. "OK."

We ran from the library, giggling after hiding my phone. A knock at my door snapped me back to the horrid present.

"Can I come in, Peaches?" Dad said.

"I guess."

He poked his head in and awkwardly worked his way inside but remained silent.

"What, Dad?"

"I need to tell you something before your brother finds out."

Nothing good came from these talks. I braced for the worst.

"With the new birthdays, your brother is sixteen, and you're fifteen."

"What the shit, Dad?"

"Come on, Peaches, no swearing."

"Yeah, that has to stop. Keeping a girl from swearing is a man's way of controlling her." I read that nugget in Teen Cosmo on the drive to Seattle.

"Hold on. That's not what I'm doing."

"Maybe not, but control *is* why men play that game. You have to let me swear." I was so proud of how well that came out I almost ruined it by smiling.

"I'll try. I just want you to be the finest person you can be. You're my angel."

"Thanks," I said half-assed. "Are you sure we can't fix David's new birthday?"

"It's Cordy now, and no. If you don't make a big deal about his ribbing, maybe he'll stop."

"Just tell him not to do it?"

"You know how that backfired with that monstrous zit you had?"

"He was ruthless."

"Yep. It's best just to laugh it off."

I looked away, dejected. "All right," I said.

"That a girl. Nothing's changed. We'll say your brother was held back two grades and you moved up one. That'll be easy to pull off. You're mature for your age."

I sank in my chair, ignoring what I think was a compliment. "Let me deal with this," I said, holding my hand up defensively.

"Life will get better," Dad said.

I wanted to scream that life would be better if you hadn't killed my boyfriend.

Grandpa had my brother and me out in the detached garage for our first P.E. class. Bepa was in a tank top, which enhanced his muscular frame. Cordy looked at him with admiration, hungry to learn the art of fighting. I

21

wasn't sure I was up for it. That morning, I'd crumbled in the shower, crying until the water turned cold. Dad let me skip all my classes but P.E.

"There's an old saying that bravery is being the only one who knows you're afraid," Grandpa said. "That's rubbish. You are direct descendants of the Cameron Clan. We are the fiercest of the fierce. If anything, we are too brave going into battle, charging in with almost suicidal courage. What our family needs to control is that. You must go into the fight with your wits intact."

I was ready for courage. My insecurities tended to overwhelm me. I feared the strength wasn't in me.

Grandpa steadied the punching bag from behind.

"Oldest first, Janis.

"I'm the oldest," Cordy said.

Grandpa gave him the stink eye, and Cordy backed off.

"My new name is Bailey," I reminded Grandpa.

"Sorry, you first, Bailey. Give it all you can."

I put everything I had into my swing. The bag barely moved, but it was satisfying hitting it.

"You're coming in too wide. It's all arm and no body," Grandpa said. "That approach leaves your shoulder and face open. I want you to pivot and throw your weight into the punch." He threw a couple of forceful jabs at the bag.

"My turn," Cordy said and swung wildly.

"Hold up there, champ," Grandpa said. "Bring your right leg out front and pivot from your waist down. Protect your head with your other hand."

Cordy followed Grandpa's directions to a T.

"Perfect. Did you see that, Bailey?"

"Get out of the way," I said and pushed my brother aside. I thought I really smacked the bag this time, but Grandpa was soft on his praise.

"Looks like we have to build your strength up first. Help me bring out the bench press."

That initial week was painful. By the third, we were training four hours a day. The different fighting techniques left nasty welts, or as my father calls them, war wounds. Cordy says they're fun marks. Dad probably had us homeschooled to avoid explaining all the bruises.

P.E. was back in session. Dad had my brother and I change into old T-shirts and meet in the garage.

"Today, we learn what to do if faced with a knife attack."

"Wait, what?" I said. "Before we go any further, you need to tell us what you and Grandpa do for a living."

"Ya think?" Cordy said.

Dad's forehead wrinkled and he rubbed his temples. "I'm not ready. Just give me time, Peaches."

"Fine, but you need to tell us."

"I will. Now back to our lesson." He picked up a large hunting knife from the counter and pointed the blade threateningly at Cordy's stomach. "What are you gonna do, punk?"

Cordy froze, and Dad rushed forward, stabbing him in the inside top of the leg, yelling, "Artery." Then under his arm and in his neck. There was blood everywhere.

"Stop it!" I screamed and grabbed Dad's arm. "What the fuck, you lunatic?"

"It's just a prop." He pushed on the blade with his finger. Fake blood squirted out of the handle.

Cordy let out a long, terrified scream and ran from the garage. I wanted to chase after him but was frozen.

"What the hell is wrong with you?" Grandpa asked Dad a short time later. "Cordy's in his room, bawling."

Dad stormed off to the house and dragged Cordy back to the garage. My brother was a mess.

"Quit crying," Dad demanded.

"Why did you do that?" Cordy said through sobs. Wiping his tears away wasn't helping to stop them.

"I was showing you how quickly a knife attack happens. Your assailant will strike fast with little warning. What is the first thing you should do?"

"Run," I joked.

"There's no shame in that," Dad said. "Attack me." He tossed the knife over.

I gathered a month's worth of rage and lunged for him. Within seconds he had my wrists pointing toward me and the blade pressing into my neck. The fake blood was cold as it dripped into my shirt. I tried my hardest to block the tears.

"That ruled!" Cordy said. "Teach me."

Dad fed off his enthusiasm. "The trick is to knock their hand up using the top of your forearm. No arteries are on that side, so a cut's trivial. With the knife away from your body, secure their arm and break the wrist backward with your other hand."

"I want you to attack Cordy," Dad told me.

Before he readied himself, I flew at him, screaming. I sunk the knife into his neck and held it tight. "You're dead," I taunted.

"Beginners luck," Cordy said, brushing it off. "Go again."

I circled to the corner of the room and charged with my arm out wide, so he could easily disarm me. Cordy knocked my arm away and bent my wrist back.

"Good," Dad said but gave me a knowing look. "Again."

I ran around Cordy to attack from the rear. He was focused and able to disarm me.

"That was awesome!" I said.

"Again."

"Come on," I said, "that was impressive."

24

"It was," Dad agreed. "Sorry. Good job, Son. Again."

We had the move down within the hour. Throughout the week, Cordy and I would ambush each other with sneak attacks. The only rule was no fake blood in the knife. Keeping on guard kept my mind occupied, which kept me from overthinking about Stefano.

Next up was disarming someone with a firearm. We were using a plastic training pistol for this exercise. I had the weapon aimed at Dad's stomach and wasn't about to fall for his shenanigans.

"Is that a new necklace?" he said.

"I can't believe you noticed." Before I could finish the sentence, he knocked my shooting hand toward the sky and forced my wrist back, pressing the barrel to my forehead.

"A perp won't aim a gun at your stomach the way you did. They'll point it at your head," Dad said, showing me how scary it looks. "They want you to stare down the muzzle paralyzed in fear. Your instinct will be to raise your arms. Do this, but not in an I-give-up way. Move your hands like you're saying, whoa, easy, to distract your assailant. Then tilt your head to the side so you aren't shot in the face. At the same time, reach out, and grasp their forearm, pushing the gun toward the sky, then break the wrist backward with your other hand, so the gun is now on them."

"Shouldn't we try to get away?" I said.

"If there's a fair amount of distance between you and the shooter, sure, but the false sense of power from a gun causes people to stretch the moment out, offering time for you to react. If they haven't drawn, you have extra seconds to close the distance. Your grandfather has a thing for handling this situation."

Dad pressed the call button on the intercom. "Hey, Pop, can you come to the garage? I want to show the kids that trick you do to disable a shooter."

25

"Come on, son. They're not old enough to see that."

Cordy and I begged to see the move. Grandpa eventually relented.

Bepa entered the garage, buckling his belt. "You asked for this," he said. "I don't want any crying tonight about nightmares."

I rolled my eyes at him. If they were going to teach us their weird skills, they needed to treat us older.

Dad brought the rubber punching dummy out from the corner and hid low behind it. He reached around the side with the gun as if it was the dummy's arm.

Grandpa recoiled with a hand out protectively, and his other dropped by his belt buckle. Within seconds the dummy had a throwing star embedded in his head.

"My eye!" Dad screamed and fell back with the dummy. Grandpa ran over, grabbed the plastic gun, and pretended to drain the magazine into his target's skull.

I grabbed onto a post to steady myself. Was this how they killed Stefano?

"One round should be enough at that range," Grandpa said. "But to be sure that your target stays down, it's not a bad idea to double-tap. Watch the trajectory. You don't want the bullet to ricochet and strike anyone." He retrieved his throwing star and held it up. "If you leave a weapon, you're leaving fingerprints."

I wanted to scream but couldn't speak. That did not just happen. It didn't happen. Everything's OK. I dropped to a knee and worked to catch my breath.

"What the hell?" Cordy said to Grandpa.

"You begged me to show you this trick," Grandpa said. "I knew this would happen. Wrap it up. We're going to the arcade."

I crawled into a run and locked myself in the bathroom. I wanted to cry, but the tears wouldn't come. A warm washcloth on my face helped calm me down. I found my family in the living room waiting, oblivious to my feelings.

"Can we swing by the giant hat and boots?" Cordy said. "I love that park."

"Of course, champ." Grandpa ruffled his hair.

"Cool," Cordy said, thrusting his arms in the air.

"I've never understood that expression," Bepa said. "If cool things are good, why don't we call lame things hot? How can hot and cool be the same? They can't be further apart."

"Maybe to stay positive?" Cordy said, smiling.

Grandpa couldn't argue with that logic.

We spent an hour at the park before heading to the arcade. Cordy and I wanted to go to GameWorks, but Bepa found the place too commercial. Instead, we decided on the 8-Bit Arcade in a town a few miles south called Renton.

Grandpa never has luck with parking. We ended up blocks away from the arcade. It was our first sunny day in Washington. The temperature was a comfortable seventy-five degrees with no trace of humidity. I was beginning to understand the allure of the Pacific Northwest.

Grandpa carried a purple Crown Royal sack brimming with quarters and kept tossing the bag in his hand. He stopped when he saw the homeless people on the block.

"I hope no one asks me for change," he joked.

As if on cue, a homeless man asked if we could spare some.

We all looked at each other. Cordy was the first to laugh. He usually is. His laughter was contagious, and the three of us joined in. It felt good to laugh, but the man looked crushed.

"We're not laughing at you," Grandpa managed to say. He opened the sack to offer a few quarters.

The man's eye's lit up when he saw all the change. "What are you, a leprechaun?" Cordy and I were in hysterics.

Grandpa pulled out his wallet and handed the man a ten-dollar bill.

"Bless you," the homeless man said.

"You'll get through this," Bepa said. "Good always balances out the bad."

"I sure hope so," the man said.

Inside the arcade, Dad and Grandpa headed to the Golden Tee golf game. Out of respect, Cordy and I watched their first round. Grandpa played miserably on the second hole, going for his sixth shot before making it to the green.

"This isn't your hole," Dad said.

Cordy responded with his usual, "That's what she said." But in this case, it nailed our funny bone. The best part is it got us sent away on our own.

Chapter 3

My father always has Support get us a fixer-upper. That's fine when the work is complete, but it means a year of living in constant construction. Dad's first major project was to divide Cordy's and my bedroom. I made a big fuss about having to share a room with him. He's a chronic masturbator. It's disgusting.

Dad was super secretive about the project, refusing to let us go near the rooms. We had to sleep on the couch for a week.

Cordy and I heard the dust shields coming down in the hallway and jumped up from the kitchen table. Dad saw us approaching, and a rare smile spread across his face. Where one door once stood, there were now two.

"We're ready to pick out the paint," Dad said. "Then I'll lay the carpet. Your room is on the left, sweetheart." He kissed me on the cheek. Cordy ran to his door.

I stepped into my room, not sure what to expect. The space itself was only about six feet wide, but that was all right; I finally had a place to call my own. Closest to the entrance was a bed built into the wall. Above it was cupboards.

"To work with such tight quarters, I built pocket beds. Your brother's is above your closet. Don't worry. I made the divider between them solid. You won't hear or feel anything from your brother's side." Dad tore off the plastic on the adjacent wall, revealing a window nook. "I've ordered a foam pad. We can select the fabric today if you want. It'll be a perfect area to get lost in your books."

I started crying. I couldn't help it.

"What's wrong, Peaches?"

29

"I love it," I said, hating that I was crying. I was still furious at Dad.

That Saturday, we were prepping the room for paint. Applying tape around the windows in the nook took forever. I tossed the roll in the corner, happy to be through with it.

"I'm done taping."

"You don't tape off areas; you mask. Use the god damn correct term," he said in what Dad thought was a loving fashion.

I closed my eyes and counted to ten. Not today, I thought.

For the walls, I chose a cheerful yellow called Daffodil to force happiness upon myself. Dad insisted on white for the ceiling and floorboards. The carpet was a dark blue to make changing the wall color easier when I grew bored with the yellow. I adored my new room; it was my sanctuary.

Bepa was the focus of the next project. He wasn't genuinely comfortable until there was a quiet area to garden, and what we wanted most in our household was a calm grandfather. Bepa and Dad built a horseshoe-shaped raised bed surrounded with protective chicken wire matching the gate's height. It was a spectacular garden.

My father couldn't convince either neighbor to pitch in for our new fence, so we aimed the lumber's good side toward our yard.

A clear coat brought out the richness in the grain. For the alley side, a semi-transparent grey stain created the illusion of wear. The last thing we needed was to draw attention to our house. The Central District wasn't as glamorous an area as it sounded. There were dangerous parts to it.

The love interest in the teen romance novel I was reading kept reminding me of Stefano. My thoughts drifted to the first day I met him. We were walking our rental bikes toward Central Park. You're not allowed to ride on New York City's sidewalks, and I wasn't about to make a death pact to join the traffic.

We reached the entrance. Horse-drawn carriages were lined up waiting for customers. The park was just as I imagined.

"What do you want to see?" Stefano said, holding out a map.

"Can we do it all? I've never been here."

"Depends on how much time you have."

It was a quarter to two. "About an hour and a half. If I'm lucky."

He let a sly smirk slip, and for the first time, I felt uncomfortable. My father's voice entered my head; *Boys are not to be trusted.* I brushed the thought away.

"We can do the loop in an hour. There's time to stop wherever you want."

Stefano tied his jacket to his waist. That's when I noticed it. We both wore white T-shirts and distressed jeans, mine more than his.

"We match," I said.

He glanced down at himself then over at me. "You wear it better." I would have taken that as a compliment if he wasn't staring at my tits when he said it.

Stefano set his kickstand and retreated to the shade of a metallic wall. Leaning against the cool metal refreshed us to our core. He wrapped my pinkie in his. Electricity shot from his finger and raced throughout my body.

We hopped on our bikes and peddled along the paved trail. I was surprised at how hilly the park was. I expected the terrain to be flat like the city.

A half-hour later, we reached the end of the park in Harlem. My earlier concern was for naught. Stefano was a gentleman. He even kept to my pace.

"Someday, we'll take a rowboat out on The Lake," he said, coasting next to me.

"The large one? I said.

"That's a reservoir. The Lake is the one with the restaurant. It's literally called The Lake."

"I'd be up for a row," I said dreamily.

Stefano stopped his bike in front of me. "Come here," he said, and with a hand placed under my chin, drew my lips to his. My body went limp, sending my hand slipping off the handlebars. He caught me by the armpit, putting me safely back, and leaned in for the kiss.

We continued along the pathway to the far side of the reservoir.

"Follow me," Stefano said. "My favorite building is around the corner."

As soon as we reached the street, I knew which structure Stefano came to see, the one looming tall and ominous like a castle. The place looked haunted.

"That's the Dakota. Have you seen Rosemary's Baby?"

I hadn't and shook my head.

"It's an old horror flick my grandpa and I watched. The movie's slow, but I loved this spooky building."

"Who do you think lives there?" I asked. A cabbie laid into his horn as he passed, startling me.

"The only one I know is some lady married to one of the Beatles, or a Beach Boy. I can't remember which. He was shot to death in the entryway."

"Weird. I bet he haunts the place."

"Yeah, but instead of moaning eerily into the night, he's singing a stupid sixties song, driving all the tenants mad."

"Not his wife."

He shrugged with an air of indifference. "We're making good time. Care to relax by the fountain? It's not far."

"Sure."

I appreciated that Stefano chose a populated area of the park to rest. The Fountain was in the middle of a stone patio, butting up to the lake he wanted to take me out rowing. We locked our bikes and walked hand-in-hand down the sweeping staircase to the shady side of the fountain. Stefano plopped down with his legs flat on the stone pavement, and I nestled in front of him.

A statue of an angel came into view as I leaned my head back. Beams of sunlight streamed through Stefano's dark hair. He was almost too striking to look at. I felt like the luckiest girl in the world. It was a feeling I could get used to.

"I wish I could stay here all day," I said.

Stefano squeezed me tight, and I felt his heart beating against my back.

"I'm stoked that we met," he said. "I hope I don't wake up and find this was all a dream."

He was so cool I was at a loss for words and played with the bracelet he gave me.

"You're so quiet."

"I'm just enjoying the moment." What do I talk about? Books? No. Movies? Maybe.

"So what do you do in school?" he said.

"Try not to be noticed," I responded before I could stop myself.

"I bet. You're so beautiful. It must be hard."

I didn't believe him for a minute, but coming from someone so handsome, meant a lot. "You're very sweet."

"That was a stupid question," he said. "What do you like to do?"

His question depressed me. I like to hang out with friends, but the click girls made sure that wasn't an option. I missed my old school and the friends I had.

"What do you like to do?" I asked right back.

"I love music. I'm learning to be a DJ."

"Like on the radio?"

"No, spinning records."

"Oh." I laughed at my ignorance. "You're so handsome I don't think I could dance to your music. I would just be staring."

"You'll be in my booth," he said, wrapping his arms around me.

I caught a glimpse of his watch and was shocked at how much time had passed. "I hate to do this, but I should get back to the library and check in with Dad."

"Of course," he said.

After dropping off our bikes, it was a brief ride on the MTA to Bryant Park. We were strolling along 42nd when I spotted my father. I gasped and hid behind Stefano.

"Dad's here. I'm in so much trouble." I peeked around Stefano. My father was nowhere in sight. He must have gone to the main entrance.

I had seconds to beat him to the children's section. That would be the first place he looked, being that he still thought I was his little girl.

"I have to go," I said and kissed Stefano quickly but passionately.

"Can I get your number?" he said.

"I can't have a boy calling," I said, climbing the side steps.

"When can I see you again?"

"Next Saturday. Or if I'm grounded the Saturday after."

"I'll be on that stoop every Saturday at noon."

My smile grew so large I feared it looked silly. I raced to the children's section, relieved that Dad wasn't there. With my phone retrieved and a random book in hand, I rushed to a chair and pretended I was asleep. I was wearing Stefano's leather bracelet. Shit! Footsteps were approaching, and there was a light touch on my shoulder. I jolted my body, pretending to be startled.

"What are you doing in the city?" I said, confused. With my wrist, I wiped imaginary drool from my chin.

"You fell asleep, Peaches. Come on; I want to take you out for ice cream."

"My phone," I said and searched for it.

"Here it is." He picked it up from the ground. "Your ringer is off. You have to keep that on."

"I'm sorry, Daddy. It wasn't on purpose."

"I know."

Out of the corner of my eye, I saw him deleting all the texts and voicemails he'd sent. That gave me hope. I turned my head to let him clean up the mess I created.

"This library is amazing," he said, handing my phone over.

"Best library in the world," I said.

"It's also New York City. You should be more careful."

"I can take care of myself. I don't like that you keep such close tabs on me."

"You're still my little girl."

"I'll be sixteen in three months. Your daughter is growing up."

"Don't say that. It kills me. Let's go get that cone."

Part of our homeschool P.E. curriculum included Bepa taking me to the track at the local high school twice a week to work on my quick starts and sprints. He was so serious about it, which bugged me. But then he explained that it could one day save my life. Of course, he didn't explain why.

We were stopped at a red light after a strenuous training session. Tents lined the sidewalk, with trash strewn everywhere. I felt bad for the people living there.

"What's up with all the homeless in Seattle?" I asked. "I didn't see anything like this in New York."

"It's all about the weather," he said. "On the East Coast, you can freeze to death on the streets. Because of that, they have a Right to Shelter Law."

"I don't get it. The people in this city seem so nice. Does it take freezing to death to house all the homeless?"

"Apparently."

"Grandpa, you passed it," I said, smelling the fresh aroma of pizza wafting through my open window.

"Oh, crap."

Bepa U-turned in the middle of the street, almost sideswiping a car. Lucky for him, the other driver swerved out of the way.

I was looking forward to pizza. When Mom died, I became the family chef. It was that, or we ate processed food. I was a cook out of necessity.

"Why don't you go in," Grandpa said, rolling to a stop in the lot. "I have a call to make."

I looked at the entrance of Central Pizza and back at Bepa. I was subconsciously moving my chin around nervously like Mom. "I can wait for you outside the car."

He pulled forty dollars from his wallet. "Don't be ridiculous. Go in."

I wasn't sure how to explain myself, so I blurted out, "I don't like cashiers."

He stared at me, trying to suppress a smirk. "You're just shy. That's normal for your age."

Warmth flooded my cheeks at the exposed insecurity. I wasn't just shy; I have nothing of interest to add. The only person I've ever been comfortable with outside the family was Stefano, and he was gone. A tear dripped from my eye.

"Bailey, everything's OK. You know who else was shy growing up?"

"Who?"

"Your father."

"Shut. Up. Dad's the most socially brave person I know. He can strike up a conversation with anyone."

"He wasn't always that way."

"But Cordy's not shy," I said.

"Your brother takes after the old man," he said, slapping his chest. "Don't worry; I can help you through this. The trick to confidence is acting. What I want you to do is act like you're social. Over time you'll find yourself wondering when the acting stopped and the confidence began."

"I don't know if I'm ready," I said.

He chuckled. "That's what your father said when I taught him this trick. Don't you dare let him know I told you this."

"I won't," I promised.

Grandpa peered around me. "This should be easy. The cashier is a young woman. After you're through with the formalities, pick something of hers that you like and offer a compliment. It could be her hair, eye shadow, a button, anything that will put the topic in her court. If the conversation stalls, discuss the weather. You can do this."

"Formalities. Pick something I like of hers. Weather," I said out loud and left the car before I talked myself out of it.

"Posture," Grandpa reminded me. How did I let that slip? The house mantra is: *You stand in your height proudly, not shrink away from it.*

I entered Central Pizza, feeling as if I were on death row, walking to the gas chamber. Each step toward the cashier felt heavier. I hated myself, but at least I was standing tall.

"Hi," the woman at the register said, looking up at me. "Damn, you're a tall one."

"Thanks," I said, acting like it was a compliment. "I'm here to pick up an order for Callister. Wow, I love your earrings." My tone was peppy and hopefully not too forced. I was doing pretty well with my fake confidence.

The girl touched an earring and rubbed it between her thumb and forefinger. "My boyfriend gave me these. He died in a car accident last month."

I threw the money on the counter and fled.

Grandpa was giving me a pep talk when the cashier knocked on my window. She set the pizza and change on our hood and walked away.

"Wait up there, Miss," Grandpa said, stepping from the car to give her a tip.

Back in the driver's seat, he asked what happened. I explained the situation, and he cracked up. It wasn't often that I got to laugh with Bepa. I didn't waste the moment.

"The good news is it can't get any worse than that," he said. "We'll try again tomorrow. Where *you* shine is in self-reliance. You've always been your own girl. When you were younger, your mom would search for you at bedtime. You know where you'd be?"

I shrugged my shoulders.

"Already in bed, having tucked yourself in, same as your father used to. Once you add confidence, you'll be as unstoppable as him."

I liked the sound of that.

Grandpa had me return to Central Pizza the next weekend to build confidence and set things right. Apologizing to the woman was easy. I had been doing that my whole life. We ended up having a lengthy conversation about dead boyfriends, which was therapeutic.

From there, I went straight to 7-11 to keep the confidence rolling. My interaction wasn't perfect, but I pretended to be at ease, which put me at ease. Grandpa was right; within a month, I chipped away a portion of my social phobia. School was even getting easier. I asked more questions during class instead of my usual silent panic when I was lost.

Dad's lessons were odd at times. He had sent me to my room to practice administering injections on an orange. My studies on dosages were levels above Cordy's.

Bepa pounded on the door. It startled me so bad I almost pierced my hand.

"You mind if I come in?" he asked.

"Not at all, Grandpa." I set the orange aside with the needle stuck in it.

"Your English teacher sent a note to your father, but I said I'd speak to you."

I grew flush, not knowing what I did wrong.

"Sorry."

"It's nothing bad. You kids have such a guilty conscience. Why did you say sorry if you don't even know what your teacher wants?"

"I don't know."

"Were you sorry?"

"No."

"Of course not. Don't be sorry. You have an equal seat at this table called life."

"I do say it too much. What should I do if someone bumps into me? Sorry just comes out even if they're in the wrong."

"You're saying sorry to be polite. You can still be polite without appearing weak. Tell them, excuse me. I'm not saying never apologize. If it's warranted, that's a sign of strength, not weakness."

"I'll work on it, Grandpa. So what did my teacher say?"

"What?"

"Sorry, you were saying my teacher sent a note."

"You just said sorry again."

"Sorry. What the hell? I can't stop saying it."

He laughed. "You will. Your teacher said that you've been participating more, and your confidence has improved tenfold. Her words. I wanted to tell you how proud I am of you."

"Thanks, Grandpa. For everything."

I missed the first train to New York City and didn't arrive at the library until one. Would Stefano wait for me? I walked to the side entrance and found it empty. Do I stay or search for him? I sat on the stoop, distraught.

Maybe it was for the best. I had looked up what a lack of empathy does to a person. Everything I read pointed to me heading into a toxic relationship. It could be a sign of narcissism, or worse, he could be a sociopath or a full-blown psychopath. What I couldn't find was empathy coming in later in life, like he said happens in his family.

"Sup girlfriend?"

I turned my head, and on the landing was my Stefano. He was more stunning than I remembered. How could a man this handsome be attracted to me?

It was blisteringly hot outside, yet Stefano was in jeans. His T-shirt had a sketch of an alien frog with eyes stretching far above his body. I didn't recognize the band, Daniel Johnston. I would be looking up the album on the train ride home.

"It's so good to see you again," I gushed.

"It's good to be seen. Care to join me for a walk through Times Square?"

"I can't. Dad will find out."

"We'll be fine. Give me your phone."

I handed it over, and he navigated to the GPS settings to disable my tracking.

"It'll look like you're in the library."

40

We were at a street vendor's stall ordering an Italian soda when Dad called.

"I'll meet you back at the library."

I raced down the sidewalk, knowing I couldn't answer with all the street noise around. From inside the doorway, I called him back.

"What's up, Dad?"

"Where are you?"

"I'm at the library."

"No, you're not. I just called."

"I was in the bathroom. That's a long train ride."

"Turn your GPS back on."

"Dad, I'm not a kid anymore. I don't like you tracking me."

"Turn it on!" he barked.

I spotted Stefano out on the stoop and flagged him over to activate the GPS.

"Are you happy?" I asked my father.

"Keep it on," he said, ending the call.

"I have to stay here," I said, disappointed.

"That's cool," Stefano said, handing over my Italian raspberry soda. It was no longer layered. From rushing over, the drink was now a milky pink hue. I found it to be delicious.

"We can have fun here," Stefano said. "Show me around?"

"I would love to." I was excited. We were on my turf.

A librarian made us finish our drinks outside. She gave us a map of the library to keep us busy.

I wanted to blow Stefano's mind right away and brought him up three flights to the Rose Main Reading Room. The space is massive, as long as a football field. Arched windows high above supply an abundance of natural lighting. Many a day I have spent studying in this magnificent room.

Stefano stared up at the gilded wood ceiling. I'd had the same reaction of awe the first time I stepped into the room.

"I don't have words to describe the beauty." He sat at a desk to take in the ambiance.

The location proved too quiet for us. In the rotunda, I showed him one of the animals hidden in the library's architecture. That led us to the second floor on a quest for more. After discovering a lion's head, Stefano ran down the hall to the study rooms and peered into one. A college-age woman said, "Occupied." A room two down was free, and he pulled me inside. Dad would not have been pleased, which added excitement to the act.

I backed Stefano into the desk, and he fell over with me on top. My fingers weaved through his thick and luscious hair as we kissed. His hand was wandering toward my breast. Luckily an older librarian walked in.

"Hey, you can't be in here," she said.

We jumped up, embarrassed. Well, I was embarrassed. Stefano berated the poor woman for interrupting us. I wanted to say something, but she was being a bitch. Stefano and I ran from the room, hand-in-hand.

"I'm starving. Can you leave for lunch?" he said.

"Maybe, but it's my treat this time." I had enough money from babysitting.

I texted Dad, and we headed into the city. We found an air-conditioned café a couple of blocks over. It was a welcome relief from the heatwave.

Stefano got into an argument with the waitress about substituting an item. I told her I wasn't ready and to come back.

"I'm not trying to control you," I said. "The way you were treating that woman made me uncomfortable."

"But I want rice. It's not that big a deal."

"It is a big deal. You're being an asshole."

"Fuck you!"

I couldn't believe what I was hearing. "No, fuck you. Make this right, Stefano, or I'm leaving."

He stood up, muscles clinched, but sat back down.

"Fine. But you can't get all salty, threatening to leave every time I do something stupid."

"I'm not going to stick around if you behave this way. You'll end up losing me." I hoped he didn't see I was trembling. Confrontations were a struggle. I was so proud of myself.

"I can't help it."

"Try harder."

"What do you want me to do?" He folded his arms defiantly.

"Apologize to the waitress and order rice on the side. Is that so fucking hard?"

"I guess not," he said.

After we ordered, Stefano placed a USB drive in my palm. "A mix inspired by our first date," he said.

"That is so sweet." I melted, blindsided by his kindness.

"Here, listen to the song I made from John Lennon's Imagine." Stefano handed over a pair of earbuds. "He's the guy who was shot in front of the Dakota."

A familiar tune from Grandpa's era began. There was layer upon layer of complementary beats added, making the song modern and danceable. Stefano wasn't just dabbling in the DJ world; he was talented.

"I have something for you." I removed a diamond earring from my ear. "It was my mom's." I expected him to protest that it was too personal, but he excitedly replaced his earring with Mom's.

"It looks cute," I said and kissed him.

"Get a room," a man in the booth next to us yelled. It was the first time anyone said that to me. I felt like an adult around Stefano.

Chapter 4

There was one area in the house where my brother and I weren't allowed. That would be what Dad and Bepa call the Lair. A sliding bookshelf in the basement kept the entrance hidden. Even if we wanted to, there was no getting past the solid metal door.

My father assembled Cordy and me in the basement for our third lock-picking session. The lesson this evening was on padlocks. We already mastered deadbolts; with the right tools, it's pretty simple. The only thing a lock offers is a false sense of security.

Dad's phone screeched with a loud warning. He pulled it from his pocket so fast the phone slipped out of his fingers, and he scrambled to pick it up. His reaction to whatever was on the screen scared me. He unholstered his Glock and slammed a full magazine inside. Dad handed the pistol to Cordy but thought better of it and gave it to me.

"Indexing!" Dad yelled. He startled me so badly I could have accidentally fired. I moved my finger off the trigger. "You have fourteen forty-caliber rounds in there. That's a lot of firepower. Get to Cordy's room and lock the door. Go!"

Grandpa met Dad in the kitchen. They raced out the back, packing heat. Cordy and I high-tailed it to his room.

There were sounds of a scuffle in the backyard, screaming and yelling, and then a gunshot. Cordy and I looked at each other wide-eyed.

"We're all right," Dad called out after ten of the longest seconds. "Don't you move," he said to someone outside. "I will end you."

45

"What do you think it was?" Cordy said, making a game out of guessing.

"I don't want to play," I said.

"I think it was a gang hit," he said.

"You're not helping."

The doorbell rang a few minutes later, and I opened Cordy's door to see who it was.

"Go to your room," Dad ordered. "While you're in there, I want you to list the four main rules of gun safety."

I deserved that for resting my finger on the trigger. On the way to my room, I caught a glimpse of the strangers in our kitchen. Cordy was close in his guess. They weren't gang members per se, but a couple of neighborhood thugs. Grandpa was sitting at the dining room table drinking tea with them. The guys were quite menacing, which made the image odder. The man closest to me was large but held his tea daintily with his pinkie raised. He thought that was the funniest. The tall and lanky boy quieted him down so he could listen to the police at the door.

"No, sir. It was fireworks," Dad said to the officer. "I saw the blast from the back window. It was a brilliant blue explosion from a mortar. If you drive through the alley, you can probably still smell it. Sure, no problem. I appreciate your service and for arriving so fast."

I peered around the corner after Dad passed. The guys fawned over him for not turning them in.

"We don't care for the police," Dad said. "They roughed me up in my youth."

"Come on, son," Grandpa said, "that's not the lesson here. You were roughed up at a party because you stupidly tried to grab a responding officer's firearm. I'm not blaming you, but it was your fault."

"Oh, shit, Daddy," Big Boy taunted. My father's back was to me, but I knew the terrifying glare he was sending. Both boys straightened up in their seats.

"You *should* like the police," Tall and Lanky said, "being able to get them to believe your bullshit like that."

"All you have to do is be polite," Dad said.

"Yeah, that's not how it works in our world," Big Boy said. The reality of the statement silenced my father.

"Let's get back to the subject," Bepa said. "It wasn't wise what you did tonight. If my son hadn't been on top of his game, you'd be dead. You're smart kids. Use those minds to better yourself. The way to stick it to life isn't stealing; it's succeeding. Success is key. You don't have to make millions to be successful. It can be a decent career and a place to call home. Success is whatever makes you truly happy." He paused to let his message seep in. "I want to see you back here at noon tomorrow. You have to make a thing right."

I ducked into my room to look up the Scottish proverb, but the saying was all Grandpa.

The boys were coming down the hall as I was returning. I physically ran into Big Boy. His body was solid as a brick wall.

"Aren't you a tall glass of milk," he said.

"I'm Janis. I mean Bailey," I said, sticking out my hand.

"Well, which one is it?" Tall and Lanky said.

"This is my granddaughter, Bailey."

"Granddaughter?" both boys said.

"She's sixteen," Grandpa said as a warning.

"I thought you was in your twenties," Big Boy said. "I'm Leroy, but my friends call me Tubs."

The nickname his friends gave him was as mean as mine.

"Can I still be your friend if I call you Leroy?" I said and shook his hand.

"Of course," he said, flattered by my comment.

"I'm Demoine," Tall and Lanky said.

"It's nice to meet you, Demoine."

"The pleasure is mine, sugar."

47

"She's more like fine honey," Leroy said.

"Stop," Grandpa said roughly. "All this sweetness is giving me the diabetes."

That got Leroy rolling in a deep, bellowing laugh. I let them pass and joined Dad in the living room. Cordy entered a short time later. We sat in silence until my brother couldn't take it anymore.

"Well? What the hell was all that?" he said.

"Just misguided youth trying to break into our garage," Dad said. "I thought it was something else. Your grandpa and I sure scared those kids."

"What do you mean you thought it was something else?" I said.

"Nothing," Dad said with a forced laugh. "They won't attempt that again. Grandpa is having them come back tomorrow to help weed. Give them honest work."

"Is that safe?" I whispered.

"Sure, your grandpa will be in the garden with them. He'll get those boys straightened out."

I believed he would. Grandpa is very persuasive.

Cordy grew bored and retreated to his room to play Minecraft. When I heard him chatting with the online players, I turned to Dad.

"What did you mean when you said you thought it was something else?" I asked again.

"That was nothing," he said gruffly.

"It wasn't nothing, goddamn it! I need to know what you guys do for a living."

"I suppose you're right." He slapped my knee. "Let's go find Bepa."

He was in the kitchen looking spent. Dad refilled his glass with scotch and poured another for himself.

"It's time for the talk," Dad said.

"The boy's not old enough."

"Just her. Cordy's in his room playing that damn game."

48

Grandpa took a long swig off his drink. "You sure you're ready for this?"

"I've been ready for months. Spill it."

"All right." He sat silently, gathering his thoughts. "This is going to sound a little out there. We come from a long line of families called Hunters."

"What do we hunt, vampires?" I joked.

"No, but they are monsters," he said with a straight face.

What the fuck? I was only kidding.

"We call them the Dread. They're pure evil, cursed from the sours of the earth. Their day-to-day life is fairly normal, except for a severe lack of empathy. Without frequent sexual encounters, though, they change. The Dread needs a connection every three days, or something in their brain flips, causing them to become homicidal. We've lost many innocent lives to these creatures."

A severe lack of empathy? Was Stefano a Dread? Is that why they killed him? That's crazy. I wasn't prepared for this. Hitman, sure. Mafia, fine. But monsters? It didn't sound real. They had to be talking about people who just act monstrously.

"This doesn't make sense," I said. "If they change because of a lack of sex, why don't they just have it regularly?"

"A lot of them do," Grandpa said. "And that's how they hide so well. But sometimes they slip. Others grow fond of the change. It's the latter who we focus our energy on. We never target a Dread unless they've harmed or intend to harm someone. That was your mother's rule. She was adamant about it."

"The whole thing sounds made up," I said.

"I speak the truth," Grandpa assured me. "The story dates back a thousand years in Italy. Legend is that witches cursed the invading Moors, turning them into the Dread. I don't believe that garbage. There was a darker, evil force at work." He took another drink from his scotch.

"The Moors conquered most of Sicily, but the Sicilians fought back with the help of the French Normans. By 1070, the Normans were winning the war, but they couldn't defeat a holdout of Dread. Their leader, Robert Guiscard, called upon the Pope to find the fiercest of the fierce to help end the war. That is where our family came into play. Our bloodline runs to Angus de Cambrun, the first Chief of what is now known as Clan Cameron. Our family were great warriors."

"We still are," my father interjected.

"Aye. That we are." They clinked their glasses. "Our relatives were called by God to fight in Sicily, to fight the Dread. The journey was in the guise of a pilgrimage of the Western Catholic church. During the year 1072, our kin were vital in the fall of the Dread's stronghold of Messina. This dealt a severe blow to the Moor's power in Sicily. It took another nine years to retake the land. If it weren't for the king of Sicily's tolerance, the Dread would have perished. He protected the Moorish community, and the Dread among them stepped in line to show a false love toward King Roger. For years, the Dread laid low. It was easy for the attractive to blend in, keeping the change at bay with a steady flow of sex. The unattractive and the rapists were ultimately exposed and killed off. Because of this, the Dread evolved handsomely into some of the finest looking Sicilians. But don't let their appearance fool you. They are pure evil." He looked deep into my eyes, drilling the point home.

"After the battle in Messina, our forefathers returned to Scotland as heroes. It wasn't for another hundred years that our bloodline was back in the fold, and we've lived as Hunters ever since."

Dad took over the story. "Our daughters are the ones who lead the charge. You, Bailey, are the omnes videntes venator, the all-seeing Huntress. Technically what you have is a hyper form of Mirror-Touch Synesthesia. Or as we call it, The Mirror's Touch. When you're close to a

50

Dread, there's something in their chemistry that allows you to feel what they do."

I ran to the bathroom and threw up. Stefano *was* a Dread. That is why Grandpa felt the urgency to kill him. They were protecting me. But from what? They said they only kill a Dread that poses a risk. What threat does a sixteen-year-old boy present? Was my boyfriend a monster? Had I been foolishly ignoring the signs? I hoped his death was quick and painless.

There was a knock on the door." You all right in there?" Dad asked.

"I'll be out in a minute," I yelled.

I splashed water on my face, sucked back my emotions, and returned to the kitchen. My anger overtook my reasoning. "Did you have my boyfriend killed?"

Dad feigned ignorance. "What boyfriend?"

"I was in the hall when you and Grandpa said you had to eliminate him."

"He was a Dread," Dad yelled

"I didn't know that!" I screamed. "I didn't even know what a Dread was."

"If you hadn't been sneaking around, we could have figured it out together," he said. "Look, we didn't kill the Rosotti boy. Your grandfather and I went to talk to his family but found their house on fire. We saw a news crew filming and got the hell out of there. Support arranged our move that day."

I was doing everything I could not to cry. "If you didn't know I had a boyfriend, how did you find out about him?" I said in a nasty tone, knowing I had him.

"You and your boyfriend tripped our security when you were trying to sneak into your own window. I sent his picture to Support. Their response is what made me read your diary. I would never have violated your trust if it weren't an emergency. You have to believe me."

"I don't *have* to do shit."

51

"Is this why you've been in such a mood these past few months? That you thought we killed him?"

"Yes," I admitted.

"Oh, honey," Dad said, going in for a hug.

"Fuck you."

He was taken aback. "Fair enough. I'm sorry, Peaches. We were doing what we thought was right."

Getting away with telling my father off was disarming. "Can I have the picture that you sent to Support? I don't have any of him. It would give me closure."

"If I still have it."

"Thanks. I hate to tell you. I don't think the Mirror's Touch is strong in me. I could only feel him when we touched, and that was only at the end."

"It will grow stronger with time."

"Did mom have the Mirror's Touch?" I said.

"No, your mother was wed into the family," Dad said. "The Touch passes down from the father's side. The gene is dominant. It always prevails."

"This seems too coincidental," I said, "that the very people who were called upon to fight the Dread have daughters that can find them with this weird power."

"The gift you have is one of the reasons the Pope chose our kin. Don't take this path lightly. Your destiny is a perilous one. That's why we train you so hard."

I looked over at Dad. "Are there other Hunters?"

"Yes, but we don't know how many or who they are. For our safety, we're not allowed to speak to the others."

"OK, but if Huntresses have this power to sense the Dread, how have they survived so long?"

"That's a great question, Bailey. Look at you."

"Just answer the question, Dad."

"Your mother couldn't take a compliment either. The reason it's hard to track the Dread is they charm everyone around them."

"The monsters," I said.

"This is serious. The Dread's support structure is vast. They become the center of the neighborhood, so no one wants to turn on them. Plus, they hide well. It's as if they disappear."

From my experience with Stefano, Dad was right about the hiding, but I couldn't see the Dread charming a neighborhood. Their anti-social behavior would eventually emerge no matter how hard they tried to suppress it. My thoughts were drifting heavy to Stefano. I didn't want to cry in front of my father.

"What's wrong, Bailey?"

"Nothing," I said. "This is just a lot to take in."

"It will be old hat in no time. I'm proud of you, honey."

"Thanks, Dad. I need some time to think." I kissed Grandpa on the forehead and headed to my room to comfort myself with Stefano's music. He set me up in New York with a private email address on our second date. I usually checked these at the library, but there was no hiding now. I brought up the first note Stefano sent me.

```
Janis. My heart aches for you when
we're apart. I'm sitting on my bed,
wishing you were here in my arms.
We've only known each other for
eight days, but they've been my
favorite so far. What I do to
escape this wanting is to disappear
into my music. I like you, Janis.
Don't take that lightly. I like you
more than life itself.
```

I sent him a response knowing I wouldn't get an answer. I never do. I shoved my face into my pillow and cried.

A new email chimed, sending my heart racing. I was disappointed it was from my other account, but shocked at what Dad sent—a grainy picture of Stefano laughing at me climbing in the window. My boyfriend was so beautiful.

Once my tears dried, I went to find my father to get that hug.

I took my training more seriously after learning about the Dread. The Mirror's Touch gave us the advantage of detecting them. Hunting the Dread was a different story. How could I track and kill Stefano's kind?

Cordy didn't understand why I suddenly became so devoted. I let it slip that Dad and Grandpa were hitmen. In a way, they kind of are. He went all-in after hearing that.

A Mixed Martial Arts academy was in our neighborhood. I wanted to join as soon as I learned of the place, but it took months for Dad to agree. I was seventeen when he finally signed me up.

My sparring partner was three years older than me. Mary was an angry ginger who reveled in pushing my boundaries in the ring, but I was now what I jokingly called five foot twelve, so my reach was well beyond hers. Aside from the family, the gym was the one place I treasured my height. It gave me an advantage.

"Is that all you have, you freckleless cunt?" Mary said after I landed a solid hit.

It took a moment for her statement to register. I thought she said feckless. "Did you say freckleless?" We started laughing. I liked Mary's laugh. It was deep and throaty like an olden day movie starlet, but it didn't match her appearance. She had a unique, almost elfin look. Her face was narrow with a cute dimpled chin and a sultry mouth that turned up mischievously at the edges. I found her stunning.

54

"Tom's not paying money for social hour," my trainer, TJ, said.

He was a no-nonsense older tough guy, exactly what I pictured a coach would look like with his round, expressive face and crazed but focused concentration. He even wore a stereotypical coach's black stocking cap. I bet Grandpa picked him so I wouldn't crush on my coach.

We assumed our positions, and TJ struck the bell.

"You punch like a T-Rex," I said to rile Mary up. She charged in, and I landed a one-two jab to her head. Each connection sent a rush of satisfaction through my body. I was made for fighting.

Mary fell forward and wrapped her leg around mine, tripping me. I was quicker and sprawled back, turned, and placed her in a reverse choke. TJ had me release my hold, and we both popped to our feet. Mary was strong but no match. I returned the few punches she landed with more forceful ones of my own. I was about to land a Superman blow, a specialty of my long reach, when her coach threw in the towel.

"No offense, Mary, but I need to find Bailey a new partner," TJ said. "If she would have thrown that punch..." He shook the thought off.

"I can do better," Mary said.

"You'll have another chance," her coach promised.

I liked how nuts the people at this gym were. This girl pretty much had the crap beaten out of her, and already she was asking for more.

TJ pulled me aside. "Do you know why you're able to beat Mary so easily?"

"My reach?"

"That helps, but no, people can get around a long reach. What makes you a strong fighter is you never let rage overtake you. That keeps you fully in the moment. I hope you don't mind me asking, were you bullied?"

I dropped my gaze, embarrassed. The click girls are who I imagined I was fighting. It gave me strength. Even

55

the name they made up for themselves is grating. What I wouldn't give to beat the fuck out of those two.

"Bailey, this is nothing to be ashamed of. Bullying is what stops you from flying off the handle. You've compensated for the better. Don't lose that. And don't ever let anyone bully you again." He hit me on the shoulder and headed to the water cooler.

"Want to get a coffee?" Mary asked, switching to friend mode.

"I would love a coffee," I said, hoping my response wasn't too eager.

We had to run laps for trying to duck out of training early. It was another hour before our coaches allowed us to leave.

Mary changed into a T-shirt with a low collar, showing off her freckles. She has so many they're a statement of beauty.

"Let's get out of this neighborhood. It scares me," she said. The area she was referring to was twelve blocks from my house. It scared me too.

"Do you have a car? I rode the bus." I didn't want her knowing I walked.

"Sure, follow me."

The inside of Mary's Subaru was roomy for a tall frame.

"I like your car."

"It's Dad's. Oh shit, I love this song." She cranked the stereo, and we sang along to Adele like old friends.

Mary drove to a trendy café in the gay district of Capitol Hill. I enjoy that part of town. The people go out of their way not to judge, making me feel comfortable in my height.

The barista called our names, and we retrieved our mugs from the counter.

"Can we sit outside?" I said. "This neighborhood was made for people-watching."

"Of course." Mary followed me to the door.

"Banana or peach?" she asked as we made ourselves comfortable at a street-side table.

I was confused. Were we having dessert with our coffee? I grabbed a menu from the table.

"Well, banana or peach?" She tilted her head toward a boy waiting for the light to change. But then I wasn't so sure it was a boy.

"I don't think we're supposed to be playing this," I whispered.

"Come on. I'm so sick of this PC bullshit."

"With your muscles, haven't you ever been told you look like a boy?"

"Not to my face."

I laughed. "Imagine you were born a different sex than you actually were. How foreign your own body would feel. You wouldn't be truly happy until you were the correct gender."

"I realize the plight of the pronoun," Mary said. "Don't worry. I know this person. Banana or peach?"

"Fine, she's a peach. Her hips gave her away."

"Yeah, that's my lesbian friend Linda. She's pissed at me 'cause I told her she's dressing so much like a boy that it's confusing my gay friends." She did a triple take to show how they react when they realize she's a girl.

"That can happen when you expect the pole and get the hole," I said.

"The pole and the hole. You're a riot."

"Sorry to go off on a rant there. I was bullied in my last school. My transgender classmate Kayla was the only one who stuck up for me. She was pretty cool."

"Hey, no sweat, sister." She leaned back in her chair with the sun on her face and closed her eyes.

"Speaking of old schools," I said. "Have you ever beat up someone you knew?"

She leaned forward abruptly. "One time. It was fucking epic. Get it out of the way quickly. Once you reach a certain level, you can get in a lot of trouble."

"I wish I could. Those bitches are on the East Coast." A gay couple holding hands gave me a smirk as they passed.

"I'd almost pay your way to see that. So, you're not from around here. I had a feeling you weren't. Don't worry; there aren't many who are."

"How about you?" I said.

"Born and raised in California. Seattle works for me, though. The climate is much better for my complexion and my confidence. So, what got you into fighting?"

"The family business. I needed to know how to protect myself." Why hadn't I lied? Fuck!

"Is the business why your grandpa won't let you go professional?"

"Yeah." I took a sip of my coffee so I wouldn't have to look at her.

"That's too bad. I haven't seen anyone take to the sport so naturally."

"You're too kind. What about you? Why did you get into fighting?"

She thought about the question. "Same story, my parents, although I do it because they're such pacifists. I fight because it drives them nuts. My parents want me to be a nurse. Another kind of fight."

"I like you," I said. "You're so open."

"Life is too short to be boring," she said. "So, do you have a boyfriend?"

"I did, but my dad and grandpa killed him," I responded dryly.

Mary didn't believe me for a second. Laughing about it somehow chipped away a piece of my sorrow. It had been a while since Stefano crossed my mind. That saddened me.

"Do you have time to go shopping?" I said. "This is the only neighborhood I can find shoes in my size."

Mary laughed. "That's because of the drag queens."

"Well, duh, they have fabulous taste in footwear."

"Let's go." Mary took my hand. I was uncomfortable with that initially, but the contact felt nice.

That evening my thoughts kept drifting to her. I'd never experienced such an immediate closeness with another woman. I contemplated whether I should dabble in what my brother calls the Devil's pond.

The following Tuesday, I was looking forward to getting back to the gym to see my new friend, but Mary wasn't around.

My coach was avoiding eye contact. "Bailey, there's no easy way to say this, so I'm just going to come out with it."

Was he kicking me out of the gym? I knew that body slam was too much.

"Mary was jumped last night. She's in a coma."

My chest tightened. "Oh my God. Is she OK?"

"I don't know. Here's the address. Forget about today's workout. Your head wouldn't be in the fight."

"Thanks, TJ," I said and headed out.

Mary was in Harborview Medical Center. Getting beyond security was an exercise in patience. The officer was thorough to a fault. I finally made it past the riff-raff and located Mary's room. She was unconscious, with a bandage securely wrapped around her head. Mary's parents were seated at her side. I'm not sure why I expected pacifists to be weak looking. Both had a ruggedness to them, especially her father. He looked like a lumberjack.

"Hi, I'm Bailey. Mary's friend."

"Our daughter spoke of you. I'm Ben, and this is my wife, Tara."

"What happened?" I said. "I saw her two nights ago."

"She was mugged," her dad replied. "Took a solid hit to the side of her head. I doubt Mary had more than ten dollars on her."

"Damn this city," her mom said, staring out the window. The comment sat weird, almost forced. She reminded me of Mary. It was all in the lips. Even with her sullen expression, the uptick at the sides was there.

"They must have sneaked up on her," I said. "That girl can take care of herself. How bad is it?"

"The doctors don't know yet," her dad said. "She's in an induced coma until the swelling goes down.

"Her brain activity registers normal," her mom added, "That's keeping us going."

I sat on the other side of my friend and held her hand. "Hi, Mary, it's Bailey. We were supposed to go to the movies tonight. We'll go real soon. Keep fighting." She was motionless. It killed me seeing her that way.

Her parents had me read Mary's book aloud while they left for lunch. When we were alone, I closed the novel to talk.

I had my headphones on her when they returned. My favorite song from Stefano was playing. I hoped the frantic beat would trigger her awake, but she remained lifeless.

The fourth day I visited, I was happy to find Mary had been discharged. That was all they could legally tell me, but it sounded like good news.

I headed to the gym to get her address, but it wasn't on file. Her family was as private as mine.

On the way out, this jackass, Carl, challenged me to a fight. Once in the ring, I envisioned my sixth-grade principal and had him on the run. I struck Carl with a right hook to the chin. Out of the corner of my eye, I saw Mary. Her head was still bandaged. Carl used my broken focus to high-kick me in the ear. Even though I was wearing protective gear, the force of the blow knocked me off my feet. He went in for a choke, but I sprawled backward, breaking free.

"Come on, you pussy," Mary taunted.

I charged my opponent with four head shots to disorientate him, then threw a Superman jab. It should have been a walk-off knockout, but as Carl was wobbling, I picked him up and brutally body-slammed him onto his back. The small crowd that had gathered cheered. TJ was leaning against the back wall. I hadn't seen him come back from lunch. He shook his head disapprovingly.

"You are such a badass," Mary said.

I climbed out of the ring to join her. "I'm amazed that you're up and around. How's the noggin?"

"Hurts like hell. I thought you toughened me up, but man, I got walloped." Mary stopped speaking, and her face tightened.

"What's wrong?" I said. "Should we get you back in bed?"

"It's not my head." She was fighting back tears. "I'm on my way to Africa this afternoon. My parent's Peace Corps assignment came through. I can't fly in case of a blood clot. We have to take a train across the country to make it in time, then a ship. I couldn't leave without saying goodbye."

"What? No," I said, failing to hold back the tears.

"You're going to make me cry." She gave me another hug.

"Can I see you off?"

She hesitated. "Of course. Get changed. I'll meet you out front."

Mary was waiting outside in an Uber.

"I make such a cool friend, and now you're leaving," I said. "Life is a dick sometimes."

"You have that right. I like you, Bailey. You're like a sister."

"I thought the same thing. We have this weird energy between us."

Inside the car, Mary and I peppered each other with questions. The route was way too fast to learn anything meaningful.

61

I'd noticed King Street Station's brick building when my family was exploring downtown Seattle. The tower looks a lot like the one in Venice's St. Mark's Square, which I learned about in history class. Although, that one doesn't have a clock.

I walked through the entrance and marveled at the high ceiling carved in a bright white ornamental relief.

"This is about as far as you can go," Mary said.

I was sure I could go further but didn't press. "Here's my email," I said, handing it over. I hugged her as a horn blasted from the yard.

"That was my train. I am so sorry."

And with that, another friend was gone. Once again, I was alone. My destiny seemed to be one of depression and isolation. All I had was my family.

Chapter 5

Throughout the year, Dad and Grandpa sent me stories of the Dread and their kills. Each new murder brought me one step closer to the hunt. The gruesome details made the decision easy. Dad said he would know when it was time, but I knew it was.

I waited until he was three drinks into the night before I dared ask if I could join the business. There was one condition. I would never kill.

"I'm almost eighteen. You know I can handle myself."

"It's dangerous," he said. "Are you sure you're ready?"

"As ready as I'll ever be."

"Let me discuss this with Pop. Why don't you get out of here? You're ruining my buzz."

"All right, Dad," I said and kissed him.

Three weeks later, I was heading out on my first case. Bepa was in the driver's seat, with Dad riding shotgun. Their long wigs offered the guise of aging hippies. Grandpa's fake soul patch worked hilariously well with his mustache. They were having a ball acting stoned. Dad's drooping eye effect was perfection. I wore a floppy tan leather hat over my blonde wig. It would be tough ditching the colorful sundress when this was over. I wanted to be this woman.

I had no idea where the van came from, and I wasn't about to ask. In our family, it's best not to know certain things. "Deniability can one day save your life," Grandpa told me.

The joking abruptly ended as Grandpa rolled to a stop on a dimly lit street in West Seattle.

"Bailey, this isn't a stakeout," Dad said. "We didn't want you to overthink the real task. Our mission is to take out a Dread."

My heart dropped, but I wasn't scared. A strange and unfamiliar calm overtook my nerves. I was ready for the fight.

"You'll be fine," Grandpa said.

"I believe you're right," I said. "I'm not afraid. Why am I not afraid?"

"That's the Cameron blood in you," Grandpa said with a Scottish accent.

"When we're near the man, let us know if you can feel him," Dad said. "Your role is to confirm he's a Dread."

"I will," I said but wasn't sure I could.

"It's like we're in a low-budget surfer movie," Dad said as he shut the back door of the van.

"I can see the title up in lights," Grandpa said. "The Van with the Tear-Stained Mattress."

It took a few seconds to get Grandpa's dark humor. We burst out laughing and climbed back inside to avoid drawing attention to ourselves. It was a while before the laughter subsided.

The three of us walked down the block and turned onto a quiet dead-end street. Our target lived in the apartment above the garage of the last house on the right. The shadow of a laurel offered a safe vantage point.

Dad peered through binoculars. "That's him," he said after a man passed by the window. My pulse raced with the excitement of the moment. "The owner of the main house should be at work for another two hours."

Grandpa put on a large pair of military goggles. "Someone's tied up on his bed. We still have time; there's heat rising from the body."

Dad handed me a Glock, and I pulled the slide back to check for a round in the chamber.

"You'll want to wear these," he said, offering me flesh-colored earplugs. "Even with the suppressors, firing indoors can be deafening."

The significance of our mission was heavy. We were here to kill a Dread. I didn't know if I could be a part of this.

Grandpa gave the word, and I reluctantly made my way up the steps to the side door. An odd sensation washed over me from inside the house. I wasn't quite sure what was causing the feeling.

We were dangerously in the open. Grandpa unscrewed the light bulb above the doorway for cover. Dad removed a metal device from his backpack, attached it to the door's peephole with suction cups, and then raised the lower part to connect with the top. He held onto the handle with gloved hands.

"You guys ready," Dad whispered. We gave him the thumbs up. He motioned for me to move over, so I was out of gunshot range, I suppose.

Grandpa knocked, and I sensed a man walking to the door. Somehow we were connected like I was a passenger in his shoes. It was as clear as if I were him. This man was evil, through and through.

Dad looked at me and mouthed, "Well."

I nodded and smiled, relieved and horrified that the Mirror's Touch was working. I pointed to the door and then at my gun to show him the Dread was packing.

Grandpa had his heat vision goggles on. A pistol was cocked and ready in his hand. I felt the man grip the door handle then back off. He bent slightly forward, and I was him as he brought his eye to the peephole. Grandpa pointed his finger and Dad released the lever on his device. What I thought was the handle arced upward and pierced a spike through the peephole. There was confusion in the man but no pain. His gun slipped from his fingers, falling loudly to the floor. He was stuck to the door and struggled to get free. Dad wrestled with the lever to pull the spike back. Both the man and I dropped to the ground. I woke up in the car disoriented.

"There's my talented daughter," Dad said from the driver's seat.

"I was him. I felt him die. What the fuck?"

"Are you OK?" he said.

"I think so. How did I get here?"

"We carried you."

"The Dread faded to black, into nothingness. Is there no God?"

"There is a God," Grandpa replied with indignation. "That creature is heading in the opposite direction."

A few miles from our house, Dad pulled into the back of a secluded lot to swap cars with his own. Grandpa used our Dyson to vacuum out the van. Dad and I were on fingerprint duty, wiping any trace of our presence.

When we were safely home, Grandpa retrieved the good scotch from the cupboard and two tumblers. I grabbed a glass and followed him into the living room, where Dad was kneeling by the fire, burning our disguises.

Grandpa poured father and himself a drink. I held my tumbler out, and he set it upside down on the coffee table.

I wish he would have poured my drink. The guilt from killing one of Stefano's kind was overwhelming.

"Wasn't that a little over-the-top, introducing me to the business by driving an eight-inch spike through a man's eye?"

"The order was to terminate," Dad said. "There wasn't time to check things out. Just be glad you didn't see it. That wouldn't have been pleasant."

"No, I just felt it," I said.

Grandpa and I sat at our breakfast nook two days later, easing into the morning with a cup of his pressed brew. The expensive beans are one of Bepa's few splurges. I sipped my coffee, savoring the robust flavor while taking in the soothing aroma.

"How are you doing, Grandpa?" I asked.

"I'm good. The Seattle Storm was a crossword answer today, and I knew it. Look at me getting all local."

"No, I mean, how are *you* doing?"

"Honey, you don't have to worry about me. I'm just fine. It's you we need to comfort. How do you feel?"

"Comfort? Why?" I thought I was hiding my sadness.

"Your connection with the Dread was broken through death. That can be traumatic for a Huntress. You're mourning. It will go away in a few days."

That explained the weird funk I was in. It was as if there was a hole in my heart like I'd lost a friend.

Bepa slid the newspaper over and tapped on a picture of a man in a hospital bed. The caption stated that he was in critical condition but expected to make a full recovery.

"The Dread we killed was torturing that man for his amusement," Grandpa said. "He eventually would have killed him. Who knows how many lives we spared? What we do is squash evil to save humanity." He accented this statement by angrily closing his hand into a fist. "Don't ever feel guilty about our role."

Bepa opened an envelope and counted out ten $100 bills. "This is from Support," he said. "Welcome to the business."

I felt dirty taking the money.

"Now that you're working with us, you'll need access to the Lair. Follow me."

I was excited to see the Lair. They used it as a carrot, saying I would gain entry when I joined the business.

We descended the stairs to the basement. Grandpa rolled the bookcase aside, exposing the steel door. He handed me a set of lock-picking tools and went back to his paper.

"I'll double that money if you can break in."

I tried to pick the lock, but the tension wrench wasn't working. It was as if the plug was frozen in place. Without that turning, you can't manipulate the pins.

Grandpa set his paper aside when he'd had enough. "You won't crack that one. The housing is also a combination lock. I wanted you to see how secure the room is."

I glanced closer at the handle. A marking arrow was above the keyhole.

"Up is north. Turn it left to west."

I rotated the handle and stopped where I thought was west.

"Right to southeast, left to north and right to east. Here's the tricky part. Insert a quarter of the key and turn right. Good. Now push it all the way in and return full left."

The handle engaged, and I heard multiple deadbolts slide out from the doorframe.

"That was excessively complicated," I said. "This monstrosity had to be Dad's idea."

"Of course," Grandpa said. "A punch code would have been sufficient."

I opened the door to the Lair, expecting, well, I'm not sure what I was expecting, but it wasn't a bleak metal room. There was a desk with dual monitors and a rack with network equipment. Two chairs were in front of the desk with a coffee table between them.

Grandpa pushed against the paneling on the opposite wall; it opened inward from the middle like louvers. There were all sorts of tools and gadgets, plus an arsenal of pistols, rifles, and weapons, neatly in their place, just as I envisioned Dad would have. This was more like it.

Bepa sauntered over to the desk and relaxed in one of the chairs in front. "Come join me," he said, patting the seat next to him. "What we do isn't easy. This role can screw with your head if you let it. The key to sanity is forgiveness. It's that simple. I want you to close your eyes and visualize the Dread we killed. Get a clear image in your head."

I shut my eyes and relived the spike piercing his brain.

"Close-em back up," Grandpa said. "Picture him when he was walking to the door. Feel his body. You are him. Now let him go. Forgive him. Forgive him for what he did and tell him it wasn't his fault, that his actions were beyond his control, from an evil force a millennium old. Tell him you forgive him."

I brought the Dread back and forgave him. "I don't feel any different," I said.

"Keep forgiving until a weight lifts off."

It was three more times before I felt a change as if a breeze passed through my body, blowing a portion of the guilt away. "I do feel better," I said, "but there's still something heavy inside."

"You are so perceptive. We're only halfway there. Now forgive yourself."

I closed my eyes and forgave myself. One time was all I needed for the remaining guilt strangling my psyche to lift. I opened my eyes, shocked, and smiled at Grandpa.

He slapped my knee. "From now on, you'll be the main contact for Support. Your father will show you the ropes when he gets home. He knows all that computer stuff."

"I'm sorry, what?"

"You're the contact. And quit saying sorry. I thought we talked about that."

Dad was back twenty minutes later and joined us in the Lair. He didn't seem surprised to see me in there.

"Hi, Bailey," he said, greeting me with pride. "This is the big day. Why don't you have a seat at the desk?"

I was settling in my chair when Dad shook his head. I walked to the business side of the desk and sat in the comfy executive chair.

"The house is behind an onion network that puts our location in random spots around the world." He handed me a keychain with digital numbers displayed. "You'll need this for the login code. It updates every five minutes."

Dad selected the 'change user' icon on the computer and typed in Peaches.

"How come you call me Peaches?" I said, looking up at him.

"Because peaches were your mom's favorite."

How had I not figured that out? All this time, he's been saying I was mom's favorite.

"Log in using the numbers on your fob."

I entered the digits and was forced to change the password. Dad showed me how to access the dark web and find the encrypted email system we use to communicate with Support, plus their secure messaging tool.

"You're our contact with Support now," he said and walked to the door. "When a Huntress is involved in her first kill, Support prefers to talk with her. That's the way it has been for a thousand years. Eventually, you'll be in charge of the business."

Dad saw the panic on my face.

"You'll be fine." He leaned over and kissed me on the cheek. "The way you moved your chin nervously there reminded me of your mother."

"I need to know something. I am so sorry to ask. How did she die?"

The color drained from his face, and I immediately regretted asking. He turned his back to me and leaned on the doorframe for support.

"We were on a hunt. I didn't want her there, but she insisted. Your mom was shot by a Dread, murdered in cold blood. The son-of-a-bitch got away. I will get him," he said, slamming his fist into the wall. "You rest assured."

"I'm sorry for bringing it up," I said. "I needed to know."

"It's all right, sweetheart," he said and slumped from the room. Dad would be drinking his dinner tonight. Supper would have to be early to get ahead of him.

I finished composing my email to Support, and ten minutes later, an IM popped up:

Hello, Peaches. This is Support. I have the honor of welcoming you to the fold.

> I am humbled by this role.

That is good to hear. Your job is a challenging one that takes a level head. Do you have any questions for me?

> I did have a question. Why is Support so adamant about having the Huntress of each family as your main contact?

You're not just the primary contact. Eventually, you'll be in charge. Women are tuned into the moment and usually won't make rash decisions if they understand they are responsible. Men get lost in the fight. Their animal instincts kick in, causing them to ignore all sense of reason.

There would be fewer wars if generals were women. So do all Dreads have to be killed or are there some that we can just observe?

That is up to your family. If you allow a Dread to live, will he take a new victim? The Dread's life is not the only one in your hands.

I will go into each assignment thoughtfully. Can I ask about our history?

Your grandfather has already discussed that with you. A family must teach a family's history, and the past cannot be written down. We are here to assist you in the now. Do you have other questions?

I wanted to ask who killed my boyfriend, but I wasn't sure how to broach the subject without exposing myself as a risk.

I'm good. Thank you.

No, thank you. And
welcome to the hunt.

Upstairs, I pulled my father aside. "If we're doing this as a family, we have to be in it as a family. I'd like you to bring Cordy into the business. He'll be invaluable on the technical side."

Dad gave me a bear hug. "I knew you wouldn't disappoint. Cordy, come here."

My brother walked into the room. At six-one, he's physically a man. Remnants of mom's soft facial features were balanced with his robust European nose and dimpled chin.

"What's up?"

"Your sister has been brought into the business."

"What the hell?" Cordy blurted out.

"Boy, for once in your life, you need to shut up and listen."

Cordy wisely held his tongue.

"As I said, your sister has been brought into the business. Her first directive is to bring you in early. I am not about to question Bailey's first act."

"Thanks, sis."

"Don't make me regret this," I said.

"Come with me," Dad said. "I'll show you the Lair, and as soon as your grandpa gets back from the store, we have a story to tell."

Cordy turned to me and mouthed, "Holy fuck!"

I smiled as I watched them head for the stairs. My next order of business came to me. I was ditching the silly costumes. Maybe have reversible jackets so we could change our look on the fly.

My role, in the beginning, turned out to be a lot of waiting. It had been a month without a new assignment. I was walking up the steps of my local library when I sensed a Dread seated inside. Astonishment surpassed my rush of concern.

I returned my stack of books and followed the Mirror's Touch to the computer room. The connection was so strong it was as if I was walking up to myself. I concentrated on what he was writing, but the man was a hunt and peck typist. Even if he did know how to type, I wasn't sure I could follow what he was saying. I made a note to take a typing class.

Once in the room, it was apparent who I was getting a read from—the stunning man in his early twenties at the end console. He had a tightly manicured beard and a perfectly coiffed medium-length haircut. His lips were full and kissable like Stefano's. I was so drawn to him I had to stop myself from staring.

I headed to my car and pinned on the brooch-camera Dad gave me. Before going back in the library, I tucked my hair under a baseball cap.

Controlling the camera from my phone, I captured the man's profile.

The Dread rose to speak with the librarian at the main counter. Their conversation soon became heated. It reminded me of Stefano. I walked past him and snapped a shot of his face.

I moved my car across from the parking lot entrance and pointed the dash camera his way. He was leaving the library. I climbed out and hid behind the driver's side door. The Dread disappeared around back for a long while. It confused me, but he came back into focus.

Following a Dread in a car proved easy. It was trippy feeling him floating down the road. I tracked him while keeping a safe distance, but a traffic light foiled my plan. After a feeble attempt to detect him, I went home to run a trace on the plates.

The car was an old Honda registered to a twenty-two-year-old woman living ten blocks from my home. Jesus, why was he so close? It would be least noticeable if I jogged there.

I sensed the Dread three houses away. The Mirror's Touch was more defined than at first, maybe because I already made contact with the man. He was somewhere near the back, sitting at a table.

Pretending to catch my breath, I crouched to attach a tracking unit under the Honda's rear wheel well, then continued on my run.

That evening, I created a database for Dreads. I was on a mission to document as many as I could find. But for now, I had dinner to prepare. I was making a vegetarian lasagna for the family. It was as healthy a meal as my brother would eat.

I called for Cordy twice, but he still wasn't at the table. I found him in his bedroom, lost in virtual reality, jabbing his fists in the air. I knocked him on the head, and he jumped back, startled.

He lifted the visor to his forehead. His bright blond hair had aged to a dirty blond. It was sticking up in places from the exercise.

"You scared me."

"Dinner's on."

"Thanks, I'm starving." He followed me into the kitchen. "Yes!" he said, seeing what I cooked. The quick shuffle caused his junk to sway back and forth in his soccer shorts. I hated how he wore them commando. It was so gross.

"Dude, can you put on underwear?"

"What the fuck? Quit looking at my dick."

"Dad?" I begged.

"Listen to your sister," he said, totally ignoring my brother's swearing.

Cordy returned in jeans and dished himself an ample helping of lasagna. Before taking a bite, he pulled out his phone and began texting.

"No phones at the dinner table," Dad said.

"I'm chatting with a school friend who's deaf. It's the easiest way for us to talk." He used air quotes for the word talk.

"Shit, sorry about that," Dad responded sheepishly.

"Just kidding," Cordy said and put his phone away.

Oh, Cordy, why?

"Give me the phone," Dad said sternly.

"I said I was kidding."

"Hand it over."

Cordy reluctantly placed his phone in Dad's hand. He slammed it flat on the table, shattering the screen, and handed it back.

"What the hell?" Cordy said.

What did you expect? I wanted to tell him.

"Let's eat," Dad said as if nothing happened.

I thought it would be best to wait a while to tell Dad my plan since it involved Cordy.

"How come we never say grace anymore?" I said.

Grandpa looked over at his son accusingly.

"The things I've seen," Dad said, "I don't know if I still believe in God."

"But how can you know for sure?" I said. "Atheism is just as large of a leap."

"Christians are atheists too," Dad said.

We all looked at him like he was crazy.

"They're atheist to the many gods of the past, but you're right; we can't know for sure. I guess we're agnostic."

"Then there's hope," Grandpa said.

"Not for me," Dad said. "The apple in the Garden of Eden doesn't represent knowledge; it represents religion. Organized religion ruins everything. Look at what happened in Hawaii. The natives were in paradise until Christians arrived and made them cover up in shame."

"Don't listen to him," Grandpa said. "The Christians brought salvation. Your dad is understandably upset that God took his wife. If you want to be religious, more power to you."

Dad was noticeably irritated. He walked over to the bookshelf and plucked Grandpa's Bible from its cherished location.

"Do *not* manhandle my Bible," Grandpa said. He tried to snatch the book, but Dad held it out of reach.

"My beliefs have nothing to do with Caroline's murder. I tried reading this once." He thumbed impatiently to the Book of Genesis. "In the beginning, God created animals then man, but the very next chapter, in the story of Adam and Eve, God creates man *then* animals. Which is it? Were the animals first, or was it man? How could such a colossal error be written in the voice of an infallible God? I quit reading at that point."

"Maybe God added that as a test?" Grandpa said, taking the Bible from him.

"You don't test perfection with an error," Dad said. "It doesn't matter. We can't join a congregation anyway. Getting wrapped up in the community would blow our cover."

"I, for one, don't need religion," Cordy said. "Spirituality comes from within."

After patting his heart, he brought his arms out wide, exaggerating the statement, which resulted in him knocking over his milk. Dad glared at him in dire frustration. It had been a while since he spilled anything. It used to be if there were a glass of milk ten feet from him, he'd manage to knock it over.

"Hear ye. Hear ye," Grandpa said. "Gather round for the tale of Cordy the Spiller."

"Knock it off!" Cordy yelled and pounded his fists on the table. He hardly ever raised his voice, especially at Grandpa. "I am not Cordy the Spiller. I am. A human being."

The family had watched The Elephant Man a few nights back. We found the movie reference hilarious.

After dinner, we retreated to the living room to watch Law & Order. Dad was well into his fourth glass of scotch.

Cordy grabbed a handful of Doritos and shoved one in his mouth.

"These chips taste upside down."

We all looked at the bag. It was right-side up. Not that that would make a difference. None of us knew quite what to say, which made him laugh.

At the commercial, I gathered my nerves. "I know you have a hard rule where Cordy can't go out on missions until he's eighteen, but I may have come up with a way he can safely assist us."

"Absolutely not," Dad stated bluntly. "Look at the games he plays. He's a petulant child."

"I'm a childishly sulky child?" Cordy crossed his arms defiantly.

Dad hated anyone challenging his English. It made him feel stupid. Cordy's incorrect attempt must have really struck a nerve.

"I don't like him messing with my mind."

"What do you mean?" I said. Cordy was being a brat, not messing with his head.

"He makes me think," Dad smirked at his unintended humor.

"His games are what gave me the idea," I said, "One of his video games. What if we order a drone? He could follow us to provide an eye in the sky."

"Come on, Dad, can I?" Cordy pleaded.

Grandpa looked at me with pure adoration. "That's a damn fine suggestion, Bailey." I ate his compliment up.

"Whatever," Dad said.

Two weeks later, Support sent information for the Amazon locker where I would find the delivery.

The drone must have cost a fortune. It had night and heat vision, tracking, and autopilot. Cordy would master it in a week, of that I was sure.

After watching the tutorial, the men headed out to the vacant lot at the end of our block. I stayed home to check on the GPS I planted on the Dread's girlfriend's car.

I opened the tracking program. A day earlier, the vehicle arrived at a Greyhound bus station, then the signal ended. I went on a brisk walk to the Dread's house. Crime scene tape stretched across the porch. I pulled up the local news on my phone. The Dread murdered the woman. Fuck! I ran home for my car.

At the bus station, I found the Honda in a far corner of the lot. I made sure no one was watching before I bent down to retrieve the tracking unit. It was gone. Had I placed it under another wheel well? No, it was this one. I distinctly remember which way the car was facing.

My fingerprints were on it. How could I have been so careless? I turned to leave and almost twisted my ankle on the metal device crunching beneath my sole.

I meticulously collected every piece of the broken tracker, all the while obsessing on the notion that I was responsible for the Dread's girlfriend getting killed. An innocent person was dead because of me. That's not something you can just brush off.

Back home, I thought about contacting Support to see if the man was on their radar but couldn't figure out an excuse for letting him get away. Do I tell them anyway? I didn't know what to do.

An IM from my cute classmate, Chase, popped up on my laptop. This was a surprise. We never spoke outside the classroom. I liked him. Chase wasn't afraid to use his brain.

Hi, Bailey.

> Hey, Chase. What's going
> on?

I'm in downtown Seattle.
Dad's at a conference all
day. Want to meet for
coffee?

> I would love to.

Chase sent me the address of a coffee shop downtown by Westlake Center. I let him know I would be there in an hour, and danced in excitement.

Rummaging through my closet was discouraging. All I had were clothes that emphasized my muscular frame. I longed to be feminine, girly but that doesn't play well in the ring. A breezy pair of white pants and a loose-fitting hoodie would have to do. Not knowing how tall my classmate was, I wore the flattest tennis shoes I owned.

My friend was recognizable by his short blond hair with the flip in front. He was relaxing at a curbside table, enjoying a cup of java. I was relieved to see that he was tall and robust. The last thing I needed was to come off as a giant. No one picked on me at my online school. I didn't want the harassment to start all over.

Chase looked over casually as I approached. He rose, and I stuck out my hand like an idiot. He pulled me in for a warm hug, setting me at ease.

"It's so dope meeting you in person," he said. "You're exactly as I pictured."

I insecurely folded my shoulders inward.

"Don't do that. You're beautiful," he said.

I tried to suppress the smile growing, but it was too real. I wanted to tell him, "You're not so bad yourself," but chickened out.

Chase *was* pretty hot, with his Scandinavian features accented by a cute turned-up nose. He was the epitome of boy next door.

A spunky waitress stepped out to take my order. The lady was a stunner, but Chase kept his gaze on me.

"What can I get you," the woman said.

"Is it too late for cappuccino?" I asked. From what I'd read about Italy, the drink was more of a morning fare.

"It's never too late for a cappuccino in Seattle," she said and was off.

"How did you get in such great shape," Chase said.

I looked down at my sweatshirt, wondering how he could tell.

"I see you online in class."

"Oh, duh. You have to be in top shape when you're fighting."

"Wow, what do you do? Box?"

"MMA."

"That sport's brutal. Damn. I should let you know I'm a pacifist."

I laughed. "Everyone knows *that* from your Dalai Lama speech. Pacifists and fighters have more in common than you think. What we learn most about fighting is how to avoid it, to keep our wits, and be aware of everything around us, to be one with the earth."

"Haven't thought of it that way." He drank from his coffee, leaning back, relaxed. "What led you to Mixed Martial Arts?"

"My grandfather saw something in me," I lied. Well, it wasn't a lie, but it is not why I'm training.

81

"Your grandfather?" he laughed. "Your family is nuts."

"You have no idea," I said. "What's yours like?"

"My dad's a professor at the University of Oregon, and Mom's an author."

I perked up. "Anything I would have read?"

"No. But we have faith in her. She's talented."

"Oregon. Isn't that a red state?"

"Can be, in rural areas, but we live in Eugene. The place is liberal to a fault. Why do you ask? Are you conservative?"

I thought about that. "I don't know. My family doesn't talk politics."

"Best to keep it that way. Partisan politics reels you in when you're down, feeding you idiotic things to be upset about. Once they've got you, you'll believe anything, no matter how ridiculous it sounds. It's brainwashing."

"Why would anyone want to be a part of that?" I asked. "It sounds horrible."

"At our core, we're tribal. What's more tribal than having a common enemy? But you can be a part of something without hate. Lots of things are positive if you give happiness a chance," he said with a wink.

"I like you," I said.

My coffee arrived in a large white mug. The barista had created a leaf pattern in the foam. I poured in sugar, and a section of the design fell into the coffee.

"So, what are you doing at an online school?" I asked. "My family moves a lot. We're enrolled to give us familiarity."

Chase pressed his lips into a thin line as his glance skittered around. I regretted asking.

"We can talk about something else," I said.

"No, it's cool. Well, it's not cool. My classmates at my last school ruthlessly bullied me. That's why I'm a year behind."

"I was bullied, too," I admitted. "That's really why I'm in the program. But you, you're so handsome. Why would kids pick on you?"

"Bailey, you underestimate yourself."

"That's what the tormenting does."

He sighed. "With me, it was the jocks at first, but the whole school eventually turned on me."

"Why would they do that?"

"They thought I was gay."

"Shouldn't matter this day and age."

"It does at a Christian Academy."

"But why would they think you're gay? You're so masculine."

His cheeks grew flush. "I told a friend a secret, and it ruined me. It was something I thought every boy could do."

Chase tried to change the subject, but I wasn't having it. Not with that tantalizing nugget hanging in the air.

"Tell me."

He fidgeted before blurting out, "I can suck my own cock."

I spit out my coffee. I had never heard of anyone being able to do that.

"You must be huge?"

"More limber." He wiped up the table with a napkin.

An image of him going down on himself left a tingling below.

"The boys in your school were just jealous. If I could do that, I'd still be in my room, and we wouldn't be enjoying this fine coffee."

A lingering, awkward silence fell upon our table as Chase adjusted his noticeable erection.

"Would you like to go back to the hotel?" he asked. "Dad's working all day."

Sex was not on my mind when I accepted our coffee date. Having it presented so effortlessly was appealing.

"Yes, I would," I said.

Chase's hotel was conveniently located across the street. The desk clerk gave us a knowing look as we raced to the room. Chase had his tongue inside my mouth as the door was closing. I unbuttoned his short-sleeve shirt and let it fall to the floor. His chest was toned, naturally like he didn't work at it. Chase's skin was silky smooth, but that's all I could feel. There was no physical connection. When I was with Stefano I was immersed in the Mirror's Touch.

Chase worked my sweatshirt over my head and struggled with the bra's clasp. Once free, he explored my chest nervously. A massive bruise on my waist from Saturday's fight caught his eye. I guided us to the bed to distract him, and he laid me gently onto my back, just as Stefano had. I was already wet from the passion that was soon to erupt.

He unzipped my pants and rubbed my labia awkwardly. The drowsy pace was exasperating. I unbuttoned his jeans and worked his cock free. Knowing he can go down on himself, I expected it to be enormous, but he was about seven inches. That's no slouch, just unexpected. It was a bit of a relief as it had been a while since Stefano and I made love.

Chase climbed on top of me and forced himself painfully inside. Where was the foreplay? Seriously?

"Dude, condom!" I said, pushing him off me.

"Sorry." Chase searched the room for his bag. He held up a wrinkled condom wrapper. "Let's hope there's still life in it."

He rolled the condom down his shaft and mounted me again. His body was trembling. Was this his first time?

The sex was decent, but he was too slow and methodical. What was missing most was the Mirror's Touch. It was like eating a meal without salt.

Chase needed a bit of a kick start. I slipped off of him and positioned myself on top to set a faster pace. He fell back in ecstasy. I thrust deeply in a rolling rhythm, my body in tune with my soul, screaming out in joy. This was how I remembered sex.

I wanted to see what Chase could do. I kissed him and rolled us over, but he went right into his slow tempo. I had no idea sex could be bad. Was it me? Was I not sexy enough. All I wanted was for it to end. I patiently waited for him to finish and faked an orgasm.

Chase turned his back to me and began crying. "I am so sorry."

"There's no reason to be sorry. You were good. Very romantic."

He sobbed harder. "This was my first time with a woman. I thought someone as beautiful as you could change me. The rumors were true. I am gay."

"What the fuck? So you just use me for sex?" I was livid.

"It's not like that." He was bawling. "Mom said I could change. I can't. I'm so sorry."

I wanted to storm out, but the emptiness in his eyes tore at my heart. Did he really think he could turn straight? What a messed-up thing to put in a kid's head. At least the mediocre sex wasn't because of me.

I've never had a lot of friends. Having a gay one may prove fun. I squeezed my eyes together, thinking I could somehow force the anger away. Forgiving him in my mind did help, so well, I repeated it out loud.

"I forgive you," I said, taking him in my arms and gingerly wiping the tears from his eyes. "Your mom is mistaken. There's nothing wrong with being gay. This is who you are."

"Really?"

"Of course. I guess this explains the lack of cunnilingus."

"I was going to but chickened out at the last second."

I made the truck backing up warning noise. He didn't find the joke as funny as I did.

"Since you're gay, I want to see you suck your cock." There was no way I was leaving without witnessing that talent.

"What? No."

"Come on. When will I get a chance to see this again?"

"You won't make fun of me?"

"Absolutely not," I assured him. "At this point, you owe me."

"All right."

Holy shit! He was going to do it.

Chase had moved away from me to a recliner. I expected him to climb on the bed and do some kind of contortionist act, but he just leaned over and reached it. Not only reach it, he took three quarters into his mouth, and that was while flaccid. I had never seen a man suck a cock, let alone his own. I was wet again, but I kept that to myself.

"That's so hot."

His mouth rose toward the head. A droplet of leftover cum from our sex appeared on the edge of his lips. He sat up and bowed. I applauded his magnificent act.

"Get dressed," I said, slapping him on his butt. "I'm taking you to Capitol Hill."

"What's that?" he said.

"The gay district."

Chase was beaming in gratitude.

Later that evening, I headed to my room to "study." What I needed was to get off. My thoughts drifted to the week after my sixteenth birthday, when I lost my virginity to Stefano. We had been dating for three months. I might have done it sooner, but Dad hadn't loosened the reins until that monumental date. True to his word, he let me start taking responsibility for myself.

It was a warm fall afternoon as our train crossed upstate New York. The colors in the changing leaves were unreal, as if we were riding in a Kinkade painting. Stefano was on his best behavior. We hadn't fought once that day, not even argued.

His lack of empathy was trying. When you can't put yourself in other's shoes, you don't know where the line is. He could come across as so cruel. But aside from this affliction, no other toxic traits emerged, which was a relief. I wouldn't have put up with any narcissistic bullshit. I read about the signs like manipulation, gaslighting, belittling, controlling. If he tried any of that, I would have been long gone. One thing I didn't need to worry about was him isolating me. The click girls already did that. The good side was he love bombed me to make up for his behavior. But that in itself was a sign of narcissism, which kept me on guard.

Stefano had switched hairstyles to a medium-length cut, parted in the middle, with long hair in the front. The look was stunning. I never could get used to how handsome he was.

"Is your uncle going to be home?" I asked.

"Nope. We have his condo to ourselves. Uncle Tony's out on one of his road trips. Hasn't been the same since his boyfriend was murdered."

"Murdered? That's horrible. What happened?"

Stefano turned his eyes from mine and stared out the window. Even when looking away, his presence was captivating.

"Uncle Franco was jumped in the park by Flushing Meadows. They never caught the evil fucks. Tony used to be fun. He just mopes around now."

"I am so sorry."

"I know, baby."

I leaned over and rested my head on his shoulder. It would be just us at Uncle Tony's place. The thought of being alone made me majorly body-conscious. My sixth-grade principal had entrenched a sense of deep shame. The bastard sent me home for the length of my skirt. It wasn't even that revealing. I was sitting weird during lunch, and the hem hiked up as I rose. That was the first time I realized that adults saw me in a sexual light. It felt dirty that he would approach the subject. Grownups don't understand how much so little can screw up a child.

Uncle Tony's condo was a brisk walk from the train station. We held hands the whole way, blissful in each other's company.

Was I going to go all the way? I performed oral once with him. It was strange and fun. I would be doing that again, but was I ready for actual sex? Dad tried to keep me his little girl for so long I feared it might have affected my emotional growth.

"Welcome to la casa di Tony," he said as he held the door for me.

I expected more flamboyance in Uncle Tony's decorating taste, but his condo was masculine. The picture of him, not so much. He had the lips of a woman, large, subtle, and full. His manicured eyebrows and colorful scarf gave him the appearance of a fashion designer. Uncle Tony looked fun. It hurt knowing he was sad and alone.

Stefano headed straight for the bar. He was sorting through the bottles and chose a fifth of vodka.

"I think this goes with orange juice."

His search through the fridge was fruitless. After a trip to the corner store, I was about to taste my first adult beverage. I didn't tell Stefano that. The last thing I needed was him knowing I was such a nerd.

He hesitated in handing my drink over. "Don't think I'm trying to get you drunk and take advantage of you."

"Well, that's a disappointment," I said. That may have been too bold. I regretted saying it.

He smiled wide but pulled back.

I accepted the drink to dull my inhibitions.

Stefano put on a dance mix he created, and we headed to the balcony. Fall had produced a brilliant red hue to the Japanese maple across the way. Stefano noticed me admiring the tree.

"That maple is gorgeous," he said, "but it's nothing compared to you."

I smiled, not knowing what to do with a compliment, especially one so odd.

"That sounded stupid, didn't it?"

"A little," I said, laughing.

"You're funny. So, how'd you get away? Thought you were in trouble."

"I'm in so much trouble. Dad has all my electronics. I pleaded with him to let me come to a friend's 'birthday party.' I played that up pretty hard."

"I'm glad you're here. We never get to be alone." Stefano leaned over to kiss me gently. His mouth was sweet with orange juice. The warmth of his breath on my cheek sent an adrenalin rush below. I felt a buzz of intoxication, but it was coming from inside Stefano.

He shook the ice in his empty glass. "Ready for another cocktail?"

"Lead the way." When he let go, so did the buzz. As he turned, I threw my drink over the railing. I was scared to get drunk.

Stefano was behind the bar when I reached the front room. I set my empty glass next to his and plopped down on one of the stools.

"I dig this song," he said, handing me my refill. I followed him, petrified, to the middle of the room. My brother and I mastered the Highland Dance, but I had no idea how to express myself freely. I avoided school dances like the plague, not wanting to be that towering loser off in the corner. Worse, I didn't want to be that towering loser on the dance floor. Stefano sensed my apprehension and pulled me close to slow dance. It was easy to follow his lead and not feel too stupid.

My fear of sex was nothing compared to my anxiety over dancing. When a fast techno beat introduced the next song, I led him to the bedroom. As we crossed the threshold and I saw the bed, my nerves came flooding in.

"We can go slow," Stefano said. "If you just want to cuddle, that's cool."

The fact that he read my body language and reacted appropriately was monumental. I loved him for the effort and responded by drawing the curtains. He dimmed the lights, but I had him turn them off. There was no way I was doing anything exposed in the open.

I met him in the middle of the room and unzipped his coat slowly. Stefano gasped as the spark between us ignited. We worked at each other's clothes in a heated race to nakedness. He reached for my chest like a boy receiving his favorite gift at Christmas. It was comical how drawn he was to my breasts. I could barely make him out in the dark, playing with them, nibbling and sucking. It wasn't so much arousing as it was exhilarating. I couldn't believe what was happening.

Stefano hates how skinny he is. I didn't understand his concern. Exploring his body, he was flawless. I caressed his back and traced the contours with my fingertips. My hand found its way to his chest and wandered toward his abs, then bumped into *him*. The luscious scent of his pheromones triggered my lust further. As I wrapped my grip around it, his fingers slipped between my thighs on a voyage of exploration. I gasped at the sensations and stroked him firmly, hoping to match the pleasure I was receiving.

Stefano lifted me and tossed my body over his shoulder. The motion was effortless. He walked us over to the bed and laid me on the mattress. Everything was happening so fast. My heart was pounding out of control.

From his pants on the floor, he retrieved a condom. He fumbled for a few moments as he tried to put it on. "Oh shit. It's upside down," he said. "How is that even possible?"

Nervous laughter bubbled out of me.

"I love you," he said and kissed me.

The feeling was more than mutual, but I didn't want to stop kissing to tell him.

I was outside my body, watching my legs open to offer him entry. Stefano moved with fluid assurance as he positioned himself on top of me. His confidence should have set me at ease, but it had the opposite effect.

"Relax," he whispered in my ear. "You ready?"

"I think so."

The moment he slipped painfully inside me, a strange and enchanting transformation occurred. It was like a switch flicking on where I could feel what he was feeling. I know now it was the Mirror's Touch kicking in, but I had no idea what to think at the time. The immense pleasure Stefano felt offset any discomfort I was experiencing.

"Are you OK?" he said.

"Yeah, it feels good," I lied. Although, from his perspective, it felt amazing.

I was confused about why I could feel what he was feeling. I tried to wrap my head around what was him and what was me as our sensual touch mingled. I would have done this sooner if I knew it would be this incredible.

His smile grew wide, as if he couldn't believe this was happening. I stared at his face, enthralled. I loved this boy so fucking much.

Stefano was pumping mechanically but slowed down to shift my legs out wider. When he did this, I involuntarily clenched down with my pelvis muscles. A wonderful tightness wrapped around him, like what he felt when entering me for the first time. That was interesting. I tried it again on the upstroke, but it felt weird. A few more tries and I had the timing down. Upon every inward thrust, I tightened my inner walls around him.

"This is so fucking awesome," he said.

His movements loosened and became rhythmic as the pain I initially felt shifted to pleasure. A quiver of satisfaction from me would flow into a pulsing from him and wrap around something glowing deep inside and back to him. It was too much to comprehend. I moaned and grasped the back of his head, bringing his lips to mine. I felt his tongue advancing and moved mine playfully across the tip.

The passion was so strong nothing would have broken us apart. We kissed and groped and fucked and fondled.

I was able to keep Stefano from finishing by loosening my hips in the right places, but I could tell he was getting close. His balls shifted and throbbed from within, tightening as the rest of his body grew numb. The pressure built, rising like a shaken bottle of champagne, exploding in a series of pulsing intervals. There was a tingling, shivering sensation through it all. I couldn't read what was going on in his mind, but I felt the synapses firing in his brain as he crossed into a world of ecstasy and pleasure. It was over all too quickly. I pulled him onto me and was him as he caught his breath.

He lifted his face to mine. "Well, that was fun."

I pined for my release. "I want more. Can you grab another condom?"

"You bet. Tony may have some." Stefano used his phone to search the room with the flashlight app. That was the first time I saw him fully naked. He was delicious.

"Oh my god." He slammed a drawer shut, laughing. He found condoms in the next one over.

This time was all about me. Stefano worked tirelessly for my release. Being inexperienced, I assumed a girl always has an orgasm during intercourse. Luckily, the Mirror's Touch was there to help.

Stefano had been going at it for a solid half-hour. He wasn't about to give up. Sweat glistened on his skin as the sweet musk of his scent filled the room.

Was I doing something wrong? I reached between my legs and touched myself to wake it up. This sent the whirlwind of our merged senses shooting into hyperdrive. I jerked back but quickly returned to rub myself. Sparks emitted as waves of ecstasy rippled through my body. The pleasure soon morphed into a strange heated tightness. Pulses of electricity raced to my heart and exploded in all directions.

"Don't stop," I said breathlessly.

"I won't."

My hips quivered as the internal pressure steadily grew until it could no longer be contained. The relief shot skyward, joyfully. I fell back as my body spasmed. Gasps came out in quick breaths like I was struggling for air. My pulsing contractions gripped Stefano so tightly he ended up coming again. As he did, he rolled his shoulders skyward and rode the release home. Electrical currents ran noisily through my ears as complete darkness crept around the edges of my eyes. I was in full panic as I lost consciousness.

"Janis. Janis." Someone was patting my hand like my mom used to do when waking me in the morning. I opened my eyes, expecting to see her. Stefano's angelic face came into view. He had turned the lights up slightly. I moved to cover myself with my hands, but he already caringly placed a sheet over my naked body. I started crying. Not from missing my mom. I don't know why I cried.

I invited him under the covers and sobbed with my head nuzzling his chest.

"I love you," I said.

"Anch'io."

Stefano had me home before midnight. We made out in the side yard, then attempted to sneak me back in.

Entering through my window proved difficult, even with a hand from Stefano. That was embarrassing.

"Hold on," he said. "Why are you sneaking in? Can't you just walk through the door?"

I laughed. "Yeah."

"Sorry I was so quiet today," he said.

I wondered what was up with him. "Were you nervous?"

He dropped his eyes to his shoes. "I didn't want to say something wrong and make you mad." Stefano can be so randomly sweet.

"You wouldn't have ruined anything. I wanted it as much as you." I just didn't know it until we started.

We kissed again, and I headed to the front. I'm glad I looked back. Little did I know that would be the last time I saw him.

I missed my soul mate so profoundly I cried as I coaxed myself to orgasm. The sadness numbed my release as if to remind me how lonely my life was.

Chapter 6

Support sent us a solid lead on a porn star suspected in a string of murders. There wasn't enough evidence for the police to press charges, so they were forced to release him. My role was to determine if the man was a Dread. Once confirmed, the order was to terminate. During our first contact, support told me that it would be our decision, but I didn't question the order. Dad said they don't make such an explicit request unless there is proof that a Dread is actively killing.

The plan for our drive to California was to do it in one shot. We were in a poor man's version of a Mercedes-Benz Sprinter van. Cordy rode shotgun, navigating with a map Support gave us. The route brought us around toll cameras or anything that would record our whereabouts. Dad and Grandpa were on the futon in the back, snoozing.

The monotony was getting to my brother. To entertain himself, he kept reaching out for my hair creepily. It was driving me nuts. "Knock it off," I said quietly so as not to wake Dad.

"I was just playing," Cordy said innocently, but I could tell by his smirk he enjoyed getting a rise out of me. "This trip is sooo boring."

"Tell me about it," I said. "Let's get some coffee."

"You may have a bit of a habit there."

I ignored him and exited the freeway to the RV side of the rest area. Cordy was searching the cab for something as I parked.

"What'd you lose," I said.

"My hat."

"Really?"

"What?" He reached up and found it on his head.

"Doesn't feel like any Dread are around." I climbed out of the van to stretch my sore back.

"What's it feel like when you do sense them?"

"It's weird. Almost as if I'm a passenger in their body."

"Can you read their minds?"

"No, it's all just touch. I sometimes get a sense of mood from the muscle tension. If they've gone through the change, I can feel the evil. It makes me sick to my stomach."

"You're a superhero," he said, clearly jealous.

I knocked his hat off and ran to the booth for a free coffee. Cordy headed to the restroom, meeting back with me by a large map of Oregon.

"See that guy in the blue shirt," he said, pointing to a man leaving the lavatory. "He's looking for rest stop sex. Another point for me."

We were playing a game Cordy made up called F or W. The F was a derogatory term for gay people. I wasn't about to play if he continued to say that word. It was the least I could do for Chase. The W stood for whores. I didn't seem to mind that term.

"What? That guy? He totally looks straight," I said. "That man is *not* cruising for rest stop sex."

"He hit on me in the bathroom, said I have nice eyes, that I should smile more."

"Doesn't mean anything."

"We were standing at the urinals. He said it to my dick."

"Oh my," I said, feigning shock.

"That's two to one. Although I shouldn't have given you a point for that last rest stop W."

"Serious? Only a whore would wear a leather skirt that slutty."

"Wait, you get to say the words? That's not fair."

"Sorry, W. And while we're on the subject, we're changing F to Q."

The man walked by and I waved. He saw who I was with and picked up his pace. My laughter was cut short after noticing his wedding ring.

As I was driving out of the parking lot, we spotted the guy leading another man to the cab of a Peterbilt. That was a well-earned point for Cordy and a significant loss for the creep's wife.

My cell rang a mile away from the rest stop. "Did you maybe forget something?" Dad asked when I picked up. I turned around and saw that he and Grandpa weren't in the back. Cordy and I laughed so hard I almost crashed into the side of the off-ramp. We couldn't stop. Our laughter continued through the stop light, up the onramp back to the rest stop, and into the parking lot. Seeing Dad and Grandpa waiting by the curb only made it worse. We didn't stop laughing until miles down the road.

I was sick of the drive, and we hadn't even made it past Oregon. It took an additional thirteen hours before we pulled into Corona.

We rolled by the Dread's house to solidify our plan. The homes on the adjacent street butted up to his, so this was the only entry point. A patch of trees formed an ominous canopy over the driveway. We'd at least have darkness on our side.

Cordy dropped Dad, Grandpa, and me off a few blocks away. Dad didn't like how chatty Cordy was in our earpieces, but it kept my mind off the mission. The waiting was what I hated. Grandpa checked me over, making sure I had a knife on me, and my gun was loaded and ready. Dad insisted that we all wear Kevlar under our shirts.

I shuffled from foot to foot. The strength I had the first time out wasn't coming.

"Focus your energy," Grandpa said to me.

I wasn't sure how to do that, but it distracted me enough that I was no longer overthinking.

"OK, the bird's in flight," Cordy said. "Should be there shortly." His tone had shifted. He was all business.

"You ready?" I asked Dad and Bepa.

"We're good," Grandpa answered for both of them. His eyes were steady, emotionless.

"I'm right above you," Cordy said.

I looked up but couldn't see or hear the drone.

"Let's go," Dad said.

"Single file so I can check your identifiers," Cordy said. We changed positions. "Youngest is in the lead, followed by the middle, then the elder." I was impressed with how he kept our identities at bay.

"Affirmative," I said into the mic in my cuff.

Grandpa appreciated my use of the word and gave me a thumbs up.

Three houses away, my heart was pounding. The driveway was here, and we were entering. Everything was happening too fast. I bent over, holding my thighs to get myself under control. I'd been so confident my first time out.

"You OK?" Bepa asked.

"I'm fine," I lied.

At the end of the driveway, Dad stopped us with a single hand gesture. There was movement in the house. We huddled in the dark, hidden behind a large bush. A man stepped up to the window, eating an apple, his face caked in blood.

"Fuck, he's killed again," Dad said.

"I can feel him," I said. "The Touch is faint from this distance, but he's a Dread."

"There's only one person in the house," Grandpa said and removed his goggles.

"Only one alive," Dad corrected.

The Dread moved out of view, and a light in a side room turned on.

"Does the infrared work through the roof," Dad asked Cordy.

"That's a negative."

"It's all right."

"Masks," Grandpa said.

I rolled my ski mask over my face.

Dad and I headed for the front while Grandpa handled the rear.

"Our door's unlocked," Dad whispered into his mic.

"Hang on a second," Grandpa said. "OK, I'm in."

"Stay behind me," Dad said to me. "I love you."

He wasn't the type of guy who said I love you very often. It shook me out of the moment. I would have to speak to him about that.

We traversed stealthily through the living room and into the hall. Evil seeped from the Dread making my stomach queasy; he was fully into the change. Grandpa approached from the rear. I pointed to a door in the middle of the hall.

The Dread exited the room and froze. I could physically see evil rising from him like heat in the desert, but it was outlined in grey. He was exceptionally handsome, even splattered in blood. Our guns were drawn, but none of us had a clean shot.

"Let's all remain calm," Dad said. "We just want to talk with you."

"I have nothing to say," the Dread responded. His voice was sultry and inviting. I was drawn into his presence as if in a trance.

The Dread tried to bolt, but Grandpa blocked his path. The man opened his palms out in front of him and said, "Whoa, easy."

Dad taught us the same trick. "We're not falling for that," I said. My father chuckled to himself.

The man dashed back into the room. There was a crash as he broke through a window. My head, wrist, and shoulder burned where he sliced them.

"Target is locked in my sight," Cordy said. "It's tracking him! This drone kicks ass." That was the one time in the mission he let his professionalism lag.

99

I checked the room. There was blood on every surface. Tied to the bed was what used to be a woman. The cuts were so deep she was flayed open. This Dread needed to die.

Grandpa peered around me. "That can't be good," he said. It was a weird casual statement.

"Head out the driveway and take a left," Cordy said.

We followed his directions as he led us through the neighborhood, unmasked and exposed.

"He's gone in a house," Cordy said. "I can't tell if anyone's home. The roof's blocking the infrared here also. I shouldn't go any lower. The whir of the blades could spook him."

"Nice job, son. And great use of the word whir."

I looked at Dad, questioning.

He made sure that his finger wasn't on the talk button.

"Cordy's not doing well in English class."

"Your support is appreciated, but you called him son over the radio."

"Oh, man, I won't do that again."

Cordy directed us to the house and around the side, to the backyard. I put on my ski mask and crept up to the porch. The screen door creaked, and a woman yelled for help. Dad kicked in the door, working his way room-by-room. I passed the men and headed to the front, where I knew the man to be.

In the living room, the Dread had a frail, older woman in his arms. His gun was pressed to her temple. The terror in her eyes spoke volumes as she struggled in his grasp. The Dread's gaze darted between us, unable to tell who was the greatest threat.

"Don't come closer," he said. "I'll fucking kill her!"

The juxtaposition of his beauty against his actions was unnerving. The worst part is I couldn't help being reminded of Stefano. Did my family save him from this fate?

"We don't want any trouble," Grandpa said, setting his gun down.

"You too," the man said, gesturing recklessly to my father with his gun.

Dad used the opportunity to fire a single shot, striking the Dread above his right eye. The brain must be void of sensory receptors because I only felt the initial impact. The life drained from the Dread's body as he drifted to the darkness. I almost lost consciousness but was far enough away not to be dragged along. The evil rising from him dissipated. Dad moseyed up to the man and fired a second round, close range to the head. I hadn't prepared for the gore. It was too much. The woman fainted, and Dad caught her in his free arm. I should have been horrified, but my father looked like such a badass.

I bent down to check the Dread, expecting him to be hot to the touch because of the evil I'd seen rise from him, but his body was average temperature.

"I can see the headline now," Grandpa said. "Porn star gives last head."

Cordy didn't understand why we were laughing, which made us lose it more.

"What is happening?" the lady screamed when she woke up.

"We just saved your life from a serial killer," I said. "When the police ask for our description, there was only one man. About five-eleven. Blue ski mask. Wearing a dark blue jacket, jeans, and bright green tennis shoes."

"What?" the woman said, confused.

"Ma'am, please help us. We're the reason you're alive." I repeated the description.

"You all right?" Cordy asked.

"The subject is down. Hostage is safe." I loved how official I sounded. All those hours of watching Law and Order were paying off.

"Uh, guys, a cop just pulled up front," Cordy said.

We ran out the back to the alley.

"Another officer is about to turn onto your street. Hide."

We ducked behind a parked sedan. Gravel crunched under the cruiser's tires as it approached. A spotlight lit our hiding spot, holding steady. My heart was beating so loudly I was afraid the officer would hear it. The light panned away and we shuffled to the rear of the vehicle.

"OK. Hold it. Hold it. Go. Same direction you were heading and then take a left."

Cordy guided us to an elementary school playfield a half-mile away, to our van. The drone landed on the pavement, and my brother stepped out of the woods to meet us.

"You saved our ass," Dad said, patting Cordy on the back. My brother beamed with pride.

As a show of gratitude, Dad let him drive. Grandpa called shotgun.

A block from the freeway entrance, a cop's siren blared at us from behind. We all let out a terrified gasp.

"What do I do?" Cordy asked.

"Pull over," Grandpa said, defeated.

"Fuck, fuck, fuck!" Dad kept repeating. He cocked his gun. "Don't look back."

Cordy rolled to the curb, and the cruiser sped past.

From deep inside Grandpa came a bellowing laugh.

"Get the hell out of here," Dad said.

Cordy joined the traffic and eased onto the freeway. At the Oregon border, we replaced our borrowed California plates with the original Washington ones.

Even though it was an exhausting twenty-hour trip home, we were all too wired to sleep. That night I had my first scotch. Not as a celebration, more to numb the guilt. Yes, he was a Dread, but he was also someone's son. It

102

weighed heavily upon me. And that, I realized, is why women are put in charge.

Sleep came fast once I forgave, but I was awakened by my grandfather crying out. The panic in his voice was unsettling. My brother was already in the hall. We rushed to Grandpa's room, where Dad was at his side.

"What's the matter, Pop?" he asked.

"I don't remember my name."

"You're Tom Callister."

"My real name, damn it! What's my real name?" He was on the verge of tears. The long day left him disoriented. At least that's what I hoped.

"Your name is Aleck MacGregor Cameron," Dad said in a quiet tone. I didn't know Grandpa's actual name. It was magnificent.

"Aye," Grandpa said proudly. "I couldn't for the life of me remember."

I went to the kitchen to fetch Grandpa water.

"Thank you, dear," he said, taking a sip.

"We'll be right back," I said and pulled Cordy along.

"What are you up to?" he said.

"You and I are dancing for Grandpa."

Cordy headed to his room to change into his Highland outfit. We returned with Bepa's bagpipes and a drum for Dad. After moving Grandpa's recliner into the hall, Cordy and I set our swords in two crosses on the floor. The tears building in Grandpa's eyes fell happily. I hugged him, and Dad set the beat on his drum. Grandpa filled his pipes with air, and Cordy and I took our positions with our hands on our hips and bowed.

Performing the traditional Highland dance sends me to a different plane. There is nothing like it. I am free when I dance. I leaped and bounded along the four quarters made up by the swords, never faltering.

Successfully taking out the second Dread gave me a false sense of confidence. A few weeks later, I found myself challenging a man to an unofficial MMA fight. I had won and was on top of the world. Sure, Steve was seven inches shorter, but he was a man. The match was determined by technicalities, with me the clear winner; it wasn't even close.

On the way home, my body ached with each step. Why did I bring my car into the shop before a fight? I took a shortcut a few blocks from my house. Halfway down the street, two black guys and a white dude with the name Christine tattooed on his neck emerged from the alley. I looked them briefly in the eyes to show I wasn't afraid but kept my pace.

"Where you headed, my snow queen?" the guy in the skullcap asked. His deep baritone gave me the creeps. The speed at which the group caught up to me was startling.

Neck Tattoo stroked a lock of my hair, and I aggressively knocked his hand away. Red flags were blaring.

"I have to get home," I said, but the men blocked my path.

"We can take the scenic route," the shorter of the three said and held my arm.

"What we have here is French vanilla on a platta," Skullcap said. He leaned closer and smelled my hair, sending chills down my back.

I tried to break free, but shorty's hold was solid. All my struggling did was get a rise from the men. I looked for help, but no one was around.

"I should warn you," I said. "I'm a trained MMA fighter."

The men just laughed. I used the distraction to swing at Skullcap's nose. He moved his head and watched my fist sail past. I landed a headbutt and three kicks before succinct blows on opposite sides of my head dropped me. The gang lugged me into the alley. Dragging my feet did little to slow them. Off in the distance, a car drove by. I felt helpless as my body was tossed between a dumpster and a stack of broken pallets. Two of the men pinned me to the ground on my back.

"Don't!" I pleaded.

My sense of reasoning was nonexistent as if my brain was powering off. I screamed, and a large palm covered my mouth. Hands wrestled with the knot on my waistband, but it held. A burning pain shot across my legs from the force of my sweats being ripped apart. They didn't bother removing my shoes. I was drifting, hoping this was happening to someone else. My body shut down to the point that I couldn't move or keep my eyes open. A man climbed roughly on top of me. His breath was a rancid combination of chewing tobacco and Cheetos. He was fumbling below. I turned my head and cried.

"Get your ugly ass off Bailey," a booming voice commanded. There was a thud, and the man assaulting me grunted as he was knocked to the ground.

I opened my eyes. Leroy was in a fighting stance like a superhero.

"Why you trippin', Tubs?" Neck Tattoo said, holding his side.

"She's Tom Callister's granddaughter. You better recognize the situation."

"It's cool. My bone is clearly dry," the creep said, pointing to his hideous penis.

I cried in a mixture of relief and trauma. Demoine came running up from the street.

"Be easy," Skullcap said. "The rumors about Tom ain't shit."

"The rumors aren't true enough," Demoine said. "Tom knocked my gun out of my hand so fast; I don't know how he did it. That dude whooped Tubs and my ass. His son sat back and watched, grinnin' the whole time. I couldn't imagine facing both those guys."

"They run the mafia," I said, hoping my voice wasn't too weak for them to believe me.

"It's all good," Neck Tattoo said. "We'll bounce."

A hand touched my thigh and I cringed. "It's just me," Leroy said tenderly. He closed my legs and reached for my torn sweats. Seeing the shape they were in, he removed his massive jacket and wrapped it around my shoulders.

"Yo! Apologize," Leroy demanded.

"I'm sorry," Neck Tattoo said. I looked away until they were gone.

"There's another pair of sweats in my bag," I said, pointing to the duffle in Demoine's hand.

I was shaking so badly I needed help putting them on.

"Let's get you home," Leroy said when I was dressed.

"Don't say anything to my father. He's not in the mafia, but he wouldn't handle this well."

"Whatever you want," Leroy said. "We're here for you."

"Thank you. The reality of the moment came crashing down, and I crumbled.

The boys helped me to their car, where Leroy had me join him in the back. I rested my head on his chest.

"Can we sit here a while?" I asked.

"Take as long as you need," Leroy said and stroked my back.

"What did I do to bring this on?" I said.

"You didn't do anything," Leroy said. "Don't for a second blame yourself."

I cried, not knowing if I could ever let this go. The man hadn't penetrated me, but I still felt raped.

When I collected myself enough to stop crying, Demoine headed to my house.

"I'm sure lucky you were in the neighborhood."

"It wasn't luck. We stopped by your crib to show Tom our grades from tech school," Leroy said. "We're gonna be electricians."

"That's awesome," I said. "I'm proud of you guys."

"It was all your grandpappy. He believed in us. I haven't had a man believe in me as he did. My father died when I was a boy. Your grandpa is solid. Even paid for our first quarter and tool kits."

"That's Bepa," I said. "I want to cook you dinner for saving me. Are you free this Thursday?"

"No reciprocation is needed," Leroy said. "We're even."

"No, no we're not," I said. "Those guys would have raped me. Cooking for you is the least I can do. I'll make steak and potatoes."

"We'll be over at six," Leroy said comically fast.

The attack royally screwed me up, more than I thought it would. Seeing a therapist was too risky, and Support wasn't being very supportive. It became painfully obvious they were here to assist, not to help. There was no one to talk to about the assault. I was mad at everyone, especially my family, for missing my fight that day, even though it was me who told them not to come. They could have pushed harder.

Chapter 7

After I graduated high school, my training intensified. The three years since were a blur. I was now fluent in Italian, but that wasn't enough for my grandfather. He insisted I learn the Gallo-Italic dialect spoken in certain parts of Sicily. The task was rather daunting since I couldn't take a class; that would give my family away. I learned the language from Internet videos and the help of a used book I found. The dialect was coming to me, but it was a slow process. I was also learning Scottish Gaelic. Not on a request but to please my grandfather.

I continued honing my fighting skills and was currently practicing India's Kalarippayattu. This technique offered a deep understanding of one's body and spirit. From it, I discovered a strength I didn't know was there. I would be a champion if I could fight professionally, but it would expose our family. At least I had my brother as a sparring partner. He was stronger than me and had a four-inch height advantage, but I trained more, so we were on equal footing. The times I won, he wasn't mad. Cordy would look at me with admiration. For all the games he plays, he's a good sport.

Under my watch, there were a total of twelve Dread's deaths. None by my hand, but that didn't mean I wasn't responsible for each one. Causing another's demise was hard to come to terms with, even a Dread's. I understood why presidents aged so rapidly. Sending people to their death, be it a soldier or a terrorist, has to eat them alive. I dealt with it through meditation. It cleared my mind of the negativity, leaving a sense of peace in the void.

My life at twenty-one consisted of family and the business. Mary never emailed me back, and Chase was always traveling. He created a bullying simulator and visits schools that have purchased the program, teaching the kids how to be kind to one another. It's important work that keeps him busy. We talk on the phone, but that isn't the same.

I was shopping in the Italian grocery at Pike Place Market, gathering the authentic ingredients for Cordy's favorite dish, carbonara. I promised to make it for his alias's birthday. He was the only one in the family who celebrated both.

DeLaurenti's selection of cheese was daunting. I was narrowing my choice of Pecorino Romano when the Mirror's Touch sparked up. A Dread entered the store.

The Touch was strong with this one. I had encountered him before. If luck were with me, it would be the Dread from the library. I ducked past his aisle and turned down the next.

The man was across from me. My hand was his as he chose an item from the middle shelf. I tried to peek through the rack but was foiled by a center divider. The Dread was on the move with a cocky rolling swagger.

I was drawn to the man and headed in the opposite direction to scope him out from behind. The Dread was tall, around six foot three. He wore a burgundy short-sleeve, collared shirt and designer jeans. His black leather Hugo Boss tennis shoes were dope. I passed him, and my eyes carelessly drew to his. It was the man from the library, just not the one I was thinking of. My heartbeat seemed to stop the moment our eyes met. His muscles clinched, frozen in Terror.

"Stefano?"

His body relaxed after hearing my voice.

"Janis?"

Years of sadness and longing welled up, threatening to drown me.

"You're alive," I said, confused and threw myself into his arms. Stefano dropped the bag of flour to catch me; it exploded in a cloud of dust at his feet.

I was bawling as we kissed madly. My thoughts were swirling frantically as the patrons in the store faded from my vision. I could feel everything inside Stefano, from the stance he held himself to the blink of his eyes. The Mirror's Touch was stronger with Stefano than I'd ever felt. He was definitely a Dread. And I was definitely still in love with him.

He broke us apart. "I had no idea you thought I was dead. I would have searched the world over," he said, stroking my face softly. "Let's get out of here."

I was in shock and could only nod yes.

"I love you as a brunette," he said. That meant everything. Not just because Stefano knew me as a blonde, but as someone lacking empathy, offering a compliment was colossal.

A female clerk approached Stefano. "I'll have that cleaned up, sir. Can I help you find anything?"

I tensed, waiting for an uncomfortable interaction.

"Yes, thank you. We could use some help. What we're looking for is a medium to large exit." His comment gave us a case of the giggles, and we laughed well beyond the store.

I couldn't stop staring at Stefano. No one matched the memory of my boyfriend. Yet here he was exceeding himself. His boyish, round chin grew dominant and powerful, as had his nose, creating symmetry with his expressive eyebrows. There was something new—a scar running down his left cheek.

"My car's around the corner," he said, taking my hand. Feeling both pulses in our palms was strange, almost like a drum loop. I stared up at his beautiful face, still not believing this was happening.

"You should know, I had climbed into your room when you heard your Dad reading your diary. He almost caught me when he was putting it back."

I loosened my grip in alarm; Stefano tightened his so I wouldn't flee.

"I had to see you again. After that night we had."

"I appreciate the sentiment, but that wasn't safe."

"How was I to know? You didn't react when I told you I lacked empathy." He glanced over, eyes full of accusation. "Played that off pretty well."

"They didn't tell me of our world until after we moved to Seattle. I fucking swear."

He loosened his grip. "Don't worry; I didn't rat you out. I made up a story about a woman saying she could sense me. We had to leave New York because of your family."

"I would never hurt you," I said.

He held my gaze. "Me neither."

The air grew heavy as if it was constricting. That could have been the panic in my body. Fear and confusion were fighting for a hold in my brain. I shied my eyes away, and we walked in silence for the remainder of the block.

"If your family left on your own, why would you burn your house down?" I said. "Leaving a trail is risky."

"The house burned?" Stefano asked. "What the fuck! I bet that was our landlord. Robbie talked about building condos on the property. How could he put suspicion on us? We were always good to him. I see the treehouse survived." He touched my mom's earring. "Pop deleted my second email account. It killed me not knowing how to get a hold of you."

A woman with a 'Jesus Saves' placard was blocking the sidewalk. She had wild unkempt hair and a crazed look.

"The bowels of hell are waiting for your soul," she screeched at Stefano. I was kind of impressed with the woman's boldness. I wouldn't have led with that, but still.

112

"You know," Stefano said, "your life would have gone a lot smoother if you had just kept Carrie from the prom." The woman seemed unfamiliar with his movie reference, which made it all the funnier. I only knew the film because Dad loves horror movies. I think he watches them to desensitize us to violence.

We were heading up the hill to First Avenue when Stefano clicked his remote to unlock a white Audi. He had waited until I was next to the passenger door, probably so I wouldn't check his plates.

I grabbed the book off my seat and settled in. The novel was one of my favorites: A Confederacy of Dunces.

"I love this story," I said.

"Me too. This is the second time I've read it. I finished a Henry James novel and needed a brain cleanser."

The way he referred to a Pulitzer prize-winning novel as a brain cleanser was intimidating.

Stefano started the car, and opera music blared from the speakers. He turned the volume down using a control on the steering wheel.

"Are you familiar with Puccini?"

"Not really," I said, shrugging my shoulders.

"This is La Bohème with Pavarotti & Mirella Freni. The emotional power strikes so forcefully it's almost spiritual. I'll play something you might know. A little Andrea Bocelli. It's the song I used to get over losing you."

His admission was sad, knowing he can't cry. The tears are what helped me through the trauma.

Stefano selected a vaguely familiar song. A woman sang the opening in a haunting soprano. My Italian had advanced enough that I could follow along. When she switched to English, I recognized the catch; *Time to say goodbye*. Stefano belted out the male verses, and I melted. The crescendo in the finale blew my mind, especially how long he sustained the last note.

113

"Do you sing professionally? I said, wiping my tears.

"No, but I'm the best tenor in my class," he said proudly.

"You could be an opera star." Then it hit me why he couldn't, and I held my tongue.

"There must be something you want to do but can't."

"MMA," I said. Stefano looked at me, confused. How did my gay friend know what MMA was but not Stefano? "Mixed Martial Arts."

He feigned support, but I could tell Stefano was disappointed. Everything I know about the Dread confirms that they're monsters, but it turns out my family are the animals. We never attend operas or the symphony. We're all about the chase. About fighting. About killing — killing people like the beautiful man next to me. I felt sick to my stomach.

Stefano changed the music to the local dance station. They were playing Brixton Webber's new single. He hit the button for another channel. "That kid's a douche."

We were in the midst of downtown Seattle driving up a steep incline. Stefano jammed the gas at the cross street, and we shot off the crest of the hill. The drop sent a tingling from my abdomen, causing me to flex my pelvic muscles involuntarily. The flutter below lingered well after the car was on solid ground. Stefano smirked as if he knew the effect he'd had. We slowed at the next intersection and took a left.

He pulled into the parking lot of the Warwick Hotel. I guess we were having sex. It would have been nice to be involved in the decision, but OK. I spotted a security camera in the pay booth and turned my head away.

"This is so dangerous," Stefano whispered to me.

After paying, he raced up the ramp.

"We really shouldn't be together," he said.

114

"Yes, we should," I said fondling his bulge.

Stefano lost his concentration and almost clipped a car as we rounded the corner.

"Feeling you get hard with the Touch is super trippy," I said.

"It's not fair that you can do that," he said.

"Life isn't fair. If it were, we'd be free."

"I missed you," he said.

He slid a hand between my legs and rubbed me through my jeans. For not being able to feel what I do, he sure was spot on with his aim.

His fingers brushed the gun in my waistband and he withdrew his hand. All I could do was shrug guiltily. I never left home without it, but it wasn't because of the Dread.

"Come on," he said and stepped from the car.

The anticipation of sex raced through his veins. His pulse heightened, and mine pumped in succession. We ran down the garage stairwell to the entrance of the hotel. It proved challenging to run close to a Dread. The mind has to sync an orchestra of muscles to move a body. I felt all of his, yet couldn't make sense of any. It screwed up my stance, and I kept tripping over my feet.

Stefano stopped us at the base of a carpeted staircase. "I'll get a room," he whispered. "Meet me on the second floor by the elevators. If you run into trouble, there's an exit across from the bathrooms."

"Everything will be fine," I said.

"Yes, it will."

He let go of my hand, and a rush of energy sucked away like a string drawing from my palm. I bounded up the stairs.

"Wait," he said, calling me back, and pressed his lips to mine.

Kissing, I found, was one of the ways to use the Mirror's Touch to my advantage. The mind has a distinct reaction to good or bad kisses. It was simple to guide ours

115

to the positive. Of course, it helps if you have a man who can follow leads. He swirled his tongue playfully around mine as I met his sumptuous touch with sneak attacks, knowing which way he was heading. I felt his knees weaken, and he pulled us apart.

Stefano's eyes were are alive, comforting, and his warm smile was back. "Wow. I mean, wow." He shook his head as if trying to restart his brain. "I'll meet you upstairs." He gave me a peck and disappeared down the hall.

I ran up the steps floating in bliss. Before heading to the elevators, I checked the exit. The door locked behind me and I had to walk around like an idiot.

It took an excruciatingly long time for Stefano to reserve a room. I was getting worried. For some reason, I couldn't get a read on his location even though the lobby was directly below me. One dreadful scenario after another played through my mind. I forced out the negativity. Stefano would never cross me. I knew that. I hoped I knew that.

For the third time, the elevator chimed as a car was stopping. The doors parted, and the Touch struck me like a blow to the chest. My strength gave out as my vision narrowed. I stumbled backward, fumbling for the chair. I felt Stefano approaching and was soon in his arms.

"Are you OK?" he asked. Even his look of concern was handsome.

I didn't want to reveal a weakness in the Touch. "You were gone so long I was beginning to think this wasn't real. Seeing you there. I just…"

"It is real." He went in for a kiss, but the elevator chimed, then opened to let a boy out. "Come on," he said, helping me to my feet. We would have had sex right there in the lift, but an elderly couple was occupying it.

I studied the doors as they closed, trying to figure out what blocked the Touch. It must have been the dense layers of metal.

Stefano had selected a corner room on the seventeenth floor, far away from prying eyes. Once inside, we lunged for each other. My senses were ablaze as he explored my body. He slid a hand under my top and released my bra.

I unbuttoned his shirt and worked it over his head. He had a lean, sculptured upper body like a diver. But unlike a diver, he had a tuft of hair on his chest.

"You're so fucking sexy." I reached out and traced the outlines of his muscles.

"I run a lot. Keeps me alive."

I wish he hadn't said that.

Stefano remained silent as I removed my carry holster and set my gun on the desk. He lifted off my top and smiled.

"Man, you're ripped."

I folded in on myself, shrinking away from his gaze.

"Don't you dare," he said. "You're the most beautiful woman in the world."

The compliment embraced my soul. Stefano leaned forward to kiss my chest and held my wrist behind my back, torturously keeping me from his cock. That was probably for the best. Just the feeling of him suckling my nipple from his perspective was overwhelming.

He spun me and slowly walked us backward until my legs hit the mattress. With a playful shove, I fell onto the bed.

I drifted outside my body and was him as he moved toward me. Stefano unzipped my pants as I worked on his belt. He was calm and self-assured as he laughed playfully, putting me at ease. I won the race and rolled him onto his back. His erection stood perfectly straight and firm. The skin is darker than the rest of his body, accenting his manhood to perfection. I gripped him with both hands and still had room to slip my lips over the head. His shaft pulsed from within and my pussy answered with a quiver.

Having your cock sucked is not an all-over experience. The nerves concentrate on the front where the head meets the shaft. I focused my licks playfully as I stroked to the timing of my mouth. Heat pooled low in my belly. I was slick with need.

Rolling his balls around in my palm flooded him with a feeling that was more comforting than sexual, as if they were glad I remembered them.

Even without his groans of satisfaction, I knew how much he enjoyed me stroking his cock after removing it from my mouth. I could feel it through him. My hand gliding across the wet saliva was heavenly. A rhythmic throbbing between my legs spread his desire through my whole body. I was making him feel so good. Holy shit, I was about to come. No, that was Stefano.

"I have to finish inside you," he said forcefully.

How selfish of me. This was more than sex to Stefano. The act was keeping him from changing.

I lay down missionary style, wanting to look into his eyes as he entered me.

"That doesn't mean I can't get you off first."

Stefano flashed a mischievous smile that reminded me of his eager sixteen-year-old self. He slid down my chest, giving my breast a playful nip, then began working my pants off.

"I'm not wearing my best underwear," I said, embarrassed.

"They won't be on long enough for me to notice," he said, removing my hand from the waistband. Stefano laughed when he slid my jeans off and saw my horrible grannie panties. I was mortified. He bit a hole in the fabric and tore my underwear in half.

A filthy alley flashed into my mind, and I could almost smell the rancid scent of my attacker. My body tensed.

"You all right?" he said.

I blinked the unpleasant memories away. "Yeah, keep going."

Stefano hadn't performed cunnilingus our first time together, but any worries I might've had about that vanished the moment he settled between my legs. He was so hungry he practically covered me with his whole mouth. He flicked his tongue relentlessly across my clit, and my legs kicked out involuntarily. The pleasure I was receiving drowned out what he was experiencing, allowing me to focus solely on myself. More importantly, it blocked out my thoughts.

Stefano explored a circular path around my clit, occasionally catching it gingerly between his lips, sending sparks through me. He licked and sucked like a man starved. I suppose we both were after so long without this connection. I gasped when he drove his tongue into me.

The pleasure built with each pass across my clit. He changed his focus to one repetitive stroke of his tongue over and over. He was determined to make me come, but I was straining my hips against the cause.

Why was I fighting it? I relaxed, and ecstasy soon rose from the depth of my core.

"Don't stop," I said throatily.

Stefano picked up the pace and added a stronger flick to his tonguing. My body collapsed as my orgasm assumed control, and I forgot how to breathe. The release washed over me in flares, leaving me gasping for air.

He held onto me tightly while I recovered. Our scents merged with the energy of our souls. Having him in my arms again completed me. There was only one thing that could bring us even closer.

"I want you inside of me."

"You sure you don't want me to make you come again?"

"I need you to fuck me," I said.

"Sunshine, nothing would please me more."

He grabbed a condom from his pants then shimmied them off the rest of the way.

"The curse can be reset through a condom?" I said. I was willing to go without one—anything to keep him human.

"Certain kinds. Sheepskins were the only ones that used to work. Microthins were a game-changer."

"Enough talking," I said, ripping the condom from the package. The sensations that passed to me of it rolling along his shaft was the weirdest.

Stefano positioned himself over me, and I pulled his lips to mine. The thirst in my kiss was driven by years of absence. My heart pounded in my chest, not just from the excitement of the moment but from having him back in my life. I wanted the kiss to last forever but pulled him off me so I could look at his face. Goddamn, he was beautiful. A smile met mine and he brought his hips forward, tempting my opening with the head of his cock. He was staring deep into my eyes as he pressed inside. The simultaneity of my warm tightness forcing along his shaft and the stretching as he filled me to capacity was mind-altering.

"Your pussy is so tight," he said.

I was overloaded and answered with an appreciative moan. The dueling sensations heightened as each action merged with a reaction, building, growing. I concentrated on what was him and what was me, then clinched down in time to his thrusts, repeatedly gripping his cock. The effort was rewarded through him, passing into to me with pulsing reverberation. His cock and my pussy sang a duet in perfect harmony.

Stefano was miles ahead of me in the art of sex, but I kept up by tapping into his being. As our pleasure merged, I could no longer tell who was feeling what. It would be like pouring different paints into a churning washing machine and trying to isolate the colors. My carnal pleasure intermingled with Stefano's was too much to handle. A crackle of electricity raced through my eardrums, and I began to fade.

I woke to Stefano's face inches from mine.

"You all right?" he asked, giving me a peck. I appreciated that he pulled out after realizing I was unconscious.

"I think so," I said, catching my breath. "The Touch... holy fuck, it's awesome. Get back inside me," I demanded.

I took control and straddled him. Being the one thrusting but also the one penetrated was a mind fuck of epic proportions. Up was down. In was out. I almost gave up but stumbled on a pattern that aligned my senses. Concentrating on him during insertion and me on the withdrawal worked. I rode upon him so rigorously he was getting close.

"Not yet," he said.

"Yes," I countered. "We can keep going."

Pressure from the base of his shaft grew with force like floodwaters pressing on a dam. I slowed my movements to focus on his orgasm. His balls constricted, and the first wave shot out of him with intense ferocity. He steadied himself on outstretched arms like a newborn fawn, the spasms quaking from below.

The orgasm left him fully sated. I held still, careful not to rub the head of his cock. It was a lightning storm of sensitivity, screaming, *don't touch.*

Stefano pulled out and walked to the window. I marveled at his naked body, especially his plump yet firm ass. There wasn't an imperfect angle on him.

He grabbed another condom and lay next to me to catch his breath.

I rolled over on top of him. As I let myself relax, I felt my own weight and raised my body.

"No, you don't get to do that. Lay down."

I let go and was happy to see that Stefano could handle my weight. He made me feel light.

121

Stefano reached for his phone on the nightstand. "I want you to hear something. This is a song I made after I thought I lost you."

The most heartfelt notes of sorrow arose from the tiny speaker.

"Is that you?" I said, hearing the singer's voice.

"Yeah," he said hesitantly, like he didn't care for the quality.

"Start it over."

The song was simple but created with such passion it took me back to being sixteen. Stefano's singing was as close to crying as he could get. It sure reduced me to tears. I bawled on his chest, hanging onto him.

"I missed you so much," I said and kissed him.

"You were always the one," he said.

I melted in his arms and he grew erect again. I loved the feeling. It would be like if my clit quadrupled in size, growing and stretching.

Stefano had me lie on my stomach. He hiked me up to a kneeling position and entered from behind. My head was low, and a jolt of electricity kept racing through, causing a strange shift in my brain like it was continuously overloading. Stefano grasped a handful of my hair and tilted my head back. With my head raised, the electrical pulses subsided. He smacked me on the ass, which hurt his hand more than it did me. I liked that.

"Again," I said. He smacked my ass harder. What was I doing? "OK, that's enough."

He laughed.

Stefano went with the roughness, giving in to the passion. We wrestled around, each striving for dominance over the other. It was like being in bed with a wild beast.

He had me bent over a chair in the corner when I felt my second orgasm vying for attention. The release was blossoming as Stefano was about to come. I tried to will mine faster, hoping to ride his coattails, but only succeeded in chasing it further out of reach.

"Keep going," I said. "I'm almost there."

I rubbed my clit as he thrust harder. Heat licked across my skin, gathering below, shooting through my body in tingling pulses. Stefano pounded into me so vigorously my head bumped against the wall.

A ball of energy drew inward, growing, pulsing. Warmth spread across my thighs in a rolling quiver that reached my toes. The internal pressure was focused so tightly there was nowhere to go but out. I moaned when the release exploded through my core. His orgasm wove through mine, nourishing its energy.

My legs trembled as I felt my inner walls clamp around Stefano's cock in gripping pulses. His continued thrusts extended the orgasm. A quivering gasp morphed into another moan. I fought to hold on to him, but my arms were numb. I could hardly support my weight and slid limply off the chair, collapsing in a euphoric, sweaty mess. Stefano carried me to the bed and spooned up beside me.

"You're an animal," I said.

"I know."

"I didn't mean it that way. You're talented as fuck in bed."

"What's the use of sex if you don't have fun?"

That brought silence to the room, as we both knew the answer. I had to change the conversation fast.

"I'm a little shocked that you have no tattoos," I said.

"We can't have identifiable marks," he said coldly.

And I made it worse. "That's fucked up," I said.

"This whole situation is fucked up. But it is what it is," Stefano said.

"Yeah, it bites."

"I think it's funny that you call us the Dread. We're not the Dread. The Dread is the worry in our family that our boys won't be gay."

"Why would you dread that your kids aren't straight?"

"Our gay offspring aren't affected."

How did I not know this?

"We're by far the greatest influence of gay rights in the Italian culture," he said proudly as if the act was on purpose.

"Well, if you're not the Dread, what do you call yourselves?"

"Il Maledetto."

"The Cursed," I said. "Seems a little harsh. Where does the name come from?"

"You know your Italian. That's frightening. It's an actual curse from a witch of la Vecchia Religione, the old religion, stregheria. A young Sicilian strega cast a dark spell upon the conquering Moors. It was supposed to make the Moors impotent and cause them to take their own lives. The girl underestimated her strength, plus she mixed a few verses up, and the spell had the opposite effect. Our lineage has been cursed ever since."

"How have I not heard of streg…"

"Stregheria."

"How have I not heard of stregheria?" I said, looking over my shoulder at him.

"The Inquisition forced the coven to go underground. They went so far as to pretend to be Catholics, which worked out well since a hefty portion of the Bible was lifted from stregheria—like the story of the virgin birth. Although the stregheria's Messiah is female. If you're ever in Sicily, peek under the swaddling cloth of the sculptures of the baby Jesus. You'll eventually find one that's a girl, carved by a strega."

"I have got to read up on this," I said.

"That'll be hard. The stregherian tales are never written down."

Where had I heard that before?

124

"The legends are passed from mother to daughter. Generation to generation. Who do you think helps your family in a pinch?"

"Support."

"They're witches," he said softly in my ear.

That's where I heard that the tales are never written down, from Support. They *are* witches.

"Is that why you chose the Warwick Hotel?"

"You're thinking of Warlocks." There was the old smirk, realizing he caught me in a mistake. "Your family is also under a spell. It's why you relentlessly pursue us. The young witch visited the High Priestess after her parents were murdered by the Cursed. Realizing there was no way to break such a dark spell, the High Priestess projected herself astrally, searching for the fiercest of the fierce to fight the Cursed. That's when your kin were brought in. Why do you think you have this great power to feel us? The Mirror's Touch is a spell. I guarantee that the midwife who helped bring you into this world was a High Priestess. A Priestess of Death will be there to help you pass back through."

"How do you know all this?" And how did he know my mom used a midwife?

"My bloodline stayed in Sicily for hundreds of years. We heard the tales. Our wives even tried becoming witches to see if they could break the curse. That never ended well."

I wiggled free and sat with my back against the headboard and my arms wrapped around my knees. My mind was racing. There had to be something we could do to free ourselves.

"Maybe you and I can break it."

He sat up and positioned himself across from me cross-legged. "We can't. And because of this, you'll continue to hunt."

"I won't."

"You will."

"I won't," I said forcefully.

He held me by the wrists. "You will," he said bluntly. "The spell has become part of your nature. What I don't understand is why you always have to kill? Can't you turn the Cursed over to the police?"

"I haven't personally taken a life. That rule is because of you. Grandpa says we can't turn your kind in because they could get out, and one more victim is too many."

"You guys are so goddamn noble. If you're worried about my people getting pardoned and killing again, you'll be happy to learn that the spell vanishes around age forty."

"It goes away?" There was hope.

"Absolutely. We refer to this as the Age of Reckoning. I have a theory that it happens at forty because that's the oldest people got in the eleventh century. But don't believe for a minute that the change is going to be easy. During the Reckoning, the empathy, along with the guilt, comes flooding in. It's especially hard for those who have killed. A lot of us don't make it through this phase. After the Reckoning, we gather our families for a forgiveness celebration that lasts days."

I sat up with excitement. "Back in New York, you said the tears come later. I understand that statement now."

"Exactly."

"This explains the stories my grandfather told me of The Drea... I mean, Cursed, dropping off the radar. He thought they died."

"In a way, they do. It's a rebirth of sorts. We used to confuse it with finding God, but we know better now."

"Maybe it is a connection with God."

He shrugged and placed his hand on mine. "If there is a God, why would she allow such devastation to continue?"

"She," I said and smiled.

"I thought you'd like that."

"Why was my grandfather so adamant that you had to be killed? Is the curse stronger at first?" I felt him flinch, but he kept his hold.

"That's something you'd need to ask him. But no, the curse grows as we mature. Theoretically, you wouldn't have been in danger for a year or two. Maybe your grandfather thought I was older. The danger for us comes around seventeen or eighteen. That's when women like you, the Huntresses, can connect with us from a distance. We're in the open at that point."

Christ, I was the monster. "I am so sorry for everything."

"It's not your fault, Sunshine. We were born into this. I just hope you can put a brake on the killing. We've lost a lot of important people. Michelangelo's brother was as talented as him, but Hunters targeted him."

"How come they spared Michelangelo?"

"He was gay. I may have told you more than I should."

"I won't tell," I said. "I promise."

"I appreciate that." He retrieved a pen and paper from the desk. "There's a serial killer in Tacoma who's Cursed. Most of them are. Catching him will help put you in the mindset of turning us into the police. He's not from our immediate family, so you can do with him what you want. He'll be a test of your skills and compassion." Stefano wrote a name and folded the note in half. "This is the only one I know of, so see if you can figure out who he is without looking at his name. There's a pattern in his victim's disappearance dates that gives him away. Once you find that, you can use your gift to locate him. He doesn't deserve a quick death. This animal needs to rot in jail."

"I will get on this tomorrow. I promise. What do the detectives call this killer?"

"The Hilltop Hellion."

127

"I've heard of him." The man was a vicious child murderer.

"Be safe."

"We always try."

"Try harder." He kissed me on the forehead.

I traced the scar on his cheek with my finger. "Did a Hunter do that?"

"No. I bit it on my skateboard." He ran a finger along the scar and drifted into thought.

"Do you mind me asking a personal question?"

"I won't know until you ask it."

"How do *you* control it?"

"That's not the question I was expecting. Are you sure you want to know?"

"Yes, and I appreciate you thinking of my feelings."

He smiled. "Before I answer, I want you to know I hadn't gone through the change when we were dating. You were the only one I was sleeping with."

A weight lifted even though I was having a hard time believing him. "You have no idea how much that means to me."

"I know you more than you think. How I control it is I find married couples whose husbands like to watch. It's a safe outlet with no commitment."

"Why don't you get a girlfriend?"

"They all walk away broken." He said this like it was their fault.

"Not me," I said.

"What are you talking about? You thought I was dead."

"Yeah, I guess so. But *you* wouldn't have broken me."

"No, you're different. You're tough. Tougher than me. You have no idea how difficult it's been without you. It almost killed me."

"I wanted to die when I thought you were gone."

128

"That would have destroyed me. There would be no greater love than ours." He kissed me gently on the lips after saying this odd phrasing. "I still think this is a bad idea. Without you around to keep me in check, my social problems have grown worse."

"Nothing we can't work through," I said.

He retrieved his phone and sat next to me. "I want to show you my family, so you'll know not to hunt them."

"Of course. I would be devastated if we did."

"Here's my uncle." I recognized Tony from the photos in his condo. "He's gay, so he's no trouble. Here's my cousin. He's kind of a bad guy, so if you do run into him, teach him a lesson."

My heart skipped a beat seeing the picture. "Your cousin killed a woman," I said.

"Seriously? How do you know?"

"I tracked him back to his girlfriend's place. A week later, she was dead, and he skipped town."

"Damn it. If you find him, can you talk to the police? Don't hurt him."

"I won't."

He showed me his remaining family, then set the phone on the nightstand.

"I'll do everything I can to keep them safe."

"Thank you. Now, how about you show me yours?"

I panicked, not sure what to do.

"See, it's not so easy. How will I keep your family safe if I can't recognize them?" More importantly, how will he know when to run?

"Fine." I found a picture from the night we doled out our latest identities.

Stefano laughed.

"What?"

"Your family looks like Irish gangsters. They scare me."

"They scare me too," I admitted and locked my phone.

"Show me the rest," he said.

"We're not allowed to know the other families."

"That's so sad." He wrapped his arms around me. "Family is so important. I would be dead without them."

"You don't have to tell me."

There was a long, understanding silence.

"Care to join me in a nap?"

"I would love to."

We slid under the sheet and Stefano took me in his arms from behind. The ability to feel his every movement or shuffle kept me awake. I had to meditate to shut his body out. This sent me into a deep slumber.

I awoke alone in the room. On the end table was a note.

Janis,

I meant it when I said there would be no greater love than ours. But there's also no greater risk. We would be putting each other and our families in danger. Because of this, we can't be together. The reality of our fate hurts me as much as this note is hurting you right now. I wanted to say goodbye, but I knew you'd try to talk me into staying. You'll be better off without me.

With all my love,
Stefano

I crumpled the note to my chest in disbelief. How could this be happening again?

"Why should you be happy?" I yelled at my reflection in the mirror and started bawling.

130

I dressed quickly and checked the parking garage, hoping that Stefano's car was still there. With his license plate, I could find him, but the spot was empty. I took the stairwell and stepped into the street dejected.

On the way home, I picked up the ingredients for nachos. There's no way I could make carbonara for my brother. You have to create that with love, and I felt none.

Chapter 8

It was as if Stefano died all over again. My family kept asking what was wrong. There was no way to tell them without putting him at risk. I felt utterly alone.

To keep my mind distracted, I searched for a pattern in the Hilltop Hellion's killings. A week of intense scrutiny had me no closer to solving the puzzle. There wasn't a direct correlation between the locations of the abductions and the discovery of the bodies. The time the victims disappeared varied, as did the day of the week. I closed the folder on the computer, frustrated, and headed to the store.

I was in line at Jackson Street Grocery, trying to ignore the incessant rambling of the man ahead of me. He apologized to the checker for his short temper, saying his work had burnt him out.

"Burnt out?" she said. "You have the greatest job ever, seven days on, seven days off, working by yourself in a heated booth. How can you beat that?"

"It gets old," the man said. "Plus, the stench of the dump never goes away."

I sidled up to the candy display to see the back of the man's jacket. He worked at the South Seattle Transfer Station. Was the pattern that easy? I was so thrilled I nearly left my groceries on the conveyer belt.

Back home, I opened the calendar I made for the Hilltop Hellion and counted backward from the latest killing. From the pattern in his murders, I determined his schedule. He worked Monday through Sunday and then had seven days to kill. Literally. A Google search of *Pierce County employment seven days on seven off* returned nothing of importance.

There were three transfer stations near the area of the abductions. I checked the calendar and, to my frustration, realized that The Hilltop Hellion would be off for two more days. I prayed that he wouldn't kill during that time.

On Monday, I had Cordy help me load Grandpa's truck with the scraps from Dad's latest project.

"Do you have your sidearm on you?" I asked.

Cordy lifted the front of his shirt to show me. "What are we really doing?"

"I think the Hilltop Hellion is a Dread, and I believe I know where he works."

"No way!"

As I explained what I found, he grew more excited.

"Let's go," he said, jumping in the passenger seat, and we headed to Tacoma.

"Sorry again about not cooking carbonara for your birthday," I said.

"That's all right. I like your nachos. I'm always up for a snack dinner. So, what was up with you that night?"

"Female stuff," I said.

It irked me how easily Cordy took that as an excuse.

"Do you want to talk about it?" he asked.

"No," I said abruptly.

"Well, then shut up," he joked.

I couldn't come up with a decent rebuttal.

Cordy amused himself with a game he made up for the drive over, where you get a point if the first letter of a car's color was anywhere on the license plate. The hour flew by.

The Touch didn't register anything in the line for the Tacoma Transfer Station.

"I forgot my wallet," I told the man in the booth. "Can I make a U-turn?" He waved me on.

Algona's Transfer Station was also a bust.

134

We were waiting in line in Enumclaw, the last dump on my list, when I sensed a Dread in front of us. Another car length closer, and I was sure of it.

"He's here," I said.

"Wicked," Cordy said.

"The guy's running the booth. Be cool. Don't look at him."

I rolled to the window and casually turned my head toward the man. He had the dark, rugged handsomeness of a Dread. Could this be the face of terror? The problem is he barely resembled the police sketch. As I was taking the ticket from him, I snapped a picture with the camera in my sunglasses. The name on his ID was Georgio R.

"Was it him?" Cordy said as we pulled forward.

"He's a Dread. It would be too much of a coincidence for it not to be him. Here, check out his picture."

"Why are they so damn handsome?" he said, looking at my phone.

The bed of the pickup was full of glass and wires. I ducked into the cab for my work gloves. What I really wanted was to read the name Stefano gave me. I opened the note, revealing Georgio Romano. Look at me. I found my man.

Back at the weigh station, Georgio brushed my hand as he was passing my change over. There was an evil deep inside of him. He had embraced the Dread, channeling it into his own doing. I almost threw up. "The smell," I said to cover.

"You get used to it," he said. "I have six more hours of this."

"Well, enjoy," I joked.

He awkwardly laughed like he didn't do it often.

A few blocks away, I pulled into a gas station and ran a background check on my phone. "Look at that. Only one Georgio Romano lives in Pierce County."

"How did you know his name?" Cordy said.

"His permit was in the window," I fibbed.

Georgio's home wasn't far from where we were. I entered the location in Google Maps and was happy to see that his property butted up to a park.

"We can go in right here," I said, showing Cordy.

"What do you mean, go in?"

"We need evidence that he's the Hellion."

"Why? He's a Dread. Just call the family and we'll take him out."

"Death is too quick for this monster. He needs to suffer in jail. I found him. This is going to happen my way."

"What in the hell are you talking about, jail?" He leaned back, staring at me in bewilderment like someone had replaced his sister.

"We're handing him over to the police. There's no discussion on this."

"I don't understand," Cordy said, disappointed, "but if we're breaking in, we should have brought my drone."

"Damn it. You're right." I checked the time; it would be cutting it too close.

The park by the Dread's house was almost a bust. A wall of sticker bushes blocked our entry, but at the far end of the cyclone fence, a path was cut through the blackberries, leading to a child's tree fort. The kids were going to shit their pants when they learned they were playing on the Hilltop Hellion's property.

We watched for movement from the edge of the backyard. His home appeared to be empty, with no security cameras. The wind shifted, bringing with it a foul odor.

"I can smell the death," I said.

"That might be the skunk cabbage," Cordy responded dryly, pointing to the swamp across from us. That gave us a bad case of sibling giggles.

The seriousness of the task forced us to gather our senses. I brought out two pairs of rubber gloves and tossed a set to Cordy. The yard was isolated, but we still ran stooping low for some reason. At the backdoor, I stepped aside to watch Cordy perform his magic. He's the master locksmith in our family. The door was open in seconds.

"Oh God, it's him," he said, getting a whiff of decay seeping from the house.

"Holy crap," I said, tilting my head back.

We followed the stench down a hall to a door with a padlock on it.

"Allow me," Cordy said. "Shit, it's a combo lock."

"Look around. There has to be incriminating evidence here."

In the living room was a portrait of Georgio and a woman who I presumed was his mother. Aside from his handsome appearance, he came off as normal.

"Oh, Bailey," Cordy called out in a sing-song voice.

I found him in the kitchen. He tossed a freezer bag to me. It didn't register right away that it was a child's arm inside.

"Don't drop it," he said, reaching out.

I took a picture then handed the bag to him. "Put it back exactly as it was."

Leaving the house was more nerve-racking than entering. Even though the Dread would be at work for another four hours, I expected him to jump out at any moment. My heart was pounding as we reached our truck.

"That was fun," Cordy said. "Thanks for bringing me."

Everything is a game with that one. "I need a scotch," I said, sounding like Dad.

Back home, we found Dad and Bepa sitting at the dining room table. There was something off about their demeanor.

"What's up with you guys?" I asked.

"I received a letter from New York," Dad said. "A reporter's been looking into the day the Rosotti family's house burned. He said we were acting suspiciously in the crowd and followed us to the car to get our plates. The guy wants me to call him."

I picked up the letter. "Christ, he even has your new name."

"We have to start packing," Dad said.

"Hold on," I said. "I can take care of this. Give me your burner phone." I dialed the number, and a man answered. "Hello, is this Julian Roberts?

"It is. Who may I ask is inquiring?"

"This is Lorreta Springs. I'm a private detective working with Tim O'Donnell. I hear you've managed to track him down. I'm afraid there's a bit of a problem in that, Julian. You see, we're deep undercover. You've kind of fucked us here. I can offer a decent trade if you make this go away."

"I don't understand what you're saying. A trade?"

"Have you heard of the Hilltop Hellion?"

"Of course."

"Would you like to be the one who cracks the case?"

There was a long pause. "Go on."

"I know who the killer is. I was in his home today. There's proof of his guilt in the freezer—a child's arm. I'm certain from the stench you'll find bodies in his basement." I didn't dare turn around. Dad was surely staring daggers.

"What would you like in return?"

"For you to go away. That's all. And to delete everything you have on Tim and his family. You'll be famous, Julian. Probably get a book deal out of this."

That was all it took. "I'm in. Who is it?"

"In time," I said. "The Hellion won't strike for at least six days. Let me tell you how you solved the case. Then I'll give you his identity, even a picture. What's your email address?"

138

Grandpa threw me a pad and a pen. I wrote the email down and verified it with Julian.

"I'll send my files and call you right back."

"Thank you," Julian said. "This is huge. Life-changing."

I sent the files using a temporary email account and called Julian to explain my process. "Remember, you identified the killer at his job from the police sketch and the pattern in the days his victims disappeared. You'll have to fly in to retrace my steps where I eventually identified him. Print out the photo when you're here and take a picture so the original is on your phone. I wouldn't risk going in the house. I'll draw the layout of the inside so you can describe it."

"Thank you so much for doing this. I swear on my parent's life, I will destroy all traces of Tim's file."

"That's all I ask. Have fun," I said and hung up.

Dad was concerned that Cordy and I went out alone, but he was beaming with pride that I solved a high-profile case. He didn't understand when I told him we would have turned him into the police anyway.

"We don't operate that way, Bailey."

"Sometimes, a quick death is too good for the Dread. This monster needs to rot in jail."

"Yeah, well..." His sentence dissolved into a disgruntled mumble. "I'm proud of you, Peaches."

"Thanks, Dad."

"Can I have a word with you?" Grandpa said.

"Of course." I followed him into the living room.

"Janis."

"Bailey," I said, cutting him off. "I've been Bailey for six years."

"Bailey, sorry. I wanted to tell you how proud I am of your confidence on the phone. You've grown so far from that scared girl outside Central Pizza."

"Your trick worked. I'm not acting anymore. I haven't been in years."

Five days later, Dad called me into the living room and pointed at the TV. The graphics to the side of the reporter read Hilltop Hellion Captured.

"Look at you," Dad said, slapping my knee. "My daughter is the greatest citizen detective never known."

Julian flew in for the arrest. His face wasn't like I had pictured. It was narrow and rat-like, coming to a point at his nose. Julian's sincere eyes were his saving grace; they expressed compassion. He leaned over and spoke into the cluster of microphones.

"Sadly, we learned that the Hilltop Hellion murdered a boy the day before his arrest. I am so sorry we didn't come sooner. There couldn't be any mistakes. We had to be sure it was him. From the depths of my soul, I apologize. I have spoken with the parents. Their grief is unimaginable. The only comfort is that no other family will go through the trauma inflicted by this monster."

My heart was racing as sweat poured from me. The room tunneled in until I was gone.

"Bailey, Bailey. Are you there?" It was Dad.

My vision slowly returned and I worked myself to a seated position.

"Do we need to get her to a hospital?" Cordy asked.

"No, no, this happens," I said.

"I knew we're pushing her too hard," Dad said.

"It's not the work. It's the Touch. I faint sometimes. It's not wearing me out. I just get overloaded."

"Go see if there's a Dread outside," Dad told Cordy.

"No one's here. Did Julian say what I think he said?"

"Yeah," Dad said.

"But he only killed on his off weeks."

"Don't beat yourself up," Dad said. "You stopped a monster." He offered a hand to help me to my feet. "The best thing for us to do is drink this day away."

140

Knowing Support were witches, I was curious to learn about them and stregheria. I could only find bits of information on the web about the religion and nothing on them, not even a picture. Every time I tried to get personal, the conversation was steered toward business. They were so distant I could only talk to them through email and IM chats. It was very frustrating.

I was checking my email when a new lead from Support popped up. "Shit."

"What is it, Honey," Dad responded from the weapons cabinet. I forgot he was in the room.

"Nothing," I said, but it wasn't nothing. Stefano's cousin was back in town and had killed again. I told Support that I would verify if the man was a Dread. The order was to terminate on sight. I needed to talk to Stefano, but I had no way to contact him.

Cordy knocked on the open door. "You up for going out dancing tonight?"

I froze.

"What's the matter?"

"I never learned how to dance," I admitted.

"That's all right. I can teach you. Come on."

I logged off the computer and followed him upstairs.

"Play that dance mix you're always listening to," he said.

I hooked my phone to the stereo and brought up Stefano's mix.

"The first thing you do is find the beat. Hear it? Right there, and there and there," he said as he moved his head rhythmically. "Now, just bounce back and forth from foot to foot."

With the Highland Dance, you're rigid. I struggled to adapt to Cordy's loose movements but eventually found the rhythm.

"Now that you have the beat, bring in your upper body with whatever strikes your mood." He performed a funny double-shoulder tuck and mirrored it on the other side. I followed his lead and waved my hands above my head, knocking them on the ceiling.

"See, you're a natural. I'll find some YouTube tutorials for steps to use."

"Thanks, I appreciate this."

I didn't want to go dancing, but our family rarely did anything. Staying out of sight was part of our survival.

Cordy and I practiced dance moves throughout the day. I regretted waiting so long to learn. Dancing was a freeing way of expression.

Now all I had to worry about was what to wear. I wanted to go in a dress, but they all made my muscles look manly. A slouch shoulder top and a pair of jeans worked better. With this outfit, I could wear tennis shoes that wouldn't add too much height. Cordy whistled at me when I emerged from my room. I brushed him off with a swipe of my hand but ate his compliment up.

The first club we hit was a total meat market. Cordy had to pretend to be my date to keep the lecherous men at bay. When he'd had enough, he asked if I'd rather go to a gay bar for peace of mind.

"It won't bother you?"

"Not at all."

We ended up at a straight-friendly club on Capitol Hill called Neighbors. The relaxed vibe was a refreshing change from the last bar. There weren't just couples dancing; everyone was dancing comfortably together.

I was on my fourth drink and feeling no pain. Cordy and I were having an absolute blast. No one cared how I danced, just that I was dancing. I wasn't even mad when a guy reached for my nonexistent cock. That made me laugh. Cordy sure didn't care for the mix-up.

"It's cool. He thought I was in drag."

"It's not cool. You do *not* look like a man."

"He only thought that because of where we are."

A brunette with an adorably broad smile strolled confidently up to Cordy to dance with him. My brother didn't seem to mind. He looked over at me and shrugged. The guy worked his way closer until he was grinding his cock on my brother's like he was trying to start a fire with two sticks. Cordy wouldn't back off, which confused me. I stepped to the side of the dance floor and tried not to stare. It wasn't long before Cordy passed him over to another man and joined me.

"What?" he said.

"Is there maybe something you want to tell me?"

"No," he said, laughing. "I'm not gay."

"Why would you let him do that then?"

"Maybe I liked the attention. Don't you dare say anything to Dad."

"I wouldn't do that."

A gaggle of drunk bachelorettes stumbled onto the floor, falling over each other.

"Speaking of attention," he said, "I'm owed a little."

Cordy introduced himself to the ladies, and they were soon passing him around like a bottle of wine in a park. He seemed to favor a spunky redhead who danced with a march in her step.

A half-hour later, Cordy found me upstairs, leaning on the balcony, watching the fun below.

"There you are. Do you mind if I take off?"

"Not at all. I think she's cute," I said.

"What do you mean, she? I'm fuckin' the whole party."

I spat my drink onto the floor below. Cordy's confidence was off the charts.

143

"Hang on a second." I snagged a handful of condoms from the bowl on the upstairs bar.

Cordy was a gentleman and stayed with me until I was in a cab heading home. I longed for Stefano. Why had he gone away? That was so unfair.

Chapter 9

I had my headphones on, watching a live performance of Time to Say Goodbye. It was a month since Stefano ditched me. I was furious at him for leaving, and insanely jealous of whoever he was using to keep the curse at bay. We could have worked out a solution.

The song was interrupted by a message from Dad asking that I meet him and Grandpa to help with a case. I hid my hair under a baseball cap, hoping I could pass for a man. Before I left, I had the foresight to put on my Kevlar vest.

On the drive over, I turned to the Classical station. I was going to become cultured if it killed me.

The storage facility Dad sent me to was disconcerting. There were way too many security cameras. I put on my sunglasses and climbed the fence.

"It's me," I said, knocking on the metal door of storage unit 24.

Dad slid something heavy to the side and let me in. There was a blindfolded man tied to a chair in the back of the room. I was horrified when I recognized Uncle Tony's feminine lips. Why were so many of Stefano's family members showing up?

"Where the hell was I in this decision?" I said.

"Sorry about that. This one caught us by surprise. So, he's a Dread?"

"No, he's not," I said. That wasn't a lie. Stefano's uncle is gay. I was pissed that they detained him.

"Bullshit!" Grandpa shouted. "He's a Dread. What are you hiding?"

"I'm not hiding anything, and I don't appreciate your tone."

Grandpa walked up to Uncle Tony and punched him hard in the face.

"What the fuck! I would have felt that. How dare you. Get out of here," I demanded. "Now!" I never stood up to my grandfather. His glare was a mixture of shock and pride.

"Fine," he relented and stepped out of the unit.

"Go," I told my dad. "I'll take care of this."

"I can help," he said.

"You guys have done enough. We'll meet up in a couple of weeks," I said with a wink, hoping it sounded like we weren't living together as a family.

I approached Uncle Tony once we were alone. "You're going to be all right," I said and pressed his head to my chest. He began to sob, and I cradled him until he finished.

"Is this your storage unit?" I asked.

"It is," he said. His voice was smooth and calming.

"You might want to move to a different facility."

"Ya think."

That made me laugh. "Let's see what we can do to get you out of here."

The knots in the rope to the chair would only give on one of his wrists. I cut him free from the other.

"I'm going to face you toward the wall," I said. "Give me a ten-minute head start, so I can make sure the boys are gone. We'll call this a truce."

"Yes. Yes. Absolutely. Thank you."

"If we see you around again, I won't be able to help."

"You won't."

I turned his chair and removed the blindfold to take with me.

"Can you leave that? The tie was a gift from my grandfather."

"Of course." I placed it on his lap. "I'll knock when I'm leaving, so you'll know it's safe to turn around."

"You're very kind."

I was furious when I arrived home and slammed the front door. "Don't you ever do that to me again," I said. "I have to check our targets out. That is the rule."

"We were just..." Dad said

"Never again," I yelled, cutting him off.

"Yes, Bailey," he said.

The next day I was reading an Agatha Christie mystery, trying to figure out how the latest clue was a red herring. They always were. Solving the Hilltop Hellion case gave me a false sense of importance. I was sure I would beat Agatha at her game.

My cell phone rang, pulling me from the tale. It was the Warwick Hotel. I hadn't given them or Stefano my number. Curiosity got the best of me and I answered.

"Good afternoon, this is John from the Warwick Hotel. Is this Janis?"

"Yes?" I said, unnerved.

"I'm calling to confirm your meeting tomorrow at four p.m. Same room, 1701."

I squealed. Stefano had caved.

"I'll take that as confirmation," the man said and hung up.

I was ecstatic and troubled. Dad spotted Uncle Tony twice before he led them to his storage unit. Then there was the matter of Stefano's cousin going missing. Support asked about him again. I couldn't stall forever.

The following afternoon I told my family I was heading out to document the Dread. Dad wanted me to stay and help with a project, but I used our last fight to throw a fit and stormed out.

I wasn't comfortable parking my car near the hotel, so I left it by the stadium and rode the light rail to

Westlake Center. The manikins in the store windows were drawing me in. Was my floral tunic too casual with jeans? I had been stressing all day about what to wear. My reflection was cute, putting me at ease.

A brisk walk brought me to the Warwick. I avoided the front desk and took the second-floor elevator. Something felt amiss when I reached Stefano's room. The Mirror's Touch couldn't find him. I unholstered my Glock and held it at my side.

My heart was pounding as I knocked. I sensed Stefano as he returned from around the corner on the balcony. I reluctantly put my firearm away.

Stefano greeted me as if nothing happened. I went to slap him, and he caught my arm. The leather bracelet he wore reminded me of the one from when we were younger. It gave me pause.

"Hey, come on," he said.

"You hurt me." I looked away so I wouldn't grow lost in his eyes.

"I know. But we can't be together. You have to understand this."

I was livid. "Don't you ever say that again."

He opened his mouth to stress the truth but smartly backed off.

There was a skateboard in the corner. That explained the rip in his jeans. He must have been out riding. I was glad I didn't dress up too much.

"Thank you for letting Uncle Tony go."

"Does he know it was me?" I said.

"No, you're fine, but I knew it was you. Any other Huntress and he'd be in the morgue. You won't see Tony anymore."

Christ, had he been casing our house? I was putting us in danger. "Are you sure we're safe? My family can move."

"No, you're good. Sorry, you didn't get to solve the Hilltop Hellion case before that reporter did."

148

"No need to be sorry. I was the one who sent him the info."

"No shit. How?"

"Seven on, seven off."

"Hey, you did solve it. That must have felt great turning him in?"

"It actually did."

"Thank you for doing that. It means the world. Do you think you can keep it up?"

"I'm going to try." I looked him in the eye. "I do need to know how the hotel got my cell number?"

Stefano had a guilty look that I recognized from when we were younger. "While you were napping, I kind of unlocked your phone with your thumb."

"What the hell?"

"I needed your number in case I was wrong."

"You *were* wrong," I yelled. "I need you."

"We have to be careful," he said. "I want you to know I never stopped loving you, Janis. I brought you something to say I'm sorry." He handed over a USB stick.

"Look at you saying you're sorry. Please tell me this is what I think it is."

He raised an eyebrow. "Those are my best remixes. And some songs I made. Nothing good enough for the market, but I like them."

"I was hoping you had more."

"You'll want to keep these away from the net. If someone traces them to my SoundCloud, they have my DJ schedule, and with that, they can find me."

"I'll protect this with my life," I said, holding the drive close to my heart. I was proud that he followed through on his dream of being a DJ, but scared that it put him out in the open.

I slid my finger from his abs to his chest. The simple touch ignited Stefano's desire and he ran playfully further into the room. He hadn't said anything about my cute outfit. He couldn't get it off fast enough. I tackled him

149

on the bed, accidentally knocking his head into the wall. We both rubbed our skulls in pain. Our lust was ablaze in an inferno of passion. Stefano flipped me over and slammed me onto the mattress hard enough that I bounced. He gave me a quick kiss and worked his way down my chest to my clit. I was ready to fight for my turn with his cock, but he needed to apologize, and apologize he did. Three times. The final apology nearly tore my head off.

I was in a daze from the tongue lashing and eager to have Stefano inside me. "Let's do it on the deck," I said and wrapped half of the blanket over him.

"Oh, hell yes."

We made our way outside and Stefano steered us around the corner for privacy. Our end room has the only deck on that side. I bent over the rail and reached behind to guide his cock home.

"I should wear a condom," Stefano said.

"You don't have to" I placed his hand on the birth control in my arm.

"What if I have an STD?"

"Whatever is you is me."

"That's not right," he said, pulling away.

I backed up into his cock. The head throbbed as we made contact, with my clit answering back.

"No," he said. "I'll get tested and then, and only then."

"Grab a condom," I said, happy that he thought of me but even happier that there was going to be a next time. The little shit took the blanket with him, leaving me naked on the balcony. I wasn't too upset. He was back in my life.

Stefano returned through the slider with a condom on his erect cock. I positioned coyly in a sexy pose.

"Damn, you're too hot," Stefano said, rounding the corner.

I turned to the rail and seductively pushed my backside out. He grabbed my hips and drove himself home. The sensation he felt of his cock slamming inside me created a reverb from my reaction as the mixture churned and blended. Stefano set a punishing pace from the first thrust and wouldn't let up until he was dripping with sweat.

"Do you think you can work the Mirror's Touch so we come at the same time?" he said. "No pressure."

"I'll try."

"I can help."

He moved to the blanket on the ground and I lowered onto his cock, grinding into his pelvis for clitoral contact. I used my trick from last time to isolate and focus the Touch. It wasn't controlled in any sense of the word, more like riding a wild horse.

"It won't be long," I moaned.

Stefano slid my finger into his mouth. "Stick it in my ass."

"What?" I almost laughed.

"Do it."

Well, this escalated quickly. Without him slipping out of me, I raised myself high and reached between his legs. The skin of his hole was unexpectedly smooth. I drove my finger home. The sensation from him was an uncomfortable tenseness that ran through his body.

"Up high," he said. I rotated my finger. The sensitivity of his prostate was mind-numbing like an amplifier switching on as a thousand nerves sang out. He pulled me free. "Do that when you're about to cum."

I thrust upon him rigorously, working for my next orgasm. Stefano had ignited the fire orally. What was coming was epic, of that I was sure. My muscles constricted deep inside as I coaxed my release to fruition. I reached down and slid my index finger into him, massaging his prostate. It was as if there were two clits in sync.

151

Stefano gripped my inner thighs with both hands and slid his thumb across my clit in time with my thrusts. Sparks like a welding torch's reached across to his prostate and back, fusing us. My core was glowing, throbbing uncontrollably as my breath grew heavy.

"I'm getting close," he said.

"I am too, baby."

I massaged him and he rubbed me, the clenching constricting, growing, building, until our orgasms burst into the city air. His contractions merged with mine like dueling tornados. He pulled my upper body close to his and let out an almost animalistic howl. I moaned in succession.

Stefano's orgasm waned as mine gained intensity. I rode him tight, feeling through him what I was experiencing. The last of the quivers faded as I fell back with him—both of us working to catch our breath.

"You're my soul mate," he said, gazing into my eyes. "I love you."

His words floored me, but I kept my composure, not wanting to scare him. "I can't picture a world without you."

My head was throbbing, overloaded from the Mirror's Touch. I woke to an empty room, not sure how I made it to the bed. Stefano's presence was nowhere to be felt. If he left me again, I don't know if I could make it through the grief. The last time nearly destroyed me.

The Touch found Stefano walking up to the door, and I lay back in relief. He was carrying what I think was a shopping bag.

"Hi, Sunshine," he said smiling. "You scared me."

"What happened?"

"You just crumbled. I almost called an ambulance but you fell into a deep sleep. You looked so peaceful I didn't want to wake you." He set a bottle of vodka and a six-pack of Italian orange soda on the nightstand and crawled in bed to hold me. "I'm worried about these fainting spells. How often does this happen?"

"Apart from sex with you, it's only happened one other time when I was on my first mission. I was too close to a murderer that my father took out. They had to carry me to the car. I'm sorry. It must be horrible hearing this."

He hugged me tightly. "Everything is terrible about the curse."

We lay in silence. The reality of our world was horrendous.

"Not everything," I said and kissed him.

Stefano found drinking glasses in the bathroom and made us cocktails. He was heavy on the vodka but balanced it with the Italian orange soda.

A drink would do me good. I accepted it happily.

"This is delicious," I said.

"I knew you'd like it," he said and joined me back in bed. "Kind of reminds me of that evening at Uncle Tony's."

"The day you ruined me for sex with anyone else," I said. "It's not the same, and I'm not talking about the Touch. The connection we have is amazing."

"I'm in the same boat. No one comes close to my girl."

"Hey, I believe I have a safe way to contact each other," I said.

I showed him the secure app that my family uses. He reluctantly handed his phone over, and I had him set up within minutes. A terrible thought entered my mind. Had I taught Stefano how his family could communicate anonymously? Christ, this man was going to be my downfall.

I sent myself a text from his phone. "Watch what happens when I try to take a screenshot."

A message alerted him. He liked how the screenshot I tried was blank.

"This is perfect," he said.

I'm still concerned that you had the hotel call my phone," I said. "My number is forever linked to your room."

"No, it's fine. That was my friend, John. He thinks I'm fooling around with a married woman. That's why he was all incognito. Don't worry; he's not family. If it bothers you, we can go somewhere else."

"It's cool," I said. "Speaking of family. If we're compromised, we should have a way to alert each other. Is there a phrase you don't care to hear?"

He threw one right out, "We need to talk."

I laughed. "That will work."

"Want to see something weird," Stefano said.

"Sure."

He showed me a picture of what I thought was a male model bungee jumping. It was Stefano's cousin, the guy from the library.

"It's a suicide selfie," he said.

"Oh, thank God," I said.

"Hey, that's my cousin. He sent me that as he was falling to his death."

"I didn't mean any offense. I am so sorry. It's just Support sent me your cousin's case a week ago with orders to terminate. I couldn't get a hold of you. I was worried my family would take him out. It's so hard to reel them in. Three more women died at his hands."

"Damn it," he said. "Sometimes, the Curse is stronger than the man."

"Are you OK?" I said.

He shrugged. "I miss him. Of all my cousins, we were the closest."

I grabbed the phone and looked closer. Gasworks Park was off in the distance. His cousin must have jumped from the Aurora Bridge. There was no way he survived that far of a drop.

"He sure chose a ballsy way to go," I said.

"Jamie never was one to do things half-assed."

154

My phone vibrated with an incoming text that read Hendrix. I sat up abruptly.

"I have to go. My family needs me."

"There's no rest for the wicked."

"No, there isn't," I said, ignoring the honesty in his jab.

"I had fun today," Stefano said.

"Same here." I kissed him and dressed to catch the light rail.

A half-hour later, I pulled up to the Northwest African American Museum, next to the Jimi Hendrix Park. We picked the meeting spot because most people in Seattle would think our code word meant the Jimmy Hendrix statue downtown or his memorial in Renton.

Dad's car was parked on the far end of the lot. My family was a sweaty, exhausted mess.

"Apologies for the rush, Peaches. We're moving again."

I had pushed to move since my assault, but now that Stefano was back, I didn't want to. "Damn it. I was enjoying Washington."

"We're not going far," Dad said. "Just on the other side of town to a neighborhood called Ravenna. Pop has had a feeling for a while. We have your clothes and toiletries, so you should be good. The rest will arrive tomorrow. We even have a decoy moving truck to lose anyone following them. Your brother helped with the Lair and anything incriminating."

I was pissed. Did my family not trust me anymore because of Stefano's uncle?

"What are our new names?" my brother said.

"There's no need for that," Bepa said. "We pay cash. The house and utilities aren't in our name. Support feels we're safe."

"But that journalist found us," I said.

"He was true to his word," Dad said, "What he couldn't remove was scrubbed by Support. We should be in the clear."

"You're going to love this house," Grandpa said. "It's a duplex. You and Cordy have your own place."

"I haven't gone in our side," Cordy said. "I waited for you."

"Thanks, Brother. Hop in."

The duplex was another fixer-upper, but I didn't mind. Cordy and I would be living on our own. That was epic.

Dad handed us each a set of keys, and we ran down the driveway to the back entrance of our unit. The last key I tried fit the lock. We raced through the entryway, past the kitchen, and up the stairs.

Our new living room faced the street, with our rooms behind. The two bedrooms were a decent size, but one had an en-suite bathroom. I was hoping Cordy would be a gentleman and give me that one.

"Let's play hide and seek," he said. "If you can find me in five minutes, the main room is yours."

I gladly accepted his challenge and went outside to count to a hundred. His footsteps were clear as he bounded up the stairs. The place was empty, which should have given me the advantage, but I couldn't find my brother anywhere.

"I give up," I said in the kitchen, defeated.

There was rattling under the stairs, and a small door in the paneling popped open. No fair.

"Of course you get the room," Cordy said. "I just wanted to play."

"We're going to have fun on our own," I said. "Let's go see what the other side looks like."

The entrance to Dad and Grandpa's unit was in the front like a typical home. The living room, kitchen, and bedrooms were all on the main floor. Off the kitchen was a deck that unfortunately overlooked our entrance.

Dad challenged me to find the Lair downstairs. I had a hunch it was behind the new cedar paneling in the room next to the shared laundry, but I couldn't locate the opening.

"The whole wall moves." He slid it to the right, revealing the familiar metal door. I worked the combination and stepped inside.

"How long were you planning this move?" I asked.

"A couple of weeks. I know. I know. We thought it would be best if we kept this between us."

"That's bullshit, Dad. I thought Support was supposed to talk with me. You need to let me do my job."

I stormed out through the back, hurt that my family no longer trusted me. Could they know I was seeing Stefano or that Tony was his uncle? There was no way. I made sure the GPS on my phone was disabled.

I found my laptop in the boxes upstairs and uploaded the songs Stefano gave me. His music was the escape I needed. He wrote a song using my old name, a love song. I was listening to it for the third time when he sent me a text.

Hi Sunshine. I miss you already.

Hello lover. I'm listening to the songs you wrote. I felt like you were in my room. You're so talented. It's going to be agony waiting to see you again.

Too bad I'm not on your bed with you. I just wanted to send my love.

157

For a man who can't cry,
you're sure sweet.

I liked the safe vibe of Ravenna. My favorite parts of the neighborhood were the trendy shops and restaurants within walking distance.

Dad kept himself busy, making the duplex home. In the initial month, he upgraded our kitchen cabinets and counters. I had him install a dishwasher so I wouldn't get stuck with the dishes. My worries were for naught. Cordy turned out to be a bit of a neat freak. Mom taught us how to clean; independence was all it took to get him to do it. He ended up being a chill roommate. I appreciate how he puts my toilet seat down after using it. To be nice, I leave his up.

Speaking of bathrooms, Dad refurbished Cordy's downstairs, applying slate over the depressing cement blocks, creating a modern yet rustic aesthetic. Once it was done, Cordy stopped using mine when I was in the bedroom.

Our duplex had a large secluded backyard. Grandpa built four raised beds for the spring planting. With him occupied, life was good.

I arrived home from a five-mile jog to the sound of aggressive sex coming from upstairs. Dad and Grandpa were at the hardware store, so I headed to my room for the keys for the Lair. It sounded like the action was in the front room, but our couch was empty when I reached the top of the stairs. I entered my bedroom and could still hear the noises coming from the living room. I fell to the carpet in hysterics. The sound cut off, and my brother stepped from his room.

"What's so funny?"

158

I was laughing so hard I could barely speak. "Your porn was coming through the stereo."

"I was wondering what that noise was." Cordy wasn't embarrassed in the least.

"Sorry I interrupted you," I said.

"That's OK. I finished."

"Lovely. You have no shame, do you?"

"None at all. Fer sher."

I laughed at how he said that.

Cordy and I were in a Pontiac Aztek like the one Walter White drove in Breaking Bad. As with many things in our world, it was just there one day.

"I checked the fluids and all the lights. You should be good to go," Grandpa said, slapping the roof of the SUV.

Dad approached the driver's side to chat with my brother. "When you're heading back from Idaho, I want you to take it easy. Cruise control is your friend. That's going to be precious cargo."

It was precious cargo, indeed. I couldn't believe Dad was letting Cordy and I go on a gun run.

"I'm cool with that, Daddio," Cordy said. "No more than five over. Fer sher."

I bit my lip to keep from laughing.

Dad smiled proudly. How could he trust Cordy? Maybe he just hoped he could. It didn't matter. I would make sure Cordy kept to the speed limit, or I'd be driving.

"Can we please have an AR-15?" Cordy asked for the fifth time.

"Damn it, Cordy, you know how I feel about that weapon," Dad said.

"Grandpa would let us have one," Cordy said.

Dad glared at him. "Well, I guess my dad is cooler than yours."

Cordy didn't find that as funny as I did.

The drive across Washington State clocked in at five hours with lunch. The time flew by with Cordy as my traveling partner.

To ensure we made it to our appointment the following day, we were spending the night near the Idaho border. If I were honest, we were there a day early because I wanted to stay in the Historic Davenport Hotel. After seeing it on a travel show, I fell in love with the place. The marble lobby is early nineteen-hundreds elegance with a two-story ceiling lined with ornately carved dark wooden beams. The space is a visual paradise of history, with the focal point an enormous fireplace at the far end.

I secretly bumped us up to a Deluxe Suite. The room exceeded all my expectations. As we stepped inside, there was a sink and closet to the right. Beyond that was a marble bathroom. The separate living quarters were a straight shot down the hall from the door. Two queen beds with oversized carved headboards faced the windows. A comfortable sitting area was off to the side.

"This is a nice room," Cordy said. "There's no way Dad splurged for this. You get first choice of beds."

I didn't care which one I slept in but picked the bed furthest in to give Cordy the illusion of protecting me.

"I'll grab some ice," he said and jetted from the room.

The view below our room was the foggy glass ceiling of the lobby. Across from that was a massive outdoor patio. The atmosphere was alive with groups of people socializing. As if on cue, a train on an elevated track passed by in the distance.

Cordy popped onto the patio to my right and casually lit a cigarette. How did I not know my brother smoked? More importantly, why did he smoke? I moved behind the curtain so he wouldn't catch me spying.

He returned a short time later with an ice bucket full from the machine across the hall.

"Where's the vodka?" he said.

"In the red tote under the sink."

"This hotel is so freaky. It reminds me of the one in that boring Rosemary's Baby you made us watch. You know that spooky one? What was the name of it?"

I couldn't remember. How the hell did I forget the name of Stefano's favorite building?

"I'm drawing a blank."

"This place is totally like it."

He poured a couple of stiff drinks, using the Italian orange soda that Stefano got me hooked on. My brother closed the closet door. I didn't remember opening it, and checked to make sure no one was in there.

Cordy and I were into our second cocktail, watching the guests on the patio.

"Let's go hang out in the night air," he said.

"Sure. I have to use the restroom first."

When I returned, Cordy was spacing out in front of the window.

"Let me top these off," he said, taking my glass. He stopped next to the closet door. It was slightly ajar again. "You open that?" he asked accusingly. There was a look of concern on his face.

"I didn't do it," I said, raising my hands innocently.

He fixed our drinks, and we headed out.

"These halls kind of freak me out," he said. "I keep expecting the murdered twins from *The Shining* to be around each corner."

"I had the same thought, walking to our room."

We hung out opposite the bar so the staff wouldn't see that we brought our own cocktails. My brother pulled out a cigarette and lit it as if he'd been smoking all his life.

161

"What the actual fuck!" I said. "Why are you smoking?"

He took another long drag. "This is why," he said and flicked his ash over the edge. The ember split in half, dancing in the wind, staying lit almost to the street. I was mesmerized by the odd beauty of the flight but not deterred.

"Those things will kill you."

"Who's to say they won't one day save my life?"

"Seriously, why are you smoking?"

"The family business is nerve-racking," he said, sucking smoke into his lungs. "This takes the edge off. Do you want one?"

"What? Screw you. I'm not smoking. I can't believe you would try that." I stormed back to the room.

Cordy rushed in a few minutes later, out of breath as if he ran the whole way. He held his hand up and bent over to gather himself.

"I was outside looking up at the hotel when I said, 'This building is freaky.' A man behind me responded, 'Kind of like the Dakota.'"

"That's the one from Rosemary's Baby," I said.

"Exactly. Get this. I turn around, and no one is there. I was by the edge. There was nowhere for him to go."

I was freaking out, not sure I wanted to stay in our haunted hotel anymore. That was until Cordy fell on the carpet in hysterics.

"You little shit. I suppose it was you opening the closet door?"

"Of course. Man, I had you going."

I should have been mad, but his long game was impressive.

He headed to the bathroom, still laughing. I slid a desk drawer out a few inches to scare him. His new game was to pretend he didn't notice.

"Do you want to go swimming?" he said.

"Hell yes." I excused myself to put on a swimsuit and one of the hotel's plush robes.

Inside the elevator, the door closed, then opened. We both leaned into the hall. No one was there. Cordy and I chuckled nervously.

"Want me to teach you how to meditate?" I said. "It helps with the stress."

"I'll try anything," Cordy said. "What would really help is if I could be on the ground with you guys."

"In time."

We crossed the Idaho border the next day well ahead of schedule, offering Cordy plenty of time to make a side trip for smokes. He'd heard that cigarettes are cheaper in Idaho. We found a smoke shop in what I hoped was a bad part of town. Idaho was trashy, like a rundown strip mall. At least at the border, anyway.

A rough-looking biker was running the store. "Those crackheads aren't still out there, are they?"

"Welcome to Idaho," I quipped.

"I didn't see anyone," Cordy said.

"Fucking parking lot maggots," the clerk said. "One of the tweakers took forever to make up his mind, all the while rummaging in his coat. If he pulled out a gun, I would have picked him up and *thrown* him through the window." The man's tone flipped from anger to hospitality comically fast. "What can I do for you?"

"How much is a carton of Marlboro Golds?" Cordy asked.

"$59."

"Holy shit, I'll take five."

"Really?" I said.

"Relax. Cartons are way more in Seattle."

The man stacked five on the counter and rang them up.

"That'll be "$312.70."

"Wait, that doesn't add up," I said. "It shouldn't be over $300."

"Six percent tax."

"That's so low," Cordy said.

"Oh, we pay," the man said, looking toward the parking lot.

"Fer sher," Cordy said.

I felt safer once we were in the car with the doors locked. "Well, I'm not nervous anymore."

"It wasn't that bad," Cordy said.

"We have a greater chance of being shot in this parking lot than where we're headed."

"I thought it was fun," Cordy said.

"How do you stay so damn happy?" I said.

"It's easy if you don't modify happy with a negative. What I do is first thing in the morning I tell myself, 'This will be a good day.'"

"But what if it isn't a good day? How do you still believe it?"

"If you act happy, you become happy. It's all in the power of positivity."

"Did Grandpa teach you that?"

He laughed. "Grandpa? No. He's a grump."

Cordy pulled into the street to the freeway. He edged faster than the speed limit to keep up with the traffic.

An electrical current resonated in my ears as The Touch detected a Dread nearby. He was ahead of us, so at least we weren't being followed. With him flying so fast in a seated position, my stomach grew queasy. I had Cordy pull over in the breakdown lane so I could vomit. He thought I was upset by the mission. It made me appear weak. If I was on top of my game, I could have blamed it on my hangover.

I navigated us in using Dad's poorly drawn map. It took three times backtracking, but I found the hidden driveway. We drove about a hundred yards, and Cordy called from our burner phone.

"Is this Tony's Pizza?" he asked in Grandpa's gravelly voice. Cordy listened to the response. "Anchovies." His face was the spitting image of Bepa's scowl. He let his expression soften. "We're in."

Cordy had looked so much like Grandpa; it made me laugh. My brother joined in.

"These people are gun runners," I said. "We have to be cool."

His face grew stern again, and we proceeded forward. The dirt road led to a massive red barn where a hick in shirtless overalls waited by the open double doors.

"Fucking parking lot maggots," I said.

Cordy let out a snicker but held it together.

"Walter White, I presume," the man said, ribbing us for driving an Aztek. His rotten teeth were disgusting.

Cordy made a mockingly dumb laugh that didn't sit well with the man.

"Bring it in, asshole," he said, leading our car into the barn.

I was nervous, and not just from Cordy's bad first impression. There were blind spots everywhere, with the rafters my greatest concern.

We came to a stop inside the barn and exited our vehicle to approach the man. I don't know what the guy was thinking when he took a jab at my brother, coming inches from his nose. If he was testing to see if he would flinch, that wasn't Cordy. Within seconds the man was on his back, knocked out from a single punch. The distinct sound of guns cocking echoed throughout the garage.

"Whoa, whoa," Cordy said in Grandpa's angriest tone. I've been on the receiving end of that voice. Hearing it from Cordy scared the hell out of me. "That dude swung first. Lower your weapons."

"Put em away," a deep voice commanded. From a side room emerged a giant of a man with a scraggly beard.

"You are the spitting image of your grandfather," he said and picked Cordy up in a bear hug. The man never did introduce himself. I'll call him Sam.

"This is my sister," Cordy said.

"It's a pleasure," Sam said and offered a firm but reasonable handshake. He laughed loud and turbulently. "Man, you sure knocked Duke out. He won't be pulling that old made-you-flinch trick anytime soon."

"You should wake him up," I said. "It's not healthy being knocked out this long."

Sam snapped his fingers at two men. They headed toward Duke's lifeless body.

"Do you mind if I use my drone to scan your property for police," Cordy asked. "I have a second visor. You can watch."

"Hell, yes," Sam responded excitedly. "We'll see if you can find my lookout."

Cordy retrieved the drone from the Aztek, and they went outside. The creeps in the barn glaring at me were unnerving. I headed out shortly to join my brother.

I glanced up in time to see the drone bearing down on them. Sam hilariously ducked as Cordy swerved at the last second and landed in the driveway.

"That ruled," Sam said. "I can't believe how fast you found George. I have to get me one of those. Was that infrared?"

"Heat detection," Cordy corrected.

"That *would* work better in the day," Sam laughed. "Well, let's get to it."

We followed him back inside to a workbench where he cranked a heavy metal song, something about keeping your balls to the wall. Sam pointed to a photograph of a bug.

"That reminds me," I yelled. "I have a present from our father."

I retrieved the jamming device and plugged it in.

"This will disable any transmissions. Especially you know what," I said, nodding toward the poster. "Check your phone."

There were no bars.

"Shit, girl, this is the best," Sam said. "Tell your dad, thank you." He lowered the volume slightly. "Speaking of the old man, I know your dad prefers Glocks, but I could only lay my hands on two. He'll be equally pleased with this brand." He laid out three additional pistols. "These are Sig Sauers, the preferred firearm of the military. It's the same caliber as your trusty Glock."

"We'll take the batch," I said, "plus, all the magazines, barrels, and hollow point rounds you can muster."

"Would you happen to have an AR-15?" Cordy asked.

"Your daddy talked with me about those. It's too bad because I have the coolest." He handed Cordy a semi-automatic with a folding stock.

The visual of my brother with the rifle was disturbing. He had the ominous presence of a school shooter.

"I have something that will blow your mind," Sam said. He brought us to a room further in the back to a machine gun mounted on a sturdy A-frame.

"That is a sweet ass weapon," Cordy said.

"How did you get that," I said before I could catch myself.

"They're legal."

"That gun right there is legal?"

"It's semi-automatic. I hate to cut the fun short," Sam said, "but my next appointment is with a man you do not want to cross paths with."

"No problem. How much do I owe you?" I asked.

The cost was less than I was expecting. "Thank you," I said, shaking his hand.

Sam unplugged the jammer. "Say hi to your dad and Grandpa for me."

Two men opened the garage doors, and Cordy started the Aztek. Sam stepped into the sun to wave goodbye as if he were our uncle. I wondered if he was.

Cordy's Grandpa-scowl slipped away, and a warmth spread across his face. He'd dropped the façade like an actor. The whole thing was a game to him.

"That was fun," he said.

It was something. I don't know if I would call it fun.

Stefano and I had only been able to hook up twice that month. I was ecstatic to see the following message from him.

> My beautiful girl, can you
> meet me today at the
> Walrus and the Carpenter
> in Ballard? John was fired
> for giving away free rooms.
> Found a new place.

> > Hey, Lover. I can't make it
> > until 9 pm. Is that cool?

> Like a cucumber. See you
> then.

Ballard is a close-knit Scandinavian community built around fishing. I was such a nerd for looking that up, but a Huntress needs to prepare when venturing into a new town. I was driving along Market Street to the waterfront. There's no way I was visiting Ballard without seeing the home that was the inspiration for the movie Up. It was adorably tucked into the building built around it, just like the cartoon.

The restaurant that Stefano chose was too out in the open. I should have objected. Standing in front of the Walrus and the Carpenter, I felt Stefano seated inside. My hand was his as he downed a shot. His upper body shuddered from the strength of the liquor.

I sent Stefano a text to meet outside but received no response. He was the only Dread in the area I could sense, so I headed in. The clientele was not the weathered fisherman I was expecting—a trendy young crowd packed the restaurant. Stefano was on a stool at the bar. He wore a weathered black leather jacket and jeans with motorcycle boots. My vulva pulsed involuntarily at his sexy attire. I headed over and tapped him on the shoulder. He leaned back and smiled upon seeing me.

"Thanks, Lorene." He set a twenty-dollar bill on the counter. The look on her face told me their interaction wasn't as pleasant as he was pretending it to be.

Stefano took my hand. "Let's you and I get out of here."

I kept on his tail as he raced between buildings. He ducked behind a truck, and we hid in the shadows.

"I want to make sure no one follows," he whispered. "This new place is perfect."

"Can't wait to see it," I said and pecked him on the cheek. The connection sent our hearts racing.

We pressed along the brick wall and down a narrow alley. I was careful not to brush into anything and ruin my favorite white sweater.

Stefano crossed Shilshole Ave and headed for the protection of a grove of trees.

"Ours is the middle boathouse," he said, pointing to the massive structures across from us. "Don't get your hopes up. We're not going on the yacht. My friend from

169

college is letting me use the loft. His family doesn't use it. We can have the place whenever we want."

The door to the boathouse had a touch entry in the layout of a phone's keypad. I turned my head to give Stefano a sense of privacy.

"What's the combo?" he said as he held the door for me.

"I don't know." I hated lying to him and came clean. "5372."

"Damn, you're good."

"You should see me in bed," I said, flirting as if we weren't lovers.

Stefano flipped on the lights in the boathouse, and I understood why he said not to get my hopes up. Moored inside was an immaculate hundred-foot yacht.

"Pretty sweet, huh."

"It's magnificent," I said in awe.

Stefano punched the same number into the alarm, then cut the house lights, leaving only the staircase lit. I wasn't sure what to expect of the loft due to the unassuming rustic exterior, but it was warm and inviting. The shiplap boards on the walls and ceiling were a nautical grey. Large metal beams added an industrial feel to the room. The space was modest, with room for a queen-size bed, a sitting area with two chairs and a coffee table. Off in the corner was a dorm-sized kitchen.

"This place is perfect, I said and jumped into Stefano's arms. I loved that he was strong enough for me to do that.

"Make yourself at home while I use the restroom."

"It has a bathroom," I said in appreciation.

As much as I tried not to, I felt Stefano urinating. I couldn't figure out why he was pushing his butt out so far, and then I noticed his erection. I wondered how you peed with one.

I was relaxing on the bed when he returned. "What did you do there at the end? When you finished, you slid your finger up your taint and along your shaft."

"Can you feel me using the bathroom? That's so wrong."

"I can't turn it off," I said unapologetically. "So, what were you doing?"

"Running a finger up my urethra to get all the pee out. That way I don't dribble in my jeans."

"Genius. I used to think boys dabbed themselves with toilet paper after they pee like girls."

"That's funny. I had a babysitter who did that for me. I wasn't about to correct her."

"Come and join me," I said, patting the bed. "Not in that order."

Stefano searched his pockets. "I forgot condoms."

He checked the drawers and stopped in his tracks. Along with condoms was a wand-like massager. I snatched it from him and plugged in the power cord.

Stefano tried to take it from me, but I pushed him back onto the bed and aggressively worked my way into his pants. The device was too powerful for his balls, but when I placed it on his shaft, a tingling rose in force to his frenulum. I concentrated the vibrations there, and his cockhead pulsed so vigorously he almost came. I shut the massager off.

"I still don't think it's fair that you can feel what I'm feeling."

"It isn't," I agreed. I had an idea that I wasn't sure would work but decided to give it a go. "How about we try something to bring you in the mix. Can I drive you?

"Drive me? Like in the ass? If that's what you want, but I didn't see a strap-on in the drawer."

His adventuresome attitude stunned me. "You'd let me do that?"

"I'm comfortable with my sexuality. Plus, sex is the one place I can really connect emotionally. Nothing makes me happier than fulfilling your needs."

"You're a national treasure. But, no, I want to direct *you*. Kind of show you what I feel with The Mirror's Touch." I took Stefano's hand and intertwined our fingers, palms together. "If I want you to lighten up, I will push away. If I need more pressure, I can pull you toward me. I'll also be able to steer you around."

I moved to the edge of the bed so he could kneel on the floor. We locked fingers and I brought him in. Stefano began licking me, and I circled his palm with my middle finger. He did the same with his tongue. I played with different directions but relented.

"You're better than I ever could be at creativity. I'll stick with location and pressure."

"I'm good because you make me want to please you."

I reigned him in too enthusiastically and backed his tongue off. My mind was going blank.

"Stay with me," Stefano said.

I directed his tongue closer and raised him to the hood of my clit. "Right there. Holy fuck!"

He repeated the move he was performing religiously. My burgeoning orgasm advanced gradually like an inner tide, each time growing closer, with the final wave cresting in a tsunami.

I opened my eyes and saw that Stefano's face was soaked.

"Did I pee on you?"

"A little," he said.

"Sorry."

"Don't be. I liked it."

"Gross."

He smirked mischievously. "Thanks for giving me the Touch. That was fun."

172

I think he was humoring me. I would have had the same results just directing him verbally, but I liked the game. "Let's go for another drive," I said.

Stefano dove between my legs, and I soon gave up control. He's a master of cunnilingus. I was kidding myself, pretending I could steer him better.

We made love that evening—hot, sexy, aggressive love. By the end, we were a sweaty mess. Stefano lit the pellet stove and we snuggled under the covers.

"I'm curious about the curse," I said. "How it affects you?"

"That's still not the question I thought you'd ask. What do you want to know?"

"How long can you go before the change?"

He rolled onto his back and stared at the ceiling. "It varies with the Cursed," he said. "For me, the change is right around hour seventy-six. I've tested myself twice. Had a dominatrix tie me up near the end of the three-day mark. The first time, I was restrained for a few hours until I felt it come on."

"What is it like?"

"I've never fully changed. Both times, I backed out. The allure was so strong it scared me. I don't want to be evil."

"You're not," I assured him, "but how did you stop it?"

"By having sex?" he said like I was slow.

"Wasn't that risky? Putting yourself out there with a stranger."

"The dominatrix came highly recommended. She was all business."

"So, you'll change seventy-six hours after sex unless you do it again?"

"Yep, welcome to my world. Kind of takes the fun out of it all."

"I think it adds intrigue, like a race against the clock."

173

"It literally is." He showed me the timer counting down on his phone.

I opened the calculator on mine and was embarrassed by the easy equation. "That's ten times a month. We can do that."

"If we miss one time, I don't know what I would do. We have to keep some of my tricks around. They mean nothing to me. You're my girl."

The callousness towards the women he sleeps with was atrocious. I forced a smile and kissed him. "I want you all to myself."

"Me too, but won't it be suspicious if you're in the habit of disappearing every three days?"

"Yeah," I said, defeated.

He pulled me on top of him. "I would sleep with only you if I could. There is no one I love more. You're the top of my love. Understand *that*. Please don't make me risk changing. I went too long between sex once, and I... I almost raped someone. Thank God she was into me." He had a pained look on his face. "To not be a monster, I nearly became one. I haven't put myself in that position again."

The thought of Stefano contemplating rape was horrifying. I pushed the notion away. "What made you wait so long? That sounds risky."

He shied his eyes from mine. "I was trying to turn gay to break the curse."

"You can't *turn* gay."

"I realize that now, but that first time I tried, I thought it worked. Then I felt the change coming on. The sex with that woman was nothing to write home about, but it was miles above what I received from a man. You need emotion for sex to work right. Didn't stop me from trying, though." He looked me in the eyes. "I'm not proud of what I did. I tried everything to be normal."

"Everything?"

He smirked. "I'm embarrassed by how good getting fucked feels. You felt the prostate's allure out on the balcony."

"That thing is like an enormous clit," I said. "So I'm curious if you can't turn gay, why would you ask me to send the worst of the Cursed to jail? Won't they turn homicidal after a few days?"

"The worst of the Cursed. I like that," Stefano said. "Jail is better because it isn't long until we're hauled off to the nuthouse or placed in isolation. From there, we sit back and wait for the Age of Reckoning. The change is so dramatic the doctors are compelled to push for an early release."

I had one final question. "Have you killed anyone?"

"*That* is the question I thought you'd ask. You'll be happy to know I have not."

"Me neither."

Stefano and I stood on the porch of a married couple he often used to control the curse. Even though it was me who insisted on being there, I was nervous. At least my body confidence was in the positive. I was at the tail end of a month with no drinking and was feeling fit. Alcohol, I concluded, was the reason for most of my recent issues with bloating.

"You sure you're up for this?" he asked, noticing my discomfort.

"It's imperative." I had to see that it was just sex.

"All right," he said, smirking at my unnecessarily large word.

Stefano knocked, and a handsome gentleman with a close-cropped military haircut answered the door. He hobbled out of the way to let us in.

175

"I'm Torrance. You must be Janis. It's an honor to meet you, ma'am."

I'm not a fan of the term ma'am, but he said it with enough respect to win me over.

"Leo." He nodded to Stefano. There was a tone in his voice, agitation or anger.

I bit my lip to avoid smirking at Stefano's pseudonym. Why hadn't he given me one? Or was Leo his new name? I wasn't opposed to fucking a Leo.

"It means the world that you're fine with this," Torrance said to me.

"And what is *this*?" I said. "If you don't mind me asking."

"Well, to put it bluntly, a roadside bomb took out my junk. My wife needs sex, and I can only do so much with a strap-on. I usually watch, but tonight, I'll leave you to it." He grabbed his coat from the hall closet and headed out the door.

"Thank you," I said, "for your service."

"You too," he said.

The door shut and in walked a petite brunette with long straight hair. I wasn't expecting her to be so small. She saw me and jumped up and down, screaming, then rushed over.

"Hi, I'm Joy. You must be Janis."

"Well, aren't you a bundle of fun," I said. "It's nice to meet you, Joy."

"The pleasure is all mine. Well, not tonight." She said. "Would you like a beer? We have Rainier in the fridge.

"Do you have anything stronger?"

"Like cocaine?"

I laughed. "No, liquor."

"Let me see." She bounced off to the kitchen.

"What do you think?" Stefano said.

"She seems fun."

"We have clear rum," Joy yelled, "but the only mixer I can find is pineapple juice."

"Sounds delicious," I said. So much for the bloat.

"Speaking of delicious," Joy said, "if it's OK with you, I want to take Leo's first load. I've been jonesin' for it all week." Stefano smirked.

"That's fine with me," I said, indifferent. "I don't believe I'd enjoy that anyway."

Joy returned from the kitchen and handed over my drink. "You've never had Leo come in your mouth?"

"No. Why would I?"

"Because it tastes like candy. Better than candy. Leo's cum is the greatest in the world," Joy said, taking both our hands. She led us to a den in the back of the house where a murphy bed was prepped and ready.

She brought out her phone and selected the stopwatch. "We're going to play cock roulette. It's like Russian roulette, but the bullet is…"

"Yeah, I get it," I said, cutting her off.

"Every minute we switch. No holding back." She handed the phone to Stefano.

I didn't want to play. Joy must have noticed my discomfort.

"Come on, your boyfriend's cum is scrumptious. I can't get enough of it."

She won me over, calling Stefano my boyfriend. I unbuckled his belt and shimmied his pants low. Stefano was rock hard. He'd been erect since we arrived at the house.

"OK." I dropped to my knees. If I wanted, I could have made him cum in the first sixty seconds, but I wasn't about to do that.

"My turn," Joy shouted. She pulled Stefano's cock from my mouth and began sucking on it. He was doing everything to ignore the pleasure.

"No cheating," I told Stefano and gave his balls a comforting squeeze.

177

He let himself relax. Joy was good, but I was better. She wasn't familiar with the subtle nuances of his cock. How could she?

The alarm chimed. I ripped that big unit away and sucked and stroked in sync with my mouth.

"Time," Joy yelled. I passed Stefano's cock over, and she took it hungrily.

Our turns went back and forth a few more times. The ball was in Joy's court when I felt him getting close. Stefano flipped the phone over.

"Time," he said and coyly smiled at me.

"Fine," I said. Four strokes in, Stefano's orgasm was brimming. There was no going back. His balls shifted, and a flood of cum shot across my tongue. It wasn't as bad as I feared, but it still freaked me out as I wasn't just connected to him; I was one with the semen shooting from his cock. That is the odd sensation I feel when Stefano comes. Three more waves splashed over my tongue. I rose to find a bathroom.

"Swallow it," Joy said.

I shook my head.

"Please," Stefano said.

Christ, the peer pressure. I looked him in the eye and swallowed. It was a relief to have his cum out of my mouth, but it sat heavy.

"How was it?" Joy asked.

"It was nice," I lied.

Without any internal notice, I threw up in my hands. Not a lot, just the cum, as if my stomach rejected it specifically. I stared in horror at the load in my palms. How insulting that must have been to Stefano.

Joy thought it was hilarious. "It's all right. You won't get sick a second time."

There wasn't going to be a second time. I liked Stefano coming inside me. The curse is reset from sex. It's a fucking curse. My inside joke made me giggle, which I'm sure had me looking like a lunatic.

"You're sure quiet tonight," I said to Stefano.

"It's better if he doesn't speak, especially around Torrance. What he said last week." She smacked him on the shoulder.

"I told him I was sorry."

"Not very well. You must have the patience of steel," she said to me.

"He's actually been making a real effort around me."

"Let's hope it lasts. Leo's lucky he's good in bed. Speaking of that, do you mind if your boyfriend fucks me for a while?"

"Go ahead," I said. My stomach was rolling. I headed to the bathroom to wash up.

When I returned to the den, joy was naked and on her back, propped up on her elbows, her inviting legs akimbo. She was doing missionary, probably to appease me, but it was still sexy. I motioned for Stefano to do his stuff, to stick it to her. He put on a condom and worked his way onto the bed. I relaxed in a side chair and prepared for the jealousy that was sure to come.

Entering Joy was a wet, warm grip of sensuality. The experience of fucking a woman was mind-blowing. Something inside felt so right, like a key in a lock. The dual pleasure I experience when he fucks me obscures the true sense of what he feels. Here on the sidelines, I was getting everything.

Joy tossed her head back, eyes closed. "You're so good, Torrance. God damn it, fuck me harder."

Stefano glanced at me, and I nodded. What Stefano was doing for this couple was invaluable. In her mind, she was fucking her husband. Torrance probably leans close and answers back as if it was him inside. Stefano was a saint. He increased the pace, ramming his cock home, and I melted into my seat.

"Kiss her," I said.

"No kissing," they both responded.

179

I was jealous of their synchronicity, but the no kissing rule helped.

I sidled up behind Stefano and mirrored his thrusts. Fucking is a powerful force, the ultimate in masculinity. His cock became mine as we ravaged her pussy.

Because he already came, Stefano held out well past Joy achieving orgasm. He straightened his legs out stiff, which concentrated the pleasure to his cock. Unlike a woman, Stefano's second orgasm was identical to his first. Men are robbed in this department. Still, it felt terrific coming inside of her. He thrust slowly, easing Joy down. I rolled onto the bed, exhausted.

I wanted to cuddle but wasn't sure if that was another rule and couldn't have Joy feeling left out.

"Would it be OK if I go down on your girlfriend?" Joy said. "To thank her."

"You'd have to ask Janis."

I had never gone there but was happy that he was asking my permission. Was it gay if someone did it to you?

"Well?" she said.

"What the hell."

Joy jumped off the bed and I scooched forward. Her approach was so feminine. She kissed and caressed my thighs, drawing closer until she was circling my vulva, the light touch and heat of her breath sparking my nerve endings to life.

"Look at me," Joy exclaimed, "I'm right back at Berkley."

She concentrated on the outer edge of my lips, rubbing with almost a pulse in her fingertips. I was begging for her tongue by the time it landed. She began slowly and softly, testing my sensitivity. I leaned into her, and she delved further. It was a dance between her actions and my reaction until a seamless rhythm was established.

Joy must have had fun in college. She lived up to her name in enthusiasm, interchanging the perfect amount of pressure and gentle probing of my clit, as well as licking my labia in long, delicate strokes. She used her fingers to rub playfully. The added touch heightened my arousal tenfold.

"Your pussy is so hot," she said, glancing up at me.

Her unabashed appreciation reset years of doubt about my genitalia. I lifted Joy to kiss her love-drenched mouth. As enticing as the kiss became, there was something better to kiss below. I grabbed her head and thrust it back between my legs.

Joy was determined to make me come but was holding the release back as long as possible. She would edge me to the brink and back off, leaving me breathless and wanting. When she finally allowed the release, my orgasm was overwhelming, like a bathtub tipping over, sending the water flooding out, washing every ounce of stress from my body. My muscles quit functioning, and I lay back, unable to move or speak. My vagina was left pulsing in the afterglow.

I ordered a strap-on after our time in the boathouse. Stefano's comment about me fucking him was too enticing. An email showed up letting me know my order arrived. I deleted all traces of the note and headed to the Amazon locker.

Cordy was in the front room watching TV when I returned. I hid the box in my room and joined him for reruns of Law and Order.

The Detective, Lenny, made an inappropriate quip about the crime scene.

"Lenny's the best," I said.

A prescription commercial came on, and Cordy locked in on one of the side effects.

"Difficulty swallowing. We know who's taking that drug."

"What the shit!" I said, accidentally knocking my water over. "Do you have me bugged?"

"Huh?" He looked at me, confused, and then it hit him. "Gross. No. Are you getting laid?"

I grinned sheepishly.

"This is epic," Cordy said. "Who's the lucky fella?"

"A boy from my senior year," I managed to say.

"From your class? Who?"

"Chase Matthews."

"Shut up. Chase is as gay as they come."

"I'll have you know he's quite bi-sexual."

"Even so, you should be safer."

"I'm not listening to health tips from an orgy guy. You're the one who needs to be safer."

"Maybe," Cordy smirked. "This calls for a celebration." He headed downstairs to make cocktails. Lately, he didn't need much of an excuse to drink.

I was in my bathroom the following morning trying on the strap-on. Within seconds I was doing the dick windmill. That made me giggle. I laughed harder when I spun it in front of the mirror. A silly lyric popped into my head:

My banana is a force of power.
It's a penis head inside a flower.

I sang it repeatedly, whipping the dildo around faster and faster. Watching the spinning phallus decelerate piqued my interest, but the slight girth of the strap-on wouldn't do. I panicked at the thought of going to a sex shop. There was only one person who could help me. Was asking him worse? I hoped not.

"You decent?" I said, knocking on Cordy's door.

"Yeah," he responded groggily.

I poked my head inside. "Get up."

182

"What? Are we going for a run?"

"No, I need a sex toy," I said, embarrassed. "I can't get the nerve up to go in one of those stores."

Thankfully Cordy pulled his sarcasm back. "Sure thing, Sis."

I lost my confidence in the parking lot of the Love Pantry. Why are those places so out in the open? I started the car, but Cordy reached over and turned the ignition off. He snagged the keys and headed for the entrance.

"Come here," he said, offering his arm. I slid mine into the comforting nook and walked a little taller.

The floor to ceiling wall of dildos at the back of the shop was intimidating. There were so many phalluses, from small ass starters to comically large. I was drawn to the realistic dildos but couldn't find one with Stefano's size and skin tone. All I knew is I wanted something quiet since Cordy's room butted up against mine. I narrowed my decision to a translucent silicone model that matched Stefano's length and girth. Now I just had to pay for it.

"Give me the money." Cordy took the box from my hand.

"Thank you. I'll buy us breakfast," I said as he headed to the counter.

When we pulled into our driveway, Dad was in the backyard, working on his latest muscle car. He waved, and I smiled guiltily, hoping the black bag wasn't obvious.

My brother and I headed straight to our rooms. Cordy would be asleep in minutes. I don't understand how he can fall asleep so quickly.

The plastic packaging made a terrible racket as I worked to free the dildo. I was horrified and remained still. Dad chose the worst time to repeatedly rev his engine, making it sound like I was using a gas-powered dildo. Cordy broke out in a loud painful laugh and shouted, "Vroom, vroom, vroom." I joined in the laughter, mortified.

183

Cordy was snoring before too long. I moved to the bathroom and cut through the packaging with a pair of scissors. My new toy looked silly as I flopped it around, but it was also intimidating. I gathered the plastic to dispose of later and retreated to my bed for me time.

I sent Stefano a text with a picture of the dildo fully inserted.

> I have a new friend to
> remind me of you.

Give me five minutes to get
home.

He sent a towering picture of his hard cock. I returned the favor with a pic of me with two fingers deep.

We traded pictures back and forth masturbating the whole time. After I came, I had an idea that gave me uncontrollable giggles. The picture turned out funnier than I imagined. It was of a large salad fork with the handle sticking inside me. I sent the photo to Stefano and wrote:

> Stick a fork in it. I'm done.

It took a long time for him to respond. I was worried.

That was by far the funniest
thing I've ever seen in my
life. I wish that picture
hadn't disappeared.

> Sending again. Love you.

I woke from a post-orgasm slumber and stumbled to the front room. I saw a flash of Cordy's shirt as he raced downstairs. The hunt was on. I checked his usual hiding spots, but he wasn't in them. I flung the backdoor open. My brother was standing just outside, which made me jump.

"There you are. I thought you were playing hide-and-seek."

Cordy had a rare moment of embarrassment. I followed his eyes to Dad, who was staring down at us from his deck. He shook his head and walked away.

"What's his problem?" I said.

"Besides the fact that his son is a child?" Cordy said.

"Well, yeah."

"This is the day Mom died."

How did I forget? "Dad," I yelled, "start a pot of coffee. I'll be right over."

A week later and Stefano was still open to me fucking him. I wasn't about to let a crazy opportunity like that slip.

The boathouse exterior is metal, which blocked the Touch until I reached the door. Stefano was on all fours, his head low as a strange sensation ran through his backside. He was cleansing himself. I went on a short walk to give him privacy and to contemplate the situation. I would need a magnitude of confidence to pull this off.

Stefano didn't object when I let myself into the boathouse. The only light in the loft was the flickering glow of the fireplace. He was half-dressed in a wife-beater and boxer briefs. Visually, he was a god in his beauty, but physically his lower back muscles were taut with anxiety.

"You don't have to do this if you don't want to," I said.

"Don't put this on me. If this is what you want, I'm cool. If not, that's also fine."

"I am curious what it feels like," I admitted.

185

"I could fuck you in the ass," he said, reaching around and grabbing a cheek.

"I don't have a prostate."

"No. No, you don't," he said, almost tauntingly.

That did it. Stefano was getting fucked. I pulled the strap-on from my gym bag, and he looked relieved.

"I appreciate you not going overboard," he said, handing me a bottle of lube.

I stripped naked and secured the device in place. Stefano crawled onto the bed, defeated.

"I can't believe I'm doing this," he said.

"No talking," I commanded and bent him over.

Stefano lowered his head with a concerned groan. I doused my finger in lube and slipped it in his ass. The discomfort was so clear it felt as if I was doing it to myself. I soon worked a second digit inside.

I covered the dildo in a generous amount of lube and taunted his hole with the tip as he does to me.

"Oh, Jesus," he said.

"I'm your Jesus now."

Stefano's laugh stifled when I worked the dildo inside. I held still. There were so many signals going off, none of them good. After a rest, I felt my opportunity and pushed in further and sat motionlessly.

"Thank you for taking it easy," he said.

Stefano sunk the dildo to the base, then paused. Inserting it deeply was bizarre. It felt awesome and horrible at the same time. I held back and let him ride.

"It's getting better," he said.

I thrust slowly at first. Within a few minutes, there was no more pain—only pleasure. Off-the-charts, out-of-this world pleasure. I began pumping harder. I was a man, and man was it incredible. People talk about role-playing, but this was the ultimate. I shifted my hips, so I hit his prostate. The nerve endings sparked to life. Stefano moaned with me as the act consumed us. I fell into a rhythm, trying to emulate the sexy way Stefano fucks with his whole body.

After an incredible ten minutes, he gestured the 'time' symbol. "I need to come in you. I'm on my seventy-fifth hour."

"It feels so good. You can't hold out, baby?"

"No, I have to come inside you, and I mean inside you." Stefano handed me a sheet of paper. It was his STD results. He didn't have anything major. That was a relief as he is way more sexually active than me.

"Fine," I said and allowed him to enter me bare for the first time. The difference for him was night and day; my slickness was a vessel of ultimate pleasure as he passed my threshold, stretching my tightness blissfully around him.

He repositioned us with me bent over the bed, then removed the dildo from the strap-on and slid it into his ass. Stefano was fucking me, which I felt from both his and my perspective, and he was fucking himself, flinging me in a wild triangle like riding the Scrambler at the State Fair. It was the greatest thrill I'd ever felt in my life.

"I'm drifting," I said, my eyes glossing over. My pussy, his ass, his cock, holy fuck.

"Don't pass out," Stefano said.

"Slap me," I said.

He smacked me on the ass.

I meant on the face, but he struck me with enough force to bring me back.

Stefano adjusted the dildo. The combination of clit and prostate stimulation was a symphony of sexual arousal, and he was the maestro.

I'd never had an orgasm come on so fast and so powerful. We were in sync; the middle of mine meshed with his, weaving and melding, throbbing and pulsing. I floated up and away. The dueling release was a golden ticket to heaven.

I crumpled over, spent; my body was reduced to pulp. Stefano moved his face to mine to see if I was OK. He knew me, but this time, coming together, there was no fainting, there wasn't even a headache. What I ended up with was a weird tingling in my skin and a lightness in my head like I had been awake for days. The pleasant feeling sent me drifting to sleep in my boyfriend's arms.

Chapter 10

Grandpa's knife wound was bleeding at an alarming rate. Pressing it closed wasn't helping.

"We need to get him to a hospital," I said forcefully. Why we let Grandpa talk us into coming home instead of going straight there, I'll never know.

"I'm fine," Bepa grunted.

"You don't look fine," Dad said. "Bailey's right."

"Just leave me to die."

"No one is dying," I shouted. "You're going to the hospital."

Grandpa protested, but I held firm.

I drove, with Dad in the back, working to seal off Grandpa's wound. Cordy was uncharacteristically silent in the passenger seat.

"Stay awake," Dad pleaded.

"I'm not gonna make it. I love you."

Grandpa is not generous with his I love yous. Hearing him say it scared the hell out of Cordy and me. I sped toward Harborview.

Grandpa was unconscious by the time we arrived. The emergency crew was waiting out front with a gurney.

"What are we looking at here," a nurse with a cute bob said.

"Stab wound," I said. "Self-inflicted. Grandpa slipped in the kitchen." There was enough blood on the floor for the scenario to hold up under scrutiny.

"I don't have a pulse," a male nurse said. The team wheeled Grandpa swiftly from us.

"I have the same blood type if he needs a transfusion," Dad said as the doors were closing.

Harborview is the state's main trauma center. I learned that from Mary's stay. At least Grandpa was in good hands. Dad looked over at me, concerned, admission papers in hand.

"They won't operate without that completed," I whispered. "Fucking sign it!"

Bepa lost so much blood. Plus, the wound was in his stomach. That's a dangerous location to be stabbed. I started crying.

A couple of hours later, a doctor emerged exhausted from the double doors. The nurse at the front desk directed him to where we were now standing.

"Thomas is in stable but critical condition."

We all sighed in relief. Cordy ducked behind Dad and cried.

"He's not out of the woods. Tom has a nicked spleen and a laceration in his stomach. We've stopped the internal bleeding, so he is stable. Now the rest is in his hands."

"Thank you, Doctor," my father said. "Pop is a fighter. He'll pull through. Would it be all right if we went in and saw him?"

"You have ten minutes," the doctor said. He handed us off to the nurse, who brought us to a shared room in the emergency ward. Grandpa was asleep, looking fragile and pale. I hated seeing Bepa in this vulnerable state.

"Hi, Pop," Dad said, touching his arm. Grandpa didn't stir. "We're all here. Don't get up."

I shouldn't have looked at my brother. Dad's unintentional humor was hilariously inappropriate. Cordy pulled it off as crying, leaving me snorting like an idiot.

Back in the waiting room, I whispered in Dad's ear.

"I'm heading back to the house to set up the scene of the accident in case the police need to investigate."

"Just clean it up."

"There's too much blood on the carpet.

"All right, but take your brother. I don't want you going alone."

190

"Come on," I told Cordy.

"I'm not leaving."

Dad gave him a stern look, and Cordy followed me out.

"What are we doing?" Cordy said when we were in the car.

We have to make it appear as if Grandpa fell on a kitchen knife. Hopefully, we can get back to the hospital before the cops arrive."

"How did this happen? Couldn't you feel the second Dread?"

"I didn't. They must have help." I couldn't explain why some weren't cursed. It would give Stefano's uncle Tony away.

"What are we going to do? They saw us."

"We had ski masks on."

"That didn't sound reassuring."

"What we are going to do is keep the family safe," I said. "That begins with making sure the cops aren't suspicious."

The amount of blood on the kitchen floor was overwhelming. Using a paper towel to hide my fingerprints, I selected a carving knife. I had Cordy coat the blade with Grandpa's blood, then streaked it outward using a dishrag. With the knife dropped onto the floor, the scene was believable.

Cordy did a sweep of both halves of the duplex, bringing anything incriminating to the Lair. I rinsed out the dishrag, then texted Support to explain what happened.

We'll take care of this. Can you describe the targets?

I have pictures of one from earlier surveillance, but I didn't see the man who

191

                                    stabbed Grandpa. I couldn't
                                    feel him.

            That's all right. Once we
            find the Dread, the other
            man won't be far behind.
            Return to your grandfather.
            We'll have another family
            deal with this.

A young officer was talking to Dad when we arrived back at the hospital. He had closely cropped spiky auburn hair and the most adorably animated face. If this were a movie, the man's role would be listed as Hot Cop.

"There are my kids, back from the cafeteria," Dad said. "You can follow them to the house."

"I'm John," the officer said to Cordy. "This will just be a formality."

I walked with them at Cordy's side.

"Just us," the cop said, dismissing me.

Cordy gave me a worried glance, like he may have to take one for the team.

"You sure saved our ass," Dad whispered to me.

"Any changes with Bepa?" I asked.

"Nope," he said.

It was eight long hours before Grandpa regained consciousness. He was livid that we brought him to the emergency room.

"It's good to see you, too," Dad said.

"The risk was greater than my life," Grandpa said.

"The drama with this one," I said.

"The cops could go to the house."

"We took care of it," I said. "They've already been there. You were in the kitchen and fell on your carving knife. All you have to worry about is getting better."

"Do you remember what the guy looked like who stabbed you?" I asked. "Support is looking for them."

"Yeah, he was the 'victim.' He got me when I leaned over to check his pulse."

"Well, fuck," Dad said.

Grandpa wasn't able to come home for a week. The doctors saved his spleen, but he would be out of commission for the foreseeable future.

We were all in Dad's living room watching TV. Any normal person would have been bedridden, but not Grandpa. He was off the Percocet and walking around, showing no signs of discomfort. As high a threshold as he has for pain, it wouldn't get him back in the game.

"Don't baby me. Christ!"

"I'm not babying you, Pop. You almost died."

"I did die, but that's not going to hold me back."

"You are not fighting this soon. It would rip your internal stitches out."

Grandpa crossed his arms. "Your wife said hello."

That stopped my father cold. "What did you just say?"

"She wanted me to tell you that she loves you."

Dad got up and walked to his room.

"I don't like you lying," I whispered to Grandpa.

"I don't like lying either. It would have been nice to see Caroline. I miss the bird. She would be so proud of you."

Dad had us meet in the garage to step up Cordy's training. His filling in for Grandpa worried us. None of us knew how he would behave in a real-world fight. Dad had kept

193

him from it, hoping he would mature, but there were no more excuses.

Grandpa sauntered in as if nothing happened. You couldn't tell that he died on the operating table three weeks earlier.

"The boy's not ready," Bepa said. "Let me back in."

"What the shit?" Cordy said. "I'm ready. You've trained me since I was fourteen."

"Well, what am I supposed to do? I ain't no crippy cripple."

"Hey, come on, no bigotry around the kids," Dad said.

"You do know I'm twenty-two, don't you?" I said.

"Sorry."

"Maybe I could fly that contraption you have," Grandpa said.

We all laughed. Bepa can barely work the TV remote.

"You don't even know what it's called," I said.

He thought about it but came up blank.

"It's a drone," Cordy said.

"I know what it is," Grandpa said and stormed off to the house.

"The drone is pretty stable," Cordy said. "I could teach him."

"Can we afford a replacement?" Dad said.

"What are you talking about," Cordy said. "Grandparents are cheap. It's the babies that'll cost ya."

Cordy and I cracked up while our father remained stone-faced.

"Seriously, Dad," I said. "That was funny. You need to lighten up."

"I wish I had that luxury."

His response made me roll my eyes.

"The drone came with a flight simulator," Cordy said. "He can practice on that."

Dad looked at me for approval.

"It's nice having an eye in the sky. The drone saved us from the first night out."

"I saved you," Cordy corrected.

"Of course you did," I said. "Are we done here?" I asked Dad.

I could tell he was about to say, "We're done when I say we're done," but refrained.

"Sure, you trained hard today. I want you to know I'm proud of both of you."

"Thanks, Dad," Cordy said.

I checked my phone. There was a message from Stefano. He wanted to meet near the UW Stadium. I let him know I could be there in an hour.

Stefano had me call when I was on the footbridge crossing over to Foster Island. I didn't feel comfortable calling, but he let me know that our IM app had a new phone feature.

"Hi, Lover," he answered. "Are you here?"

"I am."

"Keep heading down the path and take the first trail on the right."

Stepping into the shade past the bridge was unsettling. "Do we need to talk?" I said.

"What? No. I couldn't be more alone. If there were trouble, I would have told you back at your house."

"Sorry. These bushes are spooky. It's nothing personal."

"I know," he said.

I turned down the side trail and stepped up my pace after sensing Stefano. He was in a seated position with his body unstable as if he were floating in the air.

At the end of the path was my boyfriend, sitting shirtless in a rented canoe. I ran onto the small dock and gave him a quick kiss.

"I missed you," he said, staring at me with a relaxed gaze.

"I missed you too. It's painful being apart."

He dug in his pocket and pulled out a ziplock bag. "For your phone."

"Look at you being thoughtful," I said and placed my cell inside, making sure the seal was tight.

"I don't want to lose the only way to get a hold of you."

Stefano steadied the boat to the dock while I stepped aboard as gracefully as I could. I misjudged the drop and fell inside with a thud. The impact made me laugh loudly. At least I didn't tip the canoe.

"You all right?" he asked.

"Are you?" I said, massaging Stefano's temples to get rid of his headache. I searched my backpack for an aspirin. One of Grandpa's Percocets was in the side pocket, but that would mess with his sex drive.

"Here, I said, handing him an Advil.

"My headache's not that bad," he said.

"It's killing me to feel you in pain."

Stefano swallowed the pill to shut me up.

"Have you been out here before?" he asked.

"I didn't even know there was a here."

"You're going to love this."

Across the inlet was the Evergreen Floating Bridge. We paddled along one of the freeway's cement support structures until there was a break we could pass through. The channel split, leading us to the right. Bare ground and sparse shrubbery lined both sides of the lane. The scenery was clean and pristine like we were inside a train set. As we rounded a corner, the noise of the traffic drifted into silence.

A lily pad spun past our boat, knocked loose by the canoe ahead of us. We let the couple pull away and paddled down a side canal surrounded by tall grass and cattails. The channel narrowed to an abrupt end. Stefano stood up to check our surroundings.

"It keeps going," he said with childlike enthusiasm.

We passed through the brush into a small lagoon — the weeds behind closed in, concealing our whereabouts. Stefano carefully spun himself around and rooted through the cooler. He assembled a plate of cheese and crackers then opened a bottle of pinot grigio.

"Well, aren't you full of surprises," I said.

"We don't get to go on many dates. I wanted to do something special," he said, smiling. "I hate that everything we do is based around stopping the change. Wouldn't it be nice just to go for a walk or to dinner?"

I've had the same thoughts, but every time I'm not helping, someone else is. The visual sickens me. "If things were only different."

"I love you."

"I love you too."

After taking a large drink, he leaned over and kissed me. The wine cascaded from his mouth into mine. It's funny how the little things can turn you on, but I wasn't about to rush into sex. The picnic we were enjoying was so romantic.

Stefano shuffled the cooler behind him, then set his plate of food on top. I handed my glass over and carefully turned around into his lap. It felt safe resting upon him. His cock grew erect and pressed against my backside. I could feel the throb of it, and in it. Stefano reached around my leg and rubbed me through my shorts. I distracted him with a bite of food.

By our second glass of wine, I couldn't hold off any longer. I set the food down in the front of the boat and unbuttoned my fly for Stefano. He slid a finger inside me and used another to tease my clitoris skillfully. I shimmied my shorts past my knees and kicked them off. I needed his mouth on me.

The canoe wobbled as I attempted to spin around. Stefano eased me back, lowering himself between my legs. I rested my thighs on the metal support strut hitting his chest. He leaned forward, dipping his tongue into me with frenzy. Sparks flew as soon as he landed. There was greediness in his advances.

The boat creaked like an old roller coaster every time my body quivered or my hips thrust in reaction to his moves. I moaned, and the boat groaned as he skillfully lapped, eager to make me come.

The sun beating upon my naked torso urged my release along. Heated pulses raced from my spine to my feet, looped in a growing array of desire. I leaned back, raising my toes skyward. The boat creaked like a roller coaster rising steadily. I imagined I was on one. My breathing grew faster and more difficult as if I was climbing too high to get oxygen. It took forever to reach the top, but the drop was smooth once I did, sending me floating upside down, a thousand feet into the calm darkness. My contractions sent a reverb rattling through my clitoris like the track was shaking my seat. The car passed over a few slow hills and jerked slowly to a stop. When I opened my eyes, Stefano was at the controls asking if I wanted to go again. As much as I appreciated the dedication, I needed him inside me.

"Fucking take me."

"Oh God, yes."

The metal supports limited our choice of positions. He bent me over the front bench and pulled my hips toward him. The vigorous thrusting moved us inch by inch to the shore, where the canoe stuck firmly in the mud. With the boat locked in place, Stefano found a steady rhythm. I closed my eyes, trying to isolate what was him or me. The Mirror's Touch meshed our sensations together like a knotted bundle of flashing Christmas lights.

He hung onto me with one hand on my thigh and his other lovingly around my back, his head pressing against my shoulder. The familiar tightening in my stomach slowly gave way to a ball of energy growing inside. I felt his release approaching and rubbed my clit to catch up.

198

"I'm almost there," he said.

"Hold on." I breathed heavily. "Hold on."

He started to come before me as his orgasm flowed into mine, bursting into infinity. His moans slowed with mine as I nuzzled my face into his neck.

"I've never connected so well with someone that we came together," Stefano said.

"That's all you," I responded.

"No. No, it's not. I know what you're doing, and it's incredible. There is no comparison."

"You're welcome," I said.

Stefano's heart was still pounding. I would have felt it without the Touch. An itch on his back called out to be scratched.

"Let me switch spots for a second," I said.

I climbed naked behind him and used my nails to attack his itch. A new one popped up, and I scratched that. Chasing them around, knowing where they were, was the best use of the Touch so far.

"That was the greatest backscratch in the history of backscratching," Stefano said."

I was going to bow as I moved in front of him but didn't want to tip us into the mud.

Stefano wrapped his arms around me as I relaxed onto his chest. "You're all I think about," he said. "That's no small statement. You give me empathy. I want the hunt to be over. I want you in my life."

"I do too, baby. I want normal."

We sat in silence, soaking up the day.

"I missed years of your life," he said. "What was it like moving cross-country?"

"I was sad. All the time."

"I'm sorry," he said. "But after that, how was it?"

"Kind of lonely. Family is pretty much all I have. I've only met one of my online classmates. But it wasn't all bad. My family is a crazy bunch. There's never a dull

199

moment." I told stories of Dad's misguided moral lessons and how frustrated he becomes when they go awry.

Stefano repeated one of Dad's outbursts back to me. "Christ, is it so hard to teach you kids to be decent people?"

"What is the matter with you?" I said in Dad's stern tone.

"He sounds fun," Stefano said.

"Yeah," I said facetiously. "My brother's cool, though. You guys would get along. He is fun incarnate. How about you? What brought your family to Seattle?"

"Nothing I'm aware of. We drove until we reached another coast. I didn't like Seattle at first. The people are so phony nice. If someone doesn't like you in New York, they'll at least be honest about it."

"It drives me nuts," I said.

"In an act of rebellion, I ended up becoming a punk."

"Didn't we all," I said.

"No, I had a Mohawk and the greatest fuck-off outfits I could muster. It wasn't until private school that I was forced to clean up my act. I stuck out so bad my first day. That evening I got a haircut and cruised the thrift shops. The following day I met my buddy, John."

"From the hotel?"

"Yep. He thought it was hilarious that I showed up as a punk. That won him over."

"Please tell me you have a picture."

"I might. I'll have to look," he said. "It's weird. People make a big deal about private schools. All they offer is a better class of drugs, but we mostly smoked pot. Our escape was skateboarding. When I'm on my board, it becomes a part of me as I glide across the concrete."

"I feel that way when I dance."

"You're a dancer? What kind? Ballet?"

"No, I perform the Scottish Highland dance with my brother."

200

"Of course you do." His tone was condescending, digging at a nerve. "I didn't mean that."

The way he shit all over my fighting, and now my dancing, tore at my core. "If you don't mean it, don't say it."

"Jesus, don't get mad. You know you're like all the rest of the girls."

I raised myself by my arms and stared him down. "Don't you dare tell me I'm like the rest of the girls. There's a common denominator here and it ain't me."

Stefano paused before speaking. "You should ask yourself, are you upset because of what I said, or how you heard it?"

I was livid, but his comment fucked with my head. Do I filter things through my own anger?

"You focused on the first thing I said, missing the immediate retraction. Apologizing that fast is fucking huge for me. Choose your battles." He pulled me close. "For the record, I would love to see you dance."

"Thank you. Someday." My thoughts were out of control. Was he getting better or gaslighting? Was it me who has been overbearing this whole time? There's no way.

"I want you to know I'm seeing a therapist for you. I've only been to one session, but I feel she's going to help."

My nerves dropped into my belly. "Isn't that risky?"

"Not at all. She's a family friend."

It sounded real fucking risky to me. I hoped he wasn't putting our families in further danger.

"Thank you for doing that for me. For us. All you have to do is make it to your forties and we're free. That's only seventeen years. We can do that easily."

"I think we can, too," he said, squeezing me tightly.

"I'm getting hot. Can we go swimming?"

"Sure." He helped me with my top.

Once dressed, he pointed toward the channel. "On to deeper water."

We paddled to the dock where we met earlier. A girl was sunbathing on it, so we ventured to the next one. Stefano laid a matching set of beach towels on the wood decking, then ran and jumped off. I followed him into the lake expecting Seattle's waters to be colder, but there was zero shock factor. The lukewarm water was refreshing.

He dog paddled over and wrapped himself in my arms.

"I have to pee." I tried to push free, but he held firm.

"Do it on me," he said.

"That is not happening," I said and swam away.

"You're no fun," he said.

The comment hurt. I was about to let him have it when something grabbed my ankle, pulling me down.

Stefano swam over. "It's just the weeds. Don't fight it."

My wits were gone, and I fought harder.

Stefano was right in my face. "Quit fighting! You'll pull yourself under. I have you."

I felt outside my body as I kicked and thrashed. Stefano slapped me across the face, snapping me back. I quit fighting, and the drag on my legs grew slack.

"What is it?" I asked, tearing up.

"Milfoil. Weeds. Slowly work them off."

I wiggled my legs and untangled my feet. The adrenalin flooded in, and I started peeing. Stefano grew instantly hard and worked his cock up my shorts to align with the stream. The most sated look swept across his face. I wanted to enjoy the moment with him but was freaking out again.

"It's OK," he said and wiped the tears from my eyes. "I should have warned you about the danger."

A vine-like weed resembling a delicate fern floated to the surface.

"That's all it was? I thought a monster had me."

"A monster does have you," he said, holding me tight. I didn't care for his comment.

Grandpa practiced flying the drone on the simulator for a solid month. On a crisp fall afternoon, the family gathered down at the elementary school's playfield for Bepa's maiden voyage. Grandpa had the drone's visor on and was ready for takeoff. I was filming the flight with my cell phone.

"Bring it straight up as we practiced," Cordy said. "When you take your finger off the control, it will hover in place."

Grandpa didn't react.

"You good?" Cordy asked.

"I'm fine," Grandpa said, clearly nervous. The rotors emitted a high-pitched whir, and the drone lifted about three feet then flew sideways, slamming into the steel post of a cyclone fence. The crash was spectacular as pieces flew into the air. Grandpa flipped up the visor and looked sheepishly at us and the broken drone. Dad busted out in a painful, full-fledged laugh. We were soon on the ground, rolling.

I noticed Grandpa was holding his side. "You all right?" I said.

"Yeah, it still hurts if I laugh."

"Well then, next time, don't crash it so fast," Dad said. "Can you fix it," he asked Cordy.

My brother headed over to assess the damage. The left support was hanging loosely like a severed arm.

"Her frame is shot, but we have parts for the rest. Just be glad I removed all the surveillance."

"Send me the part number, and I'll order it today," I said.

"Can you buy a second controller?" Cordy said. "Maybe one I can wear on my wrist."

"Sure."

That night Cordy and I watched the video of Grandpa crashing the drone at least thirty times. It never got old.

Dad, Cordy, and I were lying low, scoping out our next target. The Dread was a lead Stefano sent me. The man killed for the thrill without putting much thought into his choice of victims. His latest murder was what pushed Stefano over the edge. The girl was an art student, volunteering her talents, promoting homeless causes. She was a saint. Still, he wanted me to turn the Dread into the police. After a lot of grumbling, my family agreed.

"I can't get the drone moving," Grandpa said. "It's just hovering. I'm crashing it. I hate this thing."

"Whoa, whoa," Cordy said. "Don't touch anything. I'll bring it over." He flipped down his visor and set the drone to follow above us. "Just monitor what's happening from there."

"I need to be in the fight."

"I know," Dad said. "After your checkup."

Grandpa grunted in defiance, then popped back on to say, "Over." This made us laugh.

A cement bicycle lane passed by the Dread's house, offering easy access, although we had to hide twice from passing cyclists.

"Hold up," Cordy said. "Something flashed in the moonlight ahead." He returned a few minutes later.

"I thought there was a trip wire. We should still go around it."

"Nice catch, son."

Our family was envious of the six-car garage on the man's property.

"Next place we buy, let's get one of these," Dad said. He peered in the window. "One without dead people."

I looked inside and saw two bodies hanging from nooses. I'd watched Westerns with Grandpa, but seeing a lifeless body hanging in real life was horrifying.

"The Dread is in the house," I said. "He's having tea." I was him as he dipped the bag.

"Ooh, he's having tea," Grandpa said mockingly through our earpieces. I was waiting for Dad to chastise him like he does Cordy, but he refrained.

We shuffled past the garage and crept to the back door. Dad and I continued to the front.

Loose decking under his foot creaked and the Dread raced to the back.

"He's heading your way," I told Cordy.

Dad kicked in the door. We were chasing after the man when a searing pain in my stomach doubled me over.

I rounded the corner of a long hallway to find the Dread stuck to Cordy, with a blade in his stomach.

"That's for Grandpa," he said, pulling the knife out, then raised it to the man's neck, brutally slicing it open. I grasped my throat in agony and yelled, but no sound emerged.

Cordy let the body drop to the ground and casually walked out. The act was so callous it gave Dad and me pause.

I was shaking mad at Cordy's betrayal and told Dad to wait outside while I cleaned up the scene.

After moping the floor, I removed the man's shoes and walked a bloody trail out the door. To further mess with the police, I rinsed the soles off and laced them back onto the man.

That night Cordy's crying woke me up. It worried me enough that I texted Dad to come over.

"Son, it's Dad," he said, knocking on my brother's door. "Can I come in?"

"It's not a good time, Dad."

"Please let me in." The lock clicked open.

Cordy's bedsprings creaked as Dad sat down. "The first kill was difficult for me too. We're taking a human's life, snuffing out their existence. That's a lot to take in. But these monsters have to be stopped. You'll learn in time that it's our duty. Our destiny. We have no choice."

"I'm not crying because of guilt. I'm crying because I don't feel anything. There's zero remorse. Am I a psychopath? Am I no better than the Dread I killed tonight?"

"You are so much like your grandpa. No, son, you're not a psychopath. You are a warrior from a long line of warriors. You're as brave as brave can be. I could not be prouder."

A message from Stefano chimed on my phone. This was going to be a tough conversation. I'm glad he hadn't called.

Hi, Sunshine. What's up?

> I am so sorry. My brother
> killed your guy. I couldn't
> stop him.

Damn it. I could have
turned him in myself. I've
got to go.

> I understand. I will try
> harder.

I was on my porch stretching out from an intense workout when the distinct smell of marijuana hit my nose. Someone was getting high. I looked over at Dad's porch, but it was empty. Funny that I thought of him first. Cordy coughed loud and harshly from above. I ran upstairs, pissed, almost bursting into his room, but knew better than to walk in on him unannounced.

"Hey, Cordy. You decent?"

He screamed abruptly and said nothing.

"Let me in. I want a hit of that pot."

My brother unlocked his room and I dove for him.

"Drugs? Drugs!" I yelled while throttling his neck.

"Shhh," Cordy managed to say.

"It's not like you can't smell it outside."

"What? I have my air filter on."

"Your window is open, you dumbass."

He slammed the pane shut. "Don't tell Dad."

"I'm not telling Dad. What am I, five? I don't want to see you doing this. We're required to jump at a drop of a hat."

"It doesn't mess with anything," he said and giggled uncontrollably.

"What are you laughing at?"

"I'm picturing you jumping around your hat."

"Dude, we have to get you out of here."

"No. Let's fight."

"What?"

"If you win, I will never smoke pot again, but if I win, you're getting high with me today. That was a dirty trick you pulled at the door."

"I can't."

"Come on, think about it?"

"OK, if you win, I will think about getting high with you."

"Today."

"Today."

We ran into Dad as we were leaving the house. He was livid. "Are you smoking marijuana?" The way he overly enunciated the word was grating.

"I smelled that coming in," I said. "Old man Jenkins lit a doobie if you care to join him?"

"No, of course not," he said jokingly.

"Dad," I love you, but right now, I need to fight Cordy, and I'm afraid you can't watch this battle."

"I understand." He sulked away.

With our father's back turned, Cordy raced across the lawn. He looked foolish standing in front of the locked garage, but in seconds he picked his way inside. Dad and I looked at each other.

"He's so fast," I said.

I found Cordy leaning against the wall of the garage, trying to stifle his laughter.

"Hold it. Hold it," I said, peeking through the window. Dad stepped inside his place and shut the door.

"OK."

Cordy removed his hand from his mouth and let out the most glorious laugh. The acoustics in the garage carried it to the rafters.

"Enough of this screwing around." I threw him his gloves and headgear.

"It's on," Cordy said. "Limited contact."

That was one of his games. You perform your fighting moves, but try not to make contact. We go for points. Pulling a punch or a kick can strain the muscles, but it was for the best to protect my stoned brother.

Cordy and I met in the center of the cage. Yes, we have a smaller version of an MMA octagon in the garage.

"You'll love this pot," Cordy said. "It's called Where's my Bike?"

"I don't want to be so high I lose my bike."

"No. No. Remember in fifth grade when you landed six 50-point Skeeball shots, giving you that crazy score of 340? How you rode your bike, thrusting your arms in the air like you were the greatest human on the planet? That's how this makes you feel. It's all about the CBG."

I was intrigued but didn't want to encourage him. "Sounds nice, but you're going down."

"We have no ref, so you'll need to tap out on the floor," he said.

"You tap out," I said and rang the bell.

I shuffled my feet and went in with a couple of short jabs. Cordy responded with more robust hits. It caught me off guard how he was better, as stoned as he was. He used my distraction to throw a high round-kick, landing inches from my head.

"You're lucky I pulled that one back," he said.

I rushed in with two leg kicks in the same spot. Not being able to connect made the hits funny, like we were in a silent movie.

"Wait, wait," Cordy said, laughing. "OK, I'm ready.

I threw a Superman jab but at a safe distance. His eyes grew wide at the hit that should have been.

"Nice. That could have taken me down."

Cordy lunged and tripped me backward, pinning my shoulders to the mat. He slammed his gloved fist into the padded floor next to my head four times. That would have been a brutal end to a real fight.

"I win," he said, popping to his feet. He climbed the fence and sat on top with his arms raised triumphantly in the air.

"Have you been holding back on me?" I said. "You moved so quickly."

"Get dressed." He jumped from his perch, landing in a seamless roll.

Cordy waited until I was finished with my shower to start his. This consideration would have been nonexistent a year ago. He was becoming noticeably more mature with each new responsibility.

While he was getting ready, I found a blog on smoking pot. It said most people don't feel anything the first few times. That tipped the scales further.

"Where are we going?" I said after we sneaked off the property.

"Ravenna Park," he said, like where else would we be heading?

The park is a ten-minute walk from our house. We dropped in from the 15th Avenue Bridge and followed the trail to the main path. I was glad Cordy resisted the urge to climb the cement trellis under the bridge. I would have gone home if he tried that bullshit again.

A canopy of maples loomed at least a hundred feet above the path. Falling leaves made the sight extra enchanting.

"So, are we doing this?" Cordy asked.

I knew he wouldn't give it a rest until I did. "You have one shot. Today is it."

"Holy shit," he said excitedly and pulled out a vape pen.

"Not out in the open," I said. "What if we run into Grandpa?"

"Fine, we'll head up a side trail."

There was a clearing at the base of a maple midway up the hill. We leaned comfortably upon the massive trunk.

"All you do is hold the button and draw inward," Cordy said, taking a long drag. He rounded his mouth to blow a smoke ring but ended up coughing harshly.

"Looks smooth," I said mockingly and grabbed the vape before chickening out.

Cordy gasped as I brought the pen to my lips. "Don't take too much," he said. "Don't hold it in."

I coughed out a small cloud. "That sounds like the exact opposite instructions." I took another drag.

After ten minutes, Cordy talked me into a third. As I let the smoke out, a veil lifted and the world grew warm and brilliant. Everything was so green.

A homeless man with ragged hair and a dirt-splotched face appeared in front of us. Cordy and I screamed and then laughed.

"Can I have a hit?" the man said.

"Gross, what if you have syphilis?" Cordy said.

"Don't be rude," I said.

"Yoinks," the man said and tried to bolt with our vape. My brother caught him by the collar and lifted the guy off his feet. When the vape was safely in my hands, he let him go. The homeless man crawled into a run and dove into the dense underbrush like a frightened animal.

"What do you feel like doing?" Cordy said as if nothing happened.

"I want to see the turtles."

"Yeah, the turtles," he said dreamily.

We eased down the hill to the trail and back onto the main path. Just before the 20th Street Bridge, a wooden boardwalk winds through a marsh and a stream. We were drawn to the enormous boulder the walkway circles around. Cordy and I climbed up the sloped side and sat on top with our backs to the trail.

I leaned over and whispered, "I'm high."

"Serious?" Cordy hugged me.

"How did you beat me in a fight? Everything is so slow."

"That's the trick. It offers time to calculate your moves. Did you see how fast I snagged that homeless guy?"

"Well, he did say yoinks. You kind of knew his intentions."

That made him laugh. "To the turtles."

Cordy performed a front-facing parkour flip off the boulder and stuck his landing like a gymnast. My dismount was sloppy, but at least I didn't hurt myself.

On the main trail, a group of shirtless college boys jogged by. Their cocks were enticing, flopping around in the soft fabric of their soccer shorts.

"That's not fair," Cordy said.

I couldn't tell if it was not fair that they weren't women running topless, or if it wasn't fair that the boys were so sexy it confused him.

We reached the end of the park. There they were, three giant turtles with cement shells and realistic flippers and heads. In my stoned state, they were glorious.

A woman with a prosthetic blade for a foot raced swiftly past. We watched her disappear into the woods.

"Did you see how fast that lady was?" Cordy said. "She could be in the Special Olympics."

"Don't you mean the Paralympics?"

Cordy's cheeks flushed red with embarrassment. "In my defense, I think all Olympics are special."

Chapter 11

Support relayed our next assignment to me. The Dread in question was an organ harvester operating from a cabin deep in the woods. Grandpa was back in the mix, and for the first time, we were four. The drone hovered above on autopilot, set to follow Cordy like a dog.

"Are we fucking clear on the plan?" I asked one last time. "He's a doctor. We're turning this guy into the police."

The three men grumbled but agreed.

"Thank you."

We hiked through the woods parallel to the cabin to avoid any alarms. I was concerned with the full moon giving us away. We would have to be more mindful of its cycles.

The trees of the forest were tall with thin trunks growing sparsely. The bare ground offered a bleak canvas for eerie shadows of arm-shaped branches. In the distance, the cabin was materializing.

"This place is right out of a horror movie," Cordy said. "All that's missing is the fog."

"Keep your head in the game," Dad ordered.

"It is a pretty freaky cabin," I said.

"Yeah, it's a real fucking scary cabin," Dad said, "and these woods are spooky as shit, but talking about it will only make it worse. This forest is probably beautiful during the day. Focus."

We split up to cover the entrances. Cordy picked the Dread's lock. My watch vibrated, showing that Dad opened his. Cordy's new silent communication system was an improvement. I responded that we were heading in.

We met Dad and Grandpa in the hall. I felt a Dread faintly on the other side of the wall, but there were no doors. I pointed to his location. Cordy rejoined us after checking the outside to no avail.

Dad ran his hand across the wall and discovered a break in the shiplap. He slid the panel open, and the Dread's presence hit me full force. He had lined the room with steel. What I didn't feel was evil. The man was not into the change. That would have given me pause if it weren't for the scene in front of us. Inside the space was a brightly lit operating table. A body was on the gurney with his chest split apart. Cordy rushed forward.

"Don't," I yelled, "He hasn't changed. We're turning him in." My plea fell on deaf ears. Cordy was like a lion honed in on his prey.

The startled doctor held his scalpel up as if that would do him any good. Cordy drove his knife into the man's carotid artery. Blood shot from his neck into my face. I was incapacitated from the pain and never saw the stream coming.

"What the fuck," I said, holding my palms up, trying unsuccessfully to stop the flow from hitting me.

The doctor clasped his neck in shock. "You need to get the heart to this address at three a.m." He reached for a card but knocked it to the floor. "Save the boy's life."

Grandpa pressed his gun to the man's chin and fired upward, splattering me in gore. But at least the Dread's pain was gone.

"Damn it, Bepa!" I screamed and used my hands to squeegee the horror from my face. I was pissed. The doctor should have gone to jail, not die.

"Sorry," he said unapologetically.

"Check for a basement," Dad said. "There could be more people here."

"What about the heart?" I said.

"What about it?" Grandpa said.

"We need to deliver it to whoever is expecting the organ."

"No," Dad said defiantly. "We're leaving."

214

I grabbed a large mirror and smashed it into the wall. "A boy's life is depending on this heart. The doctor hadn't changed into a Dread. He was doing this of his own free will. We are making the delivery."

"Don't be stupid," Grandpa said.

I was crushed. "We're doing this," I said. "End of discussion."

The men looked at each other but no one challenged me. I opened the medical cooler. Packs of dry ice cradled a heart wrapped in plastic. I shut the lid casually, forcing back my urge to slam it shut.

The drop-off for the heart turned out to be inside a decrepit amusement park in Tacoma. Excessively creepy seemed to be the theme of the evening. The worst part was going at it alone with only Cordy monitoring from above. Dad and Grandpa refused to go. At least I didn't have to worry about the Hilltop Hellion being around.

Just past the entrance were the three pigs prepping for the big bad wolf. With age, the life-size plastic figures were a horrific scenario of decay and neglect. Their gaping eye sockets were void of logic, and their mouths opened freakishly wide in accusatory fashion. The following exhibit was worse. I focused on the path ignoring the horrors that became of my childhood fables.

The doctor had a sense of humor. He picked the Wizard of Oz exhibit for the drop point.

My brother's voice crackled over the receiver in my ear. "A man is crouching in the woods about fifteen feet in front of you."

I placed the cooler on the doorstep of the crumbling Palace.

"Here's the Tin Man's heart."

As I was leaving, there was a rustle in the bushes.

"Thank you."

"You're welcome. This is the last one. The doctor is dead."

A muffled voice said, "Please no."
"I couldn't stop them. I am so sorry."

Stefano sent a message for me to call. I'd been avoiding him the last couple of days. I felt horrible for killing the doctor.

"Hey, Stefano. What's up?"

"Did your family kill Dr. Everest?"

Holy fuck. I didn't know what to say. My heart was racing.

"My cousin was the pickup man. Only you would have apologized."

"I'm sorry, baby. I am so sorry. My brother was on autopilot. I couldn't stop him."

"Dr. Everest was one of the finest men I have ever known. The donors were my people who wanted to die. The organs were for children. You have no idea what you've done. I can't do this anymore. I just can't."

"Stefano, no," I said, but the call ended.

A grey tiger-striped tabby had been working my brother over for adoption. Cordy named the stray Clio, which he explained was short for cling-on. I warned him that Dad wouldn't let us have a pet. Cordy didn't feel it was a definite rule with us now being adults. His mention of rules infuriated me. Stefano wasn't answering my messages and it was all Cordy's fault.

It wasn't a surprise when I arrived home to find the cat inside playing with Cordy. Clio saw me and shot out the door like a rocket.

"I'm keeping her," Cordy said. "We were just playing fetch," he said, tossing up a ball. "She's pretty much a dog."

"What, no way? She just hisses at me."

"That won't last," he assured me."

But it did. A month after we officially moved the cat in, it still wouldn't go near me. The damn thing went on walks with Cordy but didn't give me the time of day. It was starting to piss me off.

"Your cat's a bitch."

"Well, now you know what it's like living with a sister."

I stood shocked with my mouth agape.

"Oh my God. I am so sorry. I didn't mean it, sis."

I shook my head. "I'm taking a bath."

"Hang on." He ran upstairs. When he returned, he was hiding something behind his back. Cordy handed me a bottle of Mr. Bubble. I hadn't seen that since Mom died.

"I know," he said, noticing my tears building.

"Where did you find it?" We'd searched for a year.

"Bartells."

"You're very sweet."

His cat hissed at me.

"Clio, come on. She's family."

In the tub, I burst into tears. It was a scene that played out a lot lately.

Stefano contacted me on a cold winter morning with last-minute tickets to the opera. He hadn't talked to me in two months. The outing was a gesture for me to experience one of the joys in his life. He would not be attending. At least there was contact.

I invited my brother, but he just laughed and laughed. Luckily Chase was available and more than willing. A half-hour after asking, my friend was on the freeway heading out of Portland.

Our seats were front row of the balcony. As we made our way down the aisle, I felt a large group of Dread below. I sent Chase for drinks and leaned over the railing to catch a glimpse, hoping that Stefano was among them, but they were too far under the eave to see. I concentrated hard, trying to detect a telltale sign of his movements.

Chase returned with cocktails and handed one over. I liked his floppy new surfer 'do. The juxtaposition against his blue blazer was cute. My friend had turned into a genuine hottie.

He sat down next to me. "Why are you in these seats? Aren't we in those?" He pointed next to him.

"It's all right." I'd failed to get the couple to move. My confrontation skills apparently aren't as fierce outside the ring. That was a disappointing reality.

"No. It's not all right." He turned to the couple. "Excuse me. You're in our seats."

"Sorry. My wife needs the aisle."

Chase stood up. "Yeah, no. That's not how life works. Move it, bub."

The man folded his arms defiantly.

"I'll have the usher come down here. Now get the fuck up."

"Fine. Dickhead."

"Yeah, I'm the dickhead." Chase rolled his eyes at me.

The couple rose in a huff and walked to the back.

"Oh my God, they weren't even in our row," I said. "What the fuck?"

My friend sat down in the man's seat, giving me the aisle.

"You're kind of a tough guy now," I said.

"I'm just sick of getting pushed around. Plus, if it got physical, I knew you'd have my back."

Christ, that's all I needed, to get thrown out of the opera for fighting. Stefano would love that.

Chase put his feet up on the railing. His socks and pocket square were the same blues as his eyes. The color matching was brilliant.

"Thank you for the invitation," he said. "This is a real treat."

"There's no one I'd rather be here with," I responded, toasting him. Well, there was one other person.

The opera we were seeing was La Bohème. The one Stefano first introduced to me. He told me the seated character Rodolfo in the opening would have been played by Pavarotti. Marcello, the goateed man painting at his side, turned toward the audience and began singing. There were enthusiastic shouts from the Dread below. The man was one of their own, but he was too far to get a read. The voice of the singer was familiar. It couldn't be. It was. Stefano was in the opera.

"The man on the right is my boyfriend," I whispered. Chase saw my tears and held me through the song.

A digital readout above the stage translated the lyrics from Italian to English, but I understood most of what they sang. Unfortunately, I couldn't block out the Dread below. It kept me from becoming immersed in the story.

Stefano had two roles. He must have been the understudy's understudy because neither his picture nor name were in the playbill. His second character was a bit of an asshole. He played him brilliantly. I suspected it wasn't so much acting.

His beautiful baritone sounded angelic to me. What was impressive is he's naturally a tenor.

The performance was short as far as operas go, coming in just over two hours. I was an emotional wreck by the time it finished.

219

"Can you get us backstage?" Chase asked after the players took their final bow.

"Maybe," I said but knew the answer.

I sent a text to Stefano, and he immediately called me back. I was so excited I almost lost the phone over the railing.

"Hey, Janice," Stefano said.

I began crying.

"What's wrong?"

"I finally understand Opera. You're... You're so talented."

"That means the world."

"Would it be possible for us to go backstage?"

There was a long pause. "I can't."

"I love you."

"I have to go. I shouldn't have called."

I looked over at Chase. "Maybe next time."

"That's OK. I had a fun night."

All I wanted to do was head home, but I was obligated. "Let's go to Capitol Hill and get you laid," I said, slapping him on the knee.

"My boyfriend's not going to approve."

"What? How come you didn't tell me?"

"You told your brother that I was your date."

"I couldn't have asked for better," I said.

"You'd like my Samuel. He's cute as a button."

"I do like buttons," I said dreamily. Chase didn't find it funny. I needed to work on my humor.

He scrolled through his phone and held up a picture.

"Wow! He's hot."

"Do you have to sound so surprised?"

"You do not get to play the victim here." I backtracked. "That's not what I meant."

"I know." Chase helped me to my feet. "You'd never hurt me." He placed his arm through mine.

220

"I hope you didn't mind pretending you're my date. There's bad blood between my boyfriend and my family."

"What is he, a rescue?"

I laughed at the reality of his comment. "It's more of a Romeo and Juliet situation. I've kind of been saying you and I are dating so I can see him."

"I'm totally cool being your beard," he said.

"You're the best. Let's at least have another drink," I said

"Sure, but this is my last one. I have a long drive ahead."

Chapter 12

I was out back on our hammock, wrapped in a warm blanket, absorbed in a trashy romance novel. Seattle was having a mild winter. It was the first week of January, and the sun was shining.

Stefano still wasn't talking to me. I missed him terribly and was insanely jealous of whoever he was sleeping with to keep his curse in check.

"Hey, Sis," Cordy said, startling me. "Do you have a moment?"

My brother was nowhere in sight. I carefully rolled to my side and found him lying in the grass below me.

"Hello," I said. "Of course, I have time for you."

I had forgiven Cordy. There's no way to stay mad at that guy.

"The Adult Movie Awards are in Vegas near the end of the month. I think we should go."

"I don't want to know how you heard out about this."

"You sure you want to go there?" he said, making the revving sound of Dad's car.

The mortifying innuendo shut me right up.

"OK, yes, I was watching porn," Cordy admitted. He crawled out from under the hammock and nudged my arm to get me swaying. "But that's not why I want to go. A lot of Dread will be at the ceremony. It'll be a chance to observe the enemy. Document the Dread as you say."

Cordy's idea wasn't bad. In one evening, we could identify more Dread than I had in years. I pulled up the event's web page and saw the date.

"You want to go to Vegas for your twenty-first birthday. Your real one."

223

"Well, yeah, but don't tell dad, or he won't pay for it."

"I don't want him to go."

"Of course not," he said and looked toward Dad's empty deck to make sure he wasn't listening. "Just you and me. We'll rip that city a new one."

"I am so in," I said, sitting up.

We've never been a vacationing family. The trip was going to be a blast. It took days of convincing for Dad to let us go alone. He had an uneasy feeling about the ceremony, but what parent wouldn't, sending their kids to the Adult Movie Awards? I held firm and won him over. Dad had to learn that Cordy and I could take care of ourselves.

The trip gave Grandpa an excuse to teach us the subtle intricacies of craps. He had Cordy purchase a casino game for the PlayStation.

"If you follow closely, you should be able to come out ahead," Grandpa said.

"Don't get their hopes up," Dad said. "The house always wins."

"Not if you stick with sixes and eights."

By his fifth progression, Bepa was betting with a third of his winnings. The rest, he said, would be in a growing pile to the side.

"The main thing is not to get too caught up in the excitement of the table. Keep your head, and you keep your money. Part of that is knowing when to walk away. If you don't, you'll give it all back to the house."

"How *do* you know when to walk away?" Cordy asked.

"It's the moment greed outweighs common sense."

Dad booked us into Caesar's Palace. I would have been fine anywhere, but he felt more comfortable with home base in a safe part of town.

In our line of business, there aren't many opportunities to pamper ourselves. I hired a stylist to come to our room and do my hair and makeup. After she left, I beamed at my reflection in the bathroom mirror. The person looking back at me was a stranger. Contouring makeup was close to sorcery. I was legitimately hot. And the blonde wig I bought for my disguise was now ridiculously sexy. The black cocktail dress I chose added to the effect. It was low cut with a heavy emphasis on my breasts. Having them propped up, front and center, would make navigating the lion's den easier.

Cordy had been growing out a goatee, but he couldn't get the hair on his chin to meet his mustache. I thought it was cute. The dorky wig he chose, not so much.

"Why did you go with that stupid boy's cut?"

"Because it makes me look dumb," Cordy said, "That way if I say something intelligent, people will think I'm smarter."

"That's genius."

"See? It's already working. You ready?" Cordy adjusted the bow tie on his tux. "The limo's downstairs." He took a swig off the fifth of whiskey purchased for the room.

I stole a look in the mirror and repositioned my tits. "Let's roll," I said.

I hadn't believed him about the limo, but a shiny white one was waiting for us outside the lobby. Cordy handed me a VIP lanyard. I was Gorgeous Day, and he was Jimmy Jenkins.

The evening would require an abundance of personality. On the drive over, my brother worked on my confidence until I was riding high. The mini bottles of liquor he brought helped in this endeavor.

A block from the Hard Rock, I began sensing the Dread. I'd had one-off hits all day, but the Touch was now inundated with them. There must have been sixty in the line alone. I kept getting pounded with an intermittent overwhelming blast of the Touch. It was too much. My breathing grew heavy, and I placed my head between my legs to relax.

"You all right?" Cordy said.

"I don't know. There are so many Dread." Another blast hit me, and I rubbed my temples in pain.

Cordy scanned the line, looking to see who I was reading. He checked the button camera on his suit to make sure it was recording. "I wish I had my gun or at least a knife."

"We're here to document. Nothing else," I said.

The car stopped to let us out, but I wasn't ready.

"Slap me," I said.

"What?"

"Slap me. Right across the face."

"I can't."

"Just do it!"

"Do I dare live out my dream," Cordy said and slapped me hard.

I snapped upright. "What the fuck? That was your dream?"

"You can't get upset about something you asked for. Besides, that, my sister, was a joke."

"Sorry. We're going to do this," I said, trying to talk myself into the night.

A man in a tux greeted us as we stepped from the car. "Nominee or attendee?"

"Attendee," Cordy said. "This is Gorgeous Day, lead singer of The High Beams. We're here to promote her upcoming album, Eyes Up Here."

The guy thought it was funny but not as much as us when we came up with that backstory. I'm surprised we kept it together.

"I'm Jimmy Jenkins. Agent." Cordy donned his sunglasses.

The man typed our information into a tablet and told us to proceed down the red carpet. I was hit with another concentrated blast from the Dread. What the hell was that?

"Jimmy Jenkins," Cordy shouted and thrust his arms in the air.

Walking the red carpet of the Adult Video Awards was like attending the Grammys. Camera flashes stroked my ego as we enjoyed the pageantry. I concentrated on walking in my heels. The last thing we needed was a video of me falling.

"You're a rockstar," Cordy whispered in my ear.

"It's my time!" I responded cockily.

A splendid set of shirtless male twins opened the massive steel doors for us. The presence of a thousand Dread struck me like an explosion, but there was no turning back with all the cameras. I rushed to the lady's room and made it as far as the garbage can to throw up.

I was freshening up at the sink when a stunning redhead offered me a mint.

"Thank you so much," I said.

"Don't be nervous. You're gorgeous," she said.

"I literally am," I said, showing her the name on my pass.

Cordy was waiting for me by the bathroom entrance.

"The girl that walked out with you is my favorite starlet," he said.

"She gave me a mint," I said and winked. "I hate to do this. I need to leave. Can you get us to a side exit?"

"You sure you can't pull it together?"

"There's too many of them. I feel like I'm dying."

"No problem. We can have fun anywhere in this city."

We found our way to the casino floor, but there were still more Dread than my brain could handle. Cordy led us to a backdoor and across the street to a dingy hotel. Just standing in the lobby made me feel dirty. I couldn't imagine sleeping in one of their beds.

My brother headed to the bathroom to ditch his stupid wig and emerged with his choppy blond hair. I don't know if it was the tux, but he was genuinely handsome.

"That's so much better," I said. "Did you have product with you?"

"A little," he admitted. "We weren't spending all night at the ceremony."

"You look good."

"Thanks. Do you want to lose your wig?"

"Hell no. I'm rockin' this look."

"That you are."

Cordy hailed a cab to Fremont Street. My sanity returned a few blocks away, as the last of the Touch faded. We had the driver stop by a drug store so I could get rid of my pounding headache and cover the blisters on my feet. Wearing high heels was torture.

Fremont Street has the look and feel of old Vegas. It was glorious. We walked the main drag, drinking ridiculously tall cocktails, enjoying the show projecting on the ceiling above the street.

The Golden Nugget drew us in, and we searched the floor for a table to try out Grandpa's craps technique. His six-eight strategy worked better than expected. We were up $2,500 when we walked away.

I called Bepa from the street—trying that from inside the casino brought a stern lecture from security. Grandpa said, that's it for the night. We'd used up all our luck. I was glad I called. Cordy already blew $200 on the dollar slots. The progressive prize scrolling across the top of his machine had him firmly in the casino's grasp. Greed was definitely outweighing his common sense. I drug him from his chair.

We bought another drink and hailed a cab to the Bellagio to see the synchronized fountains. Cordy was so

228

jazzed that the show was starting he opened the cab door and fell into a staggering run. The drunken fool headed the wrong direction, to the left of the lake. I threw two twenties at the driver and chased after my brother.

Andrea Bocelli's solo in Time to Say Goodbye blared over the loudspeakers. Hearing the music felt like a sign.

I caught up to Cordy on the backside of the lake. He was stumbling and falling backward, comically slow. Cordy reached out to people for help, but they reacted as if he were a leper. He landed on his butt in a low hedge. Both palms were punctured and streaming blood.

"You didn't help, and look at me now. I have stigmata!" He rushed the crowd with his palms raised ahead of him, screaming, "Stigmata!"

I dragged him away before security showed up.

"Did you hear the music?" Cordy said. "They played that song you like."

"I know. Wasn't that weird?"

We ended up on a bench at the front of the lake, but the show was over. A kid strolled by selling water from a red wagon. I bought a couple of bottles and flipped one to Cordy. He downed half of it in one pull.

"Thanks for coming. There's no one I'd rather spend my birthday with. It's so lonely being a Hunter. Do you ever feel it?"

"All the time. I'm glad we have each other. You turned out to be a cool guy."

"I like you too, Sis. He put his arm around my shoulder and slumped toward me.

This mood would not do. I wasn't about to leave him in this sad state on his birthday. "Hang on a sec." I moved out of earshot and left a message for our hotel concierge to see if he could arrange a VIP booth at a high-end strip club. Ten minutes later, he returned my call with a shockingly expensive reservation at the Palomino Club.

"I have to pee," I said, looking for a bathroom. The hotel entrance was so far.

"Just go here."

I stepped behind the bench. Halfway through, a group of women approached. There was no stopping the stream. I was mortified.

"Can you believe the moon tonight," Cordy said to distract the ladies. "Look how bright it is. Must be the desert air." The women were commenting about how beautiful the moon was. A couple even took pictures. People passing by looked up to see what was so interesting. I joined my brother when I finished.

"Where are we off to?" he asked.

"It's a surprise," I said. "You'll have to work on looking less drunk, though."

"That I can do can," he said. I couldn't tell if he was trying to be funny.

We crossed over the walking bridge to Caesars Palace to hail a cab. At the base of the stairs, a father was yelling at his young daughter. "Do you want it in the face or the hand?" The girl held out her hand with tears streaming down her cheeks. The father drew his arm back, and I caught it mid-swing. He glared at me furiously.

"Who do you think you are, bitch?"

I held Cordy back and put everything into my punch. The man's legs buckled, and he fell flat on his ass. I fished the jerk's wallet out of his back pocket and took a picture of his license. Kneeling over him, I firmly drilled a fist into his kidney.

"I'll have my people check in with your daughter. If I find out you're hurting her in any way, I will end you. That is a certainty."

The man didn't say anything, so I hit him again.

"I understand," he groaned.

"Go buy her an ice cream cone."

"Hell of a punch," Cordy said as we were rounding the corner. A police cruiser was parked in front of us.

230

"Get in," the officer said, opening the passenger door. He had the look of a retired Marine. The juxtaposition of his inviting tone was unsettling. I didn't trust it, but he was offering me the front, so I jumped in.

"I have to get you out of here," the officer said.

"To the Palomino Club," I directed.

The officer chuckled at my request.

"For the record, I'm not a stripper. It's my brother's birthday. Get in, you idiot," I yelled to Cordy.

"Off the record. Don't worry about hitting Leonard," the officer said. "He's been a thorn in my ass since the day I joined the force. That jackass finally got what was coming to him."

"My pleasure?" I said timidly.

"God damn right it's your pleasure," he said. "That punch was solid. I was impressed."

"He was about to hit his daughter. It was the least I could do. Would you mind checking in on him? I said I'd have my people make sure he wasn't hurting her."

"It would be my pleasure."

I spaced out the window at the odd situation. A short drive later, we were in the parking lot across from the strip club. I thanked the officer and opened the door to let Cordy out, then got an idea and swung it shut.

"Look sullen," I said. "With your hands behind your back like you're cuffed." Cordy played well for the camera.

"Send it to Dad," he said. "Tell him I've been arrested."

I loved the idea and fired off the picture.

The host at the Palomino Club escorted us to a private section near the stage. Matching black leather couches faced a mahogany coffee table. After we were seated, a scantily clad cocktail waitress delivered a fifth of Bushmills and two tumblers filled with ice.

"You are the coolest sister," Cordy said and filled his glass.

"You're welcome. I should let Dad know we were kidding." I sent him a text.

Women were drawn to Cordy like chocolate. Three naked dancers accosted him. I didn't need to see that. I glanced at my phone for a response from Dad. There was nothing. The club was jamming the cell reception. When I stepped outside, my phone lit up. Dad hadn't received the 'Just Kidding' text. That made me giggle. My initial note finally went through, shutting him up. I messaged Stefano begging for him to answer. He called me right back.

"Hey, Sunshine. What's shakin?" he sounded drunk.

"I just needed to hear your voice. I'm in Vegas celebrating my brother's twenty-first."

"No way. I'm down here too. A friend from the Bronx was nominated for an award tonight. Want to hook up?"

The rush of adrenalin was so sudden I threw up.

"You all right," he said, laughing.

"Yeah, there is nothing I would rather do."

"What a crazy evening. Can you meet me in the Luxor in an hour? Room 721."

"I am so there," I said.

"Don't be late. I only have two hours left."

Hearing that took a little wind out of me. Was this all about the change? I walked back inside the club to find my brother with a gorgeous brunette. I couldn't tell if she was a stripper or not. Cordy looked over at me dreamily. He was in his element.

"Do you mind if I head to the hotel?" I said.

"Oh, man. I'm not ready to go."

"Just me. I want you to stay out all night."

"You sure?"

"This is your day. Enjoy."

"You're the best."

"Happy birthday, Brother," I said and hugged him goodbye.

232

On the way to the Luxor, I stopped by my hotel to freshen up. I liked the glamorous blonde in the mirror. I decided to keep my disguise on. Why not give Stefano the extra thrill.

I rode the monorail to the Luxor. The Egyptian theme was working for me, especially how the building was a pyramid.

The security guard stationed at the guest elevators wouldn't let me pass until he called Stefano. The man treated me like trash.

In the hall near Stefano's room, I felt him inside, rubbing that hard cock through his slacks. I knocked, and he bolted for the door.

Stefano was sporting a black suit that offered the rugged handsomeness of Hollywood. "Hello?" he said, "If my cousins hired you, I'll pay, but you have to go. My girlfriend's on the way up. I've been such a jerk. I fucking love her. She can't see you."

I wrapped my arms around Stefano and kissed him madly.

"The fuck? I just told you no."

"Stefano, you're hurting me."

He let go of my arm. "Janis? What is all this?" he said, playing with the long blonde wig.

"Out hiding in plain sight."

"I am so fucking sorry. For everything. I can't stay away from you."

"I'm the one who needs to apologize. My family is uncontrollable. They turn into animals. I can't stop them."

"We'll get through it. I love you so goddam much."

I firmly pressed my lips to his and we made out in his doorway.

"Get a room," a man passing us said. He wore the proudest smile like he thought he was the wittiest man in the world.

"Do you remember that guy telling us to get a room when we were kids?" I said.

"Totally, at the café on our first official date. Believe me, I wanted to."

We entered Stefano's room and slammed the door shut with our bodies as we locked lips and intertwined tongues. He ran his hands across the front of my dress and was pleased by the lack of a gun.

My dress was the first to go. "I love this suit." I ran a thumb and forefinger down the lapel.

"This is vintage YSL. Fit this well off the rack. I swear I didn't have it altered."

"It's gorgeous," I said and worked on the buttons of his shirt.

"Of course, it had to be the most expensive one in the store."

"That's life," I said. "You pay dearly for what you want the most."

"Ain't that the truth," Stefano said and kissed me deeper. His mouth had the lingering sweetness of Kahlúa.

We were naked by the time we reached the bed. I felt his cock throb with anticipation. I grabbed hold of it and enjoyed feeling his pleasure in my grip.

"I have to taste you," he said. "I need it bad."

"Is there time?"

He brought up the curse timer on his phone. There were fifty-three minutes left.

I parted my legs. "I'm all yours."

Stefano stormed my pussy drunk and greedily. Cunnilingus was the one activity I could concentrate on without too much interference from the Touch. It would be like trying to hear a whisper with the stereo turned up full volume.

I was edging toward my third climax when I sensed a Dread approaching. I sat straight up.

"Someone's coming," I said.

"You bet someone's coming," Stefano egged me on.

"No, someone is coming in."

The door unlocked with a click. Stefano rushed over to intercept, and I covered myself with the sheet.

"Dude, I'm with a girl," Stefano said.

"Sorry, man. I need to change. I spilled my drink."

Stefano laughed. "You came in your pants."

"No, I didn't. It was a beer."

"Hurry up," Stefano said, not bothering to put clothes on. There's no way I could confidently walk around naked like that.

I recognized his cousin from a picture Stefano showed me. Luckily he didn't know me as a Huntress and wasn't seeing me how I really looked. There's nothing like hiding in the open. The man did a double-take, but I'm sure that was because I slid the sheet past my breasts as a distraction.

While he was washing up, Stefano plucked three hundreds from his cousin's wallet.

As he was leaving, Stefano held up the money. "Would you mind staying out all night?"

"Not at all," he said, snatching the cash. "Wait, aren't you playing poker with us?"

"I can't."

"What are you talking about? We're going to clean up."

"Sorry. Call Dante. He can fill in for me."

I don't think there's a better sign of Stefano's love than him giving up poker for me. The door closed, and I ran over and dove on Stefano. My heart sank as my knee connected squarely with his testicles.

"Oh my God, I am so sorry."

I was expecting pain, but there was none. Stefano was holding his balls with worry.

"Wait for it," he said.

I was about to call him a faker when the pain struck. It felt as if I was going to shit my pants and throw up all at the same time. The deep throbbing agony was like none I ever felt.

235

"It hurts so bad."

"I know," Stefano said. We rolled around writhing in pain.

"I used to hit my brother in the nuts on purpose," I said.

"Don't," he said.

"I won't. When does it end?"

"Pretty soon."

I uncoiled as the pain dissipated. Childbirth had to be way worse, but that was brutal. I cradled Stefano's package gingerly while spooning him.

"What award was your friend nominated for?" I asked to distract him.

"Best load," he said, embarrassed.

I found that hilariously disgusting but loved when something embarrassed him. "You have got to show me," I said.

Stefano moved to the bed and searched for a porno on his phone, then fast-forwarded to the end of the second scene. A handsome Italian man was fucking a petite brunette missionary style. He pulled out and shot a repulsive load all over the woman's chest and face. She was drenched.

"Darius lost three days work building that one up."

"It was impressive," I said, faking enthusiasm. "Did he win?"

"No. A guy from Digital Sin took the trophy."

I didn't want to see the winning shot. That first one was all kinds of gross.

"Wasn't it dangerous for your friend doing that at the three-day mark?"

"Terribly, but starlets know how to please."

"Sorry about your balls," I said. "We can do whatever you want. It's the least I can offer for hurting you."

"I'll take a rain check. I'm in the mood to fuck."

236

"Oh, hell, yes!" I said, ignoring that he wasn't racing against the clock.

Stefano bent me over the bed and drove his cock aggressively inside. My cry of pained pleasure morphed into grateful moans. Stefano was on overdrive, probably worked into frustration by the clips at the Adult Video Awards. I leaned back to kiss him. He used the opportunity to reposition me to my side, putting his cock at an angle, offering a longer stroke across his shaft. I reveled in his ecstasy.

He moved us in front of the dresser the TV was on and bent me over. Stefano fucked me while simultaneously diddling my clit. I could see my reflection in the black of the TV. That didn't sit well, so I tilted back to bring his reflection into view. He saw me staring and smiled. The pain I'd caused earlier brought forth an unfamiliar tightness like my mind hadn't let go of the trauma. I tried everything to relax, so my orgasm would present itself. Nothing was working. I had to concentrate on slowing my breathing before the doors holding my release unlocked. Stefano switched his finger technique to a bouncing tap, and soon the hinges burst open, sending energy racing toward freedom. I came so powerfully I thought the world was shifting, but it was just the TV falling off the dresser. Stefano caught it one-handed so he could ease me back from my orgasm.

"It's my turn," he said, "I want to look at your gorgeous face as I come."

I ate his compliment up.

Stefano carried me to the bed and laid me on my back. I spread my legs high to give him proper thrusting room. Sweat dripped from his body as he pounded into me. He moved fluidly as if he were dancing. I was hypnotized watching the rolling sexual symmetry flow from his shoulders, down to his ass, repeatedly — every movement feeding my desire.

237

"I can't come," he said, worried. "I'm too drunk." His timer showed five minutes left.

"Stop thinking about it. Just look in my eyes."

I sunk my hips, tightening my muscles around his cock in a pulsing fashion.

"Oh God, that feels so good."

He thrust deep and long as he picked up the pace. His breathing grew heavy as he ravaged me, fucking as his life depended on it. My moans increased in volume as I urged him on until I was almost screaming.

"You're doing it," he said breathlessly. "I'm going to come. You're so hot."

There was no residual pain in his balls. They shifted and pulsed as his release shot into me in waves. I moaned with him, enjoying the ecstasy spreading across his face. His eyes were closed and his upper lip quivered as he gasped. At the end, his core involuntarily shook in a slight quiver.

Stefano fell on top of me, resting his head on my breasts as I stroked his shoulders lovingly.

"Can you stay over?" he asked. "I'd like to wake up next to you."

"Of course. I'll set the alarm for nine, so I'm out before your cousin comes back."

"Three hours from now?"

"That's Vegas." I didn't know if that was Vegas. It just sounded right.

"How do you keep going?" he said.

"I've been mixing vodka with energy drinks."

"No, how do you keep going? We live in a weird world. What do you do to make life worthwhile?"

The question stumped me. Was it fighting? Helping to run the business? That would be a horrible response. The answer was staring me right in my face. "You. You're the one who keeps me going." His hair was silk as I combed my fingers through.

238

"You're sweet, and of course, my answer is the same, but I was talking about life itself. For me, it's music. When my grandma played me an opera as a boy, something woke inside. The emotion from hearing the performance was a high that I keep chasing."

I couldn't help but think that his grandma steered him toward opera because she thought it was a world a Hunter would never be a part of.

His tone was comforting as he talked about his passion. I must have passed out at some point. It was five minutes before my alarm. I rolled with my back to him and wiggled under his arm. He screamed in my ear and wildly thrashed until he was on the ground. I peered over the edge of the bed. Stefano's expression was blank like he was no longer in his body. His eyes shifted so he was staring at me, and he slowly returned. What the hell was that? Was this the Dread in him? I crawled onto the floor and held him close.

"I don't know what just happened," Stefano said, but his tone told a different story.

"I think you should mention this in therapy."

"I have... I will. Can you be a dear and grab me a pair of the new white socks from that middle drawer," he said. "They comfort me."

"Of course."

There was a stack of new socks in the cupboard. I sat on the floor and tenderly slipped a pair on his feet. I could tell how good they felt.

"If I were rich, I'd wear new socks once and donate the lot to the homeless. That probably sounds weird."

"Not at all. In our world, finding relief is priceless. With me, it's books."

"You should read one in new socks."

It was well past sunup when I arrived at my hotel. Cordy was walking into the lobby ahead of me.

We both said, "I don't want to talk about it."

When we got to the room, Cordy removed his shoes and drifted off to sleep as he was falling onto the bed. He was seriously out when his head hit the pillow.

Later that day, I woke up in a daze. My vagina was ruined.

I looked over at my brother. He was holding his phone sideways, captivated. I realized what was happening under the sheet.

"Can you do that in the bathroom?"

Cordy screamed and lost control of his phone. It flew to the floor.

"Sorry. Sorry," he said and headed to the lavatory.

He came back minutes later.

"That was fast," I said.

"Last night was so dirty," he said. "I can't stop thinking about it."

I don't want to hear it."

"That's probably for the best. I was so drunk I pretty much blacked out. Things got way out of hand."

"I have a theory about what happens when people blackout. Remember the crawlspace under my bedroom in Greenwich?"

"That was the spookiest," he said.

"I used to have a reoccurring nightmare where my bed would roll, sending me into the darkness, while my other me flipped up in an opposite bed and lived life as me. I think when we blackout, our other me drives us around like a vehicle."

"My other me must steer from the ass because it feels as if something was shoved in there. That's not a request I would have made willingly."

We got a bad case of the giggles until my brother said, "How do you know you're not your other me?" He flashed a quick smile.

"I don't," I said. "You up for relaxing by the pool?"

240

"That will make for a perfect morning," Cordy said.

"Afternoon," I corrected.

I chose lounge chairs far away from the groups of Dread in the area. A waitress stopped by for our order.

"Bloody Mary," Cordy said. "Spicy as a mother fucker."

"Same," I said, "but hold the mother fucker. Oh, and a cappuccino."

"I'll have a coffee," Cordy said.

"Black or with cream?"

"Black with cream."

That confused the waitress.

"I have a birthday present for you," I said.

"Last night was way more than you should have spent."

"It's not monetary. We've been wondering what to do with the downstairs entryway. I'm going to let you turn it into a game room."

Cordy sprung to his feet and jumped in the air. "Yes! You are so awesome. Thank you."

"You can go as crazy as you want."

I gave Cordy the room for selfish reasons. He was always playing video games on our TV. I never got to watch my shows.

Within a week, he created a gaming area with two comfy loungers and a brand new fifty-inch flatscreen. My contribution was a high-end wireless headset so I wouldn't have to listen to the noise all day.

After seeing how nice Cordy made the room, Dad bought him an Addam's Family pinball machine. We'd discovered the game on one of our outings. In true Dad fashion, he purchased a broken one they could fix together. The toolbox he assembled for the project was impressive. There were all sorts of lights and electronic parts. Cordy was psyched, rooting through the kit.

"Look, sis, a soldering iron."

I just shook my head.

The game room ended up having a positive effect on Cordy and Grandpa's relationship. They enjoyed playing video golf together, especially on the Scottish links. It took a while to learn the controls, but Grandpa was getting pretty good. The generational bond made giving up the space worth it. Most of all, I had the upstairs living room back. Funny thing, all my complaints about not being able to watch my shows were for naught. I spent most of my time on the sofa, reading. That was the only time Clio would hang out with me. She liked the quiet.

Chapter 13

People may not know the eighteenth-century poet Robert Burns, but they've probably sung his poem Auld Lang Syne on New Year's Eve. I had a bad feeling about attending his birthday celebration but felt less safe having the family go without me. The event was held in a private club by the Seattle Center. I thought Dad was kidding about bringing scotch, but every table had multiple bottles. The liquor made for a boisterous crowd. Not that Scots need much encouragement.

We arrived early enough to snag a spot near an exit. The table I selected was stage left, next to an open passageway. I scanned the hall intensely, not just for danger but wondering if any of the attendees were kin.

A procession of four plates of haggis was marched down the center aisle by proud gentlemen in kilts. Playing them in was a trio of pipers with a drummer rigorously keeping time. The pomp and circumstance had Cordy and me giggling madly, which brought on *the stare* from Dad.

"Show some respect," he snapped.

The Master of Ceremony, Carl, had absurdly long eyebrows, which was a thing of envy from the men at my table. What was odd was Carl's strong German surname of Zimmerman. He gave an endearing toast to the haggis. It seemed a little over the top for ground meat cooked in a sheep's stomach.

I didn't dare look at Cordy. He was grunting and choking as he tried to stifle his laughter. Cordy held steady until the conversations resumed to an energetic level, then burst out in hysterics and left the table. His laughter carried from way back in the foyer. Cordy returned, but one look at me, and he spun on his heels, laughing away. The side hall he was in amplified his laughter.

"Get out," a female voice said. I looked around, confused. Was that an Italian accent? The warning repeated more urgently, and I realized it was inside my head. The surge of panic in my veins was enough to get me up.

"Everyone, out of the building!" I yelled. No one moved. "Get out!"

I lifted Grandpa by his armpits. Dad popped to a standing position and snatched his bottle of scotch from the table. In the hall, I shouted for Cordy to run.

We made it thirty yards out the back exit when an explosion blew us off our feet. Flames shot from the building as debris drifted in slow motion to the ground. A ringing in my ears blanketed the world in white noise. No one was emerging from the ruins. I gathered my family, and we headed to the car. Dad held onto his scotch with a death grip.

"Cordy," he cried.

"We have to go," I said, coaxing him along. I looked over my shoulder. The back half of the hall was missing. My brother was dead.

At the car, Grandpa seemed disoriented. I helped him into the passenger seat.

Dad wouldn't start the engine.

"We have to leave," I said through my sobbing.

Someone slammed into my window. A dark face peered in the car. It was Cordy, his head caked in soot. Tears had streaked away the ash under his eyes.

"Son!" Dad cried in relief as the family piled out of the car.

"How did you make it out?" Cordy said, wiping away the last of his tears.

Grandpa pointed at me. I wasn't about to explain the voice in my head.

"How did *you* get out?" I asked.

"I went for a smoke with the coat check girl."

"Holy shit, cigarettes saved your life. Where's the girl?"

"She was handing me her number when the blast knocked her into the bushes. I got the hell out of there."

"Well, I still don't like you smoking," Dad said.

"I love you too," Cordy said.

"Come on, let's go before the police arrive," Grandpa said.

We climbed into the car and drove the back streets to the freeway.

"All those Scots," Grandpa wailed. "They're dead because of us."

My phone rang. The number was from a foreign country.

"Hello," I said hesitantly.

"Hi, Bailey, this is Support. Is your family safe?" It was the same Italian woman who warned me about the bomb. I was talking to a witch, a strega.

"We're all safe," I said.

"La famiglia è al sicuro," the strega said to someone with her. "There is a lot of Dread movement in your area. Find a discreet hotel for your family. A sniper killed the couple that bought your last home."

"Holy fuck, OK."

"It doesn't appear the Dread know where you live. To be safe, we should move your family."

"Thank you for letting me know. We'll find a place to hunker down. And thank you for the warning about the bomb."

The woman ended the call without responding.

My phone vibrated with an IM from Stefano. "It's Support again," I said.

Janis, are you OK?

I think so.

Thank God. Don't go home.
I've heard terrible things.

We're heading to a safe
house. I can't talk right
now.

Something bad is
happening. Let's run away,
you and I.

I can't leave my family in
danger.

We'll bring them with us.
Please.

I'll think about it. I love you.

I love you too. More than
anything in the world. Be
safe.

Chapter 14

I was on the tail end of a munition run in Idaho. The drive was solo, but not by choice. Stefano wasn't answering my messages.

Support texted me earlier that I should head back to the house. They must have cleared it.

The return trip from Idaho was like a trek through molasses-soaked sand. Each mile ventured became more tedious than the last. Having to obey the speed limit was a nightmare of patience.

My street came into view, and I was relieved that the journey was nearly complete. Our family hadn't been home for a week. It was nice pulling into the driveway.

Stepping around my car, I was overcome with the Touch. A Dread was motionless somewhere inside my home. He was well into the change, but I couldn't get a fix on his location. The monster could be anywhere. I unholstered my pistol and took cover. Keeping tight to the house, I sidled up to my door and peeked inside. The kitchen appeared empty, but the Dread could be hiding out of sight.

I unlocked the deadbolt as quietly as possible and entered. The downstairs bathroom was clear. So was the kitchen. A floorboard creaked under my footing, and the Dread's location crystallized. He was on the other side of the wall, sitting in a chair in Dad's basement. The Dread looked around groggily and tried to stand, but his arms and legs were bound. Clio hissed in that direction. I turned to head for the door and saw a note taped to my fridge.

Bailey,

That Dread from the storage unit tracked us down again. He has your brother. We've gone to rescue him. There's a Dread in the basement. He says he knows you. Kill it. We need to have a long talk.

Dad

Clio stared at me with apprehension. She looked scared, as scared as a cat can emote. I'm sure I was showing enough for both of us. I grabbed her treats and scattered a handful on the floor.

"Stefano?" I called out from the basement entrance.

"Hello, Janis." His voice was strange, gravely. I crept over to get a peek. Stefano was in a chair, bound in chains to the radiator. There were cuts and bruises all over his body. My family had done a number on him, although it felt as if he was enjoying the torture.

"Come closer," he hissed. Stefano was all Dread. Except for the evil tracers rising from his body, nothing physical changed about him, yet I no longer recognized the man in front of me.

"Are you in there, baby?" I hesitantly asked as I inched closer. He was lusting to kill me. The thirst was so intense I could almost read his thoughts.

"Get me out of these," the Stefano creature snapped. He fought with his chains to the point of drawing blood.

I was repelled by what he'd become. The evil poured from him like poison. I embraced my courage and approached. There was only one way to bring him back, but I wasn't sure I could do it. Keeping what I thought was a safe distance, I unbuckled his belt. He struck fast, biting me on my shoulder.

248

"What the fuck?" I said, pushing his head away. "Back off." He'd broken the skin. Blood was soaking through my T-shirt in an oval teeth-mark pattern.

A firm wrenching on the chain cinched his neck back. The Stefano creature growled at me like a demon.

I unbuttoned his Levi's and shimmied them and his underwear down. He had pissed himself. The stench was unbearable. I cleansed him with a rag, but it wasn't helping. Soap and a dousing with a bucket of water did the trick, although it enraged the Stefano monster.

Stroking his flaccid penis wasn't working. I fingered myself seductively. This visual usually resulted in an instant rise from Stefano, but the curse was fighting against the cure.

I took his cock in my mouth and let his senses guide the pleasure. His nerve endings sparked in flight, but he still wasn't fully erect. Stefano's smug expression got the worst of me. I wrapped my hand around his neck to choke the look off his face. His cock grew instantly hard. Seizing the opportunity, I straddled him.

"You disgust me," the Stefano creature said.

"I love you, too," I responded and dug my finger into the wound on his chest. He moaned in delight but covered his enjoyment with a scowl.

I rode his cock high, focusing on the head while steadying his shaft with my hand. My thrusts were strong and fierce. I needed him to come.

"Let's have another taste." He wriggled in my grasp, biting at the air.

I could feel his orgasm approaching.

"You're fucking ugly," he said.

The remark was crushing, but I kept my pace. It wasn't Stefano saying those horrible things. I squeezed my muscles around the head of his cock and felt him unload inside me.

His release was like a curtain rising in the morning. A bright ray of energy swept away Stefano's anger. Within minutes my boyfriend was back, and I removed his chains.

"I am so sorry, Janis," he said, rubbing the feeling into his sore wrists. "I was a passenger in my body. Why did your family do this?"

"I don't know," I said.

Stefano veered his eyes from mine in shame. I grabbed the back of his head with both hands and brought his lips close. He turned away.

"I've been here for days. My breath."

I didn't care and kissed him anyway. Stefano pressed his forehead to mine and held onto me.

"How did you end up at my house?" I said.

"My family is tired of running. I came here to warn you. Things grew fuzzy after that." He rubbed the back of his head.

"Your uncle has my brother. My dad and grandpa are out looking for him. They left a note in my kitchen."

"Shit, hang on." Stefano tried his phone, but there were no bars. We moved to the backyard, and he dialed.

"Why would you think I was dead? It's OK, Pop. I'm fine." He listened to his father intently. "I'm on my way. Stall. I need to explain something important. Promise that you'll wait for me before you do anything. Dad? Dad?"

"Fuck, I lost the signal." He stared at the phone. "Your family is walking into a trap. We have to get to the woods by North Bend, to this old hunting cabin." He held me by the shoulders reassuringly. "We'll make this right."

"We have to. They're the only family I have."

I led Stefano to Cordy's room to fetch some clothes. He showered while I packed a small arsenal. Who knows what we were heading into. I had to guess at the inventory. Clio stepped into the Lair and rubbed upon me lovingly. Now I knew she was concerned.

The time it took Stefano to shower was military fast. When I returned to my bedroom, he was already in pants. The cuts on his chest were bad, especially the one I molested.

"I should dress those wounds," I said.

"No time."

"We'll do it on the way," I said and kissed him on the cheek.

We planned on driving in Stefano's Audi, but it was gone. I ran back inside for my keys.

At the base of I90, I looked over at Stefano, frustrated. "I just drove down this freeway."

"And we'll drive down it again," he said.

"I need to know something. How did you know where I lived?"

His heartbeat raced. "I was stationed across from Harborview waiting for a stabbing victim when I saw your family pull in."

"What the fuck! Did your family stab my Grandfather?"

He looked me straight in the eyes. "That wasn't us. I was contacted by the family that did. They needed help watching the hospitals. No one thought a Hunter would go to the main trauma center. I went there to humor them."

"We had to go. He was dying. How did you find the house? I would have felt you."

"I put a tracker on your car and removed it once you came back to the hospital. Your brother almost caught me. He was back out so fast."

"How did Uncle Tony find us?"

"Who knows?"

"I don't like this."

"I don't either. I had to know where your house was in case anyone was talking about it."

Stefano and I parked behind his Audi. The hood was warm, offering hope that Dad and Grandpa were close.

We weren't that far into the trail when I sensed a Dread standing guard.

"Hold up," I whispered. "One of the Cursed is up ahead."

"I'll take care of this." Stefano sprinted down the path to intervene. I tried to get his attention, to tell him I had a stun gun, but he took off so fast.

From around the corner came, "Holy shit, cousin. You scared the crap out of me." I couldn't make out the rest of the conversation. Stefano was handed a pistol. He swung fast, driving the butt into the back of his cousin's head. The pain of the impact was excruciating. My connection fluctuated as his cousin drifted in and out of consciousness. The man threw his arms out protectively as Stefano delivered a final blow. My legs gave as his cousin hobbled backward, falling to the ground, and our bond was lost.

I ran down the path to find Stefano tying his cousin's hands behind his back with the man's belt. I recognized him from Stefano's room in Vegas. I covered his mouth with a strip of duct tape.

"Knocking a person out is a lot harder than it looks in the movies," Stefano said.

"Tell me about it," I said, rubbing the back of my head.

"Oh my God, you felt that, didn't you?"

"Yeah," I said, unable to hide the trauma.

He leaned over and kissed the top of my head.

His cousin woke up, and a dull pain throbbed from my head. We both winced, and I raised my hands gingerly to the back of my skull, expecting a lump.

His cousin looked at Stefano, confused, and then over at me. A stifled, "What the hell?" came through the tape.

"His pupils are normal," I said, "You didn't hurt him too badly."

"Sorry, Marco. I'm in love with a Huntress. We're here to end this."

His cousin quit struggling but kept looking back and forth between us.

"I have to knock you out," I said, breaking into my medical kit to find a syringe. "This is the good stuff. You'll like it."

I used Marco's weight on his license to adjust the Fentanyl dosage. With the drugs administered, I backed away so I wouldn't go with him. I felt Marco's and my pain drift into a void, and then there was one. I checked Marco's wrist, concerned, but found a slow pulse.

"He's out," I said.

We removed the restraints and rolled him onto his side.

"He said that my uncle Carlino is on sniper. Dude's aim is dead on."

I had a terrible thought. Did his uncle shoot the couple who bought our last house?

It was a few miles to his uncle's position. We jogged the whole way.

"We're close." I bent over to catch my breath. "Your uncle is up the hill on the right."

"How do we get the upper hand?" Stefano said. "He was a Navy SEAL."

"Do you think you could distract him so I can get a shot with my stun gun?"

"If we spook him, we're dead. I should go at this alone."

"All right." I pulled the gun from my pack. "You have one chance, so keep your finger off the trigger until you have a clear shot."

"Is it strong enough? Carlino is tough. I saw him walk away from a car wreck as if nothing happened."

"He'll go down and stay down. We tested it on my father. He was knocked right the fuck out, and he's a big guy. Hit him anywhere there's muscle."

"I can do this," Stefano said, taking the stun gun from me.

"Do you know your uncle's weight?" I asked as I prepped my supplies.

"One ninety?" he said, not sounding confident.

"You have to be sure. Too strong a dose will kill him."

"One eighty," he said.

I adjusted the dosage between the two and placed the syringe back in my supply box.

"Stunning your uncle may knock me out," I said. "Have you ever given an injection?"

"Never," he said.

"Shit. If you have to, find a prominent vein in the crease of the elbow."

We made our way along the path, making sure not to step on any branches or twigs. It was slow going, which was nerve-wracking. Every second counted.

Uncle Carlino was ahead of us. "He's about a hundred yards away," I whispered. "Up the hill on the right. He's lying on his stomach with the sniper rifle lined up in front of him. I can feel his hands on it."

"I love you." He gave me a quick kiss.

"I love you too."

Stefano hiked up the hill and called out for his uncle.

"Leo, come up here," Uncle Carlino said. "Shit's about to go down."

We weren't too late. An odd jolt in my chest synched my muscles in a continuous pulse. Stefano's uncle dropped. I almost fell with him but used all my strength to power up the hill.

An abundance of the Touch overloaded my senses. A horde of Dread was assembled below. We had reached the cabin.

Carlino was painted in forest colors and wore what looked like a coverall made of ferns. I flipped him over and pinned his arms behind his back. Stefano slapped a piece of duct tape on him so he couldn't warn the others.

"Can you get the probes out," I said through clenched teeth. Being so close, I was nearly incapacitated.

Stefano yanked on the wires and my strength came back, but so did Carlino's. He wrestled under me.

Finding a vein on his camouflaged arms was a challenge. I tapped in a spot where I thought there should be one. With a quick thrust, I jammed the needle in, but he moved, and I sunk into his flesh.

"Quit struggling," I said. "I need to knock you out. If I mess this up, you could die. That will be on you."

"You'll be fine," Stefano said to him.

His uncle struggled more, and I drilled my knee into his back. The pain was excruciating. Carlino let out a muffled scream and relaxed his arm.

I found a vein and plunged the needle home. Stefano secured his uncle so I could back away. Seconds later, he was out. Stefano and I fell on the dirt, exhausted.

I looked through the rifle's scope. The crosshairs were centered on Cordy's forehead. He appeared more irritated than scared. I shifted the barrel to the left and adjusted the view wider. A crowd was in the field below, next to a rustic cabin. Dad had his gun to someone's head. To my horror, I realized it was Stefano's grandfather. Bepa's Glock was aimed at Stefano's father. The rest of the Cursed had their guns drawn on my family. We were grossly outnumbered. Stefano and I needed to get down there fast.

I checked Carlino for additional weapons. A gun was strapped to his side and one on his calf. I rolled him onto his stomach, and he disappeared in his fern camouflage. We hid the sniper rifle and followed the path leading to the cabin.

"You should know that my dad has a gun pressed to your grandfather's head."

"What? No?" he said, stepping up his pace. I grabbed his arm to hold him back.

"Our wits have to remain intact," I said, repeating a lesson from Grandpa. "We'll get everyone out of this. And for your information, your uncle Tony and half your family have their guns on my father."

We were close. I could feel every movement the Dread were making. It was overwhelming. Thankfully the danger was all in the field. I crept up to the side of the cabin and peered through a slit in the tall fence. Dad and Stefano's grandfather were on the other side.

"You're all murderers," my dad said.

"If you kill a killer, the number of killers is still the same," Stefano's father countered.

"But not the number of victims," Dad said.

"Killing is our curse," Stefano's father responded. "What's your excuse?"

"Don't play games with me. This guy killed my wife."

I looked over at Stefano, shocked. Had his grandpa killed my mother?

"I didn't kill her," Stefano's grandfather said. "That was you."

"Liar!" my father yelled and drilled the muzzle painfully into his temple.

"Yours was the only shot," Stefano's dad shouted. "His gun jammed. You killed your wife. Your bullet ricocheted and struck her. It was an accident."

"That's not true," Dad said, crying out.

It couldn't be true.

"The bullet hole is still in the wall. Stick a pencil in it. You'll see the trajectory could not have come from us."

256

"Don't mess with me," my dad said. "I will bring wrath upon you like you've never known."

"My son speaks the truth," Stefano's grandfather said. "She didn't suffer. I doubt she even knew what happened."

My dad cocked his gun.

"You're outnumbered," a man said. "We have a sniper on the hill aiming at your son's head."

"Just kill them," Uncle Tony said.

Holy fucking shit!

Stefano ran around the side of the fence. "Stop. You need to listen to me." My grandfather lined his gun on him.

"Don't hurt him," I yelled to Bepa.

"She's a Huntress," a man said.

Stefano leaped in front of me as a shot rang out. I felt the bullet strike him in the chest. As we were falling, the air filled with the thunderous roar of firepower. The Dread were dropping one by one, disappearing from my radar. Stefano faded, and the world grew dark as I followed him into the void.

I woke up in Stefano's arms. His body was lifeless. I couldn't feel anything inside of him, and not just him; I couldn't sense anyone.

The woods were eerily silent. Cordy was the only one standing, but that was because he was tied in that position. His head hung lifelessly to his side. Bodies were strewn across the field. There was no movement anywhere. Everyone I knew and loved was gone. Everyone.

Chapter 15

I shook Stefano and screamed, "Wake up!" His head rolled lifelessly to the side. "Don't leave me here alone," I wailed and fell on top of him, crying.

Was that a breath I felt? I brought my face to his, and Stefano's eyelids fluttered. I thought it was my imagination, but his eyes opened partway.

"My sweet baby," I cried.

He grasped my arm, and I held onto him, sobbing. I could feel his chest rise, but that was all. There wasn't the slightest hint of the Mirror's Touch. Our connection was lost.

I looked around. Everyone was still, Stefano's family, my family. I buried my head in my boyfriend's chest and cried. Blood from his wound drenched my face.

"Janis, check this out," Stefano said, physically turning my head. A bullet was floating above us, hanging in the air.

"Are we dead?" I asked. Had I been hit? Stefano reached for the bullet.

"Don't touch that," a woman's voice warned in an Italian accent. Stefano retracted his hand.

Two women emerged from the woods as if materializing from thin air. They were dressed in flowing outfits and adorned in earthy necklaces and bracelets. One of the women wore dark clothing from a bygone era. Her partner's hair was long and blonde, accenting her beige dress. They had a natural beauty and exuded confidence on a level far exceeding anyone I'd ever known. These were clearly witches.

The strega in dark clothing reached us. Her medium-length black hairdo was perfectly coiffed but looked as if she woke up that way effortlessly. The strega was around thirty with flawless skin. She had a warm oval face with a robust, rounded nose that matched her chin. Her eyes and arched brows were her dominant feature.

There was a small wooden box in her hand. She opened the lid and moved the box under the bullet; it dropped inside. She walked through the area, collecting all the floating rounds.

The blonde strega approached and kneeled in the grass next to Stefano. I was comforted and terrified by her all at once. She had the kind, weathered face of an elementary school teacher. Her dark fiery eyes expressed who was in charge. She lifted Stefano's shirt and waved her hand over the bullet hole in a slow circle. He groaned in pain.

"Hold still. It will be over soon."

"Oh God, no, help him," I pleaded.

"That is what I am doing, my child."

The woman's hand shook rhythmically, and the back of the bullet emerged from the wound. It wavered as if stuck, then flew to her hand. She redirected its path with an invisible force from her fingers, and the strega in black captured it in the box.

"You're losing him," the woman in black said.

"I know."

I rushed to Stefano's side but the blonde strega pushed me away. She placed one hand upon his back and pressed the other to his chest. Her words were from an unfamiliar dialect. I realized it was a spell when a flash of blue shot from her palm. The witch fell backward, knocked out.

Stefano took in a loud breath. I wiped the blood away from his chest but found no bullet hole. I checked his other wounds, and they were all gone. Even the scar on his cheek had vanished. The woman began to stir.

"I feel fantastic," Stefano said, propping himself up on his elbows. "Who are you?"

"I am Nera, The Priestess of Death," the strega in black said from across the way. "This is Bianca, our High Priestess.

Their names were aliases. Nera means black in Italian, and Bianca is white. "You are streghe?" I said.

"That we are."

Stefano looked at the bodies in the field. "Can you save our families? Please!"

"They are fine," the High Priestess said. "We have them in…" She looked at Nera. "Animazione sospesa?"

"Suspended animation," I translated and burst into a warbled cry.

"What is this?" Stefano said, wiping at the tears streaming from his eyes.

"You're feeling for the first time," the High Priestess responded.

"I can't feel anything," I said about the Mirror's Touch.

"That is because the curse is broken," the Priestess of Death said.

"Broken?" Stefano said, confused. "How?"

"Through your love. We waited a thousand years for a Huntress and the Cursed to perform a selfless act in… it's like together. Tandem."

"A thousand years," the High Priestess said, exasperated. "Taking a bullet for your love was the most selfless act I have witnessed. Janis, yours was freeing Uncle Tony, knowing it could bring great risk to your family."

The witches were using the names we called each other. They had been monitoring more than I was aware.

"Why would you wait so long?" Stefano said. "Couldn't you just tell us to do a selfless act?"

"Because then it wouldn't be selfless."

"I don't understand how you got here so fast," I said.

The High Priestess smiled at me, her eyes all-knowing. "I can transcend time and space. We stood by

261

while these three days played out, hoping the ending was as Nera foresaw."

"It was your voice that warned me of the explosion," I said.

The woman nodded toward the Priestess of Death.

"Thank you," I said to the woman. "Thank you so much. Did you help us in the woods? Detaining Stefano's family seemed too easy."

"Would you like me to say no?" the High Priestess said. "Or tell you we had nothing to do with his gay brother walking away from his post to take a nap in the woods?"

I laughed, but thoughts of what could have been shut me up.

"We also remove evidence from your kills. You Hunters can be careless."

"I thought we were thorough," I said.

"Something is always left behind," the High Priestess said. "A strand of hair, a flake of skin." The last part was spoken in Italian.

She reached out and held Stefano's hands. "I apologize for the streghe's curse. We are sorry for the horror your lineage has gone through. For a thousand years, there hasn't been a day that wasn't filled with regret. On behalf of all streghe, I apologize profusely. I know that won't help, but it is hopefully a start."

Stefano couldn't control his tears. The High Priestess gathered him in tenderly.

"Let it out," the Priestess of Death said. "You have a lifetime of emotions built up."

Stefano managed to pull himself together. The High Priestess approached me. "I thank you for your dedication and drive. Your kin truly is the fiercest of the fierce."

"It was both an honor and a nightmare," I said.

"You have a favor to ask," the High Priestess said, gazing into my soul.

262

"I do. Is there any way you can make everyone forget that Dad was the one who shot my mother?"

"You have a kind heart. Gather up all the guns and bury the ammo. When the task is complete, none of you will remember that terrible day."

"Thank you." I helped Stefano to his feet.

"I want you to know that I tried everything to change your mother's life path," the Priestess of Death said. "She was needed elsewhere. Your mother is special."

The strega's words struck heavily. My mom is so special she was needed elsewhere. As much as I missed her, that helped, especially knowing there was an elsewhere.

The Priestess of Death strolled with me, pointing out the weapons on people's bodies. She could see them as if they glowed from under the clothing. By the time we had all the rounds safely buried, I forgot what we were talking about. It was something to do with my father.

The streghe had us move our families into the hunting cabin. We placed the elders in chairs, and the rest were leaned against the far wall. The Priestess of Death locked the door and checked that the windows were secure.

"Change of plans," the High Priestess said, "We may need guns as a deterrent. You are a rowdy group. Each of you choose a gun. But no bullets. Enough with the violence."

I almost corrected her misuse of bullets but didn't want to sound like my father.

Stefano went straight for an AR-15.

"Dad won't let us have those," I said, taking it from him. "He thinks they promote murder."

"Don't all guns?"

"No," I said and handed him an empty Glock. "This is the one that most cops prefer."

After clearing my weapon, we returned to the cabin. Stefano and I stood as a barrier between our families.

The High Priestess began chanting with the wooden box raised eye-level. Her upper torso weaved in a circle, following the flow of her words. Our families sat up and swayed in succession. They raised their heads as one and opened their eyes. The visual was unnerving.

The High Priestess smiled warmly. "Please, remain seated," she said. "You are all safe."

My Dad rushed to his feet and searched for his pistol.

"Dad," I said, holding my hand out to make him stop. "It's cool. Just sit down and listen. You're freaking everyone out. Sit down."

"Fine," he said in frustration.

"Everything's all right," Stefano reassured his family. They were looking around nervously and checking themselves for wounds. "This is Janis. I'm in love with a Huntress. She's my rock, my groove."

"What the fuck!" Cordy said.

"Dude, just chill," I said.

"You sneaky little bitch," my father said.

"Really, Dad?"

"This is a time for celebration, not fighting," Bianca said. "Please, introduce us?"

I tucked the Glock into the back of my waistband. "This is Bianca. She's a High Priestess. Over in the corner is Nera, the Priestess of Death."

Nera emerged from the shadows and the families gasped.

"They're Sicilian witches, streghe. Bianca and Nera have graced us with their presence in a grand act of peace. Our war is over. The curse is no more." I was expecting a cheer, but there was only confusion.

"Thank you, Bailey," the High Priestess said, using a name Stefano had never heard. Although, in all fairness, he hadn't told me he was now Leo.

Bianca glanced at me as if she could read my thoughts. She turned back to the families. "It is true. The thousand-year spell has lifted. The Dark Times are over." She explained what Stefano and I did to break the spell and brought the families up to speed. The Rosotti's were having an easier time dealing with the news. Probably because they understood it was a curse that caused all our problems. The men who had been afflicted were overcome with emotion. My family looked at them like they were weak.

"You don't believe me?" the High Priestess said to my brother.

"Well, yeah. Witches. Spells?"

"The Mirror's Touch is gone," I said. "I don't feel anyone in this room."

"I'll prove it." Stefano pulled a hunting knife from my bag. My dad jumped up.

"Dad, Jesus. Chill," I said.

Stefano stood with his back to mine. "Did you feel that?"

"Huh?" I looked behind me. "Oh, honey, what have you done?

Stefano had cut a deep gash in the top of his forearm. Tears streamed down his face from the pain. The families were stunned into silence, realizing I hadn't felt it. He held his arm out to the High Priestess to heal it.

She shook her head. "I can't fix what is self-inflicted."

Stefano searched for something to use as a tourniquet.

"Let me have that knife," my grandpa said.

Without thinking, Stefano handed it to him. Grandpa cut out a large section of his T-shirt.

"I can help you with that, son," my dad said and rose. I nodded. Grandpa passed the fabric over and tossed the knife to the floor by my bag.

After my father dressed the wound, he hugged Stefano. The gesture was monumental, as the men in my family are not huggers. Stefano put everything into his embrace. I imagine it was the first one he fully understood.

"Hey, Cody," I said. "I can prove they're witches."

"How?" he said, folding his arms defiantly.

"The doors are locked. Where did they go?"

He looked around. The streghe had vanished.

"Holy fuck!"

"We'll need the Dread to refrain from sex, so we know for sure the spell is broken," Grandpa said, then grimaced. "I apologize. That sounded like an order. Can you please refrain from sex so we know that the curse is over? If it is, we'll celebrate with a truce."

Stefano's grandfather joined Bepa. He wore a tidy white beard with a sweeping haircut. If it weren't for the debris in his hair, he would look like an aging model. "Our boys will do the test, that you can be sure. There *will* be a great celebration."

"Look, no disrespect to your grandfather," Stefano whispered, "but you and I are waiting a day for this test to begin." He took my hand and led me to the door. It had always been me who initiated this simple act of affection. All I felt from Stefano was regular human contact, and I couldn't be happier.

At the door, I turned to face the room. "We had to knock out Carlino and Marco. We'll leave them by the trail. Their empty weapons will be hidden a few feet away. Don't give the men anything. Just let 'em sleep off the Fentanyl. The witches sent the third man into the woods for a nap. Do you know where he was posted?"

"I do," Stefano's Grandfather said.

Our families followed us from the cabin as we left.

266

"Wait!" Stefano's grandfather said as we headed for the trail. "Thank you. Thank you both." The families surrounded us in a group hug.

"I appreciate the love," Stefano said, "but Janis and I need to be alone."

"Your knives are in my bag," I said patting it, so my family wouldn't obsessively search for them and find the ammo.

"Bailey," Dad called out and threw the keys to the Audi. I tossed him mine.

At the crest of the hill, Stefano paused and held my chin softly. "I love you, Janis."

"I love you, too. More than anything."

"Do you feel the connection?" he said.

"I have always felt the connection."

"That's just it. Even though I forced emotion, the connection was always there. Our love is real. It wasn't a spell."

We had finished moving his cousin to the trail when tears welled in Stefano's eyes. "I had to fake so much." He lowered his eyes, fighting back the tears, and met mine again. "I didn't want to lose you."

"Honey, because you tried so hard, it made you act better than a lot of men. Your effort made me love you more."

"Away from you, I was such a prick. I just didn't care."

"You couldn't care."

"I was so horrible," he said and bawled.

Stefano was an ugly crier, and I appreciated him more for it. He cried a lifetime until his sides hurt. He apologized for his weakness, but I put my finger to his lips.

My family passed us earlier on the trail. I was glad they left first. The emotions back at the cabin were surely flowing as the Reckoning struck the Cursed.

"Let me get that arm taken care of," I said.

After cleaning the wound, it took twelve stitches and a layer of surgical glue to seal it. Stefano cut himself deep. He enjoyed the tears from the pain.

We walked in blessed silence — a sense of calm talking hold.

"So, is Bailey your birth name?" Stefano said. "The streghe called you that."

"No, that's the name I was given in Seattle. For safety, I was never told my birth name. I know I'm a Cameron."

"Until you find out, do you want me to call you Janis or Bailey?"

"Janis is fine."

"My name is Gian Perroni Lombardo."

I dug the name Gian. It was unique.

After a stop to purchase bottles of celebratory Prosecco, Gian drove me straight to his place east of Capitol Hill. The building was an early twentieth-century brick structure with a grass courtyard behind tall stone walls.

We rushed inside. Gian was eager to have sex, where we were on equal footing.

"Welcome to my crib," he said, holding the door for me.

He lived in a trendy one-bedroom condo on the third level. The door was solid steel, with thick metal lining the hall-facing wall. It was applied artistically, but I knew why it was there. The Dread understood the shielding qualities of metal.

I loved the original hardwood floors and the arched doorways in his living room. Gian removed large metal plates from his windows. Light came flooding in. The thought of him living in the dark made me sad.

He put on a CD that was a mixture of reggae and classical guitar. The relaxing vibe was a pleasant release. I noticed he had a balcony and walked outside. His place butted up to a patch of evergreens.

"That maple is gorgeous, but it's nothing compared to you," he said, making fun of his younger self. It got him laughing. He was genuinely laughing. I think he realized what was happening because he burst into tears.

"This does remind me of your uncle's condo," I said.

"The view is what sold me," he said, handing me my glass along with a white dress shirt. "Although I don't get to come out here much."

I tossed my bloody top on the floor.

"Did I do that?" He touched the bite mark on my shoulder.

I put on his shirt to cover it up. "That wasn't you," I said and buttoned low to make room for my chest.

He kissed my wound through the fabric. "To a long life."

"I'll drink to that," I said, toasting with the Prosecco. It tasted of victory. "Do you mind if we chill for a while? That was a hell of a day."

"Not at all."

Gian headed to his room while I relaxed in one of his comfortable patio chairs. He returned with a warm washcloth and tenderly wiped the remnants of his blood from my face. I'd missed a little when we cleaned up in the stream at the base of the trail.

"Can you believe we ended the Dark Times?" he said.

"They were dark fucking times," I said. "What should we call this? The Light?"

"The Blithe," he said.

"Is that from a prophecy?"

269

"Prophecy? No, I just came up with the name. The word in the positive means happy or joyous."

The definition has a darker meaning, but I thought it fit with all the shit we'd gone through. "To the Blithe," I said. "Long last the happiness."

I kissed Gian and found it to be my favorite part of losing the Touch. Feeling my own tongue was always strange. I chased his around, not knowing where it would lead. Our passion boiled over.

"I'm gonna rip that shirt off you," he said.

My muscles synched as my heart raced. "Please don't. I had a bad experience a few years back."

He rested his forehead to mine. "We can stop if you need to."

"I'm OK," I said.

"We're going to talk about this another day."

"Thank you." I liked this new thoughtful boyfriend.

He lifted my shirt gently off. I kissed him and worked his over his head, then undid his pants, pulling his cock free. All I could feel was its girth and hardness. The heat rising off it brought his scent across my face, drawing me in. I slipped him into my mouth and slid my tongue along the soft edge of the head.

"We should probably go inside," Gian said.

I looked around at the surrounding porches. An older gentleman in the adjacent condo was pretending he hadn't been watching. I waved Gian's dick at him. He nodded with a wink.

"That's a nice cock you have there," the man said.

"Thanks, Don," my boyfriend said, embarrassed.

Gian took my hand and led me to his bedroom. Mounted on the ceiling was a scratched-up skateboard with lightbulbs for wheels.

"That board saved my life. Every day it shines its luck upon me."

A painting of a European town nestled into a mountainous landscape drew me in. "Is this village real?"

"That's Novara di Sicilia. Of all the paintings in my room, you chose the town of my ancestors."

"Your village is gorgeous," I said.

"I want to travel there someday." He was lost in the painting.

"The world is ours. We can do whatever we want."

Gian backed me into the bed and I fell onto the mattress. He worked my pants off aggressively. His mouth was on me, but I wanted my share. I rolled him to his back and flipped myself around to take his magnificent cock in my mouth. My hips sank in appreciation to his face.

The sixty-nine position was too much with the Touch. Now I could enjoy it. I stroked and sucked him, pausing briefly to focus on whatever creative trick he was performing.

Even though I lost the Mirror's Touch, I could feel Gian's energy, his passion. I slowed my oral offense as he kicked his into high gear. The more he worked himself up, the harder it was for me to concentrate. His drive to satisfy fed my soul, nourishing my release. A warmth flowed inside my body, and I thrust my head back, noticing the galaxy projecting on his ceiling. I literally saw stars as I came. That made me laugh at the same time as I orgasmed. The added joy was a magical elixir.

"How was that?" Gian asked, his face glistening.

"It was brilliant," I said in a daze. "More."

Gian was eager to please. He brought me to orgasm a record three additional times before I was begging for his cock to be inside me.

I threw him onto his back and straddled his hips, driving him home. The absence of the Touch further highlighted what was happening to me. I felt him everywhere.

"It's still incredible," I said. "Better. I can feel everything you're doing to me."

271

Gian reveled in the magnitude of my comment.

I was overcome with a hunger I never experienced. I wanted his cum. Was this a side effect of the curse lifting, or was I just really worked up?

"Tell me when you're close." I slid the tip of my tongue out with a smile.

"Really?"

"Yeah," I said, raising my eyebrows with a sinister smile.

He lasted another fifteen minutes. "It's coming," he moaned.

I slid off him and dove for his cock, shoving it in my mouth. Once there, I panicked. This may have been a mistake, but it was too late to back out.

He squeezed my head in a warning and came in a fury across my tongue. I liked the taste, the texture; everything about his cum was delectable as if it was made specifically for me.

Ten minutes later, he was raring to go for a second round.

Gian mounted me from behind. We must have fucked for an hour before my release came knocking. I wasn't about to fake it with him. I would have gone all night if I had to.

I was perched above his headboard with Gian pressing me tight against the wall, driving into me forcefully.

"I'm close," I said.

He kept the pace, exhausted. Without the feel from his perspective, I could bring myself to new heights. Each time I clenched my muscles against his thrusts, my clit would throb deeply. Streaming trails of electricity shot across my core.

Gian was a machine. His eyes were closed as he pounded into me, a smile spread wide. I stared at his beautiful face, thankful for how lucky I was to have him in my life. Thankful for the curse to be lifted. Thankful to be free.

"Keep going," I said.

He was so exhausted all he could say was, "OK. OK."

My orgasm exploded into a full-body tremble. I screamed out as Gian concentrated in short, determined thrusts. I pressed my forehead to his shoulder and crumpled inward as the contractions gripped Gian's cock tightly. He pulled out and fell backward onto the mattress, taking me with him. I wrapped my arms around him and we both burst into blissful tears.

He couldn't stop. I cried with him until he could cry no more.

"You'll have to give me a few minutes," I said, cuddling up.

"It's not a necessity to come inside you anymore," he said. "We're in control now."

"We can have sex so much more now that we don't have to."

He smirked at my silly reasoning. "Can you draw a bath while I change the sheets?" he said.

"Sure. If we're taking a bath, I should cover that wound again."

I put on a second coat of antiseptic, then used more surgical glue on his sutures.

Gian's bathroom was surprisingly clean. If I run a finger across my brother's tiles, the grime touches me back.

I like to enter a tub with it half full. Gian slid in behind me. The chase was over. We were safe.

"I forgot the drinks," he said, raising himself from the warm water. The old Stefano would have made me get them. I used the opportunity to dunk my head.

Gian returned with two champagne flutes full of Prosecco. He placed the bottle on the floor.

"For your safety, I've never been able to ask this," I said. "What do you do for a living?"

He took a sip of prosecco. "You pretty much already know. DJ, a little set design. When possible, I'm an understudy. Acting helped me learn how to fake empathy. I hope you don't mind that I did that."

"You were cursed, baby. There's no reason to apologize. Now that you have empathy, I'll have to teach you how to forgive and let things go."

"You're a saint. I can't thank you enough for your patience."

"It was love."

"I love you too."

"You know you can go for main roles now," I said.

"Maybe."

"There's no maybe. You're very talented."

"I appreciate your support," he said, rubbing his face against my neck. "but there are far greater performers than me. Where I make real money is at the poker table, especially against dumb millionaires. Their ego won't let them see how bad they're losing."

"We should totally go to Vegas again. Craps is my game."

"Nice. So what do you do for a living?"

I panicked. There was no way I could tell him that Support, the witches, paid us to kill his people; that's not a thing you get over. Our income was cut off. What would we do? I had one skill, and that was stripped away. Killing was our trade. You can't turn that into a business, at least an honest one, especially hearing from the strega how sloppy we were. I could always go pro in the MMA, but that would be a conversation for later. I had to say something.

"We flip houses. My dad is a master carpenter." That last part was not a lie. Dad is a craftsman. "I'm not really into it."

"You could do the design," Gian said encouragingly.

"Why, because I'm a girl? Sorry, that came out snottier than I meant."

"No, not because you're a girl. You have an eye for what's beautiful."

"I sure do." I leaned back and kissed him.

"I didn't mean it like that," he said. "You knew which painting has an emotional connection. My uncle Emilio painted that. It would be easy to use that talented eye for design. I could help."

"You know what I want to do now that the Dark Times are over?" I said.

"What?"

"Make friends. The life of a Huntress was a lonely existence."

"We'll have a circle of friends like you wouldn't believe," Gian said and held me tight. "You'll soon be wishing for a night to ourselves."

"I would love that."

We refrained from sex after that evening—oral included, which was unnecessary as that never stopped the curse. Reports were coming in from Gian's relatives that the curse had truly lifted, but my family was stubborn and needed to see for themselves. It was the seventy-fifth hour since I brought Gian back from the Dread. We were gathered around my father's dinner table, having just finished a fabulous meal of grilled halibut and jasmine rice. Dad flipped his old Dean Martin album to the second side. At least he was trying.

Grandpa looked at Gian. "How much time do we have?"

He unlocked his phone. The timer showed twelve minutes remaining. "We should know soon."

275

Clio was on my lap, asleep. Ever since the curse was lifted, her attitude toward me softened. She still wasn't sure what to make of Gian.

At the one-minute mark, I held my boyfriend's hand. He squeezed gingerly.

The alarm sounded, and Gian clicked go on the stopwatch. Five minutes later, and there was nothing. Ten minutes and we were growing emotional.

"It was pretty consistent," Gian said. "I haven't gone this long."

"Let's not get too comfortable," Grandpa said.

"Enough," I professed, "The curse is no more, you stubborn, stubborn men. I'm bringing out dessert."

I returned with plates of homemade tiramisu and embraced Gian from behind. Dad shuffled in his seat uncomfortably. His apprehension made me hold Gian tighter.

"What is this?" Gian said, looking up at me with a glowing smile. "How did you know?"

"Grandma Rosetta shared the recipe when we were visiting the other day."

The desert was his favorite. I hoped I made it with the right amount of love.

Gian lifted a forkful of my sweet confection to his mouth and melted in appreciation. Grandpa perked up as if Gian was changing.

"It's perfect," Gian said.

"Your mother dropped off a present for this moment," my brother said. He fetched a bottle and five tiny glasses.

"Is that great-grandma's limoncello?" Gian said.

"Yep," my brother said.

Gian filled the glasses. "You sip this one."

"Can I make the toast?" Dad said.

I was a little concerned. He was still upset that I betrayed the family.

"I insist," Gian said.

Dad raised his glass. "The two of you were trouble," he said, looking at Gian and me, "but trouble is what we all were. The strength that made you disobey our families is the strength that healed our worlds. We were given a new life because of your love. To Gian and Linsey."

I adored the musical flow of my given name. Linsey Lombardo would be even better. I sipped the limoncello and was surprised by how strong his great-grandmother made them.

"This is delicious," my father said. "Your mother would have enjoyed this drink, Linsey."

Gian held his eyes shut, but it did little to stop the tears slipping down his cheeks.

"Are you crying because of your haircut?" my brother asked. That busted the whole table up.

Gian feigned a mockingly stupid laugh. "Good one."

There was a knock at the door, and Maxwell answered. That's my brother's given name.

In walked Gian's uncle Tony. The funny thing was his real name is Tony. He gave up long ago trying to change himself for people.

"Hey, Tony." Gian embraced him warmly.

Tony was dressed in a black T-shirt and jeans. He moved with nervous apprehension.

"I'm sorry to interrupt your dinner. I have to speak with you," Tony said to my dad.

"Sure, what's up?" Dad said.

"You murdered my boyfriend!" The anger was abrupt and unexpected. "Franco wasn't a Dread. The curse didn't affect gay people. My boyfriend was the man you killed in Flushing Meadows." He held up a grainy security image that looked like Dad and Grandpa in disguise. "You slit his throat so forcefully he was almost decapitated. You ruined me."

Dad went white. "Support sent a terminate order. They said he was a Dread."

"The witches sent you?"

"I swear on my father's life."

Grandpa looked over at him, then at Tony. "We didn't know. It was before Linsey became our eyes."

"I understand your pain," Dad said to Tony. "I lost my wife in the fight. There isn't a day that goes by that I'm not torn apart by her murder."

"What you talkin' about?" Tony said. "You're the one that killed your wife."

"Stop," Grandpa told Tony, putting himself between them.

"No, he needs to know the truth."

I had a weird déjà vu as my phone vibrated with an incoming message. It was the streghe apologizing, saying the truth spell hadn't taken. I was thoroughly confused.

"What are you saying?" Dad said.

"Yours was the only round shot that day. I've been to the barn. Even if we had fired, the bullet hole by the door is too low to be one of ours. It was from your round ricocheting."

"No," Dad said.

"Yes." He stared into Dad's eyes. "You know it's true."

"Oh my God." Dad fell to his knees. It tore at my heart to see him cry, but so did the truth. I almost threw up.

"What have you done?" Gian said.

Tony just shook his head.

"Did you know?" I asked Gian.

"No," he said and held me as I bawled. Fuck the Dark Times.

"You need to go," Grandpa said to Tony.

"Wait," Dad said, getting to his feet. "I want you to know that your boyfriend was brave to the end. I am sure at that moment he was thinking of you and all the love you

278

gave. Your boyfriend passed, content with the life you shared."

Tears were streaming down Uncle Tony's cheeks.

"I am so sorry for what I did," my father said, "I was following orders. I will not ask it of you, but someday I hope you will forgive me."

"And someday, I hope you will forgive me for taking your son," Tony said, "and for almost getting your family killed."

Dad and Tony hugged. The horror of it all was too much.

His uncle held me tight and whispered, "Thank you for saving my life at my storage unit."

"You're welcome," I said.

"I'm sorry I broke my promise." He turned to Gian. "I had no clue that this was your girlfriend's family. I would never have put them in danger if you told me." He closed his eyes tightly. "That came out wrong. I'm not blaming you."

"I know what you mean," Gian said and walked Tony to the door.

Dad was on his phone. "Hi, Daryl. I'm doing well. Do you still live in Pennsylvania? Great. Can you do me a favor? There's a barn outside Scranton. I need you to check something." Dad gave him the information and hung up. We tried to comfort him, but he escaped to his room.

I was checking in on him the following afternoon when his cell rang.

"No," he wailed.

It broke my heart. I found him curled in the fetal position at the foot of the bed. I laid behind him and held tight as he cried.

"Mom's death was not your fault. I forgive you."

An intense nightmare left me screaming myself awake. Maxwell had slit my boyfriend's throat so effortlessly, so brutally. I saw the skateboard mounted above the bed and realized I was safe with Gian.

"What's wrong?" He moved a tuft of hair off my face.

"It was just a nightmare." My heart was still pounding. I held onto him tightly.

"I think it's time for that talk. You up for it?"

He meant the talk I promised we would have about my assault. Maybe it would do us good to get it out in the open.

Gian kept pushing for more detail, saying that I needed to work through it, to own it. I tried, but each time I started, the horror of the day overwhelmed me.

He stroked my shoulder gently as I cried. "Let's stop. It's not your fault. You did nothing to provoke it."

"Leroy said the same thing, but it sure feels like I did."

"That's the trauma trying to keep the memory alive. My psychologist can take that away."

"You can get rid of it?"

"It's more taking power away from your attacker. I had it bad. So much so, it turned into PTSD. Remember when you woke me in Vegas, and I freaked out so much I almost hit you?"

"I thought that was the curse."

"It was from being hunted," he said, shying his eyes.

I felt like shit for having blamed Gian for something that was my kin's fault. "Baby, I'm so sorry."

Gian was silent. I wouldn't be sure how to respond to that either. "You talk about how lonely it was as a Huntress. Imagine how isolating it was for the Cursed, knowing any venture outside could be your last. Many a night, I ate a meal alone, brought by the same trusted delivery driver."

"You weren't looking through your peephole, were you?" I said, horrified.

"No. Wait, was that kill yours?"

"It was Dad," I said, not letting him know I was there.

"That one really freaked out the community. What the fuck?"

"I'm sorry."

He didn't try to comfort me. "Being hunted sucked. There isn't one of us who hasn't been transported around in a metal box like a vampire or wrapped themselves in a steel blanket to hide."

I put my hand lovingly on his shoulder, but he shrugged it away.

"You should see Dr. Killourie," he said. "She's my therapist. You can be open with her."

"What if she has me talk about my experience as a Huntress?"

"She *will* have you talk about that, but patient-psychologist confidentiality will keep her from saying anything. Plus, once she hears who was killed, she won't feel bad. Those were murderers."

"The woman your cousin killed wasn't a murderer."

"That kind of guilt is why I want you to see her." He laced his fingers in mine and gave me a quick peck.

"When did you do this?"

"Last Thursday."

"Wait, you were sad that whole weekend. How could this be a positive thing?"

"That was part of the healing process. I was back to normal by Monday. Better than ever. We're in a good place. I want you to go into this new phase of our lives fresh. Pure."

"I don't know."

"After my session, I was at peace. The change was noticeable like I emerged from a cocoon of darkness. I felt free for the first time in my life. Please, do it for me."

"Fine, set up an appointment."

"You won't regret it," he said, nuzzling his cheek against mine.

My therapy session was being held at Gian's apartment. Dr. Killourie hadn't arrived yet, and Gian was trying to convince me to take Ecstasy for some reason.

"I'm sorry I didn't tell you what type of therapy this was."

"Dude, what the fuck?"

"It worked wonders for my PTSD. Please trust me. It'll help with your trauma."

"You know I don't like drugs."

"I know, Sunshine, that's why I was afraid to tell you, but I wouldn't ask if it didn't work. You won't get too high. You'll just be happier than you've ever been. This is pharmaceutical grade MDMA. There's nothing added. Doctors used to prescribe it to their patients."

"Yeah, used to. What kind of psychologist would let me do this?"

"A family friend. Please trust me. Please."

"Fine," I said, folding my arms.

"Thank you. Dr. Killourie wouldn't let me do it again so soon, or I'd be taking it with you. She didn't want me to become depressed."

"I don't want that either," I said.

"You'll only be sad for a little while. It takes a few days for your brain to replenish all the happy."

Gian held the capsule up to me, and I downed it with water before chickening out.

When Dr. Killourie arrived, Gian headed for the door.

282

"Can I have a pair of your new socks?" I needed the comfort they offered him.

"Linsey, you can have them all," Gian said warmly and left.

"God damn, I love that man," I said.

I liked Dr. Killourie. She was a short, confident blonde with an air of cool that wasn't forced. I bet she was fun outside of her practice.

It had been forty minutes since I swallowed the capsule. There was an odd feeling in the pit of my stomach. I wasn't sure if it was nerves or the drug.

"I'm scared," I said.

"There's no reason to be scared," she said, which I found ironic since I was signing a release saying this wasn't therapy and that I absolved her of anything that should happen during our time.

"This doesn't void patient-doctor confidentiality, does it?"

"Absolutely not. Gian told me everything in his session. Your history as a Huntress is safe with me. I don't believe I would be long for this world if I blabbed."

"No, you wouldn't," I said. For my family's security, I didn't try to reassure her that she was safe.

"You don't have to worry about anything. MDMA therapy isn't legal in Washington. I would lose my license if this got out. Especially doing it for someone who doesn't show signs of PTSD."

"I like the idea of concern for your livelihood better than my veiled threats. I didn't mean my last comment. And if this is going to risk your license, we don't need to do it."

"It's all good. Gian wants this, and I want him to be happy. Why don't you have a seat wherever you will feel the most relaxed."

Having never had therapy, I headed straight for the couch like I'd seen people do on TV. Dr. Killourie placed a bed pillow behind my head and a soft blanket over my body.

"Are you feeling anything yet?" she asked.

"Not yet, Dr. Killourie, but my nerves are out of control like I swallowed a sun."

"Linsey, I don't have a doctorate. You can call me Lorie."

"Thank you. Wait, you're Lorie Killourie?"

"Think about that realization on my wedding night," she said. "It shouldn't be much longer. Your analogy of swallowing a sun is spot on. The drug is beginning to crest like a sunrise. You're going to feel incredible, better than you ever have. While we're waiting for it to kick in, I'll explain the process for this therapy. MDMA has a positive success rate in treating PTSD because it prohibits the amygdala lobes in your brain from activating. This is where the fight or flight center lives — the caveman brain. Trauma is the body's emotional and physical response to a negative experience. PTSD is the reaction to this memory. Your brain doesn't know the difference between a real danger happening now or something from the past. Your mind says, holy shit, heart is pounding, or pulse has increased; something is going on. You get tunnel vision, and in a way, you relive the trauma. MDMA is so successful in therapy because it floods your mind with serotonin and sort of deactivates the amygdala. This removes the fear and pain so you can look at your trauma pragmatically."

"That's why I felt like I was reliving my assault when I was telling Gian about it."

"Exactly. This session will be intense. Three to eight hours. Whatever it takes. I'm going to have you tell your story. The more detail you can give, the more effective the therapy. MDMA allows you to get in your mind without facing the trauma. You'll reframe the experience, reframe how you think about it, what you know, how you respond. You can't go back in time and

284

change what's already happened, but you can teach your brain to think in a way that no longer tortures you, to make sense of your experience, to let it go, or to resolve it. What makes the narrative effective is you're taking your power back. It will no longer be someone else's story. You will look at yourself and say, this is mine. This is what happened to me. This is how I interpret it. This is the meaning I take from it. This is how I will be free."

"That sounds wonderful," I said. I had a grin that wouldn't leave. I felt terrific. Amazing, in fact. "It's definitely kicking in."

"Why don't you drink some water," Lorie suggested. "Hydration is important on this drug. Do you need gum?"

"Oh my God, yes. I'm grinding my teeth like mad."

She threw me a pack. "I want you to tell me a time that you felt betrayed."

"When my father read my diary. That sounds stupid, but it led to something unimaginably horrid."

"It's not stupid at all. There was obvious trauma in it. You went right there. Having your diary read is the ultimate betrayal. The one place you felt safe with your thoughts was taken from you."

The Ecstasy helped me calmly tell my story where I thought Dad and Grandpa murdered Gian. There was no anger or rage. I talked through the situation until I owned it. The betrayal no longer lived in my head, and I was honestly able to forgive my father. In the past, when I forgave, I felt light; now, I was almost weightless.

"We're at a good place to take a break. I know the drug makes you super horny, but I have to ask you to stop touching yourself."

"I am so sorry," I said, mortified, not even realizing I was doing it.

"No need to apologize. It's just the therapy won't work if your mind is focused on sex. You have to be one hundred percent in the story."

"Is that why you didn't want Gian to take it with me?"

"I did that to protect his mental health. If this session works, I recommend never retaking the drug. It can permanently deplete your serotonin when you do too much, leaving you joyless. All the time here will be for naught."

"You don't have to worry about us. We'll be good." I couldn't stop staring at Lorie's face. She had an interesting heroin chic look to her. "Has anyone told you that you look like a young Madonna?"

"Thanks," she said, unsure if it was a compliment.

"I think it may be your confidence. I've never seen someone move or sit with such ease."

"Linsey, you were on the way to becoming the leader of your family business. You broke a thousand-year curse. If anyone should have confidence, it's you."

I shrugged my shoulders.

"We'll work on that too."

It took six hours to tell my story. I had more trauma than the near-rape, from my mom dying, sending the Dread to their death, the boy being killed by the Hilltop Hellion, to silly issues like resenting my brother for his constant happiness.

"How do you feel?" Lorie asked. She looked as exhausted as I felt.

"I feel light, free as if my body is exhaling a giant sigh of relief."

"You've figured out your puzzle. Where things were unclear, trapped, they are now understood. I really feel this has worked."

"I do too."

"How about we soak up the sun for a bit, and then we'll wrap up."

I didn't believe her about the sun, but it was shining upon the deck. The park across from me was breathing life into my soul. I felt incredible, as if I was a part of nature. Lorie eased into the lounger next to me.

"Now, what you're going to do is learn to deal with the trauma in case it ever rears its ugly head. You're probably chilled from coming down. Does Gian have an electric blanket?"

"I have no idea. How about I take a bath?"

"I still need to talk with you."

"I don't mind." My inhibitions were nonexistent.

Lorie's eyebrow lifted in concern. This was the line for her. This.

"I can make it a bubble bath."

"Sure. I guess that will work. Yell when you're in."

Gian didn't have Mr. Bubble. His pomegranate dish soap would have to do.

Stepping in the warm water was trippy, like I was returning to the womb. As I relaxed my back, my legs fell to the sides of the tub, creating a loch. My breasts added to the illusion, floating in the water like islands. I brushed my vulva lightly with my finger, producing underwater sparks. I backed off. Lorie told me I needed to focus. I didn't want to fail her.

I sunk my chest under the suds and called for her. She put the lid down on the toilet and took a seat.

"Thanks for covering yourself. We should be able to wrap this up quickly. You did really well today. What we're going to use as a guide to recognizing your body's sensations is a feeling thermometer. Trauma can start with a weird pit in your stomach or tightness in your shoulders. Maybe you're hot like you're flushing. Your hands could be sweating. Whatever it is, your system is activating. You'll want to recognize the signs so you can keep yourself from reliving the trauma. To do this, you'll distract your mind by energizing other parts of your brain. I start with finger tapping.

"I. Am. In. Con-trol," Lorie said while tapping in beat with a finger at a time against her thumb.

"Whoa," I exclaimed.

She laughed. "While you're doing this, you're also consciously slowing down your breathing. Tapping makes your brain perform a physical task. If you can speak the words aloud, that's even better because you're activating the auditory parts of your mind, giving your brain something to do other than freak out.

"Holy shit."

"I know, right? Another trick is to reach into your long-term memory. Your brain doesn't access long-term memory when you're in a panic. This confuses your mind and keeps you from going into the amygdala. You can deactivate this by naming off things. It could be hot actors, or dog breeds, whatever you want. Just name them until you're in control. My hope is you've let your trauma go and won't have to do any of this. You'll know you are no longer a victim when you don't have to classify yourself as such. I believe that is where you are. We had a productive session here."

"It was wonderful. Thank you."

"No, thank you. Hearing about the Dark Times from a Huntress was fascinating."

"We're in the Blithe now," I said.

"Yes, you are," she said, clearly not understanding what I meant. "But you should know that after the MDMA wears off, you're going to feel blue for a few days. Gian has a supplement that will help replenish your serotonin. Maybe you could pretend Seattle's weather is causing your sadness."

"That won't be hard." It had been gray and foggy all week.

"Don't get up right away. I'll text Gian. It was a pleasure meeting you, Linsey."

"I have to get up. I want to give you a hug."

"Of course." She held a towel out at eye level.

Lorie felt delightful in my arms. I absorbed her kindness like a sponge.

288

I climbed back in the tub and relaxed for a while. Gian was taking forever to return. I put on his robe and stepped into the bedroom. Gian had placed a soft fleece blanket on his bed and was rolling around naked. He patted the spot next to him. I ran and dove for my love.

"How do you feel?" he asked, breaking our kiss.

"Fucking horny."

"No, from the therapy?"

"Better than I've ever felt in my life. Thank you."

"I'm so glad you trusted me," he said and grabbed hold of the back of my head and thrust my lips to his.

The only downfall of Ecstasy was I couldn't for the life of me reach orgasm. I got close enough to ride the precipice, but the release never came.

Chapter 16

Our family offered to hold the truce in a mutual location, but the Lombardo's insisted that it was held at our duplex as an offer of trust. I took charge of my family's planning after hearing their ridiculous ideas. The day was finally here, and I was filled with nervous excitement.

A loaf of haggis was roasting in the oven. I had a feeling our guests wouldn't care for the dish. As a backup, there were bangers and mash warming on the stove. The Lombardo's meal would be miles above our Scottish offerings. You can't compete with Italian cuisine.

My front door creaked open, and Dad entered the kitchen. He was nursing a scotch to chase away his pre-party jitters.

"How are you holding up?" I asked.

He shrugged.

"I love the suit," I said.

"This old thing," he said about his new purchase.

The sausages were ready. I set the burner to low and wiped my hands on my apron.

"What is that awful smell?" Dad said, wrinkling his nose.

I showed him the haggis.

"Your grandfather is going to love you."

"He already does," I said. "Dad, I'm sorry for betraying your trust. Will you forgive me for putting the family in danger?"

"Forgiveness is a gift," he said. "You don't ask for a gift."

He'd asked the same thing from Uncle Tony, but thought better of pointing it out.

"Of course, Dad. I *am* sorry, you have to know that."

The doorbell rang. It was Gian and his immediate family, all carrying plates of food or bottles of liquor. The aroma of their dishes was heavenly. I directed them to the food table outside. Thankfully, the weather cooperated, but just in case, I'd rented a party tent for the food and a larger one with outdoor heaters for the guests. For being the first of March, it was a miracle it wasn't raining.

"Hi, Linsey," Gian said and gave me a peck on the lips.

"Hey, lover," I responded.

I had been getting acquainted with his relatives for the last few weeks. His mom, Leonora, greeted me with a pinch on the cheek like her own. She had cut her auburn hair shoulder-length. The look went well with her warm, inviting face. Leonora is beautiful, but it's an everyday beauty that puts you at ease. Of everyone in the family, she was the one I connected with the most. That could just be me happy to have a mom again.

Gian's father hugged me, and he, like my father, was in no way a hugger. Mr. Lombardo's two-day stubble was perfectly manicured, his salt and pepper hair combed back and to the side. I love his eyebrows. They slant outward, taking a forty-five-degree turn at the edge, accenting his eyes. Looking at him and Leonora, it was easy to see why their kids were so attractive.

I felt bad for making my family dress up. Half of the Lombardo's extended family looked like they were going to a swanky invite-only party, while the rest were overdone, almost to the point of being tacky.

"Hello, Sis," Gian's brother said, smacking me on the shoulder. He had his hair slicked back and was wearing a dark green bowling shirt.

"Hi, Dante. How are you doing?"

In monotone, he repeated back, "How are you doing?" Then he switched to a thick Italian accent. "You say it like this, How you doin?"

292

When I'd met him a week ago, he had no trace of an accent. Now he was overly embracing his heritage, almost to the point of being stereotypical. I found it adorable.

"Your accent is coming along nicely."

"Get a load of this joker." He pointed to me and walked away.

Gian's gay brother, Luca, hugged me warmly. He's a total cutie.

Grandpa Salvatore and Grandma Rosetta arrived shortly after. Rosetta's long silver hair was elegantly tussled as if she were heading out to a photoshoot. The couple was aging gracefully, but you could see how worrisome their life has been if you looked closely.

A few distant relatives of Gian's were at the bar in the backyard. Everyone appeared grateful and happy for the celebration. Our families were making an effort, and for that, I was pleased.

Two members of his family were standoffish, his uncle Carlino and cousin Marco.

"You know we've met before," I said to Marco.

"Yeah, in the woods," he said, rubbing his head.

"No, Vegas. I was the blonde in your hotel room."

He looked at my face with no recollection, then down at my breasts. I propped them up from below. "Hey, look at that. It was you."

I was chatting up Grandma Rosetta when a flash of red hair drew my attention. Walking to the door was Mary. Our eyes met, and we screamed, jumping up and down. I had no idea she was coming and rushed in for a hug.

Mary's hair was beyond her shoulders. The look went well with her porcelain complexion. She carried herself without a care in the world.

"I never thought I'd see you again," I said.

293

"Sorry about disappearing," she said. "Support pulled us from the city. I was made by a Dread. The fucker got away. Oops, sorry," she said, looking around.

"You were a Huntress?" I whispered, shocked.

"That I was," Mary said regally and bowed with a roll of her hand. The noble gesture was meant for a laugh, but it filled me with a sense of pride.

"Did you know I was?"

"Kind of. When you were talking about your family, you used generic terms the same as I would. Plus, you said your grandfather killed your boyfriend. I pretended you were joking, but it wasn't a foreign concept. What gave you away the most was your conversation with my parents. They said only a huntress could be that confident."

I relished the compliment. "Do you think we're related?" I said.

"Holy shit! I've asked myself the same thing. I felt such a closeness to you I thought I might be gay."

I blushed but didn't admit the same.

Gian sidled up to me.

"You?" he and Mary said, both in an accusatory tone.

"Is this Gian?" Mary said.

"That's me," he said.

"Your boyfriend was the one who put me in a coma. He's the reason I had to leave the country."

"She was out to kill me," he said. "The scar on my face was from her. Luckily, I had my skateboard with me that day."

"The one over your bed?" I asked.

He winked. "I hit her good."

"How were you able to sneak up on her?"

"I hid behind a steel fence at a construction site and jumped her as she passed."

294

"We could stand here all day fighting about who was trying to kill who," Mary said. "Besides, I can't even see your scar."

"The High Priestess healed it," he said.

"You got to meet the witches?"

I moved in to intervene. "Look at this. My boyfriend who I thought died, and my best friend who I lost, together. I, for one, couldn't be happier."

"I dig your hair color," Mary said to me. I dyed it golden blonde like it was when Gian first met me.

"Can I get you a drink?" Gian didn't know Mary's name and wavered. I introduced her.

"I'm actually Joan."

Ever since the curse had been lifted, Gian was overly affectionate, but with Joan, he offered a handshake.

"Get in here, you big baby," she said.

Gian was rigid in his hug.

"Oh, just accept it," she said and held him tighter.

Joan took a hand from each of us. "Thank you for breaking the spell. I feel like my soul is free. I've become a better fighter because of it."

"You're still fighting?" It didn't have the same allure as it used to. My feminine figure was even coming in. My arms were starting to look girly in my new black cocktail dress.

"Honey, I was in the same boat. Go to the gym. It's so much better without the curse. You have a real shot at being a champion."

"I don't know."

"I think you should," Gian said. His support was surprising. It was the first time he showed appreciation toward my sport.

"I guess I could be talked into a fight," I said. "So what are you going to do with yourself? Now that the chase is over."

"Help people. That wasn't a cover. Next month, the family is traveling to Mali to re-dig a well we built. The women in the village blew it up."

"What? Why would they do that?" I asked.

"It turns out, walking miles for water was the only break they got from their husbands. The women suggested the wells be built far enough that they wouldn't join them. We're adding a covered gazebo for socializing. They'll love it. What are you going to do?"

"Probably join the family business flipping houses. Gian says I would be good at design."

"You would be," Joan said.

"As for Gian, he's going to become a poker champion."

"I love you so fucking much," he said. His eyes lit up. "Great-Grandpapa."

"Gian." Enzo embraced him. His great-grandpa looked like a crazed artist in stolen clothes. He has a magnificent wide mustache that curls at the ends. There's a clear distinction between it and his beard. A pair of round wire-rimmed glasses topped off his look.

"Where's Pippa?"

"Poor girl's not feeling well," Enzo said in a warm and comforting tone.

"That's a shame," I said, "I was looking forward to meeting her."

"You're all she talked about."

"That's sweet."

"Mr. Cameron," Enzo said to my grandfather.

"Enzo, it is an honor. Please, we're friends. Call me Aleck."

"Friends. I like that, Aleck."

Grandpa was wearing his kilt. It gave me a great sense of pride.

"Is Uncle Tony coming?" I asked Gian.

"I couldn't talk him into it. Tony is the one that needed this most."

I had a horrible thought. Was Tony the one who stabbed grandpa?

For the truce ceremony, there was a single table and two chairs. The remaining furniture was stacked in the basement for later. I wanted the ceremony to be a focal point.

Our families flowed out into the sunshine and encircled our patriarchs. I scanned the area to see if anyone needed a chair, but everyone seemed able to stand.

My grandfather and Gian's great-grandfather, Enzo, met at the table, and shook hands. Cordy stepped out of our father's side of the house, carrying Grandpa's bagpipes. Gian walked with Bepa to the front of the garage.

Grandpa filled the pipe's bag with air while Gian adjusted his microphone.

"Aleck has asked that I join him for a tribute to our fallen kin," Gian said.

He nodded to Grandpa, who struck the first notes of Amazing Grace. Gian's voice was as haunting as the pipes. The families shared a touching moment of unplanned silence after the last note.

My grandfather returned to the ceremonial table, where he picked up the folded parchment between the gentlemen and broke the wax seal.

"We meet here one month to the day of that fateful event," Bepa said. "I come to this truce with open arms. But before we begin, I offer my sincere apology. Your family was under a terrible curse. We do not judge any of your prior deeds. We welcome you like kin. On behalf of the Cameron Clan, I apologize for the suffering our bloodline caused."

Enzo sat stern. The ends of his curled mustache quivered briefly. "Aleck, we do not hold your family accountable for the atrocities that fell upon our people." He stared deep into my grandfather's eyes. "You were also caught in a spell acting on centuries of manipulation. Time

297

will heal our wounds. But for me, I offer you my unconditional forgiveness."

The gentlemen shook hands and a cheer flowed through the families.

"There has been too much violence," Grandpa said. "For all the pain we have inflicted, I would like the last blood spilled to be a Hunter's." He looked down at his folded hands. "Hunters. That name sickens me now." He removed his ceremonial dagger from the sheath and cut a deep wound into his palm. From his coat pocket, he retrieved a quill. The crazy bastard signed the treaty in blood.

I paused the ceremony to find a gauze roll and a washcloth to dress the wound. With a kiss on Grandpa's forehead, I stepped away.

"Thank you, dear."

"I'll stitch that up for you later."

"I didn't mean to go so deep." He turned and faced Enzo. "For your signature, I offer a pen finely crafted from Sicilian olive wood." He handed the instrument over delicately.

"Thank you, Aleck. This pen is magnificent and far less painful."

The crowd cheered with the final stroke of Enzo's signature.

I set a fifth of Glenfiddich on the table with two glasses. Grandpa smiled, seeing the bottle, then did a double-take. It was a Glenfiddich Special Old Reserve distilled explicitly for the Clan Cameron.

"Where did you get this?"

"I've had it for a while," I said.

"You're two glasses shy," my brother said, producing them from behind the woodpile.

"Thank you." Dad filled the four glasses with scotch. He gave one each to Gian and me. The remaining two were for Enzo and Bepa. Most of the guests already had a cocktail.

"We would not be here today if it weren't for the forbidden romance between our families," Grandpa said. "The risk Linsey and Gian took in the name of love has ended a thousand-year curse. The magnitude of your actions will not be forgotten. The Cameron Clan thanks you from the bottom of our hearts."

The four of us shot our drinks, wasting a good scotch.

Gian produced a bottle of grappa and set it on the table.

It was Enzo's turn. He poured four glasses, then raised his. "Gian and Linsey came up with a term to describe this new period of our lives. The Blithe. It means joyous and happy. I can't think of a more fitting name. To the Blithe."

Grandpa couldn't hide his disgust in the drink and ended up giving a little shake of his enormous body. Enzo chuckled to himself. I almost threw up after downing mine.

"Grappa is an acquired taste," Gian whispered to me.

"It tastes like it was acquired from a gas pump."

"And that's the good stuff," he said with a smirk.

The crowd roared after we slammed our empty glasses down.

"If I may," Gian said. Grandpa gestured that the floor was his. My boyfriend filled Grandpa's and my glass with scotch. For him and Enzo, he poured grappa.

Gian raised his glass. "We are all guilty. Whether we killed or abated, led or fought back in self-defense, bombed, sniped, lost control, refrained, or enjoyed the kill, we all have blood on our hands, whether we killed or not. When the Reckoning happened, the Cursed felt the empathy we were lacking. We finally understood. I wish our families teamed up and worked together years ago, but we were not ourselves. Now we are free, and we can

299

love, and I love each and every one of you." There were tears streaming down his face.

The families came forth and hugged Gian and me.

"Before the party's in full swing, there is one additional surprise." I handed an envelope to my grandfather.

"What is this?" Grandpa asked.

"Open it."

When Bepa saw his name on the passport, his eyes lit up in surprise.

"How did you get this so fast?" he said. "We mailed the forms two weeks ago."

"I asked Support for a favor." I held my freshly filled glass up high. "I would like to welcome back Aleck MacGregor Cameron officially."

Dad placed an arm on my shoulder. "You're good people," he said.

"So are you, Dad," I said and gave him his passport. My brother let out a huff. "I wouldn't forget about you."

He flipped to the first page. "Maxwell," he said proudly. "I will never get sick of my given name."

I wanted to tell him that Max still sounded like a dog's name but thought better of it.

Dad pulled Gian and me aside while Maxwell helped bring out the tables and chairs. "Thank you for not asking me to speak."

"I wouldn't do that to you, Dad."

"Much appreciated. I have a gift for you. Well, it's from Support. But first, I want you to know that I do forgive you, unconditionally."

"Dad, thank you." I hugged him tightly.

He handed us a thick envelope. The top page was a vacation itinerary for Scotland and Italy. "You're going home."

"Is this for real?" Gian said.

"You leave in three weeks."

Gian's passport hadn't come through yet. There was a problem with his birth certificate not having a raised emblem. We had been putting off getting the replacement. I realized now why support kept pushing for us to get it done.

"This calls for a celebration," Gian said and headed to the DJ table in the garage. My dad and brother added a wooden dancefloor to the octagon. Disco lights were attached to the top of the cage. Later in the evening, we could close the garage doors to keep the noise inside.

Gian spoke into the microphone. "Normally, I would DJ, but I want to dance with my Sunshine. We'll have to make do with a recording." He pressed play on his MacBook and strolled to the floor. I slipped my arms around his waist as he went in for a kiss. Joan asked my brother for a dance, and they joined us.

The party was still raging at dawn with no sign of relenting. I was in my kitchen, reducing two batches of sausage gravy on the stove, when an elderly Italian woman walked in. She had a confident pose about her.

"Hello. You must be Linsey. I'm Gian's great-grandmother, Pippa." She stuck her hand out.

"Oh my gosh, it is a pleasure to meet you," I said, wiping off my hands.

We embraced, but I felt trepidation from her. She backed away slightly and held onto my wrists. Her hair was pulled back, accenting glamorous cheekbones. Pippa had the elegant appearance of an aging actress.

"I apologize for missing the truce," she said.

"That's all right. You weren't feeling well."

"It isn't all right. I was being stubborn. It's just..."

"There are no more secrets," I said.

"A Hunter killed my brother. Don't worry. It wasn't your family. His murder happened years ago in Italy."

"Still, it breaks my heart," I said.

301

"Mine too," she said. "It was harder to forgive than I thought. Enzo told me how you are always looking at my Gian. He's never seen a couple so in love. Enzo likes you, and if Enzo likes you, I like you. I should have been here." Tears welled in her eyes.

I told her in Italian that we were all under a curse. "That doesn't make it better. I am so sorry," I said. "For everything."

"You speak the language beautifully," Pippa said. "Linsey, you have nothing to be sorry for. You are the reason we are here. You are the reason we are safe."

"That means the world," I said. "Would you like to dance with Gian and me? He told me how much you enjoy it."

Pippa smiled warmly. The wrinkles on her face were a roadmap of the woman's life. There were laugh lines, places where she cried, worry, sorrow, but most of all, joy.

"Dancing would make me happy," she said. "But first." She reached into her purse and pulled out a sachet filled with mini liquor bottles, each with a yellow bow. "Limoncello!"

She had us drink two before she was ready. My buzz was back.

"OK, here's the plan," Pippa said, covering the bowl of biscuits with a towel. "We'll call everyone in for breakfast." She grabbed my arm. "That's when we sneak off to dance." Pippa retrieved the sachet and stuffed the rest of the liquor back in her purse. She wasn't ready to share. I just adored her.

"Let's go," I said.

Outside, I yelled, "Breakfast is on," and motioned to the door. "The left pan is vegetarian."

"You were in there so long," Gian said to Pippa and me. "Everything all right?"

"Of course," I said. "We had a few things to discuss."

"Yes, discuss." Pippa raised her hand in a toast and fake hiccupped. "Your girlfriend wants the three of us to dance. Are you up for it?"

"Nothing would please me more," Gian said. "Let's pick you out a song." He held Pippa's arm for support and walked her over to the DJ table. "I made you a mash-up of St. Louise Blues and Blue Boy's Remember Me. Would you like to dance to that?"

Pippa squealed. "Yes. Yes. Yes. Wait, have you heard Remember Me?"

"I don't know?" I said.

"Play her the original."

"OK, but then I get to play the original St. Louise Blues."

"Of course," Pippa said.

I've never heard a song more danceable than the one Gian played. It drove my body to move.

"Enzo, come dance with your wife," Pippa yelled through the open garage doors.

Enzo groaned as he worked himself to his feet. It took him a great deal of effort to reach us. The long evening had taken its toll.

"I'll have one of those limoncellos first," he said.

Enzo slammed his drink, walked to the center of the dance floor, and the song started. He moved his head back and forth, real hip-like. The rest of his body soon caught up. Enzo wasn't feeble; that was all an act. The old man could groove. People were clapping along when Enzo had Gian pause the music.

"I don't mean any disrespect," Enzo said to the crowd. "Please, no clapping. I can't hear the beat."

Gian put the song back on and Enzo picked up where he left off. It was cracking me up how smoothly his grandfather danced.

"Come here," he beckoned me.

Enzo held my wrists and swayed with me to the beat. Gian and Pippa joined us, and we danced as one. His great-grandparents are the coolest.

Chapter 17

Gian's passport arrived the day before our flight to Europe. That was cutting it way too close. With the stress and worry behind, our trip was off to a euphoric start. My boyfriend graciously offered me the window seat. His thoughtfulness was all the more special with us being in first-class.

"Excuse me, Gian and Linsey," our stewardess, Trudy, said. "The rest of the passengers are about to board. I can't make it back for a while. Would you care for another glass of champagne?"

"We would love a refill," Gian said.

Trudy returned with two flutes and removed our empties.

The one time I had flown before, a woman in first class made a joke as I passed about us heading to steerage. Even though I wasn't doing anything wrong, I felt guilty holding my champagne now. I lowered the glass to my side as the people passed, and stared out at the tarmac.

My boyfriend rested his hand on my knee, and I lost myself in his beauty. This part was not a curse. Gian is so handsome I get high looking at him. He is my drug, and I'm hooked.

Gian was understanding during take-off when I squeezed his hand in a death grip. Bepa says there are no atheists when a plane is crashing. I squeezed even tighter. It was surprising that the Reckoning hadn't brought Gian to my frightened state, but he was getting better at controlling his new emotions. Gian was strong; he would get through the Reckoning just fine.

"When did you know you loved me?" he asked to distract me from my fear of flying.

305

"When I first hugged you outside the library. Being in your arms completed me."

He smiled dreamily. "I had a feeling when I first saw you at the train station. I knew for sure on our ride in Central Park. Remember when I stopped on that stone bridge to kiss you, and that scary looking dude was approaching?"

I nodded. That guy freaked me out.

"When I stepped forward to be the hero, you were right with me, standing your ground. It intimidated the man so much he took a wide path around us. Your strength was intoxicating."

We were four hours into the flight when the blinds were drawn. Everyone around us soon fell fast asleep. I tried to do the same, but Gian was restless. His squirming was keeping me up.

"What's wrong?" I said.

"I'm horny," he whispered, frustrated.

I reached under Gian's blanket and felt his stiffness. There was no way two people of our stature would fit in the restroom. Joining the mile-high club was right out.

"Why don't you unzip your pants?" I whispered.

I didn't have to ask twice. My hand found him, and I wrapped my fingers around the girth. There was a small window of opportunity as Trudy headed up front to straighten out the kitchen. I bent over and sucked his incredible cock. The naughtiness thrust my libido into overdrive. I sat up, relieved to see Trudy still in the kitchen. Getting caught in the act would be mortifying. I stroked Gian rhythmically, adding an s-stroke movement to my uptake. It wasn't long before Gian warned that he was close. I slipped my other hand under the blanket and aimed into my palm. There was half a mimosa on my tray. I tilted my hand, and his goodness slid into my drink with a splash.

306

"To our adventure," I toasted and shot the mimosa.

"How am I going to be able to sleep after that dirty move?" Gian said.

He was out within minutes. Now I was the one who was too horny to sleep.

The flight across the pole was eleven hours. I thought that was long, but the people near our seats were saying how quick the journey felt.

From Glasgow, we flew in a prop plane to an airport closer to the Cameron Estates. The plan was to take a taxi. Gian and I were old enough to rent a car, but you needed to have a driver's license for at least twelve months to do so. Our new ones barely arrived.

We followed the couple seated in front of us to baggage claim. At our carousel was a man in a proper driving uniform, holding a sign for Cameron.

"Is that for us?" I said.

Before Gian could respond, the driver approached. "Mr. Lombardo, Ms. Cameron, my name is Gregory. I'm yer driver. Ye must be exhausted. I'll retrieve the luggage, and we'll be on our way."

"Fabulous," I said.

Each time one of our bags dropped onto the belt, Gian would try to grab it, but Gregory was having none of it. My boyfriend resorted to pointing out the luggage.

With all our bags on the cart, we headed outside. A steward opened the rear door of a sedan parked at the entrance.

"Nice," Gian said. "What model of Bentley is this?"

"A Mulsanne Speed," Gregory said. "Yer looking at the most powerful four-door automobile in the world."

Gregory stored our luggage and slid into the driver's seat with a tone of satisfaction.

"I love the simplicity of the back," I said. "It's classy without the cheesiness of a limousine."

"Limousin?" Gregory said. "Are ye talking about the cattle?"

"What? No," I said. "A stretched car where the passengers ride in the back. A limousine."

"Ah know," Gregory said. "I am in the driving business. Was having a wee bit of fun with ye."

Gian took Gregory's side and laughed at me.

"How long of a drive is it?" I asked.

"About an hour and a half. We could make it an hour if ye prefer."

"An hour and a half will be fine," I said.

"Thank ye, ma'am. One more ticket, and ah will lose ma license. It is hard to say no to this automobile," he said.

Gregory was a riot. He gave us the skinny on the towns near our castle and narrated our journey to boot. Near the end of our trip, he pulled up to an open iron gate attached to brick pillars.

"We're here," I said. "Those are the gates to Achnacarry."

"And another Cameron is home," Gregory said. "How about we put the bonnie lass up with me so she can look out the front window?"

I jumped out and walked through the entrance. The iron gates bore the sheaf of arrows from our crest, signifying our prowess as warriors. I was standing on Cameron land. I *was* home.

Gregory pulled halfway through the gate, and I joined him in front. We drove into a canopy of beech trees. The branches were twisted eerily like a haunted forest. On the left, a field of wild grass opened to the hills of Lochiel. We entered another patch of trees as the road wound along the forest.

The Clan Cameron Museum came into view directly in front of us. As the road bent, the museum shifted to the side. Gregory slowed to a stop. He nodded in the opposite direction. Off in the distance beyond the field was the Achnacarry Estate, the new Cameron Castle. I climbed out to get a proper look. Gian startled me with his embrace.

"Your castle is magnificent," he said and kissed my neck.

The streghe tried to get Chief Cameron of Lochiel to accommodate us but were unsuccessful. Sir Donald was not familiar with the Hunters, the Dread, or the Dark Times. For our protection, the family had been scrubbed from all records. None of us realized how deep a sacrifice we made.

Gregory had me return to the back so he could let me out properly. Our apartment was in the refurbished stables down the road. As we turned into the drive, the building centered in front of us like the museum had. What a fantastic way to introduce a place.

The cottage was a two-story stone structure with a walkway through the middle. We drove along the side and into a walled courtyard. I liked that the ground wasn't concrete; this was old school dirt.

An elderly gentleman with adorably large ears emerged to greet us. He wore a house kilt with a tweed jacket and a Scottish cap.

"I'm Caleb Sutherland. It is an honor to welcome another Cameron home."

I shook his hand. "This is my boyfriend, Gian."

"That's a fine name, Gian, fierce and noble."

"It's good to be here," Gian said, shaking Caleb's hand. "The journey was long, but the hangover longer."

"What is a holiday without a hangover?" Gregory said. He directed us to the check-in counter.

"Would you happen to have a local car service in town?" I asked.

"We have yer Uber," the man said, "The name's different in Scotland. We call it, Ubetter pick me the fuck up."

We were rummy from the trip. The unexpected vulgarity made us laugh.

"Perfect," Gian said.

"Here are yer keys," Caleb said. "My hip is acting up. If you don't mind, I will send ye alone."

"Not at all," I said.

Caleb couldn't stop staring at Gian. That had been a problem since we landed in Oban. I wasn't sure if it was from his complexion, handsome face, or both.

"Yer apartment is through the doors on the right and up the stairs. Enjoy yer stay, and again, welcome home."

"Thank you." I grabbed my luggage, relieved that the journey was over. Gian headed toward the stairs.

"I almost forgot. Ye have a package." Caleb placed a rectangle parcel in the crook of my arm.

I wasn't expecting our apartment to be so modern. The only touch of history was the Cameron tartans used for the drapes. My favorite part was the high ceilings; they reminded me of the inside of a finished barn.

"Did you see the way the townsfolk stared at me?" Gian said. "I feel like a freak."

Gian *had* noticed. "Honey. They stared because you're so handsome."

"Thank you for the attempt there," he said, "but it's like I'm in a zoo."

"I love you, Gian, but you need to lose the attitude. We're at my family's estate. I don't want any negativity."

"I wasn't negative. I was being real," he barked but pulled back. "I'm sorry. That flight was so long. I'm just grumpy from the trip. After we take a shower, we'll see how well the bed functions."

"Do you honestly believe you're getting some after that little display?"

"Yes," he laughed and headed to the bathroom.

I set the package on the kitchen counter and sliced the seal open. Inside was a bottle of Mr. Bubble. The note read, *Have fun on your trip. Maxwell.* My brother added positivity when it was needed most.

I joined Gian and was happy to see how large the tub was.

"Can we take a bath," I said, setting the bottle on the counter.

"Is that Mr. Bubble? Of course," he said.

I cranked the faucets, ready for a christening in the water of my ancestors. I squeezed a large portion of Mr. Bubble into the stream, and suds emerged.

Gian stepped in first and I relaxed into his body.

"When we get to your village, it will be my turn to be gawked at," I said.

"I hadn't thought of that," he said. "You're right. I'm sorry I was so selfish."

"You weren't selfish at all. You were human."

I just called him out for now being human. I felt horrible, but I couldn't take it back.

We were on a mission to stay awake the whole day. My father drove the notion into our heads. He said it helps with jetlag.

Our Uber driver brought us to Spean Bridge. At seven miles, it was the closest town, and the nearest restaurant. After lunch, we went grocery shopping to stock our fridge.

Gian and I stopped in the museum earlier to select a women's tartan skirt. With it, I wore a black wool sweater, thick black nylons, and stylish black boots. My outfit was rocking. Gian sported a pair of blue tartan slacks. He felt it would be insulting to wear the red tartan of my Clan. The tweed blazer we purchased a week earlier complemented the trousers and his light blue dress shirt. Gian looked adorable. My boy felt he was more dressed for the links.

The following day Caleb dropped us off down the road so we could hike the old military route to Achnacarry. It took longer than expected, but it was a profound experience for me to stroll on Cameron land hand-in-hand with Gian. By the time we got back to the apartment, he was horny — then again, he's always horny.

He had my sweater halfway off as we ascended the staircase. From above, a door shut. Ours was the only unit for this staircase, so it was definitely from our room. Gian froze in his tracks. A man in a full military kilt was on our landing.

"Can I help you?" I said.

"Please excuse the intrusion. My name is Brodie Mitchell. I am the lead security officer for Chief Cameron of Lochiel. Are ye Linsey Cameron and Gian Lombardo?"

"We are," Gian said.

"Then, I have the correct room."

"We didn't get too close to the estate, did we?" I said and let him into our place. "Gian and I tried to keep a respectable distance."

"No, no, you're fine," Brodie said. "I'm here about the stories of the two of ye — wild tales of how ye saved the world. A third trusted source has approached Sir Donald with the same story. The Chief sent me to investigate."

"If you're talking about the Dark Times, it is all true," I said. "I swear on my father's life."

He had a skeptical look. "Ye are a Huntress," he said, making air quotes. "And the lad is some kind of monster."

"Hey," I said, "he's right there."

Gian laughed, but his sour expression pressed through.

"My boyfriend is not a risk anymore. He changed one time, and that was through no fault of his own. I assure you the Curse is no more."

"That is the other thing. A curse? Witches? It doesn't make sense."

"It doesn't," I agreed.

"I ran background checks," Brodie said. "Ye were born, and then there was no record of a Linsey Cameron until a month ago. Gian just last week. Plus, we don't have yer family in our historical records. How do ye explain this?"

"My kin have been in the fight since the eleventh century," I said. "Our bloodline runs to Angus de Cambrun. We were removed from the records for our protection. The Cursed also had to assume a false identity. I assure you it is all true."

"But is there a way ye can prove it?" Brodie said.

I thought about that. "No."

"I have a way," Gian said. He found the utensil drawer and pulled out a dull butter knife. "Attack Linsey with this."

Brodie snatched the knife and made his move. I side-stepped, breaking his hold with one hand, and caught the knife with the other. He dove at me, and within seconds, he was on the hardwood floor with me on top, the knife pressed firmly to the main artery in his neck.

"Oh shit," Gian said, mocking Brodie.

"What the bloody hell?" Brodie said hoarsely.

I rose to my feet and tossed the knife to Gian. Brodie dusted himself off, and I found the lint roller to clean his jacket.

"Thank you," he said as he let me run the sticky tape along his backside. "I'm starting to believe this may be real. Are you a danger?"

"I assume you didn't discover any weapons in our room," I said.

"No. I did not."

"You have nothing to fear from me," I said. "I would protect Chief Cameron of Lochiel with my life."

"What about the lad," he said, pointing to Gian.

Gian was frustrated, but I was happy to see him keep his wits.

"You've heard the stories," I said. "Did they speak of the Age of Reckoning?"

"They did."

"Well, Gian hasn't made it through this period. If anything, he is too safe. I can show you."

I connected my phone to our portable speaker. Gian leaned over to see what song I was selecting.

"That's not fair," he said.

"I know, but it's the only way."

A lone piper began playing Amazing Grace. A half-minute in, Gian was bawling. I shut off the song.

"Don't take that as a sign of weakness," I said. "Up until the Blithe, Gian couldn't cry. Not a tear. All his emotions have caught up to him. He's working through them bravely."

"This is bullshit," Gian said and headed to our bedroom.

"When ye were cursed," Brodie called after him. "How many people did ye murder?"

"None," Gian said. "I never let the curse take me."

"How did ye stop yourself?"

"Through sex," Gian said. "Was this not explained?" He was distracted enough that he returned.

"Aye, it was, but this is a lot to digest," Brodie said. "What about ye? The great Huntress. How many Dread did ye kill?"

"I haven't killed anyone either."

Brodie raised his bushy eyebrows. "How many did yer family kill?"

I looked over at Gian.

"Go ahead, tell him," he said.

"Can you go in the hall?"

"I want to know."

I inhaled deeply. "I was responsible for eighteen deaths. I'm sorry, Gian."

"It's not your fault," Gian said. "Those were men who succumbed to the curse. They were dangerous."

"That doesn't make it better," I said. "Especially with your uncle's boyfriend."

"That burden is not yours to bear. We lost your mother to the Dark Times. The whole situation was fucked." Gian wrapped an arm around my back and pulled me in.

"I didn't mean to cause trouble, Brodie said. "We had to verify if ye were a threat. I'll let you get back to yer day."

"Wait, hold on," I said. "I believe I can prove the Curse is real. Search online for the number of murders this year. You'll see a noticeable decrease the last two months."

"We'll check the stats. Enjoy the rest of your afternoon."

Brodie left so quickly I questioned whether I had put both our families in danger. First, I blabbed to a psychologist and now to a high-ranking security guard. Gian was just happy to be alone. I wasn't in the mood anymore but played along, knowing I would be soon.

The following morning Gian handed me an envelope that someone slid under our door. It was sealed with a wax stamp of my family crest.

I tore open the seal and regretted the act. "I wish I had taken a picture of the envelope."

"I took some for you," Gian said.

"That was so thoughtful."

I read the note in disbelief. "The Chief has invited us for a drink today at four."

"At the castle?"

I nodded. I couldn't find my voice.

"What should we wear?"

"I love that this is your first question."

"Well, I am Italian."

The bottom of the invitation said the dress was semi-formal. We searched the internet to see what this

315

meant in Scotland. Gian would be fine in the outfit he wore the first day, and I was going to have a chance to show off the dress I discovered in town.

The clock struck three o'clock. We were forty-five minutes away from heading to the castle.

"This afternoon has stretched longer than Loch Ness," Gian said, grinning from his Scottish Dad joke.

He was looking sharp, having incorporated a tie to his earlier shirt. The result of this simple addition was stunning.

I wore a dress crafted from the Cameron Clan's red tartan. It had a wrap-effect at the bust and waist. I accessorized it with black tights and tall boots.

"That is one sexy dress." Gian pulled me into his arms.

"I'm a little nervous," I said. "How about we break into the scotch."

"I should warn you. Whisky has the opposite effect on me. Instead of turning into an asshole, I become a lover."

"Consider me warned," I said. It didn't have the sexy tone I was hoping for and we both laughed.

After our second glass, we headed on foot to the Gatehouse for Achnacarry Estate. At the base of our driveway, we paid tribute to the ruins of the original castle. Brodie was waiting in the road.

"Ye clean up nicely," he said.

I responded with a curtsy.

"Good to see you again." Gian extended his hand for a firm shake.

Brodie led us over a small bridge and along a tree-lined road. The walk offered time to ponder the situation but was short enough to see the estate off in the distance. I picked up my stride, eager to arrive.

Even though it wasn't technically a castle, the brickwork and the turret on the West corner of the estate makes it look like one. The building was breathtaking.

"How should we address the Chief?" I asked.

"Sir Donald will do," Brodie said.

He guided us past the ornate front door to a stone patio with three comfortable chairs and a table. I was disappointed that we weren't going inside, but not by much. The moment felt like a dream.

Across the lawn, past the beech trees, the river Arkig flowed broad and rapid. To the right were rhododendrons, with a field beyond stretching a few miles.

Brodie assumed his position outside the door as Donald Cameron of Lochiel, the Chief of the Cameron Clan emerged, his shuffling gait balanced by an ornately carved wooden cane that he clutched in his right hand. The Chief's jolly face accented his unruly eyebrows. Dad had only begun growing his out. He would be jealous of the length of these magnificent brows.

Sir Donald wore a kilt, a tweed jacket, and a black Scottish beret. The outfit looked like something he would wear around the house. Classy yet comfortable. I hoped we weren't overdressed.

"Linsey Cameron, it is a pleasure to meet ye," The Chief said. He had a learned tone to his accent.

Gian and I rose to greet the man.

"The pleasure is mine, Sir Donald." I curtsied and offered my hand. His shake was firmer than I was expecting.

"Gian Lombardo," the Chief said.

Both Gian and I laughed. Sir Donald had pronounced his name with a thick Scottish accent.

The Chief's face lit up, and he joined in the laughter. "How would one pronounce yer name?"

Gian explained the soft G and said his full name with an exaggerated Italian accent.

317

"I was askin' for that," Sir Donald said, then repeated Gian's name correctly. "Welcome to my home. Sit, please."

A middle-aged woman in a servant's apron rolled a cart onto the drive. It shook on the way to the stone patio. She placed a bottle of twenty-five-year-old scotch carefully on the table, then set an assortment of hors d'oeuvres down. The oldest scotch I'd ever had was eighteen years, and it wasn't served in glasses etched with my family crest.

"Forgive me for struggling to believe the tale of the Dark Times," Sir Donald said. "It is a bit over the top, don't ye know."

"That's understandable," I said. "I didn't believe it at first, either."

"It is my duty to behave as if I do. If the story is true, ye are in our history. Although, in this war, it sounds like we won."

I leaned over to Gian. "The Cameron Clan has a long tradition of bravely fighting in the greatest losing battles."

"That we do," Sir Donald said with a chuckle. "I would like to offer a toast. Gian, would you do the honors of pouring a wee dram of Scotch?"

"It would be my pleasure."

Gian broke the wax seal and uncorked the bottle. He hesitated, probably trying to decide what a wee dram should be. He filled our glasses a quarter full and passed them over.

"Please excuse my staring," Sir Donald said to Gian. "Ye are quite stunning. And I'll have ye know I have never said that to a man."

"I'm sure you're used to people staring yourself."

"That's not from me looks," he quipped.

We shared a chuckle over that.

Sir Donald rose from his chair and held up his glass. I started to get up but Gian placed a hand on my leg.

"On behalf of the Cameron Clan, I humbly thank ye for ending the Dark Times. This was a thousand-year war that shouldn't have happened for one minute. I welcome you, Linsey and Gian, into the family and celebrate the Blithe. I'll drink a cup to Scotland yet, with all the honors three."

We toasted our glasses, and in Scottish Gaelic, I said, "Slainte mhath," which means good health.

"Slainte," Sir Donald repeated.

"This is excellent scotch," I said. Twenty-five years in a wooden cask noticeably mellowed out the flavor, revealing a stronger hint of oakwood.

"It is my preferred brand," Sir Donald said.

I continued in Scottish Gaelic, "The curse was no match for Gian's and my love. With pride, we brought peace to our land."

The Chief teared up. "The youth today aren't learning the old language. It warms my heart."

We had a prolonged conversation in the tongue of our ancestors. I understood half of what Sir Donald was saying. He explained that he would try to bring our family back into the Clan records, but it could prove difficult. The Chief realized we were excluding Gian and repeated the last part in English.

Gian insisted we continue talking in Scottish Gaelic. Usually, a boyfriend would be jealous of being left out.

"I can arrange a tutor if ye are interested," Sir Donald said, sticking to English. "To perfect the tongue."

"I would appreciate that. It's hard learning on my own. Thank you."

"It will be no trouble."

"Do you know what our relationship is? You and me."

"I had the same question," Sir Donald said. "A trace of the bloodline proved difficult. From what we can gather, our lineage connects with Angus de Cambrun, the

319

first Chief of what is now known as the Cameron Clan. My family to his first son Gillespick. And yers to his youngest, Ràild. We are cousins with a long line of 'greats' in front of it."

"It is an honor to know you," I said.

"And the same to ye."

"Can I fill your glass," Gian said.

"Please. I was wondering why it was empty," Sir Donald responded. "Yer probably wondering why we're outside. I have a surprise arranged." He nodded at Brodie, who spoke into a walkie-talkie.

A team of drummers rolled a beat, followed by the unmistakable sound of pipers filling their bags with air.

"Holy shit!" Gian said.

The song "Scotland the Brave" began as the band emerged from the front of the estate, four people wide and four deep. The first two rows were pipers, then the drummers.

Gian had tears in his eyes. How could he not?

"Don't ye go blubbering through the whole performance, ye, big baby," Sir Donald said.

Gian's laugh came bursting forth in a spray of scotch.

The troop rested short of our table, just off the main entrance. They entertained us with two more songs.

Sir Donald leaned over to me. "I hear ye are proficient with the Highland Sword Dance. Can I talk ye into a performance?"

"Of course," I said. "I would be honored."

"I was hoping ye would say that. Ye will find a traditional dress inside the house. My butler Gerard will show ye the way."

I wasn't sure if I was more excited to perform the dance or go inside the estate. On the way, I forced myself to slow my pace so I didn't appear too eager.

The foyer resembled an English manor. I could sure feel the age. The Cameron history was on every wall, in paintings, pictures, crests, armor, and weaponry. I was in awe. The estate was the real museum.

"Right this way, lassie," Gerard said, leading me to a room beyond the grand staircase.

Hanging on a hook was a Highland dress. I was surprised that everything was my size, even the dancing shoes.

Dressed in the traditional attire, I lay the swords upon the wooden floor and practiced the steps.

Gian said something that made Sir Donald laugh. They turned to me as I came through the door, and my boyfriend whistled.

"I've been waiting a long time for this," Gian said. "Thank you for asking her."

Sir Donald nodded at him.

I was nervous, standing in front of the men. Not just for the dance, but what Gian would think of my performance. From an outsider's view, the dance can look a bit silly.

A wooden dance floor was placed in the gravel. I walked to the middle and lay my swords in a cross.

Sir Donald spoke, addressing the band. "We have a treat this evening. To perform the Highland Sword Dance is our guest from America, Linsey Cameron."

"The Huntress," a piper said. "I knew that was them. The stories are true."

"Now, now," Sir Donald said. "We don't know that to be the case."

The man tilted his head like a confused puppy. "Can ye tell me that is not Gian Lombardo sitting next to ye?"

"Aye, this is in fact Gian," he said with the correct pronunciation.

"Gian," the man repeated correctly and smacked his head, acknowledging his blunder. "To the Blithe," he said and dropped to his knee.

Sir Donald's eyes lit up. "How many of ye understand what he is talking about?"

No one in the band came forward.

"Let us keep it that way," Sir Donald said. "I don't want to put this fine lad in danger of retaliation. There were a lot of deaths due to the Curse. We don't want any more."

I was grateful for his concern.

"Thank you," Gian said.

I placed my hands on my hips, signaling it was time to begin the song I requested. I wasn't just dancing for Sir Donald; I was performing for the history of my kin.

The pipers filled their bags and began. I was in a trance as I leaped and bounded around the blades of the swords. Performing the tradition on the Cameron grounds was the single most significant moment of my life. I'd never felt more proud.

Sir Donald asked Gian to help him to his feet so he could properly applaud.

Gerard came out and whispered in Sir Donald's ear.

"I apologize for cutting our visit short, but I have a flight to catch. From what I gather, a crowd has formed out yonder to hear ye play. Would you bless me with an additional song? I would like ye to lead my guests down the drive."

"It would be an honor," the outspoken piper said.

I fetched the swords and headed to the estate to change. I returned in my dress.

"Before you depart, I would like ye and Gian to take a knee," Sir Donald said.

I glanced at my boyfriend, confused, and kneeled in front of the Chief.

Brodie handed a sword to the Chief and took his cane.

322

"Linsey Cameron, for your brave service to the Cameron Clan, I dub thee Dame Linsey." He touched each of my shoulders with the sword.

Had I just been knighted?

"Gian Lombardo, for your brave service to the Cameron Clan, I dub thee Sir Gian. I don't have a knighthood award, and I'm not sure I can even perform this duty, to be honest. But I do have these family crests."

Brodie exchanged the sword for the cane and gave Sir Donald two medallions on blue lanyards. He placed one around each of our necks. The medal was heavy in my hands. If it weren't for the Cameron Clan's embossed crest, I wouldn't believe what just happened.

"Please, fill yer glasses for the stroll home," Sir Donald said.

"That's very thoughtful," I said. Gian grabbed the bottle to top off our drinks.

"I wish I could stay. Yer story is fascinating. Tell me, is it true?"

I looked the Chief straight in the eyes. "It is as real as real can be," I said.

"What a day this has been!" Sir Donald said. "It was an honor to meet ye."

"The honor was ours," Gian said.

"Ye know what?" Sir Donald said. "Why don't ye take the bottle."

"You're too kind," I said.

"It is the least I can do. I have spoiled ye. It will be a chore switching to a younger scotch. That I can assure ye."

The piper in the band who spoke earlier offered his hand. "I am Rory. Thank ye, Dame Linsey, for breaking the curse."

"You're welcome," I said, shaking his hand.

"Sir Gian, thank ye."

"Love is all it took," Gian said.

Rory smiled. "Love, it is a powerful force."

"How did you know about the Curse?" I asked.

He let out a sigh. "A friend in London was murdered by a Dread. James was a good man."

Gian sank in on himself.

"Do not feel bad," Rory said. "Ye fixed it so no one will suffer again."

Gian hugged him and his bagpipe made a horrible racket as the air rushed through.

The rest of the band offered their gratitude to the Chief. The troop fanned out from the back, on each side, until the original formation was heading toward the road. We gave them enough distance that we could talk privately.

"Did we just get knighted?" Gian said loudly over the song.

"I believe we did, Sir Gian."

At the main road, a crowd had gathered. There must have been thirty people out front. As the band turned left to the museum, we headed to our room.

I called Maxwell as soon as we were in the apartment. He asked what the best part of my day was. Boy, did I have a story for him. After we reminisced about our visit with Sir Donald, I asked what Max's favorite part was.

He hesitated. "Promise you won't get mad."

I wasn't sure how to respond.

"I talked Joan into going on a date with me." He paused and I was silent, shocked at the revelation. "I believe I love her."

"This is wonderful news," I said. "I couldn't ask for a better sister. Although, you might want to get a DNA test. We may be related."

"We already have. Joan's lineage flows straight to Robert the Bruce."

"Oh, la-di-da," I said.

"You're not mad, are you?"

"What? No, not at all. I was making fun of her noble lineage going all the way to Robert the Bruce. That's just funny with our Clan being a bunch of murderers and thieves. I can't think of anyone better for you. Joan is one of the coolest chicks I know."

"Thanks for understanding. It sounds like you're having fun in Europe. I'm super jealous."

I hadn't thought about that. "Should I quit sending pictures?"

"Send more. I'm digging your trip. You earned this. I'm proud of you, Linsey."

"You'll be here soon enough," I said. "If you really want to be jealous, we're drinking a twenty-five-year-old scotch."

"Wow, how is it?"

"Noticeably better."

I called Joan after I hung up, which was funny because Maxwell could have just handed the phone to her. She was in our backyard, chilling in the hammock.

Our adventures in Scotland were a blur. Aside from seeing me dance, Gian's favorite part was touring the whisky distilleries. We were on our lips when we returned to the stables. Our Uber driver was adamant that he watched us stumble to the door, but we awoke passed out in the middle of the courtyard for anyone to run over.

We were back in the courtyard with our luggage, wondering where the time had gone.

"Thank you, Caleb," I said. "We thoroughly enjoyed our trip."

"You'll always have a place at the Achnacarry."

"That means the world," I said. "Thank you for everything."

The Bentley was turning out of the drive as I looked back to say goodbye to the carriage house.

"Did you enjoy yer stay?" Gregory said over his shoulder.

"It was like a fantasy," I said. Brodie was walking up to Gian's door. "Can you stop the car?"

"I apologize for the interruption, Sir Gian, Dame Linsey," Brodie said, leaning up to the window. "I came to say goodbye."

Gian and I stepped out to greet him.

I held onto Brodie's hand. "Thank you for the private tour of Achnacarry." Brodie had shown us the estate while Sir Donald was away.

"It was wonderful," Gian said. "I know that's a lazy word, but there's no other way to describe the experience."

"It *was* wonderful," I said.

Chapter 18

Italy was the final destination on our journey. A driver and a handsome man with slicked-back hair, met us inside the Catania Airport in Sicily. The second gentleman was dressed exceptionally well. I was particularly fond of his black silk shirt.

"Buongiorno," Gian said to the man. "Would we happen to be related?"

"We are not familiare, but we are connected," the man said and winked. He was a Dread. "My name is Renaldo. I will be in your..." He turned to other man and asked for the translation of per sempre.

I gave him the word.

"Grazie, Bellissima."

"Prego."

"I apologize. My English is not so good. I was saying, Gian and Linsey, I will be in your debt forever."

"It was our pleasure," Gian said.

"Walk with me to your car."

We followed them through the main exit. The warm Sicilian breeze was a welcome greeting coming from the chilling winds of Scotland.

The car was a decent Alfa Romeo, but a far cry from the Bentley in Scotland. Renaldo sat up front with the driver. On our way out of the airport, we pulled into a lot of a private charter. A bright red Ferrari sat glimmering in the sun.

"Before we depart, I wanted you to see this automobile," Renaldo said. "She is Italy's finest."

Gian knew the car down to the size of the engine. I wouldn't know one from another, but it seemed this one was top of the line—which was funny in itself since they're all in an unreachable price range.

Renaldo dangled a set of Ferrari keys in front of Gian's face. "Would you like to drive to your uncles?"

"No way!" Gian said.

"She can be moody. I should give you a lesson."

Gian's stance softened. He looked relieved. Renaldo gestured to the driver's door and they were off.

I heard the throaty Ferrari engine returning from blocks away. Gian was ablaze with life as he emerged from the car. He walked around to the passenger side and held the door open for me. I slid into the luxurious cockpit and soaked up the opulence.

"We'll meet you in Novara di Sicilia," Renaldo said. "Do you need any luggage with you?"

"The red carry-on, please," I responded.

Renaldo snapped his fingers rudely at the driver.

"Don't kill yourselves in the mountains," Renaldo said. "Now is the time to be alive."

Gian is an exceptionally handsome man, but place him in a Ferrari's cockpit, and he becomes a God. He waved to Renaldo as we eased onto the road.

"This car is so awesome," he said with a huge childlike grin.

"Faster!" Renaldo yelled.

Gian raced onto the freeway. His enthusiasm was blocked by traffic. He zipped in and out, passing cars, but it didn't get us far.

Mount Etna appeared in all its glory as we crested a small hill. A puff of smoke or cloud rose from the volcano's peak.

Gian let out a stunned "Wow."

"Is it active?" I asked.

"Uncle Emilio says it's always doing a little something."

"She's magnificent."

Toll booths lined the road. We panicked, not knowing which lane to get in. I found a Telepass sticker behind the mirror and pointed the way. The gate wouldn't rise until we grabbed a ticket.

Once through, the traffic opened. I saw the sign for the speed limit. Gian was already going 60 kilometers over. He should have known better. A speed limit sign was in the middle of the speedometer.

"I think it's 90 here," I said, pointing it out on the dash.

"Cool. We should have that in America. Don't worry, we're good. Renaldo said the cops won't pull us over."

The speed limit rose to 130. Gian drove fast, but I never felt unsafe. From the passing lane, he would approach cars with his left signal on, and they would move out of our way. No one passed us. That was concerning.

The mountain loomed off to our left. Hidden in the shadow of the volcano was the lake where the young strega cast the malevolent spell. We traveled a hundred kilometers on the Autostrada in less than half an hour. I navigated us off the freeway to the small town of Trappitello. The buildings were more industrial than classic Italian. It still felt like Italy.

We found a parking spot across from a café to keep an eye on the car.

As we stepped from the Ferrari, Gian leaned in close and whispered. "I love that car. Look at me. I'm shaking with excitement."

I took his hand.

It seemed like everyone knew us. The locals inside the café practically fell over themselves to help. It was concerning when the blonde travelers did it too, but then I heard them talk; they were Sicilian.

A waitress sat us at an outdoor table. The moment washed over me. "I can't believe we're in Sicily."

"I know, it's crazy."

329

In the distance, a village sat perched high upon a narrow mountain. "Is that your town?"

"I don't think so. Novara di Sicilia is about an hour away. We should definitely visit that one."

Seattle is known for its coffee, but I'd never had a better cappuccino. Back in the Ferrari, Gian pressed a button and the hardtop retracted. I waited until we were back on the road to mock-bitch.

"They were staring at me like I was a freak. Ooh, look at the Huntress."

"Yeah, yeah," Gian said. "You were right."

"What was that?" I half-joked.

"Nothing."

It was rural driving from then on. The landscape was unmistakably Italian, lined with vineyards and stone villas. The highway crossed through the center of a town with hundreds of years old buildings — maybe thousands.

"Now, this is Italy," Gian said.

I smiled wide, taking everything in.

The road beyond the town narrowed. Gian navigated the steep inclines and sharp corners with precision. The foliage was barren, offering plenty of warning for approaching cars.

He stopped in front of a mansion that was at least a thousand years old.

"Is that abandoned?" I asked.

"Weird. Imagine what we could do with this?"

In the valley, across the bridge, stood a roadblock. A sign showed a man walking. Two massive cement blocks were moved to the side, wide enough for us to pass. I was pretty sure it was foot traffic only.

The road wasn't blocked. Half of it was in the river. An orange safety net covered most of the usable lane. We turned around, but the first choice of roads had a threatening privacy notice. The second was unpaved.

We were back at the washout, sitting in the car.

"Fuck it," Gian said.

He drove as far to the left as possible, barely squeezing through. We rode in silence. I felt better when a car passed us coming down the mountain.

The switchbacks were fun. Gian took the corners a little faster than I would have. He slowed down when we almost hit a passing car.

I had him stop for a volcano picture. The base practically touched our valley.

Near the top of our route was a deserted town. We wanted to explore, but a creepy van sat near the entrance. Gian noticed my shudder and slipped the car into gear. At the crest of the hill we entered a forest. There was a rustic camper off to the side. He slowed to a crawl.

I couldn't shake the feeling of danger. "Get the fuck moving."

The village of Novara di Sicilia sits amidst mountainous terrain, hidden far away from the tourists. The stone buildings are connected like ancient brownstones. We crossed the bridge into town and made our way along the cobblestone road. Our lineage met in these streets, fighting for the last stronghold of Messina. Gian's and my arrival closed the thousand-year gap.

The side streets were narrow. A motorcycle would barely fit. Our turn was broader, but not by much. His aunt and uncle's villa wasn't too far off the main road. Gian kept the car running for a moment.

"I had to hear the soft roar of the engine a little longer."

I spotted a man peering through the drapes. The blinds abruptly closed after he caught my eye.

"Is your dad here?" I asked.

"What? No, that's my uncle. They're twins."

The door flew open, and his uncle rushed out. He had the handsome facial structure of Gian's father. His dad must dye his hair. Uncle Emilio's was grayer, giving him a distinguished, scholarly look.

331

"Gian, why are you driving this Ferrari?" His sharp tone startled me.

"It was offered to us at the airport. How could I say no to a Ferrari?"

"Like this, *non*. The owner of this automobile is a dangerous man."

Was Renaldo someone who let the Curse overtake him? Was he a murderer? Would he continue killing, or did the early onset of the Reckoning wipe that out? What about the others? My mind raced.

Uncle Emilio circled the car. "There's no damage. Bring your luggage inside. I don't want you near this."

"Luggage is coming shortly," Gian said, "along with Renaldo to retrieve the Ferrari."

His uncle's face relaxed upon hearing Renaldo's name.

I fetched my carry-on from the trunk and followed the men inside. We found his aunt in the kitchen.

"I am Emilio, and this is my wife, Pia.

Gian's aunt was gorgeous. Her dark hair was in a half-part, falling loosely as if she were heading for a night on the town. Her natural cheek structure was the type women fake with makeup contouring.

"It is a pleasure to meet you." I embraced them both.

"I apologize for my reaction on the street. You frightened me. Benvenuto a casa, nephew. My niece," he said and kissed me on both cheeks. "Give me the keys. No more talking with Renaldo. I will take care of him."

A car pulled up outside.

"Let us say ciao and be polite," Pia said, taking the keys from her husband. "We will show our gratitude. Make it quick and make it humble."

Renaldo behaved like a gentleman, wishing us well, and left without incident. He didn't even check the car.

"Who is this Renaldo?" Gian asked.

"He is a bad man from a worse family. Come, help me select the vino," Emilio said. "I need a drink."

We followed his uncle to a cellar with an arched wooden ceiling that resembled the inside of a barrel. Full racks of wine lined the walls.

"Ah, this one will do." He kissed the dusty bottle. "It is d'annata, vintage as you say. Linsey, what would you like?"

"Maybe a Chianti?" I said. It was the only Italian wine I could remember.

"Aziano Chianti Classico will please your palate. I am sure of it," he said and handed me a bottle.

Another staircase led to their courtyard. Pia was setting the table with exquisite plates of antipasto. High walls enclosed the space, offering absolute privacy. An Italian sonata played low over the speakers wrapping me in comfort.

"I adore your place," I said.

"Thank you, mio caro," Pia said. "We have had a beautiful life in this villa, but because of you, the safety it provides is no longer needed."

"We are searching for a villa with con vista, a view," Emilio said. "There is no more... occultamento."

"Hiding," I translated. "Your English is superb, but if you wish, io parlo Italiano."

He looked at his nephew. "My brother says that Gian is not so good with his Italian."

"I never thought I would be in Italy. Continuerò il mio insegnamento." He meant to say I will continue my lessons but used the word teaching instead of lessons, which was adorable.

Uncle Emilio opened the vintage bottle and emptied it into four glasses.

"Pace yourself, Emilio."

"Yes, darling. Tonight we celebrate the freedom that your love brings to our famiglie."

Pia saw the label on the wine bottle, and her eyes grew wide. I was honored that Emilio was sharing a special vintage with us.

A car backfired in the street, and a rifle sound echoed across the courtyard walls. Emilio was looking at me when this happened. His expression grew blank as if he was folding in on himself.

Pia reached for his hand, saving his wine, and spoke to him in Italian. "Honey, honey, Emilio, where are you? You're OK. You're safe. That was a car backfiring. Do you know where you are?"

He didn't respond.

"Darling, you are safe," Pia said. "You're in our courtyard. Come back to me. Gian is here."

Emilio's eyes darted around and his face softened. Pia helped him to his feet. They walked over to the fountain, then slowly strolled through the courtyard. The trauma my kind caused the Dread was unconscionable.

"Don't feel bad," Gian said.

Was this my fault? Now I did feel bad.

Pia joined us back at the table after escorting her husband inside. "I apologize. It has been years since this happened. The excitement of the day was too much."

"There is no reason to apologize," I said. "Would it be all right if I spoke to him?"

"Per favore."

I found Emilio pacing in the kitchen. He saw me and broke down. I comforted him in Italian. "Your family is safe, Uncle Emilio. The danger is no more. The fight is over. Come enjoy that fine wine."

The Lombardos insisted we attend a celebration that evening in the town square. Gian and I were spent from the journey but relented. We traversed narrow streets with steep steps and hills. Stone houses and shops boxed us in.

334

The history in the town overwhelmed my senses. This was Italy.

The ruckus from the throng of party-goers could be heard blocks away. The townsfolk packed the square so tightly there were tables set up on the adjacent streets. I felt no trace of the Touch, but I knew all around were the formerly cursed. A different sense was working overtime—my sense of smell. The aromas of fresh tomato sauce, cheese, and herbs wafted in the air. A feast was cooking, and it was making me hungry.

Our party was offered wine in plastic cups as we were guided to the dance floor. The crowd was impeccably dressed. Gian, thankfully, had sent my measurements to Pia. The dark blue dress she selected for me was stunning. Gian looked like a model in his new Italian suit.

I kept seeing flashes of spiritual clothing, a flowing dress blowing in the wind, wild hair flashing past. There were streghe in attendance. I searched the crowd but they didn't want to be found. Noticeably absent were Hunters. I was the sole Anglo, and people were staring.

Women carrying tambourines kicked off the traditional Sicilian folk dance. A group of young men rushed in to join them. Their style of dance reminded me of the Greeks with their arms raised high. Near the end of the performance, Mayor Russo introduced himself to our group. He motioned for Gian and me to move to the center of the dancers. We were thrust onto their shoulders and carried around the square like royalty—chants of forgiveness and appreciation echoed in Italian. The celebration was for us and the Blithe. I was embarrassed and proud all at the same time.

The atmosphere morphed into a dance party once the handsome young DJ laid down a beat. Aunt Pia whispered to Gian that it was time.

He turned to me. "We have a surprise for you. Uncle Emilio, would you entertain Linsey?"

"It will be my pleasure," he said, leading us to the dance floor.

Gian still hadn't returned when the music lowered. Mayor Russo was lit up on the stage. He addressed us in Italian.

"Ladies and gentlemen. Thank you for joining our celebration. As Mayor of Novara di Sicilia, it is my privilege to welcome Gian and Linsey into our village. We owe them nothing less than our lives."

The crowd's cheer echoed across the square.

"Like many people in attendance, I was Cursed," Mayor Russo said. "I have never publicly admitted that. When I passed the Age of Reckoning, I thought I was free, but I wasn't as long as others in my community were afflicted. The love of this couple changed the world for the better. To the Blithe." The townsfolk cheered it back. "Please welcome to the stage, Gian Lombardo and his aunt Pia."

Aunt in Italian is zia. She was Zia Pia. I found that adorable.

Zia and Gian stepped out from behind the curtain. People were on their feet cheering. Mayor Russo stood off to the side of the stage. He gestured for me to join him.

Gian adjusted the height of his microphone. "Thank you very much for the warm Novara di Sicilia welcome," he said in rehearsed Italian. "Although I have never been here, I feel like I haven't left. The thousand years of hell are over." He paused for the roar of exuberance to die down. "The following song has deep meaning for Linsey and me, but tonight we sing it to say goodbye to the Dark Times."

He walked over to the DJ booth and set a needle on a record. The opening of Time to Say Goodbye began, and the crowd went wild. He lifted the needle noisily.

"Wouldn't you rather sing this with an orchestra?" he asked Pia.

"That I would."

336

The curtain parted, revealing a half symphony. Gian and Pia took their places in front of the microphones. The conductor tapped his wand and commenced with the song. I was bawling before the singing began.

Pia's voice resonated beautifully through the square. It was hauntingly emotional. I was impressed by the quality of her singing. The soulful pitch of Sarah Brightman's soprano is hard to match, but his aunt came close.

Gian motioned for me to stand beside him. I shook my head, but he insisted.

He positioned me between himself and his aunt so he could gaze at us both. When Pia reached specific notes, I felt them to my core. Watching Gian react to these moments with closed eyes or a little grin linked us together like I had the Touch again.

My boyfriend held my gaze when he began his solo. His voice was angelic in the open air of his ancestors. He navigated through his section brilliantly.

When it was time for the duet, I gracefully switched sides. Pia took his hand, and he shifted his stance to face her.

The pitch and strength of the song rose in a crescendo, aided by the symphony. Their voices bloomed through me as we headed toward that pinnacle of musical beauty. They held the final note so long and gracefully I had goosebumps as my breath rushed from me. The audience was reduced to tears and cheered in approval.

"You performed the lyrics beautifully," Pia said to Gian. "Andrea would be proud."

"Grazie Zia Pia," he said into the mic.

"No, thank you, Gian. You and Linsey have changed the world." She raised a glass. "To our future. To the Blithe."

The family was drinking at Mayor Russo's table. From behind me came a concerned, "Don Trentino."

The crowd parted, and an older gentleman in an impeccable Italian three-piece suit and a white fedora strode confidently to our table. He had a bushy mustache and was enjoying a fine cigar.

"Forgive me for interrupting," he said. "Merda. I… I forgot the translation."

The Don looked frustrated at his limited English.

"Per favore, in Italiano," I requested.

"Tu parli Italiano," he said, relieved and continued in his native tongue. "My lineage was plagued for a thousand years with the curse. It would be an honor to shake the hands of the couple who broke it."

We rose to accept his gratitude.

"I forgive you and your family," he said to me.

Forgiveness coming from the head of a Mafia family was monumental. "Don Trentino, your kindness is much appreciated," I said.

"Gian, you are forever in my heart," the Don said. "What you did for the Cursed. There are no words. Thank you."

"Il piacere è tutto mio, signore," Gian said.

Even though Gian expressed his gratefulness adequately, the Don switched to English. "Did you enjoy driving my car today?"

"That was your Ferrari? If I'd known, I would have driven a *lot* slower."

"*That* is why you didn't know," he said and laughed. "What is the use of driving a Ferrari if you go slow? The car is in the garage, dreaming of the open road. You must give signora what she wants."

No wonder the people in Trappitello bent over backward to help Gian and me. They were terrified because we arrived in the Don's Ferrari. This is why we had scared the hell out of Uncle Emilio.

The Don turned to the crowd. "There will no longer be a division. The Cursed and the Hunters were all under spells. I do not hold a grudge."

His entourage chuckled.

"They are right to laugh. Getting me to... lasciarsi andare?"

"Let go," I said.

"Those are small words for such a large gesture. Getting me to let go is harder than pushing water up a hill. Life is now a celebration. Who knows, I may go into honest business."

That brought more laughter from his entourage. He called his family over to introduce themselves. One by one, they offered their gratitude. Renaldo tipped his hat from afar.

A dark-haired woman in her thirties was the last to approach. She leaned close to my ear and whispered in Gallo-Italic, "I can't forgive your family. Hunters murdered both my sons."

I was taken aback by her apprehension but understood. In the old language, I said, "I hope you will come to trust that we are not the enemy you once hated." At least, that is what I believe I said.

The Don turned back and gave me a bear hug. "Parli Gallo-Italic. That is a treat."

The woman apologized and broke down crying.

I pulled back to let the Don go, but he held on so he could subtly wipe his tears on my shoulder. He kept me at arm's length and winked.

As the entourage was leaving, the Don stopped in his tracks. "I almost forgot." He reached into his coat pocket, and people gasped.

"What? This is an envelope," he said, holding it out. "I want you to have a place of your own in Sicily. Maybe for good?"

"No," Gian's uncle protested. "It's too much."

A hush crept through the crowd. But the Don chuckled. "You must be Emilio. Don't worry. There are no strings attached. You will not see me again. That I promise." He gave Gian the envelope. Inside was a deed with our names listed and a ring of keys.

The Don addressed the crowd. "Linsey will remain safe. There can be no ill will toward the past. Anyone who harms her will suffer a fate worse than death." With that, the Don stepped into the night.

"Can you believe he ended with a threat?" Uncle Emilio said. "Such a low note. I would have exited on the high of his generous gift."

His wife hit his arm. "Don't disrespect the Don."

We stumbled to our new place at sun up, hoping it was furnished with at least a bed. The Don gifted us the top floor of a charming stone villa.

Our front door was solid metal. Plaster and exposed stone adorned the walls. The wide beams on the ceiling were hundreds of years old. I wasn't expecting the kitchen to be so modern. There was a six-burner gas stove with a double oven. Off in the corner sat a breakfast nook. We followed the arched brick hallway. The beams on the bedroom's tall ceiling matched the kitchens. I was happy to see a bed. We were surprised to find our clothes in the closet. His aunt and uncle must have dropped them off. That's why Emilio insisted on looking at the deed.

Further down the hall was a living room with a door to a stone terrace. Mountainous terrain stretched out far below.

"I would be fine living half the year here," I said.

Gian took me in his arms. "There aren't many things that would make me happier," he said.

The following morning on the way to the Lombardos, we passed through the town square. The celebration was going strong. It would be two more days until it wound down, never once breaking. We felt obligated to attend as most of the townsfolk wanted to meet us.

There was one day of recovery before our celebration with the streghe. A knock at the door woke me up that morning. On our stoop were two packages tied creatively with hand-spun twine. I carried them into our bedroom. Inside the larger box was a note from the High Priestess.

Linsey, this sundress was designed and created for you. We hope it will be to your liking.

I squealed and tore into the delicate crepe paper covering my gift. The streghe had crafted a gorgeous bohemian dress. I rushed to put the outfit on and spun with my arms wide. The fabric danced as if it were alive.

Inside the other box was a pair of finely crafted leather sandals for Gian. They were the type he had been searching for all week.

"The witches didn't forget about you," I said, handing them over.

"How did they know?" he said, turning the sandals in his hand. We both knew the answer. "Let's shower and head into town to find me an outfit to complement yours."

"Not so fast," I said, grabbing his cock.

It was midnight when our driver entered the streghe's compound on the shore of Lake Pergusa. The late hour was not a coincidence.

The witch's main house was massive, built in a classic Italian stone tradition. The landscaping around the loop drive was manicured to precision.

"I'm nervous," I said, unsure of what we were in for.

341

"Don't be," Gian said. "I won't leave your side."

A young blonde child came running from the house when we stepped from the car.

"Piacere, sono Marta," the girl said. "La figlia di Bianca."

"She's the High Priestess' daughter," I said to Gian, then told her it was an honor to meet her.

"I understood what she was saying. Basic Italian is coming back to me. Plus, she looks just like Angela."

Marta was staring at Gian like he was a rock star. He picked her up and kissed her cheek. She giggled and wiggled out of his arms.

The girl positioned herself in the middle and took a hand from each of us. She led us around the side of the house to a large stone patio. The landscaping below was a fairyland of shaped bushes and enchanting trails. Wind chimes and statues were placed thoughtfully throughout. Everywhere we turned provided picturesque views, especially the lake and volcano looming in the distance. The sitting areas were comfortable and informal, perfect for socializing.

I was expecting only female streghe, but there were males in attendance. They were all in casual attire, with many wearing loose headdresses of twigs and flowers.

"Madre!" Marta yelled.

Bianca, the High Priestess, waved from the lawn as she walked toward us. Her white cotton outfit billowed as if the wind and her body were having a conversation. The confidence in her gaze was intimidating.

"Venite bambini!" Bianca shouted.

A group of giggling, excited kids ran out from the villa and surrounded us. They were screaming their names, introducing themselves at once.

"Siete davvero adorabili," I said.

"No more malevolent spells," Gian scolded playfully.

342

They laughed as if he was the funniest man on the planet.

"I'm not joking. Linsey and I are very happy."

"OK, you have met them. Off to bed," Bianca said.

A groan flowed through the children, but they didn't protest. A nanny was waiting for them in the doorway.

"Your dress looks fantastic on you," Bianca said, checking the fit. "It's perfect. This will be a best seller."

"Best seller?" I said.

"The Pergusa line of clothing is our coven's main source of income." She leaned close and whispered, "And my true passion."

"You have a gift," I said. "It is the most beautiful dress I've ever seen."

"You're too kind," she said modestly.

"You speak English very well," I said.

"Communication is important in support."

The streghe on the patio and down on the lawn were strangely standoffish. "Did we do something wrong?" Gian asked. "Hardly anyone is looking at us."

"Take no offense," Bianca said. "My coven is overwhelmed by Linsey's nervousness and are offering time to relax. I have a potion that will help."

Bianca signaled to a staff member. They were the only ones in formal attire.

"I haven't been to many parties," I said as an honest excuse.

"That is nothing to be ashamed of. Being nervous at the beginning of a party is not a sign of weakness. It is your body prepping for the fun that's about to happen, pulling you back so you can be thrust to the heavens." She retrieved two glasses from the server's tray. "This concoction will help."

"What is it?" I asked.

"Alcohol."

Gian and I laughed.

I took a long swig. "Is this...?"

"Si," Bianca said, excited that I recognized the drink. "It's the cocktail d'autore of the party. We call it an OranGian."

I loved the name. It was a play on Gian's name and the French beverage Orangina. "Where did you find the Italian soda?" I said before I could stop myself.

"Don't worry. It is the silly things we say which make life interesting. As I was saying, there is no reason to be nervous. This is a party, not a ritual. If anyone uses their powers tonight, they will be banished from the coven."

"But, isn't that a witch's brew," Gian said, gesturing to a giant kettle.

"No," she laughed. "That's sangria. Lucia and I are the only ones allowed to use our powers this evening. Mi scusi, I mean Nera. Fuck!"

"I didn't think that was her name, you and her being named black and white. It would be a big coincidence."

"My name is Bianca. But please call her Nera. Do not say her real name. Do not think it."

Nera materialized with her back to us and scolded Bianca in Italian. "What the shit, Bianca? Don't pull me from the underworld like that."

I think underworld is what she said. She used the term il inferno. There's no way she could have meant Hell.

Nera paused. "They're behind me?"

Bianca nodded.

Nera turned to face us. She didn't look like someone who was braving the underworld. She had a caring glow like a new mom full of love. I adored the blood-red wrap she was wearing. I wouldn't want to be in the underworld barefoot, though. I wouldn't want to be there at all.

"Gian, Linsey, it is a treat to have you as guests at our villa."

"Gian, this is the location where the young strega cast a dark spell on your people. The curse caused Lake Pergusa to turn blood red. When the Blithe occurred, within a week, the water became green with the soul of the earth. The scientists are still baffled," she said with a laugh. "I brought you here to show you there is now only love."

"Even though we are shrouded in darkness, all I feel is light," Gian said.

"That is the mother Goddess's embrace," Bianca said. "All is well again. When you are ready, come join us and the celebration will commence." She snapped her fingers and, with a pop, was gone.

Her disappearance didn't faze Gian. He gazed upon me lovingly. "I hope our life remains as relaxed as we are right now."

"God, I hope so," I said, drawing him close to my chest.

We returned to the house, where the full party was waiting on the patio. There were around seventy people in attendance. Bianca introduced Gian and me, and the crowd clapped as we climbed the steps to the patio.

Nera was back. She spoke first. I was expecting Italian but she gave her speech in English. "Gian and Linsey. We waited a thousand years for a loving couple to break the Curse." Her voice was kind and warm. "You are forever in our hearts." She lifted her glass. "To love."

"To love," the streghe said in unsettling unison and drank.

"It is not only the Cursed and Hunters who are free. The streghe are no longer bound to a role of support. For that, we are thankful."

"Gian," Bianca said, taking his hands. "It does not seem fair that we supported the Hunters. I will have you know we supported the Cursed when a Hunter killed outside their role. We guided their demise all the same. I hope we kept a fair game. There were casualties on both sides. It was a challenge to keep a balance. Our goal was to minimize deaths directly resulting from the Curse. It was nothing personal. We were rooting for you and are honored to have you on this sacred land."

Gian nodded graciously. "I don't hold any ill regard toward the streghe."

"You're a beautiful man, inside and out," she said, touching his face. "To our newest streghe in attendance, you have our permission to let your guard down. Tonight is a celebration. You will have plenty of time to recover as nothing is planned for tomorrow. Meet our guests. Drink our drink. Most of all, be happy."

I was on the tail end of my third cocktail. The looser I became, the livelier the party grew. It was as if the witches were feeding off my growing lack of inhibitions.

Dancing is what freed my spirit the most. A band called James was playing on the lawn at the base of the patio. I loved the positive energy of their music. The lead singer moved in a unique energetic way that made me want to emulate him in dance. He was so enchanting I suspected that he was a strega, but he turned out to be just a normal guy from Manchester, England. Well, as normal as a famous musician can be.

Gian's confidence was off the charts. He had a childlike curiosity toward the witches. They scared me a little. He wanted to meet them all.

The coven was becoming more scantily clad with each passing hour. Many were naked, but they presented themselves with the poise of the fully clothed. To fit in, I ditched my panties.

Gian and I were on a walk of the lower grounds with Bianca's daughter and her boyfriend. The path I chose led to a massive round mattress suspended from an old oak. We kicked off our shoes and hopped on.

348

I was on my back, propped up on my elbows. Gian leaned against one of the thick ropes holding up the mattress. Angela and Alfonso were cuddled up across from us. The mattress was so large four more people could have fit on it.

"So, what is it like dating a strega?" I asked Alfonso.

"You can ask Angela," he said. "I am also a witch."

"I am so sorry. Was that sexist of me? Witchist?"

"Witchist, I like that. It's not sexist. The women are in charge, after all. Many of the men here are streghe. Some are quite powerful. Where I shine is in potions and concoctions. I am a healer."

"He is also an excellent chef," Angela said. "And a rocking mixologist. The Italian soda for the OranGians is from his recipe. I'll send you home with a bottle. Without alcohol, it tastes like sunshine in the morning."

"I can't take all the credit," Alfonso said. "The oranges that grow on the property are the finest in the world."

"He's humble," Angela said. "It's what holds back his powers."

Gian pushed off the ground with his foot, getting the mattress swinging. Another couple our age walked up the path. I noticed the girl earlier. She was probably trying for a stereotypical witch's look with her cat-eye glasses, but it gave her the appearance of a girl from the 50s. The man followed a few feet behind. His eyes were lowered timidly.

"I'm Chiara." There was a quirky nervousness in her manner of speaking. "Can we join you?"

"The more the merrier," Gian said. We shuffled back to give them room.

"This is my pet, Orlando," she said, gesturing to the man standing obediently at her side. He had a short comb-over like a five-year-old and a passive way of holding himself. I wondered if he actually was her pet? Like a transformed version of her cat?

"What a silly thought," Chiara said.

The only response I could come up with is, "You're a silly thought."

"That was rude of me. I'll stay out of your head. All the same, I have a personal question to ask. If you don't mind."

"I'm an open book," I said, pretending I was.

Chiara's smile was awkward, almost forced. "You experienced something very rare. The Mirror's Touch allowed you to feel what Gian was experiencing. I imagine the sex must have been incredible. What was it like?"

"Chiara!" Angela scolded.

"Angela," Chiara said in a mocking tone.

"It's all right," I said. "Get me a refill and I'll tell you all about it."

Orlando was sent to fetch my beverage.

"Don't mind Chiara," Angela said. "She doesn't have boundaries."

"You just don't know how to have fun!" Chiara shot back.

"Project much?" Angela said.

"I really don't mind," I said.

Orlando returned with two pitchers of OranGian. There's a man who knows how to accommodate.

"You asked what sex was like with the Mirror's Touch?" I said. "Where do I begin? What I felt from him was as clear as something happening to me. His body was my mine. It was like being able to suck your own dick but your mouth is a pussy."

Gian laughed.

"I could feel his cock pulse with anticipation before he even entered me. As he pressed inside, the stretch of him filling me to capacity was met with my warm and fevered embrace. I would lose track of what was him and what was me. My favorite was feeling my pelvic muscles

350

contract tightly around his cock as I came. The first time we had sex, I made him come a second time from this. What was the Mirror's Touch like? It pretty much blew my mind. The Touch was fucking awesome."

"My goodness," Chiara said. The old expression made me laugh. "Who has a better orgasm? Men or women?"

"All I have to go on is my experience with Gian, but from what I've felt, it's not even close," I said. "A man's orgasm is different, not all-encompassing like a woman's. It's focused in the genitals, and because they're outside the body, that's where the feeling lies. As good as it feels, it's nothing compared to a woman's ability to have earth-shattering orgasms. A man's is mostly different levels of the same type. Theirs doesn't grow in intensity with each release. I'm not sure a man could handle the magnitude of the female orgasm. It's the emotion that would be too much."

I felt like I was betraying Gian. "No offense," I told him.

"None taken, at all." He snuggled up behind me. The sex talk was making him horny.

"Where a man wins is the ease at which they can achieve one," I said.

"You don't have to tell me that," Chiara joked. Orlando let the comment flow right over him.

"Who receives more pleasure? Or is it the same?" she asked.

"Again, it's not even close. The clitoris has twice as many nerve endings. I looked it up because the difference was so significant. This is why it's distracting for a woman to do sixty-nine."

The questions perked Angela's curiosity. "What feels best for a man?" she asked.

"For that, you would have to ask Alfonso," I said.

"Sure, but I want to know from a woman's perspective."

351

"Gian's arousal zone is concentrated on the front, where the head meets the shaft. I believe you call it il frenulo. The sexual spark was so strong in that spot. I imagine it is the same for all men."

All three men nodded in agreeance.

"What feels best for women?" Angela asked.

I paused, not knowing how to answer. "What works for me may not work for you. As long as you're honest, it should be easy for Alfonso to know what gets you off the most. What rocks your boat? Wait, don't answer that. Let's see if Alfonso knows."

"I can do better. I'll show you."

He hiked Angela's skirt up. She wasn't wearing any panties. Her pubic hair was just a wisp at the top and dyed black to match. It was startling having a pussy emerge so suddenly.

"Santa Merda!" Chiara said.

The word holy is sacred in Italy. For her to place it next to shit was extremely blasphemous. As funny as the expression was, it shocked me to hear.

"What the fuck?" Angela said. Even Alfonso paused to look over, and he was heading toward her pussy.

Chiara grinned widely, clearly proud of the shock value.

Alfonso placed his mouth on Angela and performed a nibbling maneuver on her clit, making his cheeks quiver like a chipmunk.

"That's fucking it," Angela moaned. "It's like he's mashing my clit, pressing the nerve endings until they spark in agreement."

Gian leaned forward and kissed the back of my neck. His soft touch fluttered in a tingling wave. Watching Angela get serviced, I was already wet. I had a feeling Chiara's whole plan was to coax us into sex. I was surprisingly fine with that.

"How about you?" I asked her.

"That's easy," Orlando said. They were the first words he spoke. Chiara removed her wrap, revealing a full bush. Orlando entered her slowly, tapping and rubbing on her clit while fucking her.

"That one is second best," Chiara said.

"Oh, right. Mi scusi." Orlando pulled out, replacing his cock with an eager tongue.

Chiara grasped a handful of his hair, lifting his head. "No apologizing during sex," she scolded. "It's not sexy."

Orlando shrunk in on himself and returned to his task. Gian slipped a hand under my skirt and fingered me lightly. The faint passes and subtle teasing sent my pulse racing.

"That's it," Chiara said. "He flicks and... what are the little bites called? Oh, I know, he nibbles at the same time. Look how he's doing that. Oh God, don't stop."

"What about you?" Angela asked.

My heart dropped as if I was being called on in class.

Orlando raised his head to see, but Chiara thrust it back.

No," he said forcefully.

"I know the move that gets her going," Gian said.

I pulled the skirt of my dress up and presented myself to my man. I should have been embarrassed but was buzzed enough not to care. Gian began sucking on the hood of my clitoris as he does so well.

"Nailed it," I said, laughing, then gasped with a quiver.

Chiara shoved Orlando's head back in place.

Gian switched his tongue placement so it pressed against my clit producing the sparks Angela described. From there he moved to Orlando's flicks and nibbles. Heated pulses and waves shot out in random directions.

We were soon naked but stayed together as couples. I couldn't help staring at all the dicks. Angela saw me watching.

"Come over here," she said, moving me to the edge of the bed. "Have you ever had multiple partners?"

"We had a threesome with a girl," I said proudly.

"One cock is powerful, two is overwhelming, but three is almost too much to comprehend. Boys," she said with a quick clap, calling them over.

The guys met at the base of the bed facing me. Angela set a pair of shorts on the ground and gently guided me to my knees. Once in the position, I hesitated.

"Touch them," she insisted. "Witches don't have sexual diseases. At least not for long. Come on, when will you get a chance to do this again?"

I looked up at Gian. He nodded that it was OK. I grabbed his first out of respect and then took Alfonso in my hand. He was uncircumcised. It flowed well in my grip as I stroked it. I switched from Gian to Orlando and was pumping the two uncircumcised cocks opposingly like pistons in an engine. I gathered all three and stroked as one, then rubbed them across my face feeling the smoothness of the skin against mine. The combined scent of their manhood was intoxicating.

I took Gian in my mouth. Being curious what an uncircumcised one felt like, I replaced his with Orlando's. The loose skin fluidly rolled in my grip and along my lips. I loved the feel and tried Alfonso. His was even better. I worked the three in succession, sometimes taking two in my mouth at once. I eventually forced myself to stop so Gian wouldn't see how much I was enjoying myself.

Chiara reached around my chest and coaxed me onto the bed. Angela followed. I looked over at my boyfriend. He waved me on.

The girls met on our knees in the middle of the mattress, forming a huddle facing each other. Angela was the first to make a move, leaning in for a kiss. Chiara

354

pulled her away and tenderly pressed her lips to mine. We rotated, sometimes kissing three at once.

A hand found my breast and my clit pulsed in anticipation. I reached out and caressed one of Angela's breasts. I wasn't expecting my heart to be racing so fast.

"Can I touch you below?" Chiara asked.

Angela and I both said yes. We looked at each other surprised, then down at Chiara's hands as she cupped our pussies. I was dripping wet.

I peeked at Gian, hoping he couldn't see how turned on I had become. All three of the men were staring as they stroked themselves, each with the same childlike expression of wonder as if this was the greatest thing they ever saw. I closed my eyes, slid my hand under Chiara's, pushing her off Angela, and felt the dampness.

My inexperience was probably evident, but I made up for it with unabashed curiosity. I fingered Angela gently at first, trying to see in my mind what I was feeling. Her outer labia was thicker than mine. I delved farther into her slick folds in search of her clit. Touching another woman was so foreign yet familiar.

Chiara grinned mischievously as she coaxed me onto my back. She glanced below, then looked seductively into my eyes. Gian nodded with a grin on his face. His stroking himself really turned me on. I could watch that all day.

Angela parted my knees and nestled her face on my pussy. Chara positioned herself between Angela's legs and her hips near me. I reluctantly shifted closer to her, completing our triangle. Seeing a pussy so close was a strange experience. Her scent was alluring, almost like honey apple. I hesitated, then gave Chara a light flick of my tongue. I liked it but didn't. The more I nibbled, licked, and sucked, the more the act wasn't clicking. I was going through the motions, not doing it out of lust. Chara didn't seem to mind when I stopped. I reached up and played with her breasts.

Angela was determined to make me come. She pressed down on my clit hard, lapping repeatedly. With each pass of her tongue, a charge of electricity danced through my core. The pressure built slowly like a rising tide. I glanced skyward as my vision narrowed and the stars pushed aside into darkness. My core trembled with each convulsion. I pressed Angela's face tightly against me, riding the orgasm to completion. My head rolled back as I waited for my limbs to return to normalcy.

"I can't take it," Gian said, gently coaxing Angela aside and straddling me, driving his cock home. I gasped as my pelvic muscles quivered and pulsed against him. I wrapped my legs around his lower back and pulled his lips to mine.

We split into couples again. The bed was rocking wildly from all the thrusting. Group sex wasn't the free for all I thought it would be. I was happy to find that consent matters.

Chiara was staring at my boyfriend as I stroked him. "I want you to Suck Gian's cock," she said to her pet.

Orlando shook his head, but there was a slight wanton smirk.

"Don't you shake your head at me. Suck his fucking cock."

Well, there went consent. Maybe this was part of their game.

Chiara mouthed, "Please" to Gian. He looked at me.

"Whatever," I said.

Gian moved to a standing position, steadying himself with one of the ropes holding the mattress. Orlando reluctantly sunk to his knees and took Gian in his mouth. For not wanting to, he sure got into the act.

Angela lifted her eyebrow at Alfonso to see if he wanted to get in on the guy-on-guy action. He gave her a stern, not in your lifetime look.

Gian lasted a minute before removing Orlando from his cock. The man had the widest grin on his face.

A silly idea came to me, as a reward for Gian being such a sport. I lay down on my back with my legs spread wide, then had Chiara move on top of me in the same position, then Angela, stacking our pussies like cordwood.

Gian dove right in, moving from one to another. He was like a boy in a candy store.

As each of us was serviced, the quivering resonated through the other women allowing us to read the reaction, like a mild version of the Touch.

Familiarity replaced permission and our group melted into a writhing pile of bodies. I would lose track of Gian and not know who I was even with, but he would find me. He was always there to make sure I was comfortable.

The energy in the air eventually began to wane. Gian was inside me, thrusting in a slow rhythmic roll. I wanted to wrap up our sexual escapades with an orgasm brought on from him.

"We'll help you," Angela said, speaking from inside my head.

I wasn't sure how to respond. "Thank you," I said out loud.

Gian smirked. "You're welcome?"

Chiara focused on my breasts while Angela strummed my clit like an instrument. Currents of electricity flowed from the witch's hands to my midsection. Gian moaned throatily as his thrusts worked in tandem with the witches.

A deep ache grew from my solar plexus. The warm, intense pressure was so restricting I felt I might burst.

"Let it out from your soul," Angela said through my thoughts. "Don't perform."

A heartbeat emitted from my clit, and I became a weightless euphoric ray of light. My orgasm erupted as I

357

watched my body from ten feet above. I felt everything and nothing. My legs spasmed until, eventually, my lower half was quaking.

I let out a feral howl that was joined in chorus by the witches in the area, their energy powering my release. If it weren't for the streghe's comforting touch, I would have been scared at the orgasm's intensity. My muscles stopped working and my head fell back as everything grew black. The women eased me down and I opened my eyes. I was back in my body, my legs still trembling.

The spiritual nature of the release brought me to tears. Angela and Chiara caressed me tenderly while I struggled to catch my breath.

Gian lay down next to me, exhausted, and nuzzled his face into my breast.

"How about a drink," Angela said, slapping me on my hip. She found her dress, and the rest of us searched for our clothing.

A comfortable seating area was free on the patio by the bar. I expected a little weirdness after what just happened, but our conversation was easy as if we knew each other our whole lives. I wanted this. I needed friends.

That morning I jolted upright, scared awake from a nightmare. We were in our villa in Novara di Sicilia. I had no recollection of driving home.

In the dream, I was back on the shore of Lake Pergusa but the villas were missing. Blood-red water at the center of the lake was spreading outward. A young strega was reciting an ancient spell. The evil of her magic stunk up the air. I ran to stop her, but she hissed at me, frightening me awake.

I texted Support to check on the lake, hoping they were still monitoring. A witch reported back that it had a healthy green glow.

We spent the day relaxing. Both of us were pretty hungover. Witches know how to party.

Gian planned a picnic for us in the foothills above his village the following afternoon. Zia Pia packed a basket with antipasto and homemade sandwiches.

Uncle Emilio was kind to lend us his scooter. I was living a dream riding through the back streets of an Italian village. I smiled as I held onto Gian tightly.

We were racing toward a blind intersection when a bee flew into my top. Gian felt me freaking out and stopped the bike just as a speeding car crossed in front of us.

"Holy fuck!" he said.

The bee flew out and landed on the handlebar. It looked at me, then the road, and flew off behind us. I watched in the rearview mirror as it morphed into the Priestess of Death. No one was there when I turned around. I think all the days of celebrations were getting to me.

"Andiamo avanti," I said, pointing onward.

Gian wasn't so careless about the intersections anymore.

On the edge of town, he detoured to an ancient church. It was so old I was surprised the building was standing.

Gian whispered, "Remember when I told you about the stregherian sculptors carving the baby Jesus as the true goddess? Take a look. I'll make sure no one's watching."

I felt guilty for doing it, but I knelt in front of the statue of Jesus and Mary and peered up the baby's swaddling cloth.

"It's a girl?"

"Don't be upset."

"I'm not," I said. "I... I don't know what to believe."

"It doesn't mean anything. It's just art."

"I think it means a lot," I said.

The landscape in the hills was arid with sparse bushes and low trees. We journeyed on foot upward until the village stretched far below. There were no more celebrations or people to meet. A sense of calm enveloped my body, leaving me in a fantastic mood.

Gian found a quaint meadow to lay our blanket, then filled two wine glasses generously with a local pinot grigio. I tipped my drink back, but he stopped me with a light touch.

"A toast to our love," he said, speaking Italian.

I melted.

"From the moment we met, I wanted to spend the rest of my life with you."

His Italian was perfect. He had memorized the words. Holy crap, was this what I think it was?

"I never thought that would be possible. We have been blessed with freedom, a freedom I want to share with you."

He dropped to one knee and produced a ring. But not just any ring—my mother's wedding ring. Gian asked my dad for permission.

"Linsey Marie Cameron, would you do me the honor of becoming my wife?

"Yes. si," I said in exalted shock.

My answer reflected brightly on his face. "You make me so happy."

We cuddled up on the picnic blanket, gazing upon Novara di Sicilia. The first bottle went fast. Gian retrieved another one that was tapered evenly like a thin cone. The label was a quarter-moon, which seemed fitting after the festivities with the streghe.

"Would you like to try moscato?" he said.

"Sure. What is it?"

"A sparkling dessert wine that isn't too heavy or sweet. You'll like it."

I handed him my glass, and he replaced it with a filled champagne flute.

"To the rest of our lives," I toasted, lifting my glass.

"May they be safe," Gian added.

Moscato was my new favorite alcohol. I snatched the bottle from Gian. "What are you going to have?" I said, holding it tight.

"You," he said, squeezing me to him.

I would have ripped his shirt open in lust, but it was an expensive purchase from the village. Three buttons in, I was caressing his pecs. He lifted my top over my head and lowered me to the blanket. His lips were on mine, kissing me deeply.

"I need you in me," I said, coming up for air.

"Gladly."

"No foreplay, just go," I pleaded. "I want to feel it all."

He unbuttoned his pants and reached between his legs to steady his cock. I gasped as he pressed the head upon my labia, holding my gaze as he pushed inside.

Nothing felt better than being filled by my man. Gian thrust rhythmically deep inside me. Our intense connection was startling, almost as if I still had the Mirror's Touch.

It was exactly as if I had the Touch. I sat up.

"What's wrong?" Gian said, looking around for danger.

"I can feel what you're feeling," I said. "Something's not right."

Acknowledgments

A huge thank you to my cousin, friend, writing partner and editor, Camille English. Your thorough attention to detail and skilled wordsmithing are invaluable.

Thank you to the early readers: Vicki, Mom, Tami, Stephanie, Shelley, Robin, Niccole, Nancy, Melissa, Lori, Lisa, Deb, DeAnna, Cynthia, Connie, Debbie, and Colleen. Your feedback is much appreciated, especially Vicki's. She is always the first to read my work. Vicki is a trooper as she trudges through the initial drafts.

My deepest heartfelt thank you to my partner, Marc, for being himself. If something in this book made you laugh, it was more than likely a witty remark of his.

A huge shout out to the experts for their knowledge and patience:

Firearms: Wade, Josh, and Spike at Wade's Eastside Guns.

Self Defense: Joe Porras

Mixed Martial Arts: Claire "Grizzly" Guthrie.

Psychology: Stephanie Self-Bence, LICSW. I asked Stephanie to explain how she would use MDMA Trauma-Focused Cogitative Behavioral Therapy if it were legal in our state. She wanted it known that it would be rare for a client to let PTSD go after only one session, especially having had no prior therapy.

Stregheria:

While researching Sicilian witchcraft, I was drawn so strongly to Marguerite Rigoglioso Ph.D. it was as if she was calling to me. A paper she wrote, Stregoneria: The Old Religion in Italy from Historical to Modern Times, helped create a fictional version of the religion and the streghe. The article has disappeared, making me wonder if it was ever there.

According to Marguerite, in Sicily, the term strega is used disparagingly to describe someone who practices malevolent magic. Unfortunately, the Sicilian witches' preferred term of maga has been politically adopted in the United States. For this story, strega and the plural streghe are used as a positive to describe the witches.

I respect the secrecy enshrouding the stregonerian traditions. Portions of the rituals and history have been changed to protect their covens or fit the storyline.

Marguerite's teachings can be found at:
www.SevenSistersMysterySchool.com